Wendy Robertson has lived and worked in the north east much of her life. She trained as a teacher and later moved into teacher education, whilst continuing to write short stories for magazines, four children's novels (the last three published by Hodder and Stoughton) and, during the seventies, a column for *The Northern Echo*. She lives with her husband in Bishop Auckland.

Also by Wendy Robertson

Riches of the Earth

Under a Brighter Sky

Wendy Robertson

headline

First published in 1993
by HEADLINE BOOK PUBLISHING

First published in paperback in 1994
by HEADLINE BOOK PUBLISHING

2

ISBN 0 7472 4410 3

Printed and bound in Great Britain by
Mackays of Chatham plc, Chatham, Kent

HEADLINE BOOK PUBLISHING
A division of Hodder Headline PLC
338 Euston Road
London NW1 3BH

For Pat

PART ONE
COUNTY DURHAM
1849

Chapter One

The bucket was heavy and water slopped on to Shona Farrell's boots as she changed hands to relieve her aching shoulders.

'Here, Shona! Give it here, blue eyes!' The water splashed out again as the bucket was wrenched from her hand. She raised her head to face the narrow menace of Terry Kennedy rearing over her and her nostrils were filled with the stench of old cabbages. He was holding the rope handle awkwardly, making even more water skim over the bucket's wooden edge.

Shona drew breath then went into battle, grasping the handle and jerking it out of his hands, getting even wetter in the process. 'Now see what you've done, Terry Kennedy!' she snapped. 'Won't I have to go right back to the tap for more?'

'Let's help you, Shona.' He smiled and loomed even closer.

Her hand went out and pushed him away. Her nose wrinkled. 'You stink, Terry. You must have been sleeping with bears in your back room, never mind pigs. What're you doing here anyway? Did they tip you out of the ironworks early or are you a leisurely feller now, without wages?'

He took a short step back. 'Why, pet, I been workin' hard all day deliverin' steel screws over to the railyards at Shotwell. Special delivery from our boss to theirs. No point in going back to the yard. The lads'll be down in Showy's bar any minute. I'm meetin' Pat there. Likely your Tommo too.'

'Our Tommo?' She looked sceptical. 'Sure, he has more sense than to be found drinkin' beer with the likes of you!' She moved her gaze up and down the length of him, eyes gleaming. 'I tell you what, Terry, you can do another delivery.' She held out the near empty bucket. 'There! Fill it up at the tap and bring it here.'

He stared at her for a moment, then lifted his shoulders. 'They say y'are all right, but you're an odd lass, Shona.'

'Lucky for you I'm that odd then, isn't it? Less odd and I'd tell me brother Tommo about all this lurking around and jumping out at me like some Christmas ghost.'

He grasped the bucket, the heat of his large paw covering her hand for a split second.

Her eyes followed him as he shambled off and shouldered his way through the giggling women at the tap. He was scowling as he came back.

She held out her hand for the bucket, now brimming full. 'Now get off to Showy's bar, you clumsy snake, and tell our Tommo the bacon broth's on and I won't save it beyond nine o'clock.'

She turned to go. He watched her as, straight-backed in her gritty pit-clothes, she made her way down the narrow street. Then he lumbered after her and caught her by the shoulder. 'What is it with you and that brother, lass?' he hissed. 'What's it you and Tommo do that no one else gets a look-in?'

Shona looked at him, frowning. This was a new tack. Then she smiled broadly, her white teeth gleaming in her blackened face. She would wipe that sly, knowing smile from his leering face. She lifted her free hand, curled it into a fist and hit him hard on the jaw. Then she ran, holding the bucket away from her, trying not to spill a precious drop. His roaring voice filled the space behind her as he took up the chase.

Always quick on her feet, she moved swiftly, still looking round, fearful now of the consequences of her hasty action. The dark streets ahead were empty except for a single small figure leading a pony.

She sighed with relief as she recognised her younger brother. 'Richie! Richie! Over here!'

Boy and pony turned and the empty street was filled with the clatter of hooves and the thud of Richie's feet. Terry slowed behind her and his curses faded to a low muttering.

'Richie! Wake up, will you?' Her voice was sharp. 'You carry this water. Make the pony work for his keep.'

Her brother threw an arm over the pony's neck. 'There, Cush, tek no notice, it's only Shona! Sharp tongue. Soft heart.'

'Here! Get here!' she demanded.

They were at her side. Now the only sound behind was of heavy

4

breathing. Richie stared across at Terry lumbering towards them. 'What's that feller up to, Shona?'

'Give him no mind. Now, I want that animal to carry this water!' She thrust the bucket at him.

Richie took it from her. 'Jump up on Cush, Shona.'

She cocked one leg easily over the animal's back. Seated, her feet were only inches from the ground. She looked back at Terry Kennedy. 'Like I said, you can tell your mate Tommo that I'm home putting on the broth. If he doesn't get back from Showy's and the broth's gone, bad luck to him,' she called, jaunty once more.

'Bacon stew? Pigs! It's always pigs with you Irish!' The tall man made a snorting, honking noise down his nose. Richie and Shona just stared at him until he finally turned and made his shambling way back along the narrow muddy street.

'Bad man to make an enemy of, that Terry Kennedy,' murmured Richie as he gently stirred the pony into action. It carried them up the hill and along the lane to number seven Stables Street. This narrow house, one window wide, no different from the thirty others in the street, had been home to Shona and Tommo for two years; to Richie less than one.

He took only five minutes to get a big fire blazing on the stone hearth. Shona used a careful scoop of the water from the bucket to splash over her blackened hands and face, then poured four equally careful scoops into the great black pan they had brought with them from Ireland. She stirred the water hard to mix it with the thick residue of yesterday's broth, then placed it on the fire.

'D'you see Tommo at the works, Richie?'

'Yes. He sent me out for beer halfway through the shift. And at hometime he walked out with me.' Richie worked at the ironworks, labouring for a group of puddlers, and, being the youngest, earned extra pennies running errands and messages for the men. He endured his hard working day for the moment he could race out and see to his pony, which he kept on a loose tether on land just outside the village.

He took some bread from a shelf and pushed it inside his coat. 'I was just on my way to take Cush down to Gil Tait's. He might have some work.' He grinned at his sister. Richie lived also for the time he could spend in Gil Tait's stables. Shona knew he would vanish now.

Working at speed, she peeled potatoes and carrots and stripped down some leeks to throw into the pot. Then she sat down on one of the two hard chairs by the fire to watch it come to the boil. She stretched her toes into the warmth and rested her head against the wooden back of the chair.

There was little work to do in the dark house which was just about bare of furniture. There was the leatherbound box; the two chairs; a rough table; one bracken mattress in the corner where she slept; another in the loft where Tommo slept with Richie. That was it.

Terry Kennedy, she thought, as she allowed herself to stretch into the warmth. Half Irish himself yet hating all the Irish. What was it he had said about her and Tommo? Her mouth tightened at his sneering hint that there was something wrong between them.

Wrong? There was nothing wrong with Tommo! He was Irish and proud of it. And there was nothing wrong between them.

She had been fifteen when the two of them had walked hand in hand the breadth of Ireland from west to east. It had taken them days, following the tiny donkey-cart which groaned under the weight of the two chairs, the leatherbound box and their bundles of clothes.

They had trudged through villages consisting merely of tumbledown houses, unroofed and bare to the sky, with no people at all in them. They wandered warily through a few hamlets where gaunt skeletal figures had congregated in corners. It was hard to tell men from women. People stood humbly by the wayside begging for food or just looking with hollow misery at those with the strength to walk away out of it.

Tommo and Shona had resisted the weary blandishments, husbanding their meagre resources to pay for the boat to Liverpool. As they disembarked in a whirling fog, they talked to a Cork man who thought he was in New York. 'I've a brother and three cousins in this city,' he said. 'You can be sure I'll thrive now.'

They had finally found their own distant cousin, Anthony Shaunessy, but he was unwilling to add them to his own household of sixteen which occupied a cellar not far from the docks. He had cocked his grey head at them and said, 'But I thought you were all right, Farrells out there in Clare. Sure didn't Thomas Farrell have fields as well as the smithy! Wasn't I there once?'

Tommo's voice filled her mind again, spitting his words as he faced down his sceptical relative. 'We had to come away finally, see?' he had explained angrily. 'The fields and the smithy itself were by grace of Grandon Seley, Lord Marsteen's agent. Then there was the potatoes going bad in '45 and no cash for the rent and our own potatoes failing. And no one working their own fields, nor even the landlords', so no horses to shoe neither.'

'And Thomas, what came of him?'

'He died, just dropped dead one day.'

'And the fields were gone?'

Tommo bit his lip then and went on furiously, 'Seley threw us out. Me brother Gerard was shot for taking a shot at the landlord. They tumbled the farm while we watched. Out we were, into sheds and pig houses – and then even those roofs were taken from over us too! Then sleeping on me auntie's floor, and then her own crop getting that stinking blight too. And me sister Maire, weak from hunger 'til she died. And there was me mother crying 'til I could hit her for it! Then I had to sell me father's boots and *his* father's watch for me fare across to Liverpool. And for money to leave behind for me mother and Shona and our young Richie.' His voice tailed off as he finished.

'And your mother?' Anthony Shaunessy had peered round them into the darkness, as if he expected her to emerge from the shadows.

'Didn't she just turn her face to the wall and die too?' Tommo answered shortly. Shona remembered the bleak horror of it, how she had then insisted on coming to England with Tommo, leaving little Richie with their aunt who said she would keep him as long as she could.

Anthony Shaunessy had stared hard at them, then sighed. 'Well, I've this brother to my son-in-law, Paul Kelly. He's going to County Durham to a place where they're making iron. There're big furnaces being built by the day, he says. I'd make my way there if I were you. There's no room here. No work in Liverpool. Too many of our people.'

Tommo and Shona had pushed the cart part of the way and then sold it for money for tickets on the new railway. They had walked to New Morven ironworks from the station, Tommo carrying the leatherbound box with all their possessions on his back, Shona carrying the two chairs on her head, looking through the bars like a prisoner.

Tommo had come out of the ironworks office with the keys to Stables Street in his hand. The seventh house on Stables Street was the first proper house they'd lived in for a long time.

Now, two years later, Shona was still trying to let memories of that hard journey fade. She stood up and stretched herself, then leaned over to stir the broth. She walked across to the box and stroked its leather bands. It held so little. Two of her mother's dresses and boots and shoes not worn out but all outgrown. Even this was riches to some of the people they had seen on the road in Ireland; people walking half-naked, having exchanged the clothes from their backs for bread.

She turned the key and opened the box, reaching in to poke at the blue jug that held her pennies and sixpences. She did like to earn her own money. It was little enough for all the hours she worked, but it meant she didn't have to ask Tommo for every penny.

He wouldn't save, of course. Sometimes he earned very big money at the ironworks. When she said to him, 'Save some, a bit every week,' he would pat her on the head, saying coins were made round to go round, not flat to pile up. So his money would go on a bit of essential food for the house, a good deal of beer and too much gambling. And before the fortnight's end there would be nothing left.

He was generous in his own way, though. Sometimes he would roll in from the Puddler's Arms with some gaudy ribbons or a piece of cloth he had bought from a traveller and present it to her with a great kiss on the cheek. But normally he didn't have two pennies to rub together. He didn't know about the contents of the blue jug or in certain moods would have wheedled them out of her too.

She closed the box carefully, turning the key in the lock. Then she yawned and threw herself on the mattress for a little rest while the broth bubbled in the pot.

'Now, Tommo! Sure isn't it nice to slide through them big black gates and into Showy's?' Pat Daley slipped on to the narrow bench beside his friend and stretched out his legs like a cat.

Tommo grunted and stared into his greasy glass. He rubbed a finger against his left ear, which was still throbbing from the clanging echo which resounded through the ironworks like a great iron pulse. His skin felt stretched too tight, shrunk by the burning heat. His hand clasping the glass was bound by a rough grey cloth which protected a searing gash, caused by a boiling spillage earlier that day. His bones felt brittle and weary from the long shift.

He lifted the glass to his lips, not lowering his bandaged hand until the beer had gone. The liquid coursed down his throat and lapped through his body, cooling his parched flesh, loosening his skin to make it more comfortable on his bones. He raked in a breath and expelled it in a huge grateful sigh. Then he stood up and pushed his way through the crowd to the narrow aperture where Showy McLaglan dispensed pints. Showy was always on the hop. Blackened hands reached endlessly through the hatch to grasp mugs and glasses as fast as the little barkeeper could pour them.

Tommo pushed a few coppers on to the stained wooden counter and in his turn grabbed four pints of foaming beer, holding the glasses as gently as eggs in his two hands. He placed two in front of Pat and two in front of himself.

The first hour at the Puddler's Arms, though always busy, was usually quiet. The men spent this time silently pouring beer inside themselves, plumping out their parched bodies and making their tired brains blossom. Later on, laughter would start to ripple, passed around the room like a ball in a game. There would be calls for Manny Carling to get out his fiddle and for Gil Tait to go out and get his squeeze-box from underneath the seat of his trap, where it lay all day in a waxed cloth bag as he plied his trade through the district.

And later still, one voice then another would be raised in some soft Irish tune. The tone would grow wilder and the songs more bawdy; then the ballads would become more sentimental, setting the men thinking nostalgically of their mothers and their sisters.

After downing his second pint, Pat paused. He fingered his third glass, still half full, and eyed Tommo. 'Me mother was saying it must be terrible to be left with no family. Just you and young Richie and Shona.' He had been talking too enthusiastically to his

9

mother about Tommo's sister and she had started to ask questions about the Farrells.

Tommo shook his head. 'There's no one left but us. True there's that crew in Liverpool, but they're only distant cousins. Not blood relatives. My father moved out of Waterford to County Clare to take on my grandfather's smithy. There's his brother and some sisters back in Waterford but likely the hunger's got them too, like it got most of the rest of them. My father's sister was the one we left Richie with at first. She died of the hunger. How he didn't die as well . . .'

He stared into his beer. He knew they didn't have that much of a life here, the three of them. Shona's work at the pit stopped her doing much more in the house than clearing out the fire in the morning and putting on the pan with the potatoes and bacon at night. Richie was out all the time with horses. In terms of comfort they were living not much better now than they had out of the cart that had brought them from Ireland.

Tommo whistled through his teeth. But then wasn't it true they lived no different from other families on Stables Street? A job, a roof and beer at the end of the shift was all they could expect and all they got.

Pat watched his friend uneasily. The two of them sat there in silence. They ignored the laughter all around them and drank their way gloomily through four more pints of Showy's ale.

'Now, Pat!' The wooden partition shuddered as Terry Kennedy leaned against the wall beside them. 'Another one ower. D'you see that bugger Morrison drop his load? Took an hour to shift it! An' will we get paid? We bloody won't.'

Terry was only Irish on his father's side and was proud of the fact that he was born and bred in County Durham. In drink, he had been heard to mention more than once that he was 'No Irish tinker'. A smaller man would have been beaten for such calumny, but his size and wiry strength prevented that.

Pat and Terry worked together at the rail-siding, loading iron to be shipped out to Tyneside and Pat lifted his glass to return Terry's greeting and gestured towards a stool. It creaked as Terry sat down. 'I can't think what it is you're moaning about, Terry. You were missing half the afternoon.'

Tommo stared glumly at the newcomer, pulled back his head

10

and shouted above the growing chatter, 'So, where's your soft sound, Manny? Where's that fiddle of yours?'

There were roars of agreement, followed by whistling and stamping. In the end, shaking his head in mock modesty, Manny took down his fiddle from the shelf where it was kept and, with a flourish, placed it under his chin.

Listening to the careful measures of the slow song, Tommo put his head in his hands and stared at the pitted surface of the table. As he did the wood dissolved into the smooth face of his sister Shona. He blinked hard. Now he could see the wrinkled face of an older woman. He blinked and it too was gone. He shook his head to clear it.

Swigging off his sixth pint, he finally joined in the singing, beating the flat of his hand on the rough table in time to Manny's fiddle as it wove faster and faster tunes in the smoky air.

Tommo stood up, swaying slightly. 'Well, Pat, now for Shona's bacon stew.' He beamed his rag-toothed smile at the company. 'The darlin' sister might have her faults, but her stew is like the food of heaven.'

Terry Kennedy hauled himself to his feet and clapped Tommo on the shoulder, peering too closely into his eyes. 'The darlin' sister has her faults, but no one, not even the blessed Saint Anthony,' he looked around the room and back at Tommo, 'could deny that even in her pit-dust, no one in the county has a finer pair of eyes, a neater pair of ankles, a finer pair of . . .'

Terry's fulsome list of compliments was brought to a halt by Tommo's fist smashing into his face. Caught off balance, the blow felled the tall man and he tumbled into the space obligingly vacated by the crowd, cracking his skull on the corner of the bar. He was out cold. The music stopped and still he lay on the floor, disappointing the crowd who waited eagerly for a bit more action.

'Get rid of that!' Showy McLaglan's cross little face peered through the narrow aperture. 'Get it out of me bar! And, Manny, will yer get on playin' that bluddy fiddle of yours!'

It took two men to grasp each of Terry's arms and drag him out after the retreating Tommo Farrell and his friend Pat. They dumped him on the unpaved surface of Top Road and returned to the bar to finish their pints.

Top Road, which led away from the ironworks, was busy at this time of night. Scattered along its length were five public houses: the Red Cockerel, the King's Arms, the Queen's Head, the Black Bull and the Puddler's Arms, which was also known as Showy's bar. These were all packed to the door at the end of every shift, as men slaked their mighty thirsts.

The buildings which comprised the street between the public houses were mostly rooming houses, curtainless and bleak, shelters for the single men who were pouring into New Morven to work at the ironworks. The beds which crowded every room never cooled: the shift system at the works was mirrored in a shift system for sleeping.

One house was different. Its coloured curtains were pulled back and its neatly painted door stood ajar. Leaning against the doorpost was a tall woman of perhaps thirty years. Her dress was dark green and quite tidy, if pulled in a little too tightly at the waist. She had a pale blue ribbon threaded through her light-coloured hair.

'Now, Maudie!' said Pat, cocking his head at her as he passed.

She reached forward and pulled at his arm and he vanished from Tommo's side. The painted door closed firmly behind him. Tommo grinned into the wood panels. He was a dog, was Pat! A real dog.

His own house was in darkness when he got home. He could hear the familiar sounds of Richie's sleeping mutter from the loft. He stirred up the fire and the reflection of the leaping flames outlined the shape of Shona snuggled under the dark blankets on her mattress in the corner.

Her voice, thick with sleep, struggled through the folds. 'That you, Tommo?'

'So it is. Get to sleep.'

'Stew on the edge of the fire there for you.'

He picked up the large pan and put it on the table. He tore off a piece of bread from the lump left among the crumbs in the centre and started to spoon the food straight from the pan into his hungry mouth.

Shona pulled herself up into a sitting position, easing her shoulders away from the damp wall.

He spoke to her with his mouth full. 'How old are you now, Shona?'

'Seventeen.'

'What do you best remember? About things back there?' His voice was wistful, ruminative. The beer, Shona knew, sometimes took him like this, but she liked it.

'Home?' she answered. 'Oh . . . the fine days when the rain was really soft, no more than a fine veil. Our mammy holding on to Gerard's arm, standing laughing at Richie's antics. And our daddy standing at the edge of a field of fully grown corn. Him by the smithy fire and you sweating at the bellows. Maire sitting in the window watching for us to come home.'

He poured lukewarm water into a jug and drank it to the last drop, wiping the residue from his chin with the back of his hand. 'We're all right here, an't we? You and me and our Richie? Plenty money from the works?'

She laughed. 'Maybe. But there'll never be plenty as long as you pour it down your throat. Or on to lame dogs or horses. Or on to the wrong side in pitch-and-toss. Good job I get me own wage.'

'An't no need for you to work at the pit, Shona. Dirty work that for a woman. Pit-women, they're too . . .'

'The pit suits me,' said Shona firmly. 'I like working at the pit. To be sure, I hate the getting up in the dark, trudging down that road with the rain seeping in your boots! But I like the old men at the screens, Tommo, and the other women. And as for pit-women being too easy . . .'

'They say they do anything.'

'That's down the pit,' she scoffed. 'What woman can run away in a three foot seam? Nowhere to run. So they call them easy. And that rubs off on us who've never been a foot underground. Sure, even on the screens you've to be quick with your tongue and your feet to keep the men off you!' She pulled the blanket up around her. 'But I like the pit, Tommo, for the smiles and laughs. And the secrets the women share with the old men! Look at Mary Challoner, works alongside me. Worked in one pit where they wouldn't let you talk at the screens while you worked. But old Len Hall, he doesn't bother – as long as you fling the coal about he's quite happy. More, he's sometimes adding to the gossip himself.'

Tommo laughed. 'Aren't you singing a song now, Shona, about the dirty old pit?' He stared at her. She was sitting in the deep shadow cast by the late glow of the fire. 'You're keepin' yourself right, an't yer, Shona?'

13

She laughed and slipped back under the blankets. 'Don't you say silly things sometimes, Tommo Farrell?' Her voice was muffled and indistinct.

His head was aching now with the beer. In a few hours he would be up again, facing another shift at the furnaces. He wanted, longed, to jump in beside his sister and lie quite still.

He stood up and pulled the ladder across, setting it up to the roofhole. He clambered up the steps and threw himself on to the mattress beside Richie, who turned over and clasped him tightly round the waist. Tommo had to lie there very still so as not to wake his younger brother.

Biddy O'Farrell clambered down narrow brick steps and knocked hard at the door that faced her. A creased and dirty face peered out at her. 'Shaunessy?' she asked.

'Yes, what is it?'

'My name's O'Farrell. We're cousins of a kind.'

'We've no room here.' The door started closing.

She put her weight against it and forced it back. 'I'm not wanting to stay. I'm looking for the sons of my brother. Thomas Farrell. And his daughter.'

'Hmm. Brother and sister came, years back. Then a little'n much later. Same story.' Anthony Shaunessy let the door gape now. If the old woman didn't want space, it was easy enough to talk. 'They went off further north. On the east coast somewhere. They make iron there. A relative of mine is there too.'

'Then you'll tell me just where and I'll be on my way.'

'New Morven it was called. A village in County Durham where they make iron.'

The door started closing. She pressed on it again. 'Would you have a drink for an old woman? Hasn't it taken all day for me to find you, and haven't I the divil of a thirst on me?'

'Wait. I'll see if there's any left.' The door stayed half-closed.

Biddy O'Farrell leaned back against the wall. It had been a long walk from Waterford to Clare; all for nothing when she found her brother's and his wife's crudely marked graves. And a newer one for Marion, her sister. She relived her feeling of relief when the priest told her the boy and girl had gone to England, aiming to contact their relative, Anthony Shaunessy. Of the smaller boy he

14

knew nothing. The child had vanished the day they buried Marion. One minute he was there, the next he was gone.

The sea crossing had been rough. Biddy closed her eyes and said another prayer of thanks for her safe arrival.

'Here!' A tin mug was thrust into her hands.

She drank the water eagerly, ignoring Anthony Shaunessy and his anxious looks.

Thoughts crowded each other in her head. Now she was on the last stage of her journey and England was kinder to people than Ireland. The skies were brighter here. People stayed alive here. Those children would be safe now, in New Morven, this village in the north. And she would find a safe place with them. Wouldn't she?

For the next two days, on her way home from work, Shona kept a wary eye out for the lumbering figure of Terry Kennedy. She made Richie get water from the well for her, despite his eagerness to get off to Gil Tait's stable and his beloved horses.

Richie scoffed at her timidity. 'The feller's all mouth, Shona. It isn't like you to shy off a loudmouth.'

'It's not that, Richie,' she said, firmly handing him two buckets. 'There's something about him . . . He's such a dirty man, even being near him makes *you* feel dirty.'

Leaning against the door watching Richie lope along the street, a bucket in each hand, Shona knew that the worst thing Terry Kennedy had done was to sully somehow the thing that was special between her and Tommo.

'Tell Tommo!' As if reading her thoughts, Richie bawled it from the end of the street. 'He'll beat the pulp out of that big snake, so he will.'

Chapter Two

Biddy knew she would have to lie there, helpless, until someone came along. Heaving herself up on to her elbows, she peered at the chalky bloom on her boot as it stuck out from under the frayed hem of her long skirt. She lifted the foot out of the slushy puddle, then yelped. Red hot pokers seemed to be piercing her ankle bone. She lowered it again. The slush cooled it to lukewarm. Then the foot became cold. Too cold to bear.

She lifted her head above the frosted winter grass. The road, a rutted track, stretched away into the grey distance; at its edge, black branches scratched against the whitened sky. She rubbed one hand against the other, transferring heat from palm to finger. Then she said a rosary, fearing she would die of this cold.

Her mind strayed to another place, one springtime in Ireland. She was a child again, skipping barefoot along just such tracks or dragging her feet, peering under hedges to look for baby birds and little creeping creatures; playing with a light heart.

She didn't know then of the times to come; the way the snares of life would drag her to this foreign place. There was Peter Callan, with his black curls and bright eyes, to be taken from her before their marriage with some coughing disease. Her own fate to be a useful sister and a trusted aunt was well sewn up then: she was to be no more than another pair of hands at the stove and by the cradle.

Trying to forget the perishing cold, she pushed her thoughts onward to that heavy boat called *The Green Rose*. Didn't it hang deep in the water! Then that journey through a storm from the bustling port of Dublin to the equally bustling one of Liverpool. On the boat she had stood up on deck watching the sea, its turbulent, glittering grey stretching to the horizon.

The creaking old vessel had dipped and tossed, mimicking the

17

fear that churned away deep inside her. No one as old as she was should feel such fear. It was a relic of childhood, that stomach-turning distrust of the unknown.

A child . . . Now she was actually seeing a child. It was moving slowly along, peering into the bushes. Biddy frowned, wondering whether she had formed this from her own imagination, from her own self across the water, from the child deep inside her own old body.

Now a round young face was thrust close to hers, peering as if the old woman herself were a creeping creature of the hedgerows. A soft hand was placed on Biddy's cheek. The hand was podgy and furnace-hot, melting the ice in the old woman's blood: ice crystallised hard in her veins during three hours of lying in the white winter grass. The blood from the child's heart had such a short way to travel to that hand, so fat with food and soft with kind handling.

'Hello, lady!' It was a high fluting voice.

The twisted cord of pain inside Biddy snapped. She shook her head. Her clearing vision made out pale bright eyes and fair springing hair escaping from a white woollen cap. The child was real enough, standing beside her on the cold rutted track.

'Hello, sweetheart.' She said this calmly, as though she were on the street, basket on hip, busy with the marketing.

'What your name, lady?' The little head was round in its tight cap and the sun, low now, glinted through the straying curls, making a shadowy arc.

'I'm called Biddy.' Her mouth was stiff with cold and lack of use. She rolled a little to shift the painful weight. 'And what's it you're called, then?'

'. . . Etta.' The child took a breath. 'Lauretta.'

'Lauretta dear, Lauretta me little darlin', will you go now and tell your mammy that Biddy's down here with a bad foot and cannot get moved.'

The child frowned, then her brow cleared. 'You a grandma?'

'No, me darlin'. Not a grandma, no more a mammy. But I've had other children to take care of, another mammy's children. And here I am in this Godforsaken place and come to do the same for my brother Thomas's children.'

18

Another little frown sketched itself on the child's smooth plump brow.

The old woman sighed and tried again. 'I'm Auntie Biddy. Go tell your mammy Auntie Biddy is poorly. Tell your . . . mummy!' A family she'd once lived with in Dublin said it that way. The only Irish thing about them had been their name.

Lauretta's brow cleared again and she smiled, showing small teeth. 'I have no mummy. Only a grandma and a daddy.'

'Well then, sweetheart, go and tell your daddy about poor Auntie Biddy.'

The child smiled even more widely. 'I tell Daddy. I tell my daddy!' She padded off, the soiled edge of her petticoat dragging over clods of frozen earth on the rutted track.

A minute later Greg McNaughton watched his little daughter run towards him and sighed with relief. Laughing, he swung her aloft and on to his shoulders. 'Where have you been? I've been shouting you. Aida'll have my life for being this late. Where d'you get to?'

She pulled at his hair and leaned her face against his. 'Auntie Biddy wants you, Greg. Says she wants my daddy.'

'What auntie?' He looked back the way she had come, then peered sideways at her on his shoulder, inclined to believe her. She wasn't given to fantasy. 'Down Shotwell Lane?'

Then he was loping along, taking giant strides, so that the child was joggled up and down and had to cling to him, squealing, her fingers locked tight in his short springy fair hair.

He turned the corner and slowed to a halt when he saw the black bundle sprawled half in and half out of a ditch.

'Auntie Biddy! Auntie Biddy!' Lauretta cocked one leg over his shoulder and clambered down to the ground as though he were a tree. She bent over the bundle. 'Auntie Biddy! Here's my daddy.'

Concentrating on the cold, Biddy had hardly heard the two of them coming. She lifted her head at the child's voice and managed a faint smile. 'So I see, me darlin', so I see!' She squinted up at the tall fair man who was blocking the winter light and smiled again. 'Sure you don't look old enough to be anybody's daddy. But you'll do! I asked for her mammy.' She lifted her one good hand, palm out.

19

'She's no mother at all so I expect she thought I'd do.' The young man squatted beside her. 'Fell down, did you?'

'I got off the train and the boys there told me this was the way to New Morven. I'm walking along the middle o' this road, to keep out o' the ruts. I turn a corner – and bang! There's this feller with a wagon. Knocks me down and never looks back. Scallywag!' Her voice, weak at first, gained strength. 'Well, me darlin' boy, will you get me up or do we blether on 'til I freeze to death entirely?'

Greg's concerned face broke into a smile. Placing his hands under her arms, he pulled her free of the ditch.

She gasped with pain as he tried to set her on her feet. 'Me ankle's twisted and me wrist is as useful as unbaked bread. Can't use either of 'em or I'd'a pulled meself out of the water.'

He clasped her clay-cold hand and touched her icy face. 'By, Missis, you're frozen all right.'

'Auntie Biddy cold,' put in Lauretta.

'Here!' Greg removed his jacket and his scarf and wrapped one around her body over her shawl, and the other around her head over her bonnet. Then he lowered her gently so that she was sitting on the grass.

He looked around at her scattered bags and parcels. 'I don't know how I can carry these as well as you, *and* give a hand for our Lauretta . . . I know!'

He gathered up the packages, leapt across the ditch and put them behind a bush whose drooping twigs still clung to their red berries. Then he looked down at the canvas bag she was still clutching and prised it gently from her hand. 'Here, our Etta'll carry this for you.'

He leaned down and looped the long handle of the bag over the child's head and under one fat arm.

'Me carry Auntie Biddy's bag!' Lauretta's broad face dimpled into a smile.

'Take good care of it, me darlin'. Sure it's got all the bits of me life in there. All me papers and all me past. All me money and all me baubles.'

'Now!' Greg turned his back on the old woman and squatted down. 'Can you reach over with your good hand on to my back?'

She put her good hand on his shoulders and he grasped it, then stood up so that her legs, despite being trammelled by skirts and

20

petticoats, first dangled free, then went round his waist. Her good leg clutched at him with wiry strength.

'Now let's get your Auntie Biddy up to New Morven, Etta, before she expires with cold.'

They talked as they walked along, the old woman bouncing on his back and the child dancing along beside him, with Biddy's bag dragging along behind her.

'You're Irish,' he stated.

'Now how would you be guessing that, then?' The soft voice tickled his ear, sounding surprisingly young.

'There's Irish lads working in the railway sheds. They talk like you.'

'Me own boys don't work on the railways. Some ironworks, they work at. They came themselves just after my brother Thomas died. A feller called Shaunessy says they came here.'

'What brought you here then?'

'Well, our Paddy that I lived with and all his little ones goes to Americky, don't they? What does an old woman want in a new country? So didn't I go looking for them, my brother Thomas and his brood? Well, Lord save us, there wasn't one of that family left when I got to Clare. All dead from the famine or fled across here. Or Americky. Me poor sister Marion was the last. The rest're all here now, working in some ironworks. With no woman to mind for them.'

Greg wriggled his shoulders against her weight and laughed. 'It's some ironworks! You should see it, growing by the minute! A new blast furnace every week, seems like. They 'tice our railway lads away with high wages. They build a new street of houses every week. Money pouring into the place like leeching blood. They do say the Catholic priest's there on payday collecting a hat full of silver to build his church.' The sneer in his voice labelled him Protestant.

'You work on the railways?' She hooked her good ankle tighter round his waist.

'Everybody from Shotwell works for the railways. Just like all the New Morven lads work at the ironworks. I'm an engineer there. My brother is book-keeper. My old man designs new kinds of engine. Helped build the first ever engine.'

'Clever feller, then?'

'Oh, yes. He's a very clever feller, my father.'

Biddy dug in her chin and peered harder over his broad shoulder. She noted with widening eyes the shops in the narrow street: butchers with the white stretched pig carcases hanging high like ghosts in their dark interiors; bakers with rows of pies filling every window; one shop displayed fancy plates and cups; another filled with brightly coloured bolts of cloth.

Yellow flaring lights, roaring voices and the scrape of a fiddle spilled out into the coming night. A crowd of men stood talking and laughing under the creaking sign of the Puddler's Arms.

A heavy-faced man joked with Greg. 'What cheer, sir! Playing Atlas, are you, to some old souse?'

'The old'n wracked her ankle.' Greg looked sideways past the skewed bonnet into the old woman's bright eyes. 'What name was it you sought, Biddy?'

'Farrell. I want Tommo Farrell. Son of me brother Thomas. God love him, he's dead now. His wife too.' She flicked a stiff finger in the direction of the tall man. 'And I'm no souse, cheeky fox that you are.'

The man laughed, showing the bright pink flesh of his underlip. 'Farrell? Farrell it is you want now? Cheeky crew, them Farrells. Like the old'n here. Stables Street, you want, sir. Turn left up the alley by the Burnt Bush. Farrells'll be about seventh or eighth down that road.'

Greg turned away and Biddy clutched the broad shoulders even tighter as she heard the whisper of insults behind her. 'Ye want more than using some Proddy pig for a hobby horse, Missis!' one voice muttered.

They counted five pubs before they came to the Burnt Bush. By the time Greg was stubbing his toes on the rocks and loose stones of Stables Street, the light burden of the old woman was as heavy as any load he had shouldered in the yards of the railway shops.

They counted seven houses and stopped at one with its door hanging open. Someone inside was singing, a lilting sweet song.

Lifting the old woman lightly from his back, Greg leaned her up against the doorpost, then hit it with the flat of his hand. The song faded on the air.

Biddy hopped into the house, leaning on Greg's arm, followed closely by Lauretta.

The kitchen was stuffy and dimly lit. Heat radiated from the iron fireplace although the fire was only on a dim smoulder. The air smelled of burnt pan and boiled potato. A girl with a blackened face, dark hair dropping in long curls over her shoulders, was sitting at the table, patting scones into shape. She had a leisurely air; her movements were without urgency, as though this were all a pastime rather than work. She smiled up at them, a keen bright smile, the white teeth making her lips look redder. 'Well, who's this then?'

'I can see you're Shona, seeing you are your mother's own self. I'm Biddy, sister to your father Thomas.'

The girl simply looked at her.

'Well, your cousins in Waterford is dead now, God rest them, from the potatoes failing. And your Uncle Paddy and his Kathleen is off to Americky with their brood.' She paused again. 'They're big now and don't need their Auntie Biddy.'

The girl stood up and brushed her dusty hands down her skirt. She took a step forward, then backward as she caught the rather severe glance of the tall young man standing behind her aunt. 'Auntie . . .'

'Auntie Biddy,' interrupted Lauretta. 'Me Lauretta.'

'And I'm Greg McNaughton,' he said, looking intently at the girl with her blackened face and floury hands. 'I – we – found your aunt in the road. Her ankle's hurt.' He eased the old woman on to a leatherbound box, which stood beside the door.

Shona smiled ironically at him. 'It's kind you are, Mr McNaughton. Here – Lauretta, is it? Have a little rice cake. Just from the oven.' She tipped one into the child's waiting hand, avoiding the man's intense gaze. 'And I'll stir the fire under that kettle. I'm betting our auntie could do with a dish of tea!'

Greg put his hand on his daughter's shoulder. 'Was it you I heard singing?' he asked Shona.

'Who else?' She looked around the empty room then smiled at him, her eyes teasing. 'Father O'Reilly says I have the voice of an angel, sent by God, sent by God to make up . . .' She failed to finish her sentence, realising that the Protestants squirmed when you spoke of the priest.

A rumble of voices and a clatter of feet outside filled the

23

awkward silence, heralding the entry of two men, who shouldered their way past Greg into the room. Tommo was at the fireplace in a stride, turning round to face them, his back to the blazing fire as the steam from the kettle danced lazily around his head. Pat Daley stood, swaying slightly, in the doorway.

'What's this, then?' Tommo's hard glance ranged from the old woman to Greg. 'They said down at the Puddler's . . . said some Shotwell feller was seeking us out, with some old woman in tow.'

'Tommo!' Shona's voice was raised in protest. She turned to Biddy. 'This is my brother, Auntie. This is Tommo. And him in the doorway, that's his friend Pat. Our little brother Richie's around somewhere.'

'He has a look of my brother Thomas, the big feller,' said Biddy. 'The shoulders, the very eyes.'

Tommo pushed his hands hard into his trouser pockets. 'We need no old woman. Haven't we taken care of ourselves for two years now?' He glared at Greg McNaughton. 'We need no old woman. Wasn't young Richie delivered to the door like a parcel by John O'Carrol, all the way from County Clare . . .'

'Look, Mr Farrell!' interrupted Greg. 'All I did was find your aunt flaked out in a ditch on Shotwell Lane and bring her this way. I'll get off now.'

'She's not wanted!'

Shona started to protest but Tommo pushed her further behind him. 'We want no old woman here, brought by no Protestant bigmouth. You picked her up – you have her!'

Greg looked at Biddy and caught a glitter of a tear. He leaned over and swept her up in his arms like a baby. Lauretta carefully put the uneaten part of her cake on the table and rubbed her fat hand down her woolly coat, then followed her father through the door.

Pat slammed the door behind them.

Outside, Greg set Biddy gently on the ground and Lauretta grasped her hand, starting to cry. Biddy wiped the child's eye with the edge of her shawl. 'It's hard to believe, me darlin', isn't it?' she said softly. 'That your own'd turn you off like so much rubbish. But the hard times he had in Ireland – seeing his mammy and daddy die from the great hunger – makes him blind to his own. Thomas Farrell's boys here in County Durham were my last throw.' Her voice had, at last, lost its merry ring. Her whole weight sagged against the wall.

Lauretta threw her arms round the old woman's legs and buried her face in her skirts.

Greg sighed. 'Just wait here, will you? Stay with Auntie Biddy, Lauretta.'

In four minutes he was back with a pony and a creaking cart driven by a tiny man wearing a tall battered hat. Alongside the cart walked a boy with a lick of hair falling on to his forehead.

'This is Gil Tait,' said Greg. 'And his assistant. He'll drive us back to Shotwell.'

'For sixpence,' put in the little man, flourishing his whip and smiling, nodding and winking all at the same time.

'For sixpence,' agreed Greg as he lifted Biddy into the back and sat opposite her, Lauretta on his knee. The boy leaped up lightly and sat on the hard bench beside Biddy.

The curtains of the Farrell house twitched as the cart slowly moved away. The silvery eyes in Shona's blackened face gleamed briefly into the night. Spotting her, Biddy waved and a hand sketched some kind of response.

'Ye'll get no change out of them Farrells, Missis,' said Gil Tait. 'Hard as nails. Rough as badgers. Only one any good is young Richie here.'

'Richie?'

'Sittin' right there beside you, Missis. Dropped like a parcel at Stables Street last year. Eight year old and on his own, all the way from County Clare.' The phrase rang out like the chorus of a much repeated hymn. The driver threw back his head and winked wildly at the boy sitting beside Biddy. She looked at him with renewed interest. 'Best marrer a man could have is Richie. Working with the horses alongside me all God's hours, when he's not up at the ironworks workin' for the men. Never knew anyone for not sleeping like young Richie here.' Gil flourished his whip and set the old horse faster on her plodding way. The sky was clear now, the stars unquestionably in their place.

Biddy looked hard at the side of the boy's head but he didn't turn to look at her. She leaned back against the side of the cart and relaxed. The boy would take his time.

She smiled across at Greg, sitting opposite. 'Isn't it true that

25

boys are perverse and shy? I've never met one that age that wasn't.'

Greg stared at the boy who returned his look coldly. 'Seems from what they say things are hard across in Ireland now? Your auntie here said your parents died . . . or was it another auntie?'

The boy peered more thoughtfully at him in the gloom, then looked at the old woman beside him on the cart. Out of the folds of his rough cape he drew a pipe. He leaned over and borrowed Gil Tait's then lit his own from it. The action had the ease of long repetition, and the grace of unspoken agreement. He blinked at Greg through the smoke, then looked at the brown-spotted hands of the old woman beside him.

He sighed. 'Well, sir, as you ask . . . I was the only one there when she died, my Auntie Marion. Wasn't I there on me own with this poor dead woman? I'd seen the dead all right, including me own mother and father. But that was the only time I shed tears, when my auntie died. She and me was the only ones left, see?' He drew hard on the pipe which flickered briefly and brightly in the dark. Gil Tait glanced back at him with a look of brief surprise. 'After that I started walking. Some days I fell in with people; the last time with this family called O'Connor who were coming across to Liverpool. They talked of me staying with them but by the time we landed they all had the fever and some men took them on stretchers and I didn't see them again.'

'Came right here on your own, did you?' Greg asked.

'No. I set off north. They said there was mountains to walk through to get to here. Anyway, didn't I fall in with this man from Clare? He put me on the back of his pony. I weighed next to nothing, sir, and was no burden for the beast! He was a Clare man, John O'Carrol, though I didn't know him.'

'Yer Uncle Paddy knew him well,' put in Biddy eagerly.

The boy stared at her unblinking, and went on as though she hadn't spoken. 'The man bought me food to eat. The cloak I'm wearing now is from off his back. And he brought me here to my brother, though I know he was on his way to Glasgow. Me brother Tommo was pushing food into my face for weeks after I arrived!'

'He'd be sorry, leaving you behind like that,' said Greg grimly.

'Nothing else he could do, sir. Can't you see that? He got me a job at the works and let me save my pay 'til I had money for a pony.

His name is Cush and he lodges with Gil Tait's horses. I work there in my spare time for his keep. And on Sundays we ride through the countryside. Have you seen the countryside round here, sir?'

'I have that!'

'It's very fine when you get away from the ironworks an' the pits. Sweet rolling green, b'god, like in the old country.'

'What about your sister, Richie? The one called . . . Shona, was it?' The mocking silvery eyes were before Greg again.

'Shona? She works at the pit, sir, but on Sundays I take her for a ride on Cush out across the fields towards the fells. Shona likes the countryside just as I do, sir. And she can sing, b'god! They say that Father O'Reilly says she has the voice of an angel. But I wouldn't know that, me never being in church. Shona twitters on, so she does, about my immortal soul but I fear I have little reckoning of such things. Shona worries that Father O'Reilly'll come for me. But with the town filling up with hordes of new believers he's no time to chase up sinners like me.' He grinned ruefully.

'And your brother?'

'Tommo? Oh, he goes once every week or so to keep the priest quiet. But back home he never missed a Sunday. Didn't our own mother see to that?' He paused. 'In the end there was no one to see whether *I* did or I didn't. So I didn't.'

'May God have mercy on your immortal soul,' put in Gil Tait from the front, bringing Richie's confidences to an end. The old driver had never heard the boy talk so much.

The cart swayed along, its creaking swept up on a growing breeze and lost in the hedgerows and the whispering trees.

The old woman smiled at the boy, raising her good hand from her lap and letting it rest on his arm above the greasy ragged cuff.

Gil Tait leaned over the side of the trap and aimed a glob of spit into the hedge. 'The lad's a wonder with horses,' he asserted.

The boy's face split into a wide grin and his hand turned to grasp Biddy's thin one, before dropping it.

'B'god, ye're bloody frozen, Missis,' he said.

He leaned down to the floor and collected an armful of straw to pile into her lap, covering both her hands. Then he scooped up another handful and threw it at the watching Lauretta, so that it caught in the fine soft curls of her fair hair. The child laughed and Biddy settled back for the rest of the bumpy journey to Shotwell, speculating on the possible harm to her immortal soul which might come from consorting with Protestants.

Chapter Three

Shona stabbed the poker into the heart of the fire, raking it around to make the ash float through. Then she stood back to watch the coal glow and spurt into flame. Tommo, like all the men, had made the poker at the works.

Standing by the door with Pat beside him, her brother watched her with a wide-eyed drunkard's stare. Shona's face was red with more than the fire.

'Ye're nothing less than a barbarian, Tommo, for turning the auntie away,' she spat furiously.

'Auntie? Now is there anything to say she's any aunt of ours? She's just an old woman. The Shotwell feller was dumpin' her here.'

'Here?' She turned round to confront the two men, then surveyed the dark room. 'Why would anyone in their senses *pretend* to be an auntie to come here?' she sneered. 'What d'you think, Pat?'

He shrugged his shoulders. ''Tis a decent enough house, Shona. We got the same and fourteen of us fightin' for space.'

'What does Pat think? What does Pat think?' roared Tommo. 'Why don't you ask me what *I* think!' He picked up one of their mother's chairs and crashed it down again so that two of the finely turned spindles broke. ''Tis our house!' he bellowed.

'It's a kennel, a pigsty. And you know it, Tommo Farrell!' she screamed back at him, desperately gathering the fragments of wood to her like rejected children.

Tommo banged on the wall above the fire. 'Here is four walls and a roof. Here is a fire up the chimney and a pantry with bread and potatoes and a full side of bacon.'

'Our mother and father, Tommo – they'd think it a pigsty!'

He laughed then. 'Now haven't we got a short memory? Didn't we see how they were livin' back there in the old country, in the end?

Didn't we live like that ourselves, in the end? Like pigs in sties! This is a palace compared with that.'

Shona sat down on the remaining chair, still holding the wooden fragments to her. 'But how would the woman know of us? How would she know our father's name?'

He looked at her sullenly. 'Any aunt of ours would know better than comin' around with some bluddy Shotwell man.'

'Didn't you hear him? She was hurt, he brought her.'

'Did you see the snooty face on him, the boy-oh? *Down among the peasants.* Last time I saw such a look was in the eyes of Grandon bluddy Seley.'

Shona caught her breath. Closing her eyes, she could see the agent sitting on his horse at a distance, watching as his bullies in uniform removed the roof of the house where all the Farrell children had been born. He was holding a snow white handkerchief to his mouth. Watching him, Shona had felt hatred of the purest and most direct kind.

She opened her eyes and scowled at Tommo, lifting the poker to point at him. 'He looked nothing of the sort, Tommo. He was never like that . . . beast of a man! You're drunk. Can't see crooked from straight.'

'Drunk, am I?' He grasped the iron poker from her, threw it to the floor and moved too quickly towards her. He pulled her up from the chair by her shoulders and started to shake her.

'No, Tommo!' Pat leaped at him and tried to pull him away.

He let Shona go and turned on Pat, picked up his friend bodily and heaved him over to the narrow door and out into the dark night.

As he turned back to Shona she could barely recognise him. Standing up straight, she faced him. 'So now what will you do, Tommo? Pick me up and throw me out, just like your best friend Pat?'

'I'll show you!' His hand came up and he smacked her so hard that she was flung across the room on to her bracken bed. He came after her and, kneeling above her, shook her where she lay.

'No, Tommo! Stop it, will you?' Her jaw was aching from the blow.

He glared down at her. Suddenly he caught the trapped look in her eyes, and his temper fled. 'Oh, girl!' he groaned.

He rolled away and lay still, his face averted. She rolled in the opposite direction and pulled herself up against the wall, winding her skirts tight round her legs and folding her arms over them.

She watched the back of his head for a few minutes before she spoke, quite softly. 'Do you remember, Tommo, just after Daddy finished those chairs for Mammy he made me and Maire those little wooden dolls?'

He turned his head and looked at her, frowning. 'Dolls?'

'Yes. A little fat one for me and a tall thin one for Maire. All carved with little twirls for hair.'

He sat up. 'Yes, I remember them. Where . . . ?'

'Taken away with the other stuff by the bailiffs. Most likely Seley got 'em for his daughters. Or maybe they were burned with the other stuff. I can still smell that fire burning.' She paused. 'He made them so carefully, Daddy. Mammy telling him how.'

He leaned over and touched her arm with the back of his hand, understanding. 'You miss them still, Shona?'

'So I do.'

He stood up and pushed a hand hard over his brow and right through his long hair. When she saw his eyes again they were very clear. He was sober; the drink gone from him.

He picked up the broken chair. 'I'll take this across to Pat. He'll mend it in no time. He's a good hand with wood. Maybe he could try his hand at a doll.'

She stayed where she was. 'It's too late for dolls, Tommo.' But she was saying it to the closing door.

The door at Garth End Cottage, painted a dark and shining green, was jerked open as they approached. Lauretta was immediately enveloped in the hard grasp of a tall woman whose flowered apron did not disguise her advanced state of pregnancy.

'Where you been, you little monkey? Yer gran's been on at me these two hours. Not that she'd do owt about it hersel'.' Her scolding voice cut through the hot air as it rushed from the hallway into the night. As she was speaking she removed Lauretta's round hat, pushed her hair back from her face, patting and stroking it, smoothing it against the round cheeks. 'But, like I say to her, how can I keep an eye on that little monkey? There's the washing to do and the washhouse to scour and the supper to do.'

Finally satisfied that all was well, she stood away from the child, one hand placed precisely in the small of her back. 'So who might this be, Greg?' she said, looking down at the shrivelled shape of the Irishwoman.

'Her name's Biddy O'Farrell, Aida, and she's come visiting,' he said easily. Biddy noticed for the first time the crisp Scottish edge to his voice. 'And, Biddy, this is Aida Sedgewick who looks after us all. I might tell you she's boxed a few ears round here.' He looked around the narrow hallway. 'Where's Ma?'

'Up in her room. Where d'you think she would be? She's watching for your da. As ever!' The woman stood back and watched with raised brows as, with immense care, Greg placed Biddy in one of the elaborately carved hall chairs.

'This is my Auntie Biddy,' said Lauretta proudly to Aida as Greg went up the stairs two at a time.

In his mother's bedroom a single small lamp was fighting a losing battle against the darkness. She was in shadow, sitting in a little padded chair in the window nook, an unopened magazine on her knee. She looked up at him through the gloom. 'He's not back yet, Greg.'

'It's only seven o'clock, Ma. You know he's never back 'til half-past. Even eight. Him and Stuart'll still be sorting things out across there.'

Margaret McNaughton peered out at the tangle of buildings clustered around the tall sheds where the engines were built. 'I just thought he'd be here earlier today, November the twelfth.'

Greg frowned. 'What's that? It's nobody's birthday.'

She smiled, her face suddenly very young. 'It was November the twelfth, on the riverbank at Durham. Me and our Sarah marching in line with the other girls . . . We saw him across the river, so tall and fair. You're like him, Gregor. He was carrying that same document case he has now. And he saw me.'

Greg fumbled around. 'In Durham? Across the river?'

She smiled conspiratorially. 'We were there at school. Our Auntie Mary's little school. And he was there at some meeting of engineers.' She had had a comfortable genteel life as a girl in the Lake District, he knew. She sat back in her chair, prepared to tell her story at length. 'We didn't meet at that minute, you understand. Later that night in chapel we met. He waited outside the door.' She leaned forward again, her hand flat on the window. 'I can hear the noises, Greg. Hear the machines going. I can see the light in his window, but I can't see him.'

He pulled her chair round and forced her to look into his eyes. 'He'll be back soon. They all will.'

He thought, not for the first time, that being less useful to his father had its advantages. He did his job, both at the sheds and travelling around for the business. But he wasn't, like his brother Stuart, always under his father's industrious gaze.

He smiled at his mother. 'You'll see, Ma, they'll be back soon. Now guess what? I've a visitor for you. Her name's Biddy and she's come to see us for a few days.

She peered round him at the empty bedroom.

'Not here, Ma, downstairs. You'll come down to see her?'

She turned and looked longingly at the railway sheds outside. 'But . . .'

'He'll be back at half-past! Now come and see your visitor!' He half-lifted her out of the chair and steered her out of the room and down the shallow stairs.

Biddy looked up from the tall-backed seat and saw a frail woman dressed in dark clothes, her hair in untidy wisps round her face. She smoothed a hand over her own muddy skirt and stood up, gingerly keeping her weight from her bad foot.

'Here's Miss O'Farrell, Ma. Biddy, she's called. Biddy, meet my mother. Poor Biddy's had an awful accident with a wagon and's fallen down in a ditch, Ma. Near frozen to death, I should think.'

His mother put her hand to her mouth.

'Now, Ma, she's not badly hurt!' Greg said quickly. 'But she does need warming through and a bit of a rest.'

Margaret McNaughton pulled herself to her full height, stepped towards Biddy and put an arm round her, clutching her just a little too tight.

'Poor thing,' she said briskly. 'We must get you into a comfortable chair. Aida, some hot tea for Miss O'Farrell!' She guided the hopping Biddy into the parlour.

Aida shot a thunderous look at Greg, who followed her into the big kitchen. 'What d'you think you're doin', Greg McNaughton? Bringing Catholics and all their troubles into a good Christian

33

house!' she muttered fiercely, pouring the ever ready boiling water into the ever warming teapot. 'Bringing that old rat-bag home! Rabbits and cats I'm used to. Even that wild pony you found wandering the lanes. But an old Irish tramp! A gypsy! And yer ma in this state. Worst ever. She's always had a soft head and a soft heart but in this state she'd welcome the devil himself.'

Greg shook his head. 'Don't make out you're so hard-hearted, Aida. That's not your way now, is it? The old woman was left in the ditch for hours. How could I abandon her?' He followed her to the tall press and watched her unhook a blue jug. 'She's come all the way from the bogs of Ireland only to be turned away by her last remaining kin. They don't want her.'

'No more do we!'

'Well, *I* want her! I'm sorry for the old thing. And Lauretta likes her. And did you see Ma? I haven't seen her move as fast for weeks.'

'You're right there,' Aida conceded reluctantly.

'So what harm is there in this? Now, what about some of your fruitbread? I could smell it from the end of the street. The poor old thing must be starving!'

A merry sight greeted him as he pushed open the sitting-room door. The fire was blazing, its flickering light reaching all the corners of the over-furnished room. In one corner, Irma the parrot was squawking away. On the couch sat Biddy, with Lauretta on her knee. Biddy's hand was enclosed in that of Margaret McNaughton who was sitting beside her.

'. . . And, begolly, ye should've seen the waves! I swear they were higher than the boat. Higher than any church. Sure, didn't I spend more time on my knees saying my rosary than I have in all of ten years past? And d'ye know this little sailor boy . . . doesn't he come and tell me to get down below? But I says no, I'd rather be up there watching it than down there worrying about it!'

'Weren't you sick?' asked Margaret, her pale eyes shining.

'Well, aren't I tellin' yer, Missis, these insides were twisting like a milk churn, but nothing of me dinner, not one bit, got up and out. Will I let that happen? Oh no I won't!'

'You must've been afraid.'

'Well, like I said, I was saying my rosary. But I think I was more feared in Dublin with those high buildings. And that Liverpool! You'd never a' thought there was so many ships in the world. A angle o' masts like some great forest.' She paused. 'Being scared o' the buildings and crowds of people is one thing. Then didn't I get to he Shaunessys in Liverpool and they wanted none of me there. And some other old friends I went after, they were all dead of the 'ever, though I did find the buildings where they'd been living. Like God had just put his thumb on the whole of my family at a stroke.'

Tears were dripping down Margaret's face. 'What a terrible hing!'

'Ye've family yourself, Missis?'

'Yes. There's Greg here. Gregor, really. Then two little ones, Andrew and John, neither lasting more than a week, poor scraps. Then came Stuart, who's at work now with his father. A funny boy Stuart, always was. Hardly comes near me. There was Murray after Stuart, he was such a treasure. He got to three before . . .' Her eyes went glassy. She looked at the little girl. 'Lauretta belongs to Gregor.'

Biddy raised her glance to Aida, standing with the tray.

'Don't look at me,' she scowled. 'I an't one of them. I'm only the paid skivvy round here.' She stumped heavily out of the room.

Margaret smiled after her. 'Aida's from Cumberland. They all alk straight there. Her sister Flora came over with me when I was narried. Just about brought Stuart up, me being so poorly. He cried and cried when she went back. Flora had to take care of her father when her mother died, but Aida came across in her stead.

Greg sat down in the chair opposite them. 'Aida keeps us in order,' he explained. 'And before that her sister Flora kept us in order as far back as I can remember. Good order keepers, the Sedgewicks.' He laughed. 'Now, Ma, are you going to pour? Or will you let Miss O'Farrell faint with hunger?'

Biddy tucked into the tea and fruitbread with relish, feeling her customary strength returning with each bite.

Margaret started to ask her about Ireland.

'Was it a farm you lived on? I was on a farm myself as a child, Biddy. Near Carlisle. The byre! I loved to help my father and Mr Sedgewick with the byre. Then helping Mrs Sedgewick with the cheese . . .' Her voice became low and indistinct as she told her long and rambling tale.

Richie burst in through the kitchen door, making Shona jump. The lamps were out. She was still sitting where Tommo had left her, on a corner of the bed.

Richie looked up towards the roofhole. 'Tommo's out?'

She nodded from the shadows. 'He went off to see Pat. He threw him out earlier and now he's gone after him.'

Richie crouched on his haunches and stared into the fire. 'That old woman, Shona . . . she's a rare old thing. Like you.'

'So am I a rare old thing?'

'That you are.' He poured water from a can into a tin mug and drank it in one draught. 'The old woman must've plenty spunk in her, comin' all that way on her own. A lot of life in her. Not like Auntie Marion . . .'

'That was hard for you, the time with Auntie Marion, Richie,' Shona said gently.

He nodded. 'So it was. I told her about it, the old woman. And that man.'

'Told her?' gasped Shona. 'Told him?' When her younger brother had arrived at the house that first time, carried in exhausted by John O'Carrol, he had said nothing to Shona or Tommo about his time alone in Ireland. He said nothing later either. In fact, Shona thought, he said very little of any kind, except for the words he whispered in the ears of the horses.

'It was the old woman. And that little girl. I thought I'd tell them. She was curious, the old woman. Didn't I want to make up for our Tommo throwing her out?'

'You'd like her to be here, the old woman?'

'So I would, Shona.' He lit his pipe off the fire then came to sit beside her on the bed, stretching his legs out. He glanced at her, then peered more closely at her face. 'What's that?'

She put her hand up to her sore cheek. 'The door. I fell against it as I closed it after Tommo.'

He stared at her, frowning. 'If that door knocks you again, I'll kill him. You c'n tell him that. No, I'll tell him meself. Here.' He leaned towards her, holding out his pipe. 'Tek a draw. It's very soothing, a pipe.'

Hours later, when Tommo climbed into the loft to bed, Richie was still awake. He felt rather than saw his brother pulling off his outer clothes and spoke into the darkness. 'I was talkin' to Shona before, Tommo. Do you know what I told her?'

36

'What d'you tell her, Richie?'

'That if I ever found anybody . . . hurtin' her, I'd kill them. I'd sell Cush and buy a gun and kill them. Just like our Gerard killed the Englishman. I'd kill anyone who hurt our Shona.'

Tommo crawled under the blankets. 'I bet you would. Quite right, me boy-oh. I'd kill them meself. Now can you get down there off your high horse so we can all have some sleep?'

Chapter Four

Douglas McNaughton rolled down his sleeves and, as though unwilling to complete the task, took an inordinate amount of time to refasten his gold cufflinks.

'That should make the difference, Jamie!' he called to his foreman. He had to shout over the clamour of the test machine.

'Aye, Mr McNaughton. That's it, I think!' Young Jamie MacQuistain's gaptoothed smile lit up his face, and his hand hovered over the moving piston with reverence. 'I telt your Greg it was for his da to finish the job, as he solved the problem in the first place.'

Jamie helped Douglas back into his long black coat, in a second transforming him from workman to boss. He liked it when Mr Douglas came into the workshops, rolled up his sleeves, put on a coarse black apron and got down to work. On these occasions he was like the youngster he had once been, brimming over with excitement at the thrill of making pistons move and wheels turn on tracks. Now Jamie watched an older, graver, much sourer Douglas McNaughton walk briskly down the workshop towards the great doors.

Stuart looked up from his ledger as his father entered the office through the rattling glass door. The light from the gas mantle lit the bright edges of the young man's overlong hair, which trailed on to the green wool of his jacket. His deepset eyes were shadowed by strong, prominent brows.

Douglas pulled out his watch. 'Time we were home, Stuart. Supper'll be waiting.'

He looked at the large book. 'You said I'd to do these figures. I'll follow you.'

'Best to come now. They'll be waiting.' Douglas tucked his watch away. 'Your mother doesn't like us late for supper.'

Stuart scowled down at his pen as his father turned to the door.

'Bring your ledgers with you and work at home,' said Douglas. 'I've work to do myself.' Douglas never wasted a minute. There would be papers to read about the Society of Engineers of which he was secretary, or calculations to do for some streets of workers' houses he was involved with on the southern edge of Shotwell.

The two of them left the smoky lights and the subdued clatter of the works behind them and crossed the road to Garth End Cottage. Douglas never re-entered his home alone.

The McNaughton house was large enough to belie its rustic name, but small enough not to stand out too much among the narrow streets of railway houses. Garth End Cottage was hundreds of years older than the streets around it. Its end wall was the last remnant of a monastery which had occupied the site where now the railway sheds sprawled: the sound of iron on iron was no longer that of bells, but the clangour of an industry bursting into life.

Douglas opened the parlour door to find his wife cosily ensconced by the fire. He raised his eyebrows at the sight of the decrepit-looking woman who sat beside her, with Lauretta on her knees. On the other side sat Greg, struggling to straighten up from a lounging position.

Margaret smiled at her husband and son as they came in. 'Douglas, look! This is Miss O'Farrell from Ireland who'll be staying for a few days. Biddy, this is my husband Douglas McNaughton, the cleverest man in the world. And this is my son Stuart.'

Stuart's long face was coldly quizzical as he came forward and shook her hand. 'And we're not as clever as our father, Miss O'Farrell. But perhaps a bit wiser than Lauretta here, who's one count wiser than a rabbit.' He winked at her and laughed. 'Ireland? I hope you're not one of those assassins we keep reading about?'

Biddy looked at him steadily. Lauretta leaped out of her arms and ran to her grandfather. 'Grandpa! This is my Auntie Biddy and she falled down and me and Greg brought her home.'

Douglas pulled up his grand-daughter to face him, gave her a kiss, then placed her gently on the floor beside him.

He moved over to shake hands quite formally with Biddy. He barely looked at her, his hand cold and dry in hers. 'Good evening.' He turned to his wife. 'It's good to see you so . . . lively, Margaret. I have not seen you in such spirits in a good time.'

She laughed girlishly. 'Now, dear, don't be so silly. Aren't you late? Aida's been fretting to get the supper on the table for hours!'

He put out a hand as though to ward her off. 'Don't disturb yourself for me, Margaret. I'll take my supper in the workroom. There are costings on the new houses that need doing urgently. Did you bring those ledgers, Stuart? And, Greg, I need to check the paperwork on that new wagon order for Welling's.' He turned and walked resolutely from the room, followed by Stuart.

Greg stood up, but stayed where he was.

The workroom at Garth End Cottage was large, with heavy wooden book-cases all down one wall. The long table in the middle was the twin of that in Douglas's office at the works. He slammed the door behind him and then clasped the edge of the table for a moment before he sat down. 'Poke up that fire, Stuart,' he growled. 'It's worse than an arctic winter in here.' He looked at the door. 'Where's Greg?'

In the parlour, Margaret collapsed back on the sofa and closed her eyes. When she opened them they were quite blank.

Greg coughed. 'Now, Ma! Where'll we put Miss O'Farrell? In Aida's room?'

His mother blinked hard. 'What?'

'Miss O'Farrell'll want a wash. A rest. Isn't that so, Biddy?' he said, staring hard at the Irishwoman.

She looked from him to his mother then hauled herself to her feet. 'Yes, yes. It's polite you've all been, nobody mentioning how I must stink to high heaven!' Mrs McNaughton jumped up beside her. 'Can ye show me where to go, Missis?' said Biddy, taking the other woman's arm.

Margaret shook her head slightly, trying to dislodge the heavy weight that seemed to have wedged itself just above her eyes. It was as if there was a fly buzzing in there. 'Yes, of course. Aida's room. She doesn't use it now. Would you believe it, Biddy, she got married? What a surprise! She must be thirty-five if she's a day.' She sniffed delicately. 'Came back one day married to John Salter who has the hardware shop. Delivers here every week. Of course, he's been widowed ten years . . .'

41

Greg watched her go from the room, walking slowly to accommodate the hopping Biddy and talking twenty to the dozen. He rubbed his hands together and smiled.

'Greg!'

He looked down at the forgotten figure of Lauretta. 'Yes, pippet?'

'I like Auntie Biddy.'

'Me too, pippet. Me too.'

In the days after the arrival of the Irishwoman, Aida muttered under her breath about the extra work though now when she arrived in the mornings at Garth End Cottage, from her rooms over John Salter's hardware shop, the fires were cleared and lit, the great kettle of water was boiling on the range and the table was laid. By then Biddy had had her first drink of the day – hot water poured into her own cup and carried back to her little bedroom under the eaves.

On the very first morning, Aida had accosted Greg and Lauretta, as they brought in the brown jugs of milk and six fresh eggs – carefully placed in Lauretta's little basket – from Priory Farm which still survived on the edge of Shotwell.

She glared from them to the spotless kitchen. 'Who's been messing in here then?'

'Me and Biddy did the fires and laid the table,' said Lauretta. 'Then me and my daddy went to the farm.'

They did this journey every morning, but usually Aida had to set about the fires and the table herself.

She looked around the room. 'Where is she, then?'

'She's back upstairs with a cup of hot water,' said Greg.

Aida scowled. 'She wants nothing taking cups out o' my kitchen.'

'It was her own cup,' said Greg briskly. 'And I told her to go up with it. She needed to rest that ankle after dragging those coal buckets around. Now what about our porridge and bacon, Aida? I can hear my father stirring up there.'

Frozen by Aida's glare, Lauretta raced upstairs to tell her grandma about the morning's adventures.

So, in the days which followed, Garth End Cottage fell into a

42

different routine. Douglas, Stuart and Greg had always had their breakfast first but now Margaret rose earlier than before and had hers in the dining room with Biddy and Lauretta, sitting round a table strewn with detritus from the menfolk's earlier meal.

Aida and Stuart made an uncharacteristic alliance in their shared dislike of Biddy's presence, despite the fact that Stuart was usually offhand to the point of rudeness with Aida. He had resented her since he was twelve, when she had come, with her hard hands and vengeful ways, to replace her sister. Flora had virtually been Stuart's foster-mother since he was born, Margaret being too ill to notice him. He had hated Aida, the rawboned, fresh-faced replacement, and showed it from the first day. For weeks she would find dead frogs and mice in her pots and pans; one day she had put her hands in the sink and found herself up to her elbows in frogspawn. Then, finally, she had made her objections known. The result was a stinging beating for Stuart from his father who was annoyed at being dragged from his work. His mother had watched the punishment in a kind of panicky sorrow. But now, with the Irishwoman here, Stuart and Aida were on the same side.

'S'not right, Stuart,' she grumbled. 'Your ma spending all her time with a papist like that. Gypsy most likely. The ideas that'll be seepin' into your poor ma's head. It's weak enough as it is.'

Stuart felt a similar reaction coming up from his gut. How many years as a small boy, then as a young man, had he tried and failed to draw his mother from her bound-in grief for the children who had died before him? Then for Murray, the brother who came after him, lasting only three sickly years. His failure to help his mother, to gain her love, had made a permanent, tight knot just below his ribs. Some days he felt sick to the point of choking. And now here was this Irishwoman, to whom his mother had taken so uncannily, making it all so much worse.

The tight knot only started to loosen when he was in the tavern or at his own table with a bottle of brandy. But now he had found another way of relieving it. One day, on his way through New Morven to see a supplier in Durham, he had come upon a bear being baited by dogs. The sight of the blood, the roar of the great motheaten animal and the screams of the dogs, made his insides melt with delight.

His pleasure had been spotted by a farrier from the railyard, who later took him to dog-fights and cockfights. The farrier had no time for the Irish as such, but bigod, didn't they know how to enjoy themselves?

'The old woman's like all of them Irish,' said Stuart now into the delighted Aida's ear. 'Moves in and makes trouble. They should stand'm up against the wall and shoot the lot of 'em.'

But Biddy herself seemed to be getting younger by the day. Fresh food and water from the McNaughtons' indoor tap, clothes from Margaret's own cupboard, had made a different woman of her. And as she grew, so did Margaret's rapture with her new discovery.

Douglas McNaughton was visibly relieved at his wife's light-hearted new demeanour. Now, when he came home, he didn't have to avoid the sight of a strained white face at the window as he crossed the road. He came in to the bubbling sound of female voices in the sitting room. One night he even lingered silently at the supper table watching his wife and Biddy show Lauretta different ways to play cat's cradle with wool from Margaret's knitting, and then a game with picture cards.

But that same night in the workroom Stuart tackled his father and brother about the need for twenty more workers to meet the increasing demand from America for new wagons.

'No trouble with that,' said Greg. 'Send Jamie or one of the others down to Liverpool. Irish're coming in on every boat. Cheap enough. Pick the best. They don't ask for much.'

'Irish!' Stuart exploded. 'Aren't there other workers? Those papists are everywhere with their plots and plans! Don't you read the papers? I was talking in Priorton with this man out of Moxham's office. Says they're plotting in every town, every village. They're creeping through Britain like some disease. Even here in our own house!'

Greg looked sharply at him. 'No need for that, Stuart. Biddy's done only good in this house. Haven't you noticed how much better our mother's looking?' He paused. 'Anyway, which man from Moxham's?'

'A new clerk. Said we should keep our eye on them. He has views on the Irish.'

Douglas looked silently from one to the other, then glanced out of the window at the darkening skies. 'You can't fault them as workers. They're doing the heavy work building roads and railways, not just here but in America too. Making more work for us. I'm happy for Jamie to recruit them. And as for them in our own house, as Gregor says, only good seems to be coming from it.' He took out his watch and looked at it. 'Now I have letters to write. I'm sure there's work for you to do.'

'I want to see Lauretta to bed, Pa,' said Greg. 'Aida seems to be losing patience with her these days.'

Douglas nodded and picked up his pen.

'Well,' remarked Stuart, 'seeing that Aida's starting a family, it seems we'll have to suffer an Irish maid. If she's any mind to work at all, the old woman that's bewitching Ma this very minute.' He knew he had gone too far the moment the words were out of his mouth. In a flash Greg was towering over him, catching the lapels of his green jacket.

'That's enough!' their father said sharply. 'Greg, see to your daughter. Stuart, you'd better finish work then get some air to blow away your foul temper.'

When Greg finally got upstairs, Lauretta was sitting up in her bed talking away to one of her dolls about a piece of paper she had in her hand. He took it from her. 'What's this?'

'A picture of a funny man, Auntie Biddy's daddy. Uncle Stuart found it.'

He looked at it. It was a cartoon torn from a paper. On it were two men depicted as capering monkeys, one with a battered stovepipe hat, the other flourishing a gun. The caption underneath referred to the Irish 'problem'. An inscription underneath that, in Stuart's hand, read: 'Father and uncle to Miss B. O'Farrell'.

Greg screwed it up and put it in his pocket. 'Not Biddy's daddy, pippet. A silly picture.'

Coming down later, Greg bumped into his brother in the hall. He grasped him by the back of the neck and, clutching one arm, marched him into the parlour.

Stuart struggled. 'What's this about?' he gasped.

Greg held the scrap of paper in front of his eyes. 'This!' He stuffed the cartoon into his brother's gaping mouth. 'Next time you try to poison my daughter's mind, I'll give you a good hiding!'

Stuart leaned over and spat the paper into the fire where it sizzled and began to brown. He stood up, straightening his jacket. 'No need for that. A bit of truth never . . .'

Greg flicked the dark silk of his brother's clean necktie. 'For someone who hates the Irish as much as you, Stuart, you're spending a lot of time down there in New Morven.'

'Places of entertainment have their uses, brother, after a hard day at work. Anyway, isn't it better spending time down there than mooning around over a child and a wife whom no one knows is dead or alive . . .'

Greg leaped towards him as he dodged through the door, slamming it shut.

A minute later Biddy's voice came from the hall. 'Greg, me boy – oh, could you come in here and help your mammy? She's trying to remember where it is in Cumberland that her Auntie Harriet comes from? Can you remember?'

He sighed and turned to follow Biddy's neat, trim figure up the stairs. 'It's Wetheral, Ma, that village across there. Don't you remember?'

Stuart met his new friend Morry Smith at the point where the road to New Morven joined with the wider one to Priorton.

It was their fifth meeting. Stuart had first met Morry, clerk to Moxham the solicitor, one Friday night. The farrier had taken Stuart to an organised fist-fight in the yard of the Grapes in Priorton, and left him to go on to a drinking spree with two traindrivers.

Morry, a stranger then, had grinned sharp-toothed at the red-faced Stuart who was shouting encouragement at the heavier fighter, Black Thomas, so named for the dense black hair that he tied back into a kind of knot while he fought.

'I'll bet you've got money on the big fellow,' he'd said.

Stuart glanced down at the man beside him. 'Some.'

The smaller man pointed a ragged-nailed finger. 'A guinea on John Sargent,' he said, naming Black Tom's bandy-legged opponent. 'Just between the two of us? Morry Smith's the name. I work for the lawyer Moxham here in Priorton.'

'Moxham? Why, that's my father's man. I'm Stuart McNaughton. Done!' he said, hastily shaking the other man's curiously dry hand before concentrating on the moment when Thomas's fist would crash into John Sargent's face, causing blood to spurt from his lip.

He had not been disappointed. Black Thomas gave his opponent such a beating he had to be carried off and didn't wake for two days. Stuart won money from his new companion and their friendship was sealed.

Tonight they had retrieved their horses from the livery across the road from the Grapes and made their way down the centre of Priorton's main street, picking through the Friday revellers.

Morry Smith cocked his head when Stuart said he had to go to Shotwell. 'Shotwell? That's beside New Morven, isn't it? Now there's good sport in that place . . .'

'New Morven?' said Stuart bitterly. 'It's full of papists and gypsies. Not a decent man there. Or woman,' he added sourly.

'I tell you, there's good sport there. And money to be made out o' those Irishmen.'

'Money? They're all paupers!'

'Aye, they're all paupers – and half of them is traitors! And the constable in Priorton has money for those who know one half from the other.'

'Does he now?' Stuart had said, pulling the reins to stop his horse fleeing at the flaring light of a straw torch outside an inn. 'What kind of sport was it you said?'

Fifteen minutes later they were riding into the teeming streets of the ironworks village, Morry leading the way to the Red Cockerel, where they left their horses in the care of shoeless urchins who said they would do the two for a halfpenny.

Inside, Morry marched straight across the packed bar and through a side door into a cleared space at the back of the inn. The crowd parted with cries of: 'Let the ge'men through!'

A square pit had been dug out of the clay ground. A man with a great chest, an enormous belly and no neck was scuffing up the earth with his feet. When he was satisfied with the tilth he had created, he drew his knobbed wooden stick along the centre.

'That's Belly Aungers,' Morry said in Stuart's ear. 'He's drawing scratch. They set the dogs either side.'

Belly Aungers moved and Stuart could see the dogs and their owners on the other side of the pit.

One owner was sitting with his dog's haunches between his knees.

A smaller man was kneeling to one side of him, his head almost buried in the white ruff of his own straining terrier, tongue busy over the fur like some mother cat.

'What in heaven!' muttered Stuart, revolted.

'He's the licker,' said Morry. 'Fellow that owns the other dog pays him. Sees if there's poison or secret hooks that can defeat their champion in unfair play.'

'Pays him?'

'A pint of beer. A gill of whisky. Maybe sixpence if their dog wins.'

'It's foul! No better than beasts.'

'As you say.' Morry nodded.

Belly Aungers loomed up before them. 'Marrington Bess is the white. The brown's called Old Cur.'

Morry put his hand in his waistcoat pocket. 'And here's mine host to take our wagers. How does half a guinea on the white strike you, Mr Aungers?'

Stuart's eyes were elsewhere. He was sweating, watching with bated breath as the snarling dogs were set to face each other across the scratch line. His ears rang with the shouts of roaring men as they encouraged the snapping and straining animals.

The fight had barely begun when Marrington Bess had her neck ripped. But she fought on gamely for another five minutes, until finally she'd ripped the shoulder of her smooth-haired opponent. The roars of the men were raised a pitch, close to a scream, and Stuart sweated in silence as Bess grasped the neck of Old Cur and shook her as though she were a rat, her own blood mixing with that of her now defeated enemy.

Ten minutes later the beer that Stuart poured down his throat in the small snug behind the steaming bar was the best he had ever tasted. He felt exultant, on top of the world.

'Some sport!' Morry yelled above the roar. 'Didn't I tell you?'

Stuart, his face bright red with excitement, shook his head. 'I've not seen anything like that. Never before.'

'No? Surprises me, a sporting man like you.' Morry glanced up at the door. 'Ah, here's Mr Kennedy, by whose means we might just make our expenses. Mr Kennedy, Belly's got a pint under the bar for you.'

He kicked out a stool and, after collecting his cloudy pint, Terry

Kennedy sat down opposite Stuart and carefully placed a pile of coins in front of Morry. 'Mr Aungers sent this over.'

Morry pocketed all of his winnings except a small heap of coins which he left glinting on the table. 'Now, Terry, This is Mr –'

'McKay,' put in Stuart hastily, pretending he didn't see Terry's half-proffered hand.

'So what are they getting up to in New Morven, Terry?'

'Usual tricks, Mr Smith. Fightin' and that.'

'How about plotting and that, Terry? How about firearms? Any traitorous blackguard salting'm away?' Morry narrowed his eyes and stared coldly at Terry.

He laughed uneasily. 'These Irish. Can't turn your back on them.' He paused. 'I heard this about a big feller, name of Farrell. Seems his brother, back in what they call the old country, took a shot at the landlord. Killed a keeper. Got shot to death hissel' for his pains.'

Morry closed his eyes and tipped his head up towards the ceiling. 'Name?'

'Tommo Farrell.'

'House?'

'Stables Street.'

There was a pause and Morry opened his eyes and nodded. Terry cupped his hand and pushed the coins Morry had left into it.

Morry picked up his hat and stood up. 'Now, Terry, what about some sweeter company?'

Stuart stood up beside him, looking from one to the other.

Terry grinned at them. 'There's a new'n just up beside the Puddler's. Not much sport but she's clean, and you get a nice tot of whisky thrown in.'

Morry stroked his chin. 'Well, I do like a bit of sport.'

'Don't I know it, Mr Smith? But why not give it a try? Mebbe it'll take a bit o' teachin'.'

Morry pulled out his watch. 'I don't know that there's time for that. Nevertheless . . . you game for some minor sport, Mr McKay?'

Stuart, still flushed, grinned at him. 'Show me the way, Mr Smith. Show me the way.'

Stuart was still sweating two hours later when he returned to Garth End Cottage.

Greg was sitting on his bed, waiting for him.

'Up late, brother?' said Stuart easily.

'I waited for you, to give you a black eye for giving Lauretta that filthy drawing.' Greg peered closer in the gloom. 'Looks like somebody's beaten me to it. What've you been up to?'

'It's those Irish,' said Stuart, his voice muffled by the shirt he was pulling over his head. 'Can't keep their hands to themselves. Hooligans!'

Greg laughed, got into his own bed and pulled the cover up to his chin. 'It looks to me, brother, like someone's given you just what you deserve!'

Chapter Five

Father Stephen O'Reilly had every reason to be pleased with his Sunday turn-out in New Morven. They were a ragamuffin bunch compared with his congregation at Priorton, but there were more and more of them as the ironworks expanded.

The iron company had donated three cottages which the stalwarts in his congregation had knocked into one, to house the altar and confessional. This would, he knew, have to do until silver collections on Pay Saturday – a custom set up by his predecessor Father Peter – provided the funds for a purpose-built church. The money was mounting at a good rate. New Morven people were at least open-handed ragamuffins.

He had affection for them now, but three years previously, when he'd first arrived, he had regarded them with a combination of distaste and terror. On his first day, making his way down narrow alleyways past crowded houses, he had had to step over tumbling half-naked children and some adults who were no better clad. He put one foot painfully in front of another, walking through the muddy streets among people too unthinking for despair. But acknowledgements such as a man doffing his cap or a woman bobbing a half-curtsy gave him the courage to continue.

On that day, and on days since, he had encountered individuals made half wild by starvation in Ireland who had thrown off their sense of grace, even blaming God for their suffering. These poor souls tortured Father O'Reilly with their unseen need.

Yet, slowly, he was gathering more and more people into the long room on Sundays. And those who never came to him had at least conscience enough to swell his church-building fund from their fortnightly wage on Pay Saturday.

This morning he raised his mind above the stink of badly

digested beer and spirits, the stench of barely washed bodies, and listened to the golden voice of Shona Farrell as she sang a simple child's song of faith.

He sighed at the sheer beauty of the sound and moved his feet restlessly at the loveliness of the girl with her pale lifted face. He noted with satisfaction the heavy figure of her brother beside her. Four Sundays in a row Tommo Farrell had come now. The girl must have some sway with him. Another one back in the fold.

The priest frowned. But there was a younger one there in that house, wasn't there? Running wild with Gil Tait's horses, as pagan as any child of the forest.

After the service he stopped Gil Tait on his way out. The livery man raised his tall hat high and winked at him. Used to the mannerism, Father O'Reilly took no offence. 'What about young Richie Farrell, Gil?' he asked. 'Can't you help that boy back to grace?'

'Sure haven't I tried, Father? But doesn't the young'n go his own way? Bin his own master more'n a year now and meks his own choices.'

'A child can't make his own choices, Gil. We should all care for his immortal soul.'

'He works for hissel' like a lot of young'ns.' Gil fingered the battered brim of his hat. 'Though you'd have thought things'd be different now, with the auntie comin'.'

'Auntie?'

'The father's sister. But what does Tommo Farrell do but throw the old'n out?'

'What?' This was a surprise. The little houses in New Morven were packed, sometimes with more than one family. It wasn't unusual to have fourteen or fifteen to a house. The Farrell house was empty by comparison.

Gil sniffed. 'Didn't that big feller Tommo take offence 'cos the old woman turned up on the back of some Protestant from Shotwell? Miss Biddy O'Farrell she called herself. Didn't Tommo close the door on them? The feller as brought her was off this Shotwell family . . . well, off this family that Father Peter knowed.'

The priest frowned. 'Father Peter?' He had never met his

predecessor; when he arrived the little priest's house had been empty. 'How? In what way? Were they of the faith?'

'Ah, no, Father. Such as them who call us papists and worse.'

'Well, how was it that . . . ?'

The little man replaced his hat. 'With respect, Father, that's for you to find out. I'll be bidding you good morning. I've fares to take to the station.'

Shona and Tommo Farrell were among the last to emerge from the makeshift church, squeezing through the narrow cottage door. Shona bobbed a curtsy to the priest and Tommo touched his cap.

'Shona!' The priest put a hand on her shoulder. 'Sure it was a lovely sound you made in there this morning. And I'm hearing that your aunt is coming to stay. Now that is a good thing!'

She wriggled under his touch and glanced up at her brother. 'Well,' she said uneasily, 'we're not sure . . .'

Tommo Farrell was striding off. Shona wrenched her shoulder free of the priest's hand and raced after her brother.

Father O'Reilly scowled. His Priorton congregation never treated him with such lack of respect. This New Morven crew reminded him of nothing so much as the wild ponies on his father's hill farm: secretive, timid and arrogant at the same time. He sighed and looked at the grey skies bulging with rain which was beginning to plop in the dirt around him, splashing yet more black coal-dust mud on to his long black soutane.

Early the next morning, in that same unceasing rain, Shona was walking to the pit, manoeuvring her way though snaking black puddles. Other workers, both men and women, scurried ahead and behind her, but she always walked alone till she met her friend Mary Challoner at the junction with the Shotwell road.

At one part of the road the water draining off the fields had made a flood. She pulled off her boots and hung them round her neck, hooked her skirtèd apron to the rope belt at her waist, and set off to wade to the other side. Her breeches would get wet but there was no taking them off.

A wave of muddy water hit her face as a horse entered the flooded path. She looked up angrily into the narrow face and slight smile of the man from Shotwell who had brought her aunt to the house.

Greg pulled his horse to a stop. 'Hello . . . Shona, isn't it?'

The other pit workers stared openly as they made their sodden way around them; all curious but none stopping.

'Hello yourself!' She was angry, standing there with black pit sludge on her face and sleep in her eyes. 'And what do you think you're doin' here?'

Greg reddened. The girl's tone was steeped in insolent familiarity, with none of the respect that had made her young brother instinctively call him 'sir' during their shared journey in Gil Tait's cart.

'I've to see Mr Gardner at the pit offices. They're giving us coal in part payment for some new wagons . . .' His voice faltered at her glare. Then he tried again. 'Your auntie is well. Quite recovered from her journey, you'll be pleased to hear.'

She shrugged. 'No saying she's our auntie.'

He spurred the horse and stood waiting at the edge of the water as she sloshed her way out. She sat on the side of the road and dried her feet with the hem of her apron before pulling her boots back on.

'She has to be your auntie. Why else would she . . .'

She shot a glance at him.

He persisted. 'I'd say she looks like you. And she has your very . . . attitude.'

She stood up and shook down her apron. 'I'd say, *Mr* McNaughton, that if you'd minded your own business at first she wouldn't be where she is – in the wrong place.'

He gathered up his reins. 'You'd rather I'd left her there to die of cold? And not even a priest to minister to her? Isn't that against what you lot believe in? She'd have died untended, you can be sure of that. I must be wrong. You're not in the least like her. She has more sympathy in her hat than you have in your whole . . .' He clicked his teeth and urged the horse on. Then he stopped and turned to her. 'I'd have thought you'd want your auntie with you, Miss Shona Farrell.'

As he wheeled the horse back through the pool, more black mud flew through the air and stuck to her breeches.

She yelled after him, 'It's a fool you are, Mr McNaughton. Here am I with one brother who's sad to his soul and another a child who was never a child, and it's sympathy you're . . .' But he was cantering further and further away and her voice could not have reached him.

The pitmen who had been coming up behind her now drew abreast, two of them walking on either side of her, too close. One of them knocked her arm with his elbow. 'Now what's this, Shona Farrell? Settin' up to bosses, are ye?'

'Aye,' said the other, grasping her shoulder with a grimy hand. 'Shona knows how to look after number one. An't poor pitmen good enough for ye now?'

She shook herself free of them. 'Get off, the pair of you, crows that you are. Wasn't that just another ignorant man thinks he knows what's what?'

She ran on to the junction. As always, Mary Challoner stood waiting, a dark shape in the early morning light.

Mary flung a heavy arm around Shona's shoulders. 'Worn't that one of those McNaughton lads ye was jawin' with?' she asked, her voice full of curiosity. 'Big fellers across at the railshops they are, the McNaughtons.'

Shona matched her pace with Mary's and started to laugh. Mary always made her laugh. She had made her laugh the very first morning when Shona had been placed alongside her to learn how to work on the screens. She had felt desperate at the great dark shed and the clanking ashen greyness of the pit yard. Mary had flung an arm round her then, calling her a bonny Irish rose, transforming her shrinking fear to blushing courage.

'Big fellers at the railshops,' Mary echoed now. 'Their da's the big gaffer.' Mary's brothers worked at the railshops. 'That one, bonny as a fine new whippet he is. There was trouble, time back, over him. He's the one that married the sister to that priest o' yourn. Hell of a lot'av trouble ower that!'

Shona blushed. 'Father O'Reilly?'

'Nah. They called him Father Peter sommat.' Mary paused. 'Tho' how you lot can call'm "father" as never will have young'ns – that beats me.'

'Mary, don't!' Shona looked up at the sky, a lowering sulphureous reflection of the grey pit yard. She always thought that some devastation would follow when Mary said these blasphemous things. But then, Shona had learned early on that Mary said many bad things with a kind of hardy innocence and no harm meant.

'Hey, is you bliddy pair comin' in here to start or not?' Len Hall's thin face peered round the corner of the ramshackle building. The yard was empty. 'Ye're after the sack, I can tell thet. The pair of you's for it!'

Mary pulled Shona across the yard and planted herself in front of the narrow man. She reached up cheekily and stroked the lank hair that hung down beside his face. 'Now then, Lennie! Ye know ye canna do without us, yer sweet Irish rose and yer own Weardale flower!'

Shona scampered past her to her place at the screens, appreciating as always Mary's knack of handling Len who came from the same hamlet as her, further up the dale. Their voices chimed together with the same particular echo and Shona remembered the chill she herself had felt in Liverpool on first hearing voices which were not from her own land; the sense of panic that flowed in a great wave from her neck to her heels; the desire to run back home to a mother and father who were no longer there.

The alien crispness of Greg McNaughton's voice floated back to mind. 'I'd have thought you'd want your auntie with you, Miss Shona Farrell.' She shivered, pulled her shawl closer, and started to separate the grey stone from the black shining lumps of coal.

Aida Sedgewick stared in a kind of contemptuous terror at the figure standing before her, all in black with a large hat. 'What?' she said rudely.

'Would it be possible to see Miss Biddy O'Farrell? I understand she's visiting here.'

'Wait,' mumbled Aida, and shut the door.

She leaned her back against it to steady herself then went upstairs to Mrs McNaughton's little sitting room. Biddy was sitting with Margaret McNaughton, looking at some fabric samples for dining-room curtains; Lauretta kneeling up to a chair in which sat two dolls and a real kitten.

Aida glared at Biddy then transferred her attention to Margaret. 'There's a man here to see . . . her.'

'A man? Miss O'Farrell's relative?'

'I don't think so.' She moved from foot to foot. 'He's in black.' She lowered her voice to a whisper. 'It's a *priest*.'

Margaret put her hand to her chest. Biddy stood up.

'Is he in the parlour?' asked Margaret.

'No, he isn't,' said Aida stubbornly. 'I thought it best to leave him outside.'

Margaret stood up, her colour returning. 'Aida! What are you thinking of? Show him into the parlour. Now!'

They watched her stump heavily from the room.

'Biddy, d'you want to talk to him? Shall I speak with him?' Margaret's tone was formal, drained of its recent warmth.

'No, don't trouble yourself, Mrs McNaughton. It'll be some message . . .' Her voice trailed away uncertainly.

The priest was standing with his back to the unlit fire, a small man, too broad for his height, not much more than thirty years of age.

He took her hand and she bobbed the faintest of curtsys. 'Good day, Father.'

'Hello, Miss O'Farrell. Biddy, isn't it?'

She stayed silent.

'I was talking to your niece Shona . . .' He raised one brow. She stayed silent. 'I was thinking about her, and the young one, Richie, and Tommo, wild as he is. They're all wild. They lack a mother's hand.'

'I never was a mother, Father.'

'Yes, Biddy. But that doesn't say you have to stay with strangers.' He looked round the crowded room. The parrot squawked and the priest jumped. 'Strangers not of our kind. Your not being a mother doesn't say that you couldn't give these young people a steadying hand. Did you know the youngest has never even been inside our church since he travelled to these parts?'

'He seemed a good and thoughtful boy to me. He'd had terrible times at home.'

'Yes, Miss O'Farrell, but without the sacraments? What if he were thrown off his horse, or fell under some wheel? Just think of him dying, the suffering he will . . .'

'He'll live,' said Biddy with brief certainty. 'Too many of them have died.'

Father O'Reilly tried another tack. 'And what of yourself, Miss O'Farrell? Have you . . .'

She interrupted him without a qualm. 'There was Father

57

Anthony on that awful boat, a nice old man. And once in Liverpool, I found a church.' She folded her arms. 'But wasn't it a strange way the Lord answered my prayers? My own turning me off and me taking the charity of strangers? Strangers not even of our own kind.'

'Trials are there, Biddy, to test and strengthen our faith. It's a weak Christian who flees at the first challenge . . .'

She fixed him with a level gaze. 'Were you in Ireland lately, Father?'

'To my regret, no. Not since I trained ten years ago.'

'I just wondered about that, so I did.'

He coughed. 'Well, it's here and now that I'm talking about, Miss O'Farrell.' His voice was cold. 'My advice to you is that those young souls need you. Our little church is there in New Morven, Miss O'Farrell. The house at the end of Albion Terrace. You need the sacraments. I'll expect you.'

She said nothing.

'I'll see them, your nephews and niece, and tell them it's their duty as Christians to come here and . . .'

'I don't want you to do that, Father,' she said quietly. 'Sure it'll work itself out the right way. I'm sure of it.'

He scowled at her.

She smiled at him then, very sweetly. 'Now, Father, would you be so kind as to give me your blessing?'

Stiffly she knelt down before him.

Stuart McNaughton almost choked as he flung open the door, apprised of the strange visitor by a raging Aida. Then he turned on his heel, shouting, 'Mother! Mother!'

Quickly Biddy grasped Father O'Reilly's arm to help her to her feet. 'Perhaps it would be better if you went, Father? Indeed it was very kind of you to call. And don't worry about the young ones. I'm sure it'll be all right. It will be fine. You'll see.'

Father O'Reilly was gone when they came: Stuart, closely followed by Margaret, and then Greg with a whimpering Lauretta in his arms.

Biddy smiled from one to the other. 'Wasn't that nice now? Father O'Reilly coming to welcome me to England.' She held out her arms to Lauretta who clambered into them. 'And what would you be crying for, little sweetheart?'

58

'See?' said Stuart. 'Papists! All sweet light and reason, then they bring a priest over the threshold! Priests!'

Biddy looked from one brother to the other across Lauretta's curly head. 'Faith, isn't he just a young man about his job? Coming here with news of the young ones in my family.'

Greg glanced at Stuart. 'All I see, brother, is people trying to make their way in a hard world.'

'Oh, we know they've got *your* sympathy, Greg. You've a weakness for priests and all their kin. I wonder if *this* priest has a sister?'

Greg looked as if he'd been punched but at that moment the door opened and Douglas walked in.

Stuart turned to him. 'We were just talking about the Irish, Father, and priests and their sisters!'

Douglas's jaw hardened and he lunged at Stuart. Himself again, Greg stepped between them.

Suddenly all three were aware of a whimpering 'Oh!' and turned to see Margaret fall in a heap on the floor. Lauretta cried 'Grandma!' and, scrambling down the rigid figure of Biddy, knelt by her grandmother.

Ramrod stiff, Douglas stepped round the crumpled figure of his wife. 'See to your mother, Greg,' he said over his shoulder as he went upstairs. 'All this is far too much for her.'

Greg bent down and drew Margaret into his arms. He looked at Biddy. 'Would you be so kind as to take care of Lauretta, Biddy?'

Immediately her stiffness melted and she caught the child's hand. 'Now how about a little story before you go to your bed, sweetheart?' Her glance strayed to Stuart who was watching her with cold intensity. She held his gaze and he turned and went out of the front door, slamming it behind him. 'It's about a great man in Ireland. A great fighter called Brian Boru . . .'

Chapter Six

Showy McLaglan brought Tommo's second pint across to him, and started to rub down the table with a greasy cloth. 'I see Father Stephen's been chasin' after you, boy-oh!'

'What's that mean?'

'Didn't they say he's been across to Shotwell after your auntie? Went over there to see her, is Gil's talk.'

'Should mind his own business.'

'God's business, he'd say.'

'They're all the same, those.' Tommo took beer into his mouth in a great gulp, then pointed to the table top with the half-empty glass. 'Another one, Showy, and one for Pat. He'll be here with a thirst on him any minute now.'

Showy hovered around for around minute, then went off muttering about those without respect. He himself never missed a Sunday mass. He even went to mass on Thursdays in the proper church at Priorton, which he followed up with a visit to the market and a slap up dinner with Kevin Green, landlord of the Queen's Head. He liked to be on good terms with the priest. Didn't it offer its advantages both in this world and the next?

A moment later Pat was squeezing past the bulky bodies of the other men, carrying the mended chair above his head. He placed it carefully on the table in front of Tommo, pushing against the beerglass to make a large enough space.

He eyed his friend warily as he sat down. 'There you are, Tommo. As good as new.'

Tommo clapped him on the shoulder. 'Didn't I tell the little sister there was no one better with wood? After our own daddy, that is. He made the chair, did you know that?'

Pat relaxed. 'You're a fool, Tommo, goin' on at Shona so. She's a good one. Plenty of the boys beat their women, but I had it in me

61

head you were different. But I suppose it's hard on you, her being so . . .'

Tommo glowered. 'So . . . what?'

'So what? Such a picture. As beautiful as the day.' Pat glanced at his friend's tightening fists on the table. 'Now don't start up again with that, Tommo! The way she looks'd shine through the dark for a blind man, weaken the knees of the legless. I just meant it's surprisin' there's been no man at your door.' He paused. 'Or hers.' He put one hand up. 'Now didn't I say, don't get hot again!'

Tommo's anger drained away as fast as the beer was sponged up by his dry throat. 'S'not easy in any way, Pat. Not easy at all, her being so . . . well.'

They sat silent, each stunned in his own way at the confidence Tommo had just shared.

'You need a woman of your own, Tommo. Sisters are all right but . . .'

Pat stopped and turned his head as a murmur went around the room. Two men had entered through the creaking door. They took off wide hats as they did so. One was small and square with close-cropped hair, and wearing a dusty frockcoat; the other was younger and taller, with fair hair straggling over his green tweed jacket.

'Prowlers!' muttered Pat fiercely, turning a contemptuous shoulder on them. 'Didn't I see the wee feller in the Cockerel, snuggling up to all and sundry for the word?'

'The word?'

'Priorton constables pay good money to know where the boys who's talking against the English has their guns. Good money! To be sure they make it up half the time, to get their hands on the silver. An' false information keeps the prowlers on the leash.'

Tommo watched as Showy fluttered over to the newcomers with his greasy cloth and a tray with a bottle and two glasses.

Tommo knew about the 'boys'. They plotted and planned over their beer at the Cockerel. They saved money, sometimes levied from the other Irish, willing or not, to buy guns. They talked of what they would do when they got back home with the guns; sometimes a stranger would drop by and collect one. There would be reminiscence about O'Connell the liberator who hadn't quite made it for Ireland. Further into drink there would be lyrical outbursts about the wrongs to be righted, the vengeance to be wreaked when they finally returned home.

Pat had taken Tommo to the Cockerel when he first arrived in New Morven. But the hot watchfulness of the atmosphere had oppressed him and he'd insisted on going to Showy's which was just about the drinking and music, the crack, the singing and laughter. He knew, however, that Pat often went on to the Cockerel after they parted and that he was most likely one of the boys himself.

Now, Tommo and Pat drank another pint quite quickly, unsettled by the men in the corner who were smiling and nodding in time with Gil Tait's squeezebox.

'Give us a song, Pat!' Showy called across, shouting above the music. He turned to the strangers. 'This boy has a song for every occasion. Makes'm up himself.'

Pat stood up and hoisted the mended chair on to his shoulder. 'C'mon, let's get out of here, Tommo. Doesn't the air in here stink? Let's get ourselves to where the air is more congenial for an Irishman.'

As they walked past the corner, he spat on the floor and muttered, 'Bluddy spies!' The man in the green jacket stared at him blandly, continuing to tap on the table in time to the music.

They stood outside for a few moments, under the creaking sign. 'Now then, Pat. Where to next?'

'Home. Home to get our suppers.' Pat put an arm around Tommo's shoulders and started to walk along the street. Eventually they came to the one house that was different from its dark and dreary neighbours. The tall woman was there again, standing in the doorway. Again she touched Pat's arm.

'Now, Maudie!' he grinned.

The woman put her hand on his forearm, pulling him to a halt. He put the chair carefully on the ground.

Tommo walked on past them, hesitated, then came back. He stood still, looking very closely at Maudie Martin. She was a newcomer to this part of the street. He'd heard talk of her in the Puddler's, but had never looked at her directly.

'Now, Pat!' The girl's voice was low and husky. 'It's good to see you again. And is this your friend?' She put a hand on Tommo's arm, holding them both fast. 'Now what about the pair of you? Wouldn't you boys be likin' a cup of Maudie's special tea? It's all laid out!'

Pat chuckled. 'I bet it is! This is me friend Tommo, Maudie. And you'll have to be careful with him as he steams up easy, too ready with his fists. No tea just at the minute. Aren't we on our way home now for some nice bacon stew?'

'You know well enough, Pat, that what I've got in my tea'll keep you going longer than any greasy stew!' She took a step into the fading yellow light of the street and, linking them both closely, hustled them through the doorway.

The little room was neatly furnished, illuminated by a flickering fire. The mantelshelf was covered with pottery figures of lads and lasses in various innocent encounters. On the table was a blue-patterned teapot and cups and saucers. Standing beside them, glittering in the leaping firelight, was a tall unlabelled bottle made of blue-green glass. In the corner was a bed with brass ends, covered with a dark green paisley shawl.

Maudie turned back to lift the chair inside, then shot the top bolt on the door and drew the curtains. 'There now, isn't that cosy? Sit down, won't you, and we'll have some tea.'

She poured the tea and pushed the cups in front of them. Then she picked up the bottle. 'Will you be wanting something else in there?'

'Looks dear stuff to me,' said Pat.

'It's the best quality. The very best quality. Untainted, clean and pure.'

'So what'll it cost us then?' Tommo spoke for the first time, looking into her wide, over-shrewd eyes.

'Well, it should be ninepence . . .'

'What?'

'But since there's two of you, I'd say a shilling the pair.' She had a slight lisp but her tone was clear, reminding Tommo for a moment of Manny's fiddle in the lower reaches of a tune.

'Go on, Tommo!' urged Pat, rattling the change in his own pocket. 'We still got siller from payday, an't we?'

'All right! All right!' Tommo pushed the cup in front of her and she slopped a good measure of bright shining liquid into it.

'Now you, Pat!' She walked round to his side of the table and leaned across him to pour out his measure, allowing her breasts to fall against his upper arm. He took the bottle from her and pulled her across on to his knee. Tommo watched while she busied herself undoing Pat's jacket, then his shirt, as he pulled at her dress. Maudie laughed over Pat's shoulder, her lips wide and smiling, her eyes cold and wary. 'Aren't you gonna give a hand here, then?'

Tommo shook his head and put his hands in his pockets and leaned back so he could put his feet up on the table. He nearly fell over when his gaze met that of a child who was peering down from a hole that gave access to the roofspace.

Maudie's voice sounded muffled from Pat's embrace. 'Becky, will you get back in your bed?'

'I wan' wee-wee, Mammee! Wee-wee!'

Maudie laughed and sat up straight. 'So here's me reward for tellin' her she cannot do it where she lies, like other children do! She has to go down the yard.'

'I'll tek her.' It would be a relief to be out of the room. Tommo stood up and held out his arms. The child dropped into them and clung to him like a squirrel. 'Out the back, is it?'

But Maudie was busy with Pat again.

Outside in the yard, he pulled up the child's shift and held her over the wide channel of sluggish water that moved down through the shared space. He frowned as a memory darted at him from somewhere, of being held like this over a running stream, his mother crooning something in his ear in the old language.

'Finished now!' the chirruping voice was saying. He put the child back on her feet, then swept her up again off the foul-smelling muddy ground and sat her on the wall. Her shift was crumpled but clean and white. She smelled fresh and meadow sweet, her scent unlike the rank odour of children he came across in Stables Street.

'See the stars, Mister? I'll tell my mammy about the stars.'

He looked up to where the stars cut their crisp shape out of the blue-black of the sky.

'See them, Mister?'

He grunted, trying to ignore the hand that was pulling the hair at the side of his head, poking its little fingers into his ear.

He caught the hand and held it tight. 'All right, little'n! Stars, you can see'm all over the place!'

'Everywhere? Even across the sea?'

'Everywhere. I've seen'm meself from where I come from, across the sea. I've seen'm in Ireland.'

'Ireland. What's that?'

'It's a place. Sweet and green. There's mountains and rivers. And the sea. The sea is very big and crashes hard against the land.'

'Pretty place.' She put her cheek by his and looked up at the glittering sky.

Maudie's voice behind him made him jump. 'Are *yous* two staying out there all night?'

'We saw the moon, Mammy!' said Becky, tumbling into Maudie's arms. 'And all the stars. And they are on top of Ireland too.'

Maudie laughed and nuzzled the child's face. 'That's right, sweetie! Keep your eye on the stars!' She turned to Tommo and her voice changed, at once merrier and more distant. 'She's never seen the old country. And I don't talk of it. The past is past, I say. Too much recall goin' on.' She paused. 'Tommo, your friend Pat's gone off, aching to get to his blessed bacon stew. He says don't forget the chair. Now, do we get on with our bit of business or shall we stand out here and freeze?'

Her business with him quickly done, Maudie leaned against the door jamb watching Tommo's sturdy back, the light from the windows glimmering on it as he made his way down the street, carrying the chair easily on his shoulder. She shivered. He had been gentle and funny for such a big man. She had taken a liking to him. That was always a mistake in this business.

'Now here's a corker for you, ge'men!'

She swung round at the sound of a new voice and pulled a face at the sight of Terry Kennedy, shepherding two men to her door.

'See what I mean, ge'men? A face and form like you seen in a paintin'.'

She stepped forward into the street and bared her teeth at them in her perfunctory businesslike smile. The younger, fair-haired man took her shoulder and ran his eyes down the length of her.

'How much?' he said.

'A shillin',' she said quickly.

66

Stuart dropped his hand. 'Too much.'

'She's worth it, I tell you, Mister. Has town ways. D'you know what I mean?'

'What about two together?' Morry Smith pushed forward eagerly.

She turned away. 'No. Not two. One at a time. And it'll cost you a shillin' each.'

Stuart pulled her round again. 'Cheeky Irish bitch! A shilling it is.' He pushed her into the house before him and locked the door himself. He turned to her. 'Now, bitch. All your clothes off, every item.'

'I don't do that.'

He reached for the neck of her dress. 'For a shilling you do!' He wrenched at the buttons.

She sighed and her hand came up to push him away. 'Here, I'll do it myself.' She removed her clothes one by one, laying them carefully on the chair beside the fire. Then she half sat, half lay on the bed, her heavy breasts dropping slightly to one side.

'Now!'

He remained fully dressed, just fumbled to loosen his breeches. He was sweating and his hand was already shaking.

Then he was on her, pulling her up roughly beneath him and pushing away at her. But no matter how he pushed at her, he failed to become hard. She lay there, unspeaking.

'Come on, bitch, help me, can't you?' he growled.

She knew how to do it. She knew very well how to do it, but her hands stayed on the bed.

He started to hit her then, across the face, across her shoulders. She didn't cry out but waited for the moment when he was unbalanced by a particularly hard swing so that she could roll out from under him.

The moment came and she plunged towards a crude shelf beside the fireplace. When she turned round she had a knife in her hand, an old one of dull steel, sharpened to a lethal edge and a fine point: payment in kind from a grateful ironworker.

'Get out,' she spat. 'Get out!'

He stood up, clutching his breeches to him.

She poked the knife towards him. 'Out! You're no better use than an untooled bitch yourself. Call yerself a man!'

He lunged towards her and she brought the sharpened edge against his face, causing blood to flow.

'Now, go!'

He kept his face towards her as he edged away to the door, feeling behind him with one hand for the bolt. She stood back while he slipped out like an eel, then rushed forward to lock the door, top and bottom.

Terry Kennedy's voice started to bellow through the wood. The hammering and shouting went on for five minutes. Maudie pulled on a shift, took a shawl for her shoulders, then sat and poked the fire, watching the flames flare up until all was silent.

'What was that, Mammy?'

She looked up at Becky's face peering through the roofhole.

'It's only men, sweetie. Sure, it's nothing to worry about. You go back to bed.'

'Can't we go and look at the stars again?'

'No. They've been turned down now. They'll turn them on again another night. You'll see.'

Tommo carefully let himself in the house and placed the mended chair beside the fire. Shona stirred on her mattress in the corner as he stood stock still. Two squat candles sputtered at one end of the mantelpiece, their gleam spilling on to Shona's upturned sleeping face.

He looked at the rough grey blanket that covered her and thought of the bright soft quilt on Maudie Martin's bed. He walked across and nearly tripped over Richie curled up on the mat in front of the fire, his hand still clutching the rag with which he had been polishing Cush's bridle.

Tommo touched his brother's shoulder with his boot.

The boy stirred. 'What, what . . . no, no!'

'S'me, Richie. C'mon, will you get up from there and get yourself into bed?'

Shona sat up quickly in her stained shift, her eyes unfocused. She shook her dark head then looked across at her brother. 'What's this, Tommo? Later than ever?'

'Settle down, Shona.' He looked at his sister and thought of Maudie with her strong body cased in a fine cambric shift. He closed his eyes and saw her rearing above him, entirely naked and supremely confident about her business. He became hard yet again and moved his feet uneasily, glad of his heavy workman's breeches.

He looked round the room and thought of the bright place he had just left: its fire, its gleaming yellow lamp and soft rich cloths. His gaze came back to his sister. Sleep had robbed her face of its usual boldness. She looked about eleven years old. 'Not much of a life here for you, Shona, is it?' he whispered.

She lay back and pulled the blanket up under her chin. 'Sure it'll serve, Tommo. We've more room here than most.'

'But what about a table, even a clock on the wall? Like we had with Ma and Da back home?'

'It'd be a nice thing, a table. And another chair, to go with these two. Then couldn't we all sit around it and eat and talk like we did then?'

'I'll get you one, and a chair. Next payday. And a new dress for you. A white one.'

Her laugh was slurred and spiked with sleep. 'You'll not manage that, Tommo, you'd have to do without your beer and your gambling.'

'Three chairs is not enough.' Richie had one foot on the ladder, ready to climb up into the roof. 'We want four. One for the woman. The auntie. She should be here.' He hauled himself up the ladder.

Shona sat up again. 'Yes. Most of all she should be here.'

Tommo looked round the dark room again. Maybe the old woman would make a difference. 'All right. I've nothing against her coming. It was just that great Proddy pig that brought her.'

Richie popped his head back down through the roofhole. 'Tomorrow! I'll borrow Gil's pony cart, and take Cush. I'll get her after work.'

Tommo went across and blew out the guttering candles, then felt his way to the ladder and followed Richie into the roofspace.

As she lay back on the mattress Shona could hear the crashes as he blundered around above her in the darkness. Her last thought before she drifted back to sleep was of a tall slender man on a horse splashing through black mud. Then in her dream she was looking down and watching while a mud stain spread across her new white dress.

Chapter Seven

Stepping out of the door of Garth End Cottage, Douglas McNaughton glanced around him with satisfaction. The huddle of buildings loomed dark in the early morning. The late moon contemplated its own reflection in the clouds. There were glimmers of light from the high windows of the blacksmith's shop and the foundry, although the rest of the works was in darkness.

How many men had the blessing of creating their own kingdoms, of hammering out their own dreams in hard metal? He smiled faintly. Whatever chaos there may be behind him in the cottage, ahead of him lay order and progress.

Half an hour later, at five-thirty, Old Jamie MacQuistain, whose son, Young Jamie, was Douglas's foreman, shuffled in and pushed the railshed door closed behind him, the creak echoing up to the iron rafters that held up the great roof.

Old Jamie made his way past the boilers standing in line like soldiers to the corner of the shed where Douglas was standing holding up a lamp, peering at the innards of an exploded boiler. The back of the boiler was entirely broken, its round iron firedoor gaping open, the broken steel tubing fingering the air in mute desperation.

Douglas looked up and nodded grimly in the yellow light at the old man. 'This was a bad one, Jamie,' he said gravely. 'A driver killed and a brakesman injured.'

'Not one of ours though, is it? Do they want you to mend it then?'

Douglas felt a twinge of regret as he heard Jamie's respectful tone. This was the man who many years ago had grasped him beneath his arms and lifted him on to that first engine his father had built for Crangorrach colliery. There at Crangorrach, as a child, he had clutched Jamie's large hand in excitement as the little engine set away down its wooden tracks shooting steam into the air.

71

'Do they want you to mend it, Mester?' the old man repeated.

He smiled. 'No, Jamie. The company want a report on the damage, and an estimate for a repair.' He lifted the lamp again. 'It might mend. Or I might tell them to scrap it.'

'Looks past it to me.' He paused. 'Well, I'll just get on. Them fires'll need lookin' to.'

Jamie came across to the works only in the mornings. Douglas would have paid his wages whether he came or not but he still turned up every morning, checked the fires, tidied up the walkways and kept an eye on the men, often cocking his head to one side and giving unasked-for advice.

Douglas brushed one hand against the other and set off down the shop with him. The great door scraped again and one by one the men passed Douglas, touching their caps.

Jamie shuffled along beside him, right through the works, up the iron steps by the last gantry, to the glassed-in office. From here Douglas could watch the whole of the workshops come to life; he relished the satisfaction of seeing men setting about the complex tasks which had started out on his drawing board.

Jamie stood beside him. 'D'ya know what ah sometimes wonder, Mester?'

'What'd that be, Jamie?'

'What yer daddy would think if he saw all this. Saw who's master now. Would he think on, up there, on how he started? Wearin' thet old leather apron against that hot Crangorrach fire.'

A faint smile etched itself on Douglas's face. His father had made that first black boiler, not much larger than a kitchen kettle, at the colliery, staying back and working on it in his own time. How many nights had Douglas as a small boy raced across there, to find him musing over the movement brought about by the thrusting, boiling power of steam? How he would shout and scream and clap his hands as the crude piston started to move!

Jamie MacQuistain had been his father's apprentice, then, always by his side: a young man in his powerful prime in whose arms or on whose shoulders Douglas sat as the miracle of steam revealed itself before their wondering eyes.

Breakfast at Garth End Cottage, after the companionable mutter of prayers, was a busy if silent affair.

Biddy had continued to wait and watch. She helped Aida as far as she was allowed, even though the Cumbrian woman usually looked through her as though she were glass and never spoke to her directly.

Douglas was civil enough, dealing with the Irishwoman with the same air of distance and polite detachment that he offered his wife. Biddy shivered with the chill of it and her instinctive sympathy for Margaret McNaughton increased.

This morning, as usual, Douglas greeted them both with a gruff 'Morning!', reaching in his pocket for his battered copy of *Daily Worship for Christian Households*. The prayers dispensed with, he retired behind his paper.

On the table were plates of cold cut bacon, bread, and a great jug of milk, brought down from Priory Farm by Greg and Lauretta on their usual morning sortie. Lauretta, as was her custom, took the first crust of bread through to the parlour for Irma, the parrot. Disdaining to eat it as usual, Irma broke it up and threw it on the carpet around her perch.

Watching the bird's antics Biddy protested to Greg. 'Didn't I see too many people hungry in Ireland?' she demanded. 'No clothes for their back. No food in their belly. A crust to break their fast would be like God's manna to them. And here, it goes to a dusty old bird who throws it on the floor!'

Greg smiled ruefully. 'Would you like to pack it up in a parcel, the bread, and send it across there, Biddy?'

'Now that's silly talk, boy!'

'Well, let Irma have her fun. Can't be very nice chained to a perch all day.'

The door clicked as Stuart came into the room. Douglas lowered his paper and peered at him. 'You were late to bed, Stuart. This is no way to start a working day, blear-eyed!'

Teetotal and preoccupied himself, Douglas assumed late hours were the only cause of Stuart's morning lethargies.

'And what's that?' Margaret said sharply, indicating a red scar that ran all the way down her son's cheek.

He placed a cautious finger on the wound and gave a laugh like a fox's bark. 'Spencer Springall was in Priorton, Mother. The one who was at the grammar school with me? He invited me to his house, more properly his stable, so he could mime me up some duelling moves shown him by his grandfather who was at Waterloo. We used

73

the old boy's rapiers.' He laughed again, then winced at the pain in his face. 'Well, the battle became serious. So this morning Spencer has a great rip down his jacket and I have this cut.'

'Duelling!' Margaret moaned.

Stuart smiled across at her, pleased for once to have his mother's full attention.

Biddy stood up and, leaning towards him, peered at his cheek. 'Is there a flower in this place, round green leaves and a bright yellow head? A pulp of those heaped on it'd stop a bad scar.'

'I wish to keep the scar, Miss O'Farrell. What better way to show valour than a nice big scar? What say you, Mother?' His sheer dislike of Biddy, now having the cheek to offer him peasant cures, distilled his usual condescension into pomposity.

'Me, dear?' Margaret looked at him with deceptive mildness. 'Oh, I still think you'll need something on that nasty gash.'

Douglas had retired again behind his newspaper, ignoring this interchange.

'Spencer Springall's not at home,' stated Greg, scowling. 'He went to America to work in a manufactory belonging to his father.'

'He's just come back,' said Stuart defiantly. 'He told me about it. South America, it was.'

Greg eyed his brother. Stuart had woven wonderful untruths about his exploits ever since he had been a small boy. Flora had beaten him for it, as had Aida. But Stuart's lying was a secret well kept from their father, who saw no further than the ledgers which his son kept with such admirable neatness.

'He can't be back because . . .' began Greg.

'Oh, stop quarrelling,' said Margaret, with such uncharacteristic sharpness that even Douglas lowered his paper. 'Let us have peace!'

'Peace! It always has to be peace!' Stuart exploded, standing up.

Drawn into the fray despite himself, Douglas stood up with him. 'Yes. Your mother needs peace. It's time we were at the works.'

Biddy smiled. She knew that Douglas had been across at the works since five-thirty, doing whatever he did. This would be his second shift of the day.

Douglas caught her smiling glance and held it before he stalked out of the room, Stuart at his heels.

A few minutes later Douglas came back, stuffing a sheaf of papers into a leather satchel. 'Take these into Priorton to Lawyer Moxham,

Gregor. Contracts for new building land outside Priorton. He needs to check them and itemise the purchase agreement and write a letter confirming so to Amos Rainton.' He looked around the table. 'Take the ladies in with you in the brake. It's market day, a good one for an outing.'

Margaret clapped her hands with pleasure. Lauretta clapped hers too and shouted: 'Hurrah! Hurrah!' without knowing the reason for the celebration.

'Something up today, Mary?' Shona looked across at her friend who was leaning on her round shovel, staring at the ground. Len had set them on tipping stone into the wagon ready to be sent along the rail to the tip. Mary usually relished the job, managing as much as any man with her strong country muscles. Shona too, though more wiry, had become adept at heaving coal and stone.

Mary looked straight at Shona, her eyes wide in her heavy-jawed, ugly face. She pushed her shovel under her arm and pulled her right hand out of its mitten. Her finger ends were swollen and white. 'See those bliddy keens? And those bliddy whitlows? I said nowt'd stop us in this job, and even hands like rotten cabbage stumps dinnat.' Then she put the hand to her waist and pulled it across her stomach, showing the bulge under her sacking pinny. 'But now I'm bliddy up the stick.'

'Up the stick?' Shona frowned.

'There's a bairn in there. Off one of these bliddy miners, with their bliddy wiles. I can throw off the hard lads, easy as pie.' Tears were running down her face now. 'Them as push themselves on to yer. But the ones with soft words . . . promise you anything, they do. An' then I get carried away mesel'. The bugger is, I dinnat kna wheh's it is. Could be one of two, I dinnat kna which.'

Shona threw down her shovel and put her arm round Mary's sturdy shoulders.

Mary was bawling now. 'An' I've been up sick all night. An' the last two night. An' I'm that bliddy tired. An' me belly hurts like hell. An' me hands burn like a whiplash. More'n ever before.' Now tears were making white tracks in the black dust on her face. 'Oh!' She collapsed to the floor, pulling Shona with her.

The other women stopped work and clustered around. The old men went on working, but lifted their heads in mild curiosity.

75

Len Hall was clambering down from his gallery. 'What's this?'

One of the older women, Meg Tallent, stood in front of him, staring him in the eye. 'You want nothing here. She's lossin'.'

He took half a step back. 'Get her in that bliddy tally booth, Meg. The rest of you get back. The screens is pilin' up.'

Between them, Meg and Shona half-dragged, half-carried Mary across to the booth where the miners' number tallies hung, scoring their work for the day. They laid her on the narrow floor-space and Mary clung to Shona, retching and moaning. Meg vanished and came back with two pieces of sacking. She pushed one roughly under Mary. Black dust rose as she shook the other out to one side, then spread it carefully on the floor. She knelt beside the moaning woman, pulling away at her breeches. 'Ye'd better let it come, flower. It's doin' yer no good where it is.'

Shona held on to Mary as her body arched and she gulped down screams into painful moans.

'There, flower, it's away now. Now wait, wait!' Meg's voice was tender. Shona had never heard her use that tone before.

Another scream.

'That's it. That's the rest, flower.' She peered upwards from her place between Mary's knees into Shona's terrified eyes. 'Bliddy men! They want it cuttin' off. Ye want nowt to do with'm, flower. Nowt!'

Shona ventured: 'A baby?'

Meg parcelled the thing up, then carefully made another roll of the sacking that had been under Mary.

'Not so you'd notice, flower.' The old woman hauled herself to her feet and stumped out of the room, handling her parcels with great care.

While Meg was away, Shona desperately tried to wipe Mary's sweating face with the inside of her apron. 'There, there, me darlin'. You'll be all right soon. It's all over now.'

Mary started to cry quietly, her head turned away from Shona.

Meg returned with Len beside her and an old man hovering behind.

'In the wars, Mary?' Len's thin face loomed close. 'I got old Mac Siddons here, with his cart. He'll tek yer home. I give him sixpence.'

Mary struggled blindly to her feet, clutching at Shona. 'Good of yer, Len. But me job?' she muttered. Her face was a mess: a mixture of coaldust, tears and blood where she had bitten her lip against the pain.

'Get here on Friday and you'll still have it,' said Len. 'Ye'll loss two days' pay, but that can't be helped.'

Helplessly Shona watched her friend hobble out of the filthy kennel supported by a man on either side.

She turned to Meg. 'The baby – the thing – where d'you put it?'

Meg shrugged. 'That? On the tip. Isn't the first and won't be the last out there.' Her face hardened at the troubled young face before her. 'Now, lass, wor'll need to get on ourselves or wor'll loss our jobs too.'

After an hour Mac Siddons came back. He came up to Shona. 'That lass sent tha this. She said to give it yer, as it's your very image.' He pushed into her hand a small pottery figure of a milkmaid in a blue apron. She had long dark hair and blue eyes like Shona herself. 'She said tha's no to worry and she'd see thee on Friduh.'

Shona pushed the figure into her apron pocket and went on with her work under Len Hall's sharp eyes. The random blocks of black coal had a bitter silver sheen in the afternoon light which streamed in through the great doors.

Standing quite still, Len watched the girl as she picked up a flat stone imprinted with the perfect image of a tiny fish, complete with scales and fine fins.

She held the stone to her eyes and looked at it closely. Richie would like that one. She put it in her pocket where, as she moved, it grated against the pottery figure of the girl with the blue apron and the dark hair. She ran her fingers over the unseen shape, and murmured a phrase remembered from somewhere in her childhood: '"Lord, watch over this, thy humble servant".'

Chapter Eight

Warmly wrapped against the cold, Lauretta was clapping her hands again, this time at a dog, clad in a dainty hat and miniature dress, which walked on its hindlegs behind its master all around Priorton marketplace.

Greg had left them standing beside a man who had a great fire in an iron cauldron, and was handing out hot roast potatoes on sticks.

'We'll be at Melham's the drapers. Find us there,' Margaret called after him.

Greg made his way up a narrow alleyway and across a cobbled street, then through a single door which led up some old stone steps.

He was greeted by a bullet-headed man with a straggling beard who was standing at a tall desk, writing. His broadcloth coat was cut closer than was normal in this country town.

'Mr McNaughton?' The small eyes narrowed further. 'I'll inform Mr Moxham.'

Mr Moxham, silver moustaches quivering, came bustling out, then stopped. 'Ah, Mr McNaughton! It's *young* Mr McNaughton. I thought it was your father.' He turned to the clerk. 'Mr McNaughton senior is a genius! A genius with machines, a most gifted man, of the class of Mr Stephenson and Mr Hackworth. And you, Mr McNaughton junior, are you a genius?'

Greg laughed. 'Aye, he's a genius, sir, my father. Though I'd say more of the class of Mr Hackworth and poor Mr Trevithick. Mr Stephenson, I'd say, has a genius for the lie of the land and a gift for the improvement of other people's inspiration. But that's just an opinion. As for me? Only room for one genius in a family, Mr Moxham.' He looked uncertainly at the clerk. 'I've some business for you from my father. Regarding land.'

'Ah, business! A man of business are you now? Well, follow me.' Mr Moxham turned round with a flourish and led the way into his office which was full of chest-high tables on which were spread books and documents. He walked across to the window and stood behind a smaller table which was clear, its polished surface glittering in the pale winter sun.

'I see you looking for a chair, Mr McNaughton. You will find no chairs in my office. No one sits down to work here. Terrible bad for the heart that is. We will stand to business. Keeps it short and to the point.'

Greg smiled. He had been to this office with his father many times since he was a small boy and had heard the speech before.

He spread his father's papers on the desk. 'I see you've a new clerk?'

'Yes. Mr Maurice Smith by name. Alas, my old friend and clerk Jack Harrop just faded away. Found him leaning on his desk one morning stone dead. Upright!' Mr Moxham laughed heartily. 'A funny old stick, Harrop.'

'And this new clerk?'

'Called on me that very same day. Had excellent papers, and is a wonderful hand at writing documents. First class. Said all the right things at first. But now . . .'

'But now?'

'I am not certain of him, Mr McNaughton. Not certain of him at all. Did you see that beard? And I see a gleam in his eye when he's being most unctuous. I last saw that in a grave robber who was brought up before the assizes.'

'So he won't last?'

'I don't doubt that he won't, Mr McNaughton.' The old man rubbed his hands. 'Now, sir, to business. What is it your father requests?'

At the drapers Lauretta soon charmed the young assistant who vanished with her to the back regions of the shop to show her some new dolls.

Margaret and Biddy lingered over the final choice of dark green velvet for the dining-room curtains and Mr Melham the draper wrote down the particulars carefully in his narrow ledger. 'We will have them ready for you in a week, Mrs McNaughton. Our Mr Caperling'll come and hang them. And he'll bring Mrs Caperling to make any final adjustments.'

Biddy looked around the room with its orderly bales of rolled cloth. 'Sure you've got enough in here to curtain a town.' Her Irish tones rang cheekily against his clear-cut merchant-speak.

He turned his head to look more closely at her through his round glasses. 'That is indeed our aim, ma'am.' His voice was sharper now, losing its oily edge. 'Is there anything which strikes Madam's fancy?'

'Well, Mister, indeed if I'd a home of me own, I'm sure there would.'

'Miss O'Farrell is a guest in my house, Mr Melham,' put in Margaret, a very slight smile on her face.

'Are you visiting these parts, Miss O'Farrell?' He wondered what on earth Mrs McNaughton was doing with this creature, obviously Irish. The risks!

'You might say that, sir. I . . .'

'Mr Melham, would you kindly place some chairs by the fire?' Margaret intervened again. 'I've told my son to find us here and we must stay 'til then.'

'With pleasure, Ma'am.'

After a few minutes of fussing over whether or not Mrs McNaughton needed a cushion and whether she was warm enough, he left them in peace. He neither looked at nor spoke to Biddy.

She chuckled to Margaret, 'The wee feller has more grease in him than a Kilkenny goose!'

'Biddy, shhh!' Margaret laughed out loud in her turn. She leaned back in her chair to peer through the door. 'Look at all those people! Douglas used to love the markets so much when we were young. He used to search out the mechanical things. Once, at Hexham market, we saw a metal bear dancing to music! Can you imagine? And if there were flowers, you could be sure he'd buy some! He once bought violets and fixed them to my bonnet there and then in the street. He was so striking then, so funny! Greg is so like him now.'

'Ye sound like true sweethearts,' Biddy said, trying to square this with the chill she experienced in Douglas's presence. 'But what . . . ?' She left the question on the air.

Almost eagerly Margaret took it up. 'It was all wonderful at first. Then the babies came, Greg first. Then the ones who died, poor souls. And I was so poorly. And that . . . the business . . . of marriage didn't suit me. But you wouldn't know?'

'I know fine well the business of marriage,' said Biddy. 'Though people think I shouldn't, no ring on my finger and it being a mortal sin.'

'Well, then he became so fixed on the engineering. He's a leading member of the British Association, solving problems for manufacturers. And so fascinated by steam! Making those great monsters move. So distracted and impatient at home.'

'Men and their work!' agreed Biddy ruefully.

'Then Greg, when he was only eighteen, he did that silly thing. One of the engineers took him to Russia to fit one of the first engines there. Then, a year after, on the train coming back, he met a woman, coming here to Durham to visit her brother. And in no time he was married to her! They went to Scotland to be married and back, he no more than twenty and she nearly twice that.'

Margaret nodded conspiratorially then went on, 'They came home to Garth End Cottage. And there was Douglas, opening doors for the woman, making sure she was comfortable. There was such laughter in the parlour.' She paused. 'You saw how he reacted when that bad Stuart was insulting her.'

Unsure of quite what she meant, Biddy nodded. 'It must have been a relief, Douglas not taking against her,' she suggested quietly.

'It was at first.' Margaret looked sharply at the other woman. 'Then the attention she got, the laughter she made . . . I realised then that I'd not been properly . . . loving to him.'

She paused remembering.

'I felt like a bad woman! A bad woman, Biddy. Then there was that terrible business . . . Now he welcomes less and less of my company. Less and less. When he sees me, you'd think he sees a snake!'

'Sure that isn't so. He's a very busy man.'

Margaret was growing red and agitated. 'And Stuart is no better! Have you seen him looking at me through those strange eyes? You know, he once told me he hated me. *Hated* me!'

'Sure aren't all children the very devil sometimes?'

'No! No!' said Margaret urgently. 'He was so bad! You see, Flora, my lovely Flora, had to go home, with her mother dying. Flora had taken care of Stuart from being a baby. I'd had the poor little ones and they had died. And then Murray, so frail, but an absolute beauty . . . Of course he died. Because I was so ill with losing the other babies, Flora took charge. Well, the day she went, Stuart would be perhaps eleven or twelve. A big strong boy. Do you know, on that day he waited for me in the hallway and punched and punched me? He kicked me. He was so strong, he could have killed me.'

Biddy leaned over and held the other woman's hand tight.

'He could have killed me. But in all the struggle he kept silent and so did I. I kept silent afterwards too. No one knew. Greg was too young and Douglas wrapped up in himself . . . And then in no time Greg getting married like that. Only twenty years old.'

'Sure, 'tis a young age to be married, but lots of boys is married in Ireland at that age. The priests approve. It keeps them out of trouble.'

Margaret laughed. '*This* priest didn't approve. Her brother. He was a priest in Priorton. Oh no, he didn't approve! He was on our doorstep like the very personification of the wrath of God. Frothing at the mouth with rage! Pulling the woman out after him.' Margaret laughed again, too loudly. 'But Douglas showed him! He took the woman from him and thrust him out of the door.'

'Threw the priest out?' Biddy crossed herself, beginning to understand.

'Oh, yes. His people came and got him. He was crawling down Shotwell High Street, gibbering with rage.'

'The poor soul,' said Biddy softly.

'Save your pity! His sister wrought havoc in our lives!' said Margaret grimly. 'Do you know, that woman, she would go into Douglas's workroom and make copies of his drawings for him to send to the Association? They talked together right into the evening! There was laughter in that room!

'And the fuss when she came to be with child! She could have anything! Oh, one side of me was pleased at first. Here he was, taking an interest in his family. But . . .' Her voice faded on the air and Biddy could think of nothing to say that would make sense.

Margaret stood up and stared in the fire. 'I only once went out with her, to take some money and food to an old pensioner of Douglas's . . . an old Scotsman who lived at this end of New Morven. Never again! Those people threw stones at us, dried horse dung. They shouted names at her. The crowd milled around us and I was frightened. They were angry at the disgrace she had brought her brother, the priest. They called her a witch.

'After that day I was ill and Aida took care of me. I came out in blotches when the woman came near me. I was dizzy. She was a witch. They called her that.'

'No, Margaret! To be sure you're mistaken.'

'Those people knew she was a witch. On that very last night before she and Greg went . . . They were guyed up, with blackened faces, the women dressed as men and men as women. Carrying guys of Greg and that woman, made of straw and cloth. Uncanny! You could see just who they were meant to be, those great dolls. The woman had this great head of horsehair dyed red somehow, with white wool drawn through it to show her age. Like an old witch! They came three nights running.'

On the third they had thrust the two dolls together in an obscene congress, then cut the woman doll with knives and afterwards burnt them both. Margaret remembered that but wouldn't say it.

She was shaking now. Biddy stood up and pulled her to her feet. 'There now, sweetheart, it's all past now. All past!' she whispered but Margaret turned a tearful face.

'But it's not, Biddy. He's still gone from me, Douglas. She still has him. The witch.'

The shop bell rang and her face lightened instantly. 'Ah! Here's Greg. But who . . . ?'

Greg introduced them to Morry Smith, Mr Moxham's clerk. 'When I said we were meeting here, Mr Moxham remembered a parcel of towels Mrs Moxham wished collected. So Mr Smith insisted on coming to collect them.'

'Mrs McNaughton! I was just this minute telling your son I've the pleasure of the acquaintance of the other young Mr McNaughton. Such a great fellow! I saw him only yesterday.'

'He came home last night with a cut cheek,' said Greg.

'Ah, that. Well, Mr McNaughton, those scoundrels of Irishmen again! Waylaid us as we were about our lawful business. Brutes! I defended poor Stuart as well as I might.'

'So there was no duel?' Margaret was disappointed.

'Jewel? Duel? I know naught of any duel!'

Biddy shook her skirts, smoothed them down with her hands and looked the bearded clerk in the eye. 'To be sure those Irishmen have a lot to answer for!'

'Can I introduce you to my mother's guest, Mr Smith? Miss Biddy O'Farrell?' said Greg, grinning broadly. He turned round. 'Now where's that daughter of mine?' he said to Mr Melham, just emerging from the back regions of the shop. 'Lauretta!'

When they got home, Greg took the brake on to the livery stables. Margaret was thoroughly tired and Biddy helped her to her bed then went down to the kitchen to warm some milk herself, ignoring Aida's turned back and resentful mutterings.

Lauretta stayed outside in the narrow garden, playing with a ball that Greg had bought her from a man in the market. She had a good game throwing it into a bush and waiting for it to trickle down through the branches and roll towards her on the winter grass.

Hearing the clop of hooves on the gravel she peeped through the branches and saw a familiar face peering back down at her over the head of the pony. Behind him he was pulling a home made iron contraption with two seats at the front and two at the back, sideways on.

Lauretta emerged from behind the bush, smiling her delight. 'Funny cart,' she said.

'Me brother Tommo made it for me. At the foundry.'

'Nice pony.' She reached up her hand to stroke the white forelock.

Richie grinned back at her. 'His name is Cush.' He looped the leather bridle over a low branch.

'I got a bird. A parrot.'

'What's his name?'

'Irma.' She took his hand. 'I show you Irma.'

Aida met them at the door. 'Who's this?' she demanded.

'Richie Farrell, Missis,' said the boy. 'I saw you t'other day.'

Her face hardened. 'One of them, aren't you? Well, you can come to the back door and I'll get her for you.'

He shrugged and followed her round the back, Lauretta skipping ahead of them.

Aida made him wipe his feet on the mat before she let him in. 'I'll go for her.'

Biddy smiled broadly when she saw the boy standing there, his cap in his hand. 'Richie!' She took his shoulders and hugged his rigid body.

'Our Shona and Tommo say I'm to come to get you,' he announced. 'You're to stay with us.'

Behind Biddy, Aida was smiling slightly and nodding at the boy.

'Well, sweetheart, wouldn't I truly love to come?' said Biddy softly. 'But how can I where I was so badly used? Isn't it for your brother Tommo to come and just say he's sorry, and then indeed I can come home with you? Isn't it the only way I'll know I'm welcome?'

Richie went red. 'You're welcome, I tell yer!'

'But it was Tommo that turned me off. He has to come to me. To ask me.' She put her hand on his shoulder. 'Now you go and tell him, Richie. To be sure, I'll be in your house soon.'

He turned and grasped the door-sneck. Lauretta ran to him and caught hold of his jacket. 'Come and see my Irma!' she pleaded but he shook her hand off, shot a thunderous look at Biddy, went out and clattered the door behind him.

Aida was leaning against the dresser looking equally thunderous. 'You'll be better off with your own, Miss O'Farrell. I keep telling Mrs McNaughton.'

Biddy smiled slightly. 'Sure, don't I hear you saying it all the time? Now don't you worry, Aida, I'll be out of your hair before long!'

Outside in the lane, Richie's headlong scatter was brought to a halt by Greg who was just coming across from the stables. 'Whoa there, boy! What are you doing here?'

'I came to get the auntie.'

Greg looked across at Richie's empty iron contraption.

'She's not here. She wouldn't come,' said Richie sullenly. 'Didn't she say that Tommo's got to come and say sorry?'

'I should think so too. It was a bad thing he did.'

'But we want her, me and Shona. And even Tommo doesn't mind now.'

'Only fair she should get more than that, son. But she'll come, don't worry. She's a kind heart. In the meantime we like having her here.' It was true, Greg did regret the thought of Biddy leaving. His mother had had so much more life in her in these few days, so much laughter. 'Your sister, is she well?'

Richie looked curiously at him. 'Well? She's always well. More spunk than a butcher's dog, Shona.'

Greg laughed, watching the boy's face carefully. 'I'd think the boys all chase her. That friend of Tommo's, is he walking out with her?'

Richie roared with laughter and climbed on to his contraption. 'Pat? He'd like to. They'd all like to. The donkey even makes up songs for her. But hasn't she more sense than to take him or any man?' he finished scornfully. He made kissing noises at Cush who set off with a jerk. 'I'll bid you good day, sir. Won't it be too dark to see me own hands if I don't set off soon?' He sketched a salute with his small rope whip and, whirling it about Cush's head, encouraged him to canter.

Greg stood watching the little cart receding into the distance, a small satisfied smile on his face. Then he walked across to the works.

Entering the office he sketched a genial imitation of Richie's salute. 'Evenin', Pa! Mr Moxham sends his regards.'

Douglas grunted and made his way back to his long table. 'They brought in a broken boiler from Halsland's late last night. I need a report on the damage. Details, they need. Possibility of a mend. Cost of scrapping it.'

'It's not one of ours?'

'No. But we are requested to make a report. The company may want to retrieve money from the makers.' He turned his eyes to Stuart, who was standing beside the open fire, rubbing his hands. 'When you've finished warming yourself again, Stuart, I want a list of this quarter's completed engines, cost of manufacture, cost of upkeep of those used by the company, revenue from the coals we've led for them and the passengers we've hauled – September, October, November. I need it all in hand for the Friday meeting. I'll be down in the pattern shop.'

The noise of the workshop welled up through the door as he vanished through it.

Stuart flung himself down at his table and set to work with an ill will. Greg picked up the repair book and made for the door after his father. Like him, he'd rather be in the workshop than in the office any day.

Stuart watched his brother leave and reached into his bottom drawer to pull out a silver flask.

Greg made his way through the blacksmith's shop, standing for a few minutes to watch the blacksmith work the great bellows, judging the rhythm to get the fire to white heat.

Rob the smith shouted across to him over the noise of the bellows. 'Getting up nicely, Mr McNaughton!'

Greg looked at the white glow and from out of nowhere came the thought of the white skin of young Richie's sister. White should be cold, but like this coke fire she radiated heat. Just the thought of her made him feel warmer than he had in a long time.

It was seven when Douglas, Greg and Stuart finally got back to Garth End Cottage that night. They came upon Lauretta who was sitting on the low hall chair with a doll under one arm and her kitten in a basket on her knee.

She smiled brilliantly at her father, calling him by his first name as she did when she was excited. 'Greg! I've seen the little horse named Cush, and Richie too! But he couldn't stay to see Irma.' A small scowl marred her smooth round brow for a moment then cleared when she saw Douglas. 'Grandpa, can I have a little horse?' She jumped down from the chair, placed the doll and the kitten carefully behind her and trotted over to him. 'Can I have a little horse? I would call him Timothy. Isn't that a nice name?'

He looked down at her with his customary bewilderment. 'A horse? I don't know . . .'

'Douglas! Just in time for supper.' Margaret was standing at the bottom of the stairs, smiling tentatively at him. That smile, in its very uncertainty, always made him angry.

'No. I'll have my supper in my workroom. There are papers to see to, and I've a drawing to finish for the Society.' His tone was cold.

'Do have supper with us, Douglas!'

'Its a nice bit of pressed tongue,' volunteered Biddy standing behind Margaret.

Lauretta put out her arms. 'Carry, Grandpa! Carry into supper!'

He looked down at her, perplexed, then leaned down so she could clasp her small hands round his neck and be pulled up. 'Well, I shall have to be very quick.'

'See, Grandpa! You and me!' Lauretta peered over his shoulder into the tall smoky mirror placed above the glove drawer. He turned his head and saw her reflection beside his. He saw too an inner image of the child's mother: bright eyes and glinting red hair.

Biddy, from her place on the stairs, glimpsed the two faces side by side: the child's gaiety and the man's grimness in stark contrast. But there was about them such a similarity that she caught her breath in a tension that was only relieved when Margaret spoke in a quiet voice.

'Well then, supper. We'll all have supper and afterwards I'll play for you. The new song by Miss Jenny Lind. I bought it in the music shop in Priorton today. Do you know, Douglas, we had such a lovely time today in Priorton. Didn't we, Biddy?'

It was a relief for Shona to see Richie waiting for her at the gates at the end of her weary shift. She trudged wordlessly alongside him and the pony down the dusty road. Then she remembered the errand he had been on and stopped in her tracks. 'The auntie! Where is she? Did you leave her at the house?'

He glanced at her. 'Sure didn't the old'n stick her heels in? Said she wouldn't come till Tommo goes and says sorry.'

'No! Oh, no!' The tears started to flow then as she moaned the denial.

Richie reached out and shook her arm. 'Don't go on so, Shona! What's up with yer? She'll come soon, be sure of it.' He shook her arm again. 'I tell you what, why not ride on Cush? Seems to me like yer too tired for sense.'

His desperate offer made her smile and she reached out to hug him. He shrugged her off – the passing pitmen were watching. 'Leave off, will yer, Shona? Aren't you too tired for any sense at all?'

She climbed on the little pony and thought about Biddy. Tommo would have to go and get her. He would have to go.

She thought of the sacking parcel under the heavy stones on the pit heap. And the china doll scraping away against the stone fish in her pocket.

'I've a new stone for you, Richie. A fish with such fine scales.'

'That'll make thirteen. More'n anyone I know.'

Cush plodded along. Tommo would have to say the right things to the auntie to get her to come. She would make him. If she had to beat him there with her fist, she would make him.

Chapter Nine

'Tommo! What is it you want?' Maudie Martin opened the door six inches and peered through the narrow space.

'To stand out here and look at you, what d'you think?' He put his foot in the gap.

Maudie pushed back her hair. 'I'm not working.'

He had seen her twice now after work. 'It's just seein' you I want. Not for work. Didn't I just see the door here and think of you and the little'n?'

Maudie hesitated a second more. Then he breathed her sweet clean scent as she opened the door wider and let him in.

The room was hot. In front of the roaring fire stood a tin bath not much bigger than a chair. Becky grinned up at him through the steam, her fair bunchy curls dripping water, their ends kinked tighter than corkscrews.

Maudie knelt down and picked up a sliver of soap from the rag mat and soaped Becky's pink back. 'It's a fiendish job to keep her clean in this filthy hole. Me too, for that matter. I hate this place. Mind you, we won't always be here.'

'Are you goin' off somewhere then?'

'When I make enough money we'll get away. These places are good for the money.'

'At this game?'

Her face hardened. 'More money at this game than . . . I hear some girls work in the filth at the pit. Or in service, giving the master free bed any time he asks. With this I can save some money. For me and Becky.' She paused. 'Sit down, won't you?'

He sat on a chair beside the table, watching the bathing process with interest. 'You do this every week, do yer?'

She laughed. 'Week? Every day, don't ye mean? It takes half the afternoon, like, hauling in water from the yard. At least there's a

91

boiler here.' She nodded at the newfangled black range and the fireside boiler with its winking brass tap and matching brass bucket. 'Makes a world o' difference, that thing. We've had to go and find a stream in other places we've lived.'

She put her hands under Becky's arms and lifted her out of the bath. The child stood for a second, the fire casting a rosy light on her wet gleaming shoulders and rising childish belly, throwing the little crack down below into deep shadow.

Maudie threw a towel around Becky's shoulders and started to rub her down. 'I had the devil's own job getting it, the bath. A feller lifted it for me right from Priorton on his back.'

He could just see her charming some poor fellow into breaking his back.

She pulled a clean crumpled gown over the child's head, and thrust her towards him. 'Now you give her hair a rub, Tommo, and I'll pour you some tea.'

Gingerly, he rubbed at the child's head, which felt as fragile as an unshelled egg in his hand. Then Maudie handed him a great mug of tea and pulled the child back towards her.

Tommo drank eagerly. Tonight he had given the beer a miss, walking straight past the Puddler's Arms; Pat, in disgust, had gone off to the Cockerel. The old woman was on Tommo's mind and he had that old feeling of Shona calling him, her voice ringing in his head as it had from time to time since they were small. Then Maudie's door had loomed before him and he felt his sister retreating.

He looked at the steaming water, slightly scummy now, and stood up. 'Can I empty this for you?'

'No, I can empty it myself. I'm swilling the scullery with it after. Anyway, it's my turn next. I need the dirt of this job off me too.'

He grinned. 'An' I'll wash you, then. Couldn't I rub you down nicely?'

'No, you won't, boy-oh! I told you, I'm not working.' She was pulling a brush through the child's tangled hair. Becky squealed.

He looked thoughtfully at her. 'The little'n, whose is she?'

Maudie coloured slightly and pulled more sharply at the brush, Becky squealing, 'No, Mammy, no!'

'A religious man, not of our faith,' said Maudie. 'I worked for him once. Don't scowl like that! He was decent enough. A desperate man who pushed himself on me. And his wife knew it was his desperation, not me, that drove him to it. Mind you,' she said jauntily, 'we all had to get down on our knees for guidance. For an hour or so.' She paused. 'They gave me money, but it soon ran out.'

She put the brush on the table and pulled Becky on to her knee. 'But the two of us, we're all right, aren't we, Becky?' She stared defiantly at him over the child's head.

He hauled himself to his feet. 'I have to get home now, Maudie. There's an old auntie coming to stay. Can I see you again when you're not working? Outside, somewhere in the fresh air?'

'Out?' This was new. They never wanted to see her outside, where the women could see. 'Sunday morning? We could do it Sunday morning. Jenny Simon – she keeps the rooming house next door – takes Becky to church. She gets lots of prayers said for her, the little one. Born in sin, you see. But me, I'm beyond the pale. Sunday morning, we can take a walk then.'

'Yes. Right. I'll be here.' He made his heavy way out of the house and she locked the door behind him.

She sat her daughter on the bed. 'Now, Becky, you can tell me a story from the book while I have my bath.'

Hurrying home, Tommo thought he should buy a bath for Shona. She would like that. Wasn't she always complaining she couldn't get the coal-dust off her properly? He remembered her in Ireland at ten years old, clean and bright-bodied, emerging from the stream near the farm.

The fire was low and the silence was glum as he entered the kitchen. Shona was chopping bacon into a pan, and Richie was rubbing a leather harness. Tommo peered into the corners of the room. He cocked his head. There was no noise from the roof. 'Where is she?' he demanded.

'She wouldn't come,' said Richie. 'You're to go and get her. Said she wouldn't come, save you went and said sorry.'

'Sorry? Me?' Tommo tossed his cap into the corner.

'Didn't you push her out of the house?' said Shona.

'Well, now I've invited her in, an't I?'

'Still she says you've gotta go and get her,' insisted Richie. A faint smile sketched itself on his face. 'And say sorry.'

Tommo's hand shot out and swiped him across the face, flinging him into the corner. 'It's those bluddy Protestants, that feller McNaughton! Keepin' her there to skivvy for them for nothing to be sure.'

Richie fingered his jaw. 'Sure she looked all right to me, Tommo. Perky, she looked. There was another skivvy there. But old Biddy, she had a fancy brown dress on.'

Tommo dropped heavily into the chair. 'Well, she can stay there, fancy dress an' all.'

'We want her here,' said Shona, putting her knife down.

'She can stay there. It's her choice.' He loosened his boots. 'Is there some tea, Shona, and some bread from yesterday?'

She didn't move. 'We want her here,' she repeated. 'She's our family.'

Tommo stared sullenly into the smouldering fire.

She leaned over and turned his face towards her. 'Tommo, d'you know what happened today. At the pit? The woman I work with, Mary Challoner?'

'What about her?'

'Well, she lost a baby there and then. It came out of her. At the screens, where we were standing.'

'What?'

'It was dead. She lost it. They call it *losing*. She lost it. They put it on the tip. On the slag heap. Under a stone. Maybe a stone I'd sorted.' She was staring at him. Her wide wild eyes made him uneasy. He could feel again the tender soft-shell head of Becky Martin in his palm.

'I want the auntie here.' It was a statement without a shred of pleading.

He started to fasten his boots again. 'Right. I'll get her, the old besom. You come too, Shona. And you, Richie. And bring the pony and the cart.'

'Wait, wait,' said Shona. 'Have some bread and tea. It'll be hours before you eat and you're just from work.' She was putting the snack together while she spoke. 'And the stew's on. It'll be just nice when we get back.'

The two boys ate, watching her splash water into the tin bowl and rub her face with a wet cloth.

'Now turn round the pair of you!' she ordered. Obediently, they turned their backs to her while she changed. 'Now!' When they turned back to look at her she was wearing the blue dress she wore to church on Sunday and was tucking her bushy black hair under a blue kerchief that could barely contain it.

'What's this, Shona? No need to dress up,' said Richie.

'Didn't you say the auntie had a fancy dress? Well, wouldn't she be above coming away with a girl still in pit-britches?'

Tommo thought of what Maudie had said about pit-lassies, then roared with laughter and swung Shona round off her feet, knocking over two chairs in the process. 'Well, let's go then and crawl on our bellies and get this stubborn aul brew to come down and make a proper family of us!'

Grinning, Richie went off to get Cush and his cart, and Shona collected the lamps from the lean-to pantry.

She tied one to the iron cart and looked up at Richie. 'You go by the road. We'll go across the fields, on foot. It's quicker.'

Richie grinned at them as he gave Cush a neat cut with his little whip and set off at a lick. 'Race yer!'

Tommo took the lamp and they set off after him. It was a soft night, not cold and quite still. But soon large drops of rain began to fall and Shona had to pull her shawl tighter as she hurried along. The drops settled to a steady stream, first standing on her blue skirt then spreading in damp patches. The sky rumbled, then took a breath and split itself with lightning.

'Here! Some shelter this way!' Tommo pulled her through a hedge on to a path which skirted a meadow, making towards a great oak whose branches wove together into reasonable cover.

They reached the tree, giggling and out of breath, only to find that shelter had been sought before them. A dark figure loomed at them out of the shadows.

'Well, if it isn't the pitmen's sweetheart and the big Irishman! Brother and sister, mebbe, but anyone'd think you were true lovers,' said Terry Kennedy, sitting high on the stile which butted up to the tree-trunk.

Tommo swore and leaped forward but Shona put herself in front of him and smiled coolly up at Terry. 'Sure isn't it wet enough to fill a bucket? But aren't some fellers only good enough for filling a woman's buckets at the well?'

'It takes a kind feller to carry buckets for dirty little pit-lassies,' responded Terry sulkily.

The three of them had to stand too close for comfort in the dry patch of ground which encircled the trunk. The rain lapped down steadily round the edges of the circle.

'What're you doing up here anyway?' said Tommo suspiciously.

'I was waitin' for a bloke I know up Priorton. He owes me money.' Shona looked around. 'Funny place to meet.'

'Too many bluddy nosy folks down in New Morven and Shotwell. Up at Priorton too for that matter.'

Lightning cracked again and the tree shuddered. 'Talking of tittle-tattle, there's talk down New Morven of how a bloke's taken up with that moll Maudie Martin. D'ya hear it? A *hooah*! A good poke but . . .' He coughed and spat on to the ground. 'Bloke's got his brains in his arse who teks up with her. A little blue-eyed sister could get green-eyed over it.'

Tommo grasped Shona's arm hard. 'C'mon! Let's get on. Our Richie'll be there already.'

'What is it yer off to, then?' Terry called after them in the rain. 'A meetin' of the brotherhood? A bullet for the Mayor of Priorton? You bluddy Irish are all alike. Assassins to a man!'

As they ran along, Tommo's voice hissed through the rain into Shona's ear: 'I'll kill that animal one day.'

Shona rolled her eyes up to the pouring heavens. 'Isn't that what he's saying, Tommo? Aren't we assassins all? Now come on!'

Richie was already at the gate of Garth End Cottage when they arrived, sheltering under the sacking that had kept him dry on his ride.

Shona pulled the wet locks of hair out of her eyes and looked down at her soaking skirt in despair. 'Look at this. Look at me!'

'I don't know who ye're worrying about, Shona,' grumbled Tommo. 'Is it the auntie or those McNaughtons? The snooty feller that carried her on his back?'

'What if it is?' Shona held up her head. 'I'm good enough for any of them!'

He grinned, young again. 'But any of them an't good enough for you. Remember that, Shona.'

He lifted the lion knocker. His great rattle on the green door was followed by a clap of thunder.

'Hit it again, Tommo,' said Richie. 'They'll never hear that against all the thunder. Hit it again, Tommo! Give it a belt, won't yer!'

Chapter Ten

The continual rumble of thunder had made Margaret McNaughton jumpy all evening. Finally the cacophony was echoed by a great rattle on the door and she expelled a long chilling scream.

Upstairs, Douglas looked up from his work-table and sighed. Stuart sat back from his ledger and shook his shoulders to loosen the strain. Sweat was trickling down his brow and the pen shook in his hand. He watched his father closely for the usual signals that the evening's work was over.

Another great rattle at the door. Another scream. Greg pushed his work away. 'I'll go and see what it is.'

'Its just your mother having one of her nervous bouts,' sighed Douglas. 'There have been fewer of them lately.'

'But there's someone at the door. Didn't you hear the knock, Pa? That can't be Mother. It's not her every time. You never give her any credit . . .' Greg allowed a rare note of criticism to thread its way into his voice but, in the habit of obedience, stayed sitting. Another great rattle at the door seemed to shake the house; then a voice bellowed through the wood.

This time Margaret's scream was higher in pitch and more eerie. Greg jumped to his feet, brushed past his father and took the stairs two at a time. In the hall he pushed past the chattering Aida and the wide-eyed Margaret, now clasped in Biddy's arms.

Biddy looked across at him. 'You should open the door, boy, before this blessed house explodes.'

Greg opened the door and almost laughed at the sight that faced him. The broad Irishman, the one called Tommo, nearly filled the frame. The girl called Shona was there beside her brother, her white face gleaming with rain, her silvery-blue eyes blazing. Behind her the sharp, small face of Richie Farrell peered out beneath his over-large cap.

'Is everyone deaf in this house?' growled Tommo.

'If they weren't before, they will be now. What is it?' Greg's tone was hard.

The girl spoke. 'We've come for Biddy O'Farrell. Our aunt.'

Greg opened the door wider. 'You'd better come in. The rain's blowing right in here.'

The three of them trooped in and stood dripping water on to the black and white tiles. Greg heaved the door shut behind them and the sound and visible fury of the storm faded.

'You should'a sent'm round the back,' sniffed Aida.

'The Irish, Pa!' muttered Stuart, standing in the shadow of the landing behind his father. 'Always trouble with the Irish.'

Shona pushed herself to the front and glared up at him. 'How dare ye say that? We're hardworking people, Tommo and Richie here makin' sure ye've got iron for yer railways, me makin' sure you've coal for the boiler. Is that trouble? Comin' over from an old land ye've all laid waste to. Is that trouble? It's trouble ye make yerselves when ye rob someone of their family. And that ye've done, one way or another!'

Biddy took her arms from Margaret, whose body was relaxing now, and put her hand on Shona's shoulder. 'Sure there's no need to fluster yourself, child.' She looked Tommo in the eye. 'Was it something ye had to say to me?'

He opened his mouth but was interrupted by Douglas. 'Miss O'Farrell, you must go! There's conflict enough in this house and you bring more with you.'

'Yes,' muttered Stuart again, behind him. 'The woman's no more than a trouble-making Irish gypsy.' There was pleasure and satisfaction in his voice.

Tommo moved swiftly towards the stairs but Greg stepped in his way and Stuart took a step backwards.

'Get Miss O'Farrell's things, Aida,' Douglas ordered and went and stood behind his wife.

The maid marched upstairs, a smirk on her face.

'No-o,' wailed Margaret.

They all looked at her.

'She's my friend. She can't go. You've had your friend staying here, Douglas. Lurking in your workroom, drawing your drawings. Now I want my friend.'

'I can't think what you're saying. You've your family round you. Don't be silly, Margaret. This is madness. The woman is not your kind.' He looked at her with hatred in his eyes. 'We've tolerated this ridiculous whim because . . .'

Tommo interrupted him and smiled down at Biddy. 'What I came for, Auntie, was to say sorry for slinging you out like that. I must'a been drunk or daft or both.'

Biddy laughed. 'A grand apology, Tommo.'

'Don't go!' said Margaret. 'Stay here, Biddy, with me!'

Aida came downstairs, followed by Lauretta in her nightclothes. The maid was carrying Biddy's bag on one arm and a large cotton sack on the other. 'I'll say one thing for her, Mrs McNaughton, she's a clever one. She's going with far more than she came with.' She dumped the bags on the floor in front of Biddy, with her heavy shawl on top of them, and stumped off towards the kitchen door.

Lauretta settled herself on the bottom step to watch with large eyes.

Greg put his arm round his mother. 'Biddy has to go, Mother. This is her niece and nephew. Her family.'

Biddy shrugged herself into her shawl then turned to Margaret. 'I'll go with them. They need me now, you see, and they know it. But won't I be back to see you very soon? And we can tell our stories then, you can be sure of it.'

Greg shook hands with Biddy. It was only when her hand came away that she realised money had been pressed into it.

Margaret grasped Biddy and held her close, then let her go. She watched as Tommo picked up the large bag, Shona picked up the smaller one and Richie, with a grin, drew Biddy's arm through his. They marched out of the house, leaving only dirty puddles on the tiles.

Douglas closed the door behind them and turned towards his wife. 'Don't you *ever*, ever encourage anyone to come here and make a fool of you again,' he said coldly.

As he strode past her, she tried to grasp his arm. He shook her off and went upstairs, looking neither right nor left. She gazed after him in despair.

Greg took his mother by the shoulders and guided her into the parlour.

Settling Margaret into her chair, he felt himself sharing her despondency. With the Farrells departed, all the fire, all the heat, had gone again from the house. He went to stand at the window just in time to catch sight of the little troop making its way through the rain.

'Greg?' said Lauretta behind him.

'Yes, pippet?'

'Why's Biddy gone?'

'She went with her family. Richie and Shona and their brother've no mammy and daddy you see,' he answered absently.

'Greg?'

'What?'

'Where's my mammy?'

Margaret stopped fiddling with her shawl.

He kept looking straight out of the window. 'She's not here, pippet.'

Lauretta sighed. 'And is her name Biddy too?'

Margaret moaned.

Greg turned and picked up his daughter in his arms, lifting her until they were nose to nose. 'No, pippet. Her name is Mary Louisa.'

'And does she have pretty hair, all white and curly like Biddy?'

'No, Lauretta, her hair is sort of brown and red with a gleam on it. Like Irma's feathers.'

'And did she run away from me too, like Biddy?'

From behind them, Stuart expelled his foxy laugh. 'Did she run or was she sent, sweetheart? Is she dead or is she alive? Who knows? Well, maybe your daddy here, but like most things in this house, we don't say. You'll want to know now or you'll want to know later, I suppose. But then, I've had a mother myself and have never felt the benefit. You're better off without.'

Greg was quiet, cold and still as ice.

Stuart stood up and went to unhook his coat and hat from the crowded hall stand. He came back and smiled at them as he fastened himself into the heavy-caped overcoat. 'I think I'll just get away for an hour, now the drama's over. Have a breath of fresh air to get the stink of those . . .' He paused. 'Get the stink out of my nostrils. Trouble and smell, that's what you get with the Irish.'

There was another gust of cold wet air and he was gone.

Greg followed him into the hall, called for Aida to take care of his mother and took Lauretta back to her bed, holding her hand until she was asleep.

Then he went to the window again and looked out on the quietening storm. He thought of the woman with the red-gold hair who had entranced him from the moment he had met her on the London train: Mary Louisa, who lit up any room into which she walked and brought fire into the lives of those she loved.

The next day Shona was woken by an unusual rattling and scraping sound. Rubbing at her eyes to get them open, she could make out Biddy in the dim lamplight raking the cinders through to the hearth and taking bucket after bucket of ash out of the back door. By the time Shona was up and dressed in the pit-clothes that took an hour's wearing to soften up, the fire was clear and glittering bright, with a pan of porridge bubbling on its stand.

Richie leapt out of the roofhole first with a whoop. 'Porridge!' Tommo clambered down after him. The little kitchen seemed full of bodies. The boys sat in the chairs to eat their porridge and Shona sat on the bed.

'Have ye got any money?' Biddy asked Tommo.

'Not until next week. It's Pay Saturday.'

'I'll need to buy a bed. If I'm to sleep with Shona, I'll want a bed not the floor. Never slept a wink last night for the crawling and scurrying going round by me ear.'

Tommo looked across to the corner where his sister was crouched with a dish on her knees. Then he looked round the dark room and relaxed. The woman would solve it, his growing worry about the state of this house. 'You can have what's over after I've paid me way. And after a bed, a bath. We need a bath.'

Biddy looked at the open fire. 'You need a boiler if you have a bath.'

'Pat'll build you one. He built one for Mrs Kelly on the end house,' said Shona.

'Pat? Is that your man?'

'You saw him the first time you came. And he's Tommo's mate, not mine. He can sing, and writes songs sometimes.' Shona pulled herself to her feet and looked down at the lumpy mattress. 'A bed? I can't think when I last lay on a bed.'

'Your daddy had a nice one with brass ends. He took it off in the cart that came from our place in Waterford to the farm in Clare. I remember the day.'

'The beds all went with the rest,' said Shona. Now she remembered the brass-ended bed with its yellow quilt. She remembered climbing into the warm nest with her sister Maire, after her mother had risen to tend the cow.

'Never mind, Shona me dear. Things are better now, and they'll get even better. You can be sure of that.' Biddy took the plates from their hands and dumped them in the round dish. 'Now off with you while I get at this job. There's enough work here for ten.'

There was a new girl in Mary Challoner's place at the screens. Shona went to Len Hall who was standing at the doorway to the sheds. 'Has yon girl got Mary's job, Len?'

'Yes. She's me cousin's girl. A good strong lass.'

'You said to Mary her job was here.'

'It was but . . . ya dinnat knaa, do yer? It was all ower Shotwell last night. Mary Challoner had another one in the house. A twin. She lost that one too, and bled on they say. Dead by eight o'clock, the pair of them.'

Shona closed her eyes. At eight o'clock she had been standing in the hallway at Garth End Cottage facing down Greg McNaughton's tight-faced father and listening to insults spewing from the mouth of the foxy-faced brother. When she opened her eyes, they were all staring at her, all the pit-women.

'She was a good lass,' said Len in a low voice.

'We're all bloody good lasses,' Meg Tallent called across from her position in the corner. The old woman glared at Len as though he were all men.

He coughed. 'Right, Shona. Our Thoria here's a good lass too. I want yer to show her the ropes.' He cast his eye around the group. 'An' there's no slackin' today. I've a bliddy queue of lasses waiting for these jobs at these rates. A bliddy long queue it is too!'

Shona was aching with exhaustion and the pain of missing Mary by the time she and Richie got to the house that night.

She was greeted by Biddy, standing looking very pleased with herself by a clear bright fire in a room lit by three lamps, two of them new.

Shona looked around the room. Four chairs, two of them also new, were grouped round a large square table she hadn't seen before. Richie whooped and jumped on to a vast new bed with brass ends covered by a blue quilt that stood in the corner. The fireplace now played host to two pot stands. One held the kettle, the other a winking copper pan filled to the brim with bubbling stew.

'What d'you think?' beamed Biddy.

Shona stood quite still. 'Now where d'all this come from, Auntie?'

'Well, I gave the whole place a bit of a scrub. And these things came from Priorton. That nice little man Gil Tait took me to a place where they sell them – people needing the money and that, selling their stuff. And the stew's just from the things you've got in the pantry.'

'Did Tommo give you the money?' Shona, in her heart of hearts, was not pleased at this sight. Hadn't they managed all right, the three of them? She stood by the door and kicked at her boots to get them off.

'S'bluddy marvellous,' crowed Richie. 'Can we have some of that stew now?' He was used to the long wait for food when he got in.

Biddy was watching Shona carefully. 'I had a bit of money.' She would not mention the sovereigns that Greg McNaughton had pressed in her hand. 'How have you managed here?'

Shona shrugged. 'Doesn't the devil drive you to it when he sees the need?'

Biddy watched her closely, wondering why the girl held back so much. 'You've a lovely voice, Shona. When I first came here, I heard you singing. Who taught you to sing like that?'

Shona hitched herself on to the high bed. 'I remember singing with my mammy, but that was long enough ago. I sang with a woman at work, Mary Challoner. Songs they sing at the Red Cockerel and the Swan in Priorton.' She stripped off her shawls and carefully folded them on to the bobbly surface of the new quilt. 'Mary Challoner died last night. Of twins. She died of having twins.'

'I'm sorry to hear that. And you've lost a friend. Isn't there too much dyin' altogether?'

The door rattled and Tommo came in. He looked round the room with a grin. 'I knew you'd make a difference, Auntie.'

'You did, did you?' Biddy smiled slightly.

'So she has,' said Shona. 'It's different getting Tommo Farrell home straight from work, so it is.'

Biddy had placed the four dishes out like points of the compass on the square table. That night they sat down to a table for their meal for the first time since they had been at home on the farm.

After tea Tommo changed into a cleaner shirt and trousers, put on his jacket and cap and made for the door.

'Where to now, Tommo?' said Shona.

'I'm away to see Pat about that boiler.'

When Tommo arrived at Maudie's door it was closed. He loitered on the corner till he saw a large man, whom he recognised from the works, slip out. He leaned on a wall and stayed watching for ten minutes as the door stayed resolutely shut. Then, when he saw it open, he pulled himself off the wall out of the shadows and walked across.

Maudie beamed when she saw him. 'Tommo! Good to see you. Come in, won't you?'

He hesitated. 'I've no money, Maudie. Not 'til next week.'

Her hand stayed on the door handle for a full minute, then she opened the door wide. 'Well, Tommo, you won't get . . . *that* . . . without money. An iron rule of mine. But you're welcome to visit. Becky was talking about you. The man with the stars, she called you.'

Maudie called up to her daughter through the roofhole. 'Here, Becky! Here's your friend. The one with the stars.'

The child jumped down into his arms. She was clutching a book. Tommo sat down and kept her on his knee. She thrust the book at him. 'You read Becky a story.'

He looked helplessly at the print. Maudie knelt beside them and turned the book so she could read it. ' "The white men . . . killed the children of the red men, they shot their wives, they burned their wigwams and they took away their lands . . . the red men were beaten. They ran away into the woods. They were broken-hearted and they died. They are all dead or gone over the mountain, except a few . . ." '

Tommo put his hand on the book. 'Are ye kidding me?'

'No. That's what it says. It's about America.'

'It could be Ireland.'

'So it could.' Maudie took the book from his hands and closed it. 'Enough of that on a rainy night.' She went across and put it on a high shelf. Then from a higher one she brought down a battered black wooden box decorated with a worn brass inlay. She dipped her fingers into the box and brought out a sovereign which winked in the lamplight.

She tucked it in his hand and folded his fingers round it. 'Here, Tommo, I'll lend you this. You take my Becky and tuck her up in bed for the night. And when you come back down you can pay me. That'll keep things right, won't it?'

Becky kept him with her while she told him the tale of Freddie Stoner the spider who lived in her loft.

When he climbed back down Maudie was standing naked in a firelight so bright it might have come from the ironworks furnace. The flames played over her body, lighting the near edge with a white glow so that he could make out the fine halo of hair that covered the whole of her skin. Her heavy breasts cast a crescent shadow. The alluring fold down below was covered with fur which looked so soft he longed to touch it, to take his fingers down that silky surface and feel his way softly inwards with his fingers . . .

'Oh!' he groaned.

She put out her hand. 'Pay first!' she commanded. 'That's my rule.'

Chapter Eleven

Pat Daley came home with Tommo for three evenings straight after work, to help build a boiler in the fireplace. It was a comic affair – a lidded iron cauldron built over a hollow brick base to the level of the fire, whose hot cinders could be dragged across when the water was to be heated.

'Keep water in it all the time, an' it'll always be warm. Pull the cinders across and you'll get it hot,' Pat instructed.

They stood in a circle admiring the crude construction.

'The McNaughtons have a proper one in their kitchen, all iron, all in one with the fire,' said Biddy. 'But this is grand.'

'I'll tek Cush every mornin' to get water,' volunteered Richie. 'It'll need three buckets at least.'

The next night when Shona got in from work, bone weary, she found the kitchen full of steam and a string rigged up from the brass bed head to the mantelshelf with the blue quilt strung over it. Behind this makeshift screen was a tin hip bath filled with hot water.

'There y'are now,' said Biddy. 'A bath for ye!'

'Oh, Auntie, aren't I too tired for any old bath?'

'Just have a good scrub while I stir the broth and put in some dumplings.'

Shona looked at the door. 'Richie and Tommo . . .'

'Isn't that what the quilt's up for? Any case, Richie's away already to the horses and Tommo said last night he'd forgotten what the inside of Showy's bar looked like. Go on with you!'

Shona stripped off to her skin, dumping her clothes on the bed. Sinking into the steaming water, she looked down at her body through the glossy surface, relishing the way it lifted her breasts, making them float to the surface. She thought of Mary Challoner's body and the babies that had spilled out of it.

'Well, it's a beauty you are and no mistake!'

Shona crossed her hands over herself and looked up at Biddy who was standing beside her with a piece of soap in one hand and a small earthenware dish in the other. 'Here, I've made you some jelly-soap to do your hair, but you'll need a hand with it. Tip back and get it really wet.'

Obediently Shona sank her head beneath the water, so that her hair floated like seaweed. Then she sat there, dripping, while Biddy rubbed in her jelly-soap to the very ends of the long hair. Abandoning any hope of protecting herself from the old woman's gaze, Shona closed her eyes and let herself enjoy the hands busy about her scalp.

'There! Now dip again.'

She obeyed, feeling the water trickling cleanly through her hair and against her scalp. Biddy pulled the hair up in a dripping rope, wrung it out and pinned it on top of Shona's head.

She handed over the small piece of hard soap. 'Now the rest of you.' She came again with a towel, then vanished behind the screen.

Shona washed the rest of her body very quickly and jumped out of the cooling water. She looked from her gleaming skin to the heap of grey and greasy pit-clothes on the bed.

'I found these.' Biddy had read her thoughts. She thrust at her a thin white shift and a worn emerald green dress. Her mother's clothes, from the leatherbound box. 'Give me those pit things. I'll take them in the back and give them a good beating.'

By the time Biddy was back in the kitchen, Shona was dressed and had placed the quilt back on the bed. Biddy smiled broadly at her. 'There! It's a beauty you are. That lovely skin. Now give me a hand to get rid of this water and then you can brush your hair by the fire to get it dry.'

'Did you always boss people about back home?' gasped Shona as they heaved the tin bath into the back lane and tipped it out so the tide of water made its own way to the rough centre channel.

'Always and ever. Me without people to boss is like one hand clapping.' Biddy grinned. 'Maybe that's why they ran off to Americky, Paddy's brood. Comes a time they don't need it.'

Looking at her, Shona was not quite sure whether or not she was joking.

Richie whistled when he saw his sister sitting by the fire brushing her hair. It was nearly dry now, and shone and crackled in the lamplight. He served himself dumplings and stew from the pot and sat down at the table. 'A bath? Is it a ball ye're going to? Or midnight mass?'

She frowned at him and he laughed even louder.

Richie made short work of his supper and leaped up again to return to Gil Tait's. 'I'll be getting back now. Mind you, Auntie, you're not getting me in a bath any day except Saturday.'

Biddy roared with laughter at this. 'Saturday it is, me boy!'

'Even then, I don't know. How'll Cush know me without my smell? He'll be a wild boy on Sundays.'

On his way out Richie bumped into a large black horse in the road. 'Whoa there!' he breathed, looking up into Greg McNaughton's face. 'Ho, Mr McNaughton. This is a fine feller.' He put a confident hand on the horse's muzzle.

Greg jumped down lightly. 'His name's Juvenal.' He looked around. 'Is there something I can tie him to?'

'Shall I walk him for you, sir? He looks a bit lathered.'

'Well,' said Greg dubiously, 'he's quite a handful . . .' He stopped as he saw his great horse snicker in a friendly fashion into Richie's shoulder. He laughed. 'I'd forgotten you were the wonder with horses.' He threw the reins to the boy. 'Is Biddy at the house?'

'Aye, she's there. And our Shona. Too clean for her own good, that one,' he muttered darkly as he led the horse away.

Shona stopped brushing her hair as Greg McNaughton came into the kitchen, ushered by Biddy. He blinked down at her. 'I see what Richie means.'

'What was that?'

'Nothing.' He was red when he turned to Biddy. 'My mother was wondering about you. How's the ankle?'

'That? Haven't I forgotten about it? Haven't I been hopping around here like a two year old, Shona?'

She laughed. 'So you have. She has had us all on the hop, Mr . . .'

'His name's Greg,' put in Biddy.

'Name's Greg,' he added himself. 'You look different tonight, Miss . . . Shona.'

She put her hands tightly together. 'Out of my pit-clothes? They don't go down to the bone, you know! We're all people underneath.

We might look like beasts of burden to you but that's how you've made us look.'

'*I've* made you?'

'You know what I mean.'

'I don't know about that, Shona. My own grandfather was a blacksmith, and was often "in his black" as he called it. He was a clever man. My father said he could make iron all but talk. I used to think he looked like some god of the underworld there by his fire, with his bellows. It's a changing world, Shona. I'm but a generation away from being in the black too.'

She stood up. 'Auntie, you sit here with Mr . . . Greg, and I'll make you a dish of tea.'

Only half-listening to Biddy's tales of the purchase of the bed in Priorton and the building of the boiler, Greg watched Shona moving round the room, in her green dress with her white skin and her hair tumbling like a wild black waterfall down her back.

'Greg! Greg! Will you listen to me?'

He pulled his attention back to Biddy.

'I was asking about Aida. She must be near her time.'

He flushed again. 'I don't know . . .'

'She was pleased to see me go.'

He laughed. 'She's been singing around the place. She has Ma tucked up in her room as she likes her. In bed 'til ten, at the window after that.' He stirred in his seat. 'That's why I came, Biddy. My mother's losing all her fizz again. Won't you visit her and stir her up a bit?'

Biddy looked doubtful. 'I was coming, Greg, but there's a lot to do here . . .'

'There's no reason for you not to see your friend,' interrupted Shona. 'Nobody's tying you up here.'

Biddy smiled at her. 'I'm not tied anywhere, my darlin'. Never was and never will be.' She turned to Greg. 'I'll be there soon. You can be sure of that.'

Back in the street he took the reins from Richie and gave him tuppence. Richie pocketed it with all the assurance of any Gil Tait apprentice.

'On Sunday, Richie, where is it you walk with Cush and your sister?'

'This Sunday I'm takin' her up towards Killock Common. A good

110

half-hour ride that. Then on over to the castle. She's seen it far away but never close to. I asked her would she like to see the castle close and she said maybe she would. Just about noon-time we'll go, she being in from church.' Greg thanked him and Richie watched him jump on to Juvenal. In a second the big black horse was clopping along the darkened street.

Richie stuck his hands in his pockets, started whistling and set off to follow them as far as Gil Tait's stables. Cush would be missing him.

'What's this, Richie? Horse stealing, are ye?' Tommo called down lazily from the wall where he and Pat Daley sat.

They were watching Richie lead two ponies whose feet clicked on the frozen ground. To his left was Cush, brushed and gleaming; to his right a larger piebald, no less smart, complete with saddle.

'This is Bara. Gil's been treating her for a hurt in the leg. She got her new shoes yesterday an' I'm giving her a gentle go today to get her used.'

'Smart pony!' said Pat appreciatively. His eyes lifted again to see Biddy and Shona, in their Sunday best, coming down the street. He pulled off his cap dramatically. 'An' it's smart ye are today, ladies.'

Shona grinned and bobbed a little curtsy.

'A golden tongue gets you nowhere in this world, Pat Daley,' Biddy said. She lifted her eyes to Tommo. 'And Father O'Reilly was asking for you. He missed you, so he did.'

Tommo reddened. 'I'd things to do, I told you.' He had already been out walking with Maudie Martin that morning and would be back to her house in the afternoon. His fifth visit this week – all secret visits and all now based on the passionate exchange of equals rather than service and payment.

'And you, Richie. Father O'Reilly asks about you.'

'He can't ask about me. He don't know me.' Richie passed his hand down Bara's flank, scowling sulkily. Gil Tait had been on at him about the same thing. He looked at Shona. 'I brought you a ride.'

She came across and stroked Bara's nose. She saw herself reflected in the pony's gentle eye. 'She's lovely, Richie.'

'Well, are ye ready or are ye not?'

'Yes, yes! A minute!'

111

She flew along the street into the house. When she came back she had on her pit-breeches under the green dress and the thick shawl over her shoulders. Richie held her foot so she could leap astride the horse, then jumped on to Cush himself.

The pair of them cantered away, Shona high in the saddle, her back straight, her hair loosened under her bonnet and the green dress flowing out under her shawl and over the horse's rump.

Pat looked after them. 'Now there's a Sunday morning sight for ye!'

Biddy looked at him sharply. 'You keep your eyes to yourself, Pat Daley.'

Tommo grinned, knocked Pat off the wall and jumped down after him.

'Yeah. Keep your eyes to yourself, Pat. There's dog-racing behind the Cockerel at twelve o'clock. And hasn't Gil Tait's brother's got a flyer runnin'?'

Once out of New Morven Shona and Richie made their way off the road and into the meadows. They could see their breath on the air and the ponies' hooves crunched companionably on grass made crisp and pale by the hoarfrost.

After riding twenty minutes they could see the stones of Killock Castle rising against the winter sky. In the middle distance was the black silhouette of a pit wheel. Shona pulled the pony to a halt and Richie stopped beside her.

'At least that demon stops for one day,' she said.

'What? Oh, the pit? It's no bad thing, Shona. We'd all end up frozen in our beds if that wheel stopped for good. An' there'd be no trains, none of these new machines . . .'

'I'm not saying they should stop for good. Just that now and then . . . now who might this be?'

Making his way round the castle and joining the road leading towards them was a tall figure on a black horse, with a small figure up in front of him.

'It's Juvenal, the horse's name,' offered Richie.

They sat watching as Greg and Lauretta, sharing Juvenal's broad back, came closer and closer. Drawing abreast, Greg raised his hat and Lauretta screamed, 'It's Richie, Greg. With Cush.' She struggled to get down. 'I want to see the pony.'

Taking her with one hand by the back of her jacket, Greg lowered her to the ground. She scampered across to Richie who jumped off Cush and lifted her into his place.

'Are you riding up to the castle?' Greg asked, turning Juvenal around so he was side by side with Shona.

'I thought we'd ride round it. I haven't seen it up close before.'

'Would you like to look inside?'

She shrugged. 'Sure that would be impossible?'

He laughed. 'Not so!'

He reached into his saddlebag and pulled out a waxed cloth. He drew his horse nearer and opened up the cloth. Inside, gleaming faintly with oil, was a bunch of keys, each with its own greasy paper label.

'And where might those come from?'

'Lawyer Moxham in Priorton. Mr Shakespeare, the owner, has been on his travels to America. In the meantime, Mr Moxham has charge.'

'*Mr* Shakespeare? I thought it'd be some *lord*.' She thought of Lord Marsteen, tall and heavy, too ready with his hands, even with a twelve-year-old girl.

'No lord! Mr Shakespeare owns seven or eight pits around here. He bought the castle from Sir Reuben Smith when he was caught short gambling. I came here as a boy; played with Orlando, Shakespeare's son. He was at Priorton School with me for a while. Then he died of some wasting disease caught in London. The old man seemed to want me here more after that. I was always here. Then he went off and bought a house in Newcastle and is away all the time. Not been back for years. So I still come and go, courtesy of Mr Moxham. I deal with the bailiff, and open the place once a month for a housekeeper and her skivvies that come from Priorton.'

She smiled at him. 'Well, then. Let's see this Orlando's castle of yours!' She clicked her teeth and spurred her pony on. Smiling, Greg turned to call Richie, then followed her.

They tied their mounts to the tethering post and approached the main door. The tall windows on the ground floor were closed off with wooden shutters.

He found the key which moved smoothly in the lock and the great doors swung open.

Shona caught her breath. The inside was dim and dark and smelled faintly musty. Winter light filtered down to the hall from a great landing window halfway up the sweeping stairs.

'B'Jesus!' Richie was standing behind her with Lauretta on his back. 'We'll have the constable after us to be sure.'

'No, no!' Greg was halfway up the wide stairs. 'I come here for Mr Shakespeare. I keep the keys for Lawyer Moxham. Come on!'

They joined him on the half-landing and then followed him up to a second landing. Richie lifted Lauretta from his back and stood her on the wide sill. Shona climbed up to stand behind the child and looked out across the countryside.

'We could be birds up here,' she said. 'We can see all round.'

'See, there's New Morven right on the horizon,' said Greg. 'And Shotwell! And the chimneys of Priorton closer in to the left . . .'

There were clusters of houses in every pale green fold of land. The lower parts of the Almondshire hills were covered in trees, the winter sticks of deciduous trees and evergreens almost black against the pale frosty land. But as the land rose higher in the distance, hazed moorland lay bare of vegetation except the lowest heather and shrub.

'Now, Lauretta, count me Shakespeare's pits!'

Father and daughter started counting, beginning in the east and moving their eyes systematically to the west. They counted fourteen.

'But those two belong to the ironworks company and the three out there belong to the Dean and Chapter.'

'Nine pits of his own, that Shakespeare,' said Shona.

'Somebody has to own 'em,' said Greg. 'Do you want to go higher? There's a tower!'

Shona lifted Lauretta down from the sill and lifted her own skirt to the knees. 'Race you!' she said. The pair of them scampered ahead and Greg and Richie followed at a more sober pace.

At the very top of the staircase they stopped beside a narrow door. Greg fished out another key and as he opened the door, cold outside air swept in. They moved out on to a turreted roof.

Shona was pink-faced with exertion and her bonnet had fallen to her shoulders. She looked around in delight. 'Sure we can see for a hundred miles here. More!'

Greg, standing very near her, pointed. 'Not quite. See that, away to the left? Like a blunt finger sticking into the sky? That's the old cathedral at Durham. Ten miles away.'

Richie whistled. Shona was smiling and shaking her head at the same time.

'Have you ever been in a place like this?' asked Greg, eager to press home the privilege.

Richie sobered down and glanced at his sister.

'No and yes,' she said. 'Yes, I was once in a great house like this. *Lord* Marsteen's. Our landlord that is. And no, it wasn't like this. That was a miserable place.'

'And not a castle either,' put in Richie.

'Our brother Gerard was murdered in that place,' she said briefly. 'They had him imprisoned but let him run so they could shoot him. Dead.'

'Will you tell me about it?'

Eyeing him carefully, she told him.

Tommo had been there when it happened, that was how she knew about it. He had been in the estate office with his father who had been trying to reason with Grandon Seley, the bailiff, about the rescinding of their lease. The rent had been unpaid for two seasons and now between them lay the unmentioned fact of the scandal of the murder by Gerard Farrell of one of His Lordship's keepers.

Almost casually Seley had led them to the window of his office. They could see His Lordship standing before the great door, talking to an English officer and two of his soldiers. Suddenly Gerard had been there, running across the courtyard towards the open meadow pursued by two more soldiers. Very deliberately, the officer with His Lordship had raised his gun and shot Gerard. Her father had never described it to her, but Tommo had.

'I'm sorry,' said Greg when she'd finished. 'That's a terrible thing.'

'Hmm. A change for an Englishman to say he's sorry,' said Shona. 'But that house was a miserable place. This is different.' She put her hand on the stone rampart. 'This house feels friendly.'

Less gleeful now, Greg led the way down to a library dominated by two great desks and three tall book-cases. He opened a casement to let in a sliver of light which fell across his face on to the filmy surfaces of the wood.

Shona wandered around, touching the backs of soft chairs and running her flat palm in the dust on the great desks. She pulled a huge ledger from a shelf and read a list of numbers referring to coal revenues in the year 1838 whilst Lauretta and Richie climbed into the enormous fireplace and hollered up the chimney, making their voices echo like owls.

Using yet another key, Greg opened the desk cupboard and fished out a large ledger from a pile of six. 'There. Moxham wants me to take this to Priorton next Saturday. Shakespeare's there for an hour off the train, then on to Newcastle.' He looked across at Shona. 'You should come with me. Meet Orlando's father.'

'Saturday,' she said. 'I don't finish 'til noon.'

'Come then!' he urged. 'Get Richie to drive you in Gil Tait's gig. I'll bring Lauretta.'

She looked around the quite friendly room and felt it pulling at her. 'I can't be there 'til half-past two, I'll have to get out of my pit dirt.' The agreement was out of her mouth before she had thought about it.

'Perfect. I have to meet him and Moxham at the Gaunt Valley Hotel at three.'

Outside the castle again Greg waited while Shona jumped on to Bara. He had never seen a woman sit astride a horse: Shona sat straightbacked like a boy. He smiled. A sight like that would cause scandal in the streets of Priorton. He mounted his own horse.

They waited while Richie gave Lauretta a last galumphing piggy-back.

'You like this place?' asked Greg.

'I do,' she said, looking up again at the tumbledown gateway. 'Maybe most because it is empty of people. It's quiet, like a church.'

Now Lauretta was standing on Richie's shoulders.

'She's a happy soul, the little girl, in spite of having no . . . I have this friend Mary whose babies died and she herself. Lauretta's mother, did she . . . ?'

'She's lost to us.' He threw the phrase back as he made sounds to urge his horse forward. He reached across and transferred Lauretta from Richie's shoulders to the broad back of Juvenal in front of him, then rode on. 'Saturday, Richie! Ask Shona about Saturday,' he shouted behind him. 'Don't forget!'

Chapter Twelve

Shona peered into the smoky mirror, tipping her green felt bonnet forward over her rough chignon. She stroked a hand over her clean pale face with satisfaction.

Richie was clean too, having followed her into the tin bath and swabbed himself all over with her lukewarm water, snorting and bubbling like a frog. He was dressed in his better clothes, neatly washed and pressed by Biddy. On his curls he carefully placed the soft-brimmed felt hat bequeathed to him by Gil Tait when Gil had acquired his hard hat with the curly brim.

Richie set off for the stables at a run, with Shona's money clutched in his hand. Five minutes later he returned with Gil's gleaming second-best gig, pulled by a handsome grey horse. 'This is Liffey,' he said proudly. 'I'n't he smart?'

Biddy was not the only one to watch the pair of them as they made their way out of the village in the gig. Three barefoot boys whistled and hollered at the street corner. At the door of the livery stables Gil Tait presented Shona with a tiny bouquet, cunningly contrived from the leaves of wild carrot, scarlet rosehips and other berries. She laughed and pinned it to the side of her bonnet.

From her high vantage point on the swaying gig, Shona could see into the ale houses. They were heaving, buzzing with early customers keen to get a start on their weekend drinking.

Terry Kennedy, standing in the doorway of the Queen's Arms, made a lewd gesture at her with his finger. She responded by putting out her tongue and he turned away.

On the opposite side of the road, Tommo was standing outside a house with neat curtains, talking to a tall woman.

Richie stopped the gig and Tommo loped across. 'What's this?'

'We're off to Priorton to meet Greg McNaughton. We've some business to do,' said Richie.

'Business? What business? And who is it paying for this gig?'

'I am,' said Shona. 'It's payday.'

'Sure ye've got the brains of a flea! The pair of ye!' he growled. 'Ye want nothing with that feller and spending money on gigs.'

She looked up and down the street and then across to the tall woman, who was viewing her with open interest. 'Ye want nothing down here spendin' your money on beer and I don't know what else,' sniffed Shona.

Tommo slapped Liffey's rump angrily and the horse started down the road in a mad career, Richie struggling to hold him back.

Tommo walked slowly back to Maudie who was watching him closely.

'She's a beauty, your sister,' she said.

'Yes,' he said gloomily.

'So what's the matter with that?'

'It's too much. Like a horse that's so bluddy brilliant it might either win the race or fall dead at yer feet. Yer never know which it'll be.'

'Oh, you're a sourboots, Tommo! Come on inside and get a warm. If I have to look at the black face of Terry Kennedy over there a minute longer I'll turn to stone, so I will.'

Shona and Richie arrived outside the Gaunt Valley Hotel twenty minutes early. They were aware of the glances of passersby, looking askance at the sight of the beautifully kept gig and its ragamuffin occupants.

As there was no sign of Greg McNaughton Richie clicked his teeth and set Liffey forward again. Pulling the reins delicately to left and right, he helped the grey horse pick his way through the crowded Saturday traffic.

The road opened up into the busy marketplace and they made their way through the well laid out stalls and the higgledy-piggledy heaps of goods, towards the tall iron gateway of the Priory.

They climbed down from the gig and peered through the railings at the sparse, ruined buildings and the great park beyond, where water glittered in the white winter sun.

Richie climbed on to the wall so he could see more clearly.

'Down from there! Down from there, ye thieving Irish!' The

roar came from behind them and they turned guiltily to face a tall stout man in black boots and a shoulder-cape.

Shona pulled back towards the gig and Richie jumped lightly down from the wall. 'I'm sorry, sir, we were just takin' a look.'

As Shona began to climb on to the gig, a large hand pulled her back. The constable pushed his face into hers. 'And where would a couple of bog-Irish be goin' in a smart rig like this? Did you thieve it?'

She put her foot back on the step. 'We did not! Aren't we meeting Mr McNaughton of Shotwell at the Gaunt Valley Hotel?'

'McNaughton? I don't believe it!' He put great hands on her waist and she struggled as he dumped her in the far seat and heaved himself up beside her. 'I'll just come along and see you right there, Miss, and see this meeting of a couple of bog-Irish and the great Mr McNaughton!'

She pulled herself into the corner and glowered at him. There was no room for Richie, who jumped up on to Liffey's back and looped up the reins before the constable could take hold of them.

In this way they rode to the Gaunt Valley Hotel, arriving just on two o'clock. Greg was on the steps with Lauretta under one arm and the parcelled ledger under another. He put the little girl down and she scampered across to pull at Richie's leg where it hung at Liffey's side.

Greg looked at the large perspiring constable. 'Mr Walton, what's this?'

'Mr McNaughton?' The big constable clambered down. 'I'd expected your father.' Douglas McNaughton was a magistrate and knew all the constables. 'I found these two lurking by the Priory. I thought . . .'

'He thought we were thieves,' Shona spat. 'As if we couldn't afford a shillin' for a creaky old rig!'

Greg grinned. 'I think you owe the lady an apology, Walton.'

Red-faced, the constable touched his tall hat with his short stick and mumbled something, before turning and stalking away.

Greg was laughing out loud now. 'I thought you wouldn't come.' He put up his hand.

'Now why would that be?' She ignored his hand and climbed out of the gig herself, showing her boots and her red woollen stockings in the process.

119

They watched Richie, with Lauretta up in front of him now, manoeuvre the gig through the wide arch into the stable yard.

'Now how would that man know us for Irish, just lookin' at us?' said Shona.

He thought of Richie's open face with the round black hat, eyed her own battered bonnet with its hedgerow posy, and remembered the red stockings on the neat narrow ankles. 'I can't imagine,' he said.

In the wide hotel lobby, a dignified red-nosed man, his black coat shiny with age, looked Shona and Richie up and down with sour precision before he spoke. 'Mr Moxham? This way, sir.' He led the way up shallow stairs, along a landing to a private dining room.

He knocked loudly, then entered.

'Mr McNaughton and . . . friends, sir,' he announced in a voice that managed to be mortified and mellow at the same time.

The room was all brown wood and red velvet. The mingled aromas of roast meat, wine, brandy and cigars drifted towards them. A woman in black and white stood like a statue at the table's corner.

The two men stood up. One was tall and silver-haired with gleaming silver whiskers. The other was shorter and broader with a brown leathery face and thin hair the colour of boot polish.

This man came across and shook Greg heartily by the hand. 'Gregor, my boy! Well met – and I'm glad it's here we meet. In Mr Moxham's office there would be no sitting down. And I prefer to sit down always when doing business. And you have a daughter, I hear?' He put a hand towards Lauretta who solemnly shook it.

'Me Lauretta,' she beamed up at him.

The man laughed. 'No longer a boy, Gregor, with such a daughter.'

Greg turned to Shona. 'And these are my friends, the Farrells, Shona and Richie, Mr Shakespeare.'

Mr Shakespeare smiled at them. Shona shook his hand firmly and Richie touched his cap.

The little man turned back to Greg. 'Mr Moxham has told me the terrible things that have happened to you and your family in my absence. People can be cruel. I myself was beaten 'til nearly dead in Vienna, and my parents' shop was burned to the ground in

120

Petersburg.' He had a slight accent, the words curling at the edges, sounding well down in his throat.

Mr Moxham bustled round. 'Now if there are seats, we should sit!' He indicated comfortable chairs by the roaring fire. He signed to the woman and she brought a tray to the sofa table and started to pour cups of tea and hand around small hard biscuits. 'Mr Shakespeare here has been telling me about America.'

'A wonderful place, my dear Gregor, full of strange sights and sounds and amazing opportunities. Lots of sitting down there.' He chuckled and looked Shona in the eye. 'Especially for one of my . . . talents . . . in encouraging men to wager.'

She grinned at him. 'Oh, you're a gambler, Mr Shakespeare? Me own brother's a gambler, an' I can tell you it does you nor your family no good.'

He shook his head. 'Ah, my dear, it has done *me* some good! It got me Killock Castle from Sir Reuben Smith, and many thousands of dollars from innocents in America.' His eyes narrowed. 'As for family, my dear girl, that is immaterial. I have no family. No parents, no wife, no daughter. Now no son, as Orlando was taken. So as I say, Miss Farrell, family is immaterial.'

'Oh, sir, aren't I so sorry for that? Haven't I lost me own mother and father, me own brother and me own sister?' Her eyes shone with unshed tears. 'But then, I'm lucky. I've two brothers left, Richie here and Tommo who I know will be gambling on some lame dog at this minute.'

'Our sorrows march together, it seems.'

The silence which followed was too long. It was broken by Richie. 'And are there wild men in America, sir?'

'Oh, there are wild men, dear boy. There are those who roam the plains which are their own ancient land. And there are those wild men from England and Scotland and France who shoot them for no better reason than wanting their land.' He turned to Greg. 'Now, Gregor, did you bring the ledger? Mr Moxham and I have calculations to make on the Killock property. There is no need to wait. Mr Moxham will keep the ledger now at his offices.'

After Gregor handed the ledger over they stood up to leave and hands were shaken all round. Mr Shakespeare held on to Shona's hand and kissed it. Her face reddened and her lips twitched with suppressed amusement.

121

As they watched the little group trail out of the room, Mr Moxham turned to his client, a faint smile on his face. 'Gregor is always the strange one, always picking up waifs and strays. Now it's the Irish. Those two had the look of gypsies.'

'So they did. Did you see the girl's wonderful hat, with its berries? Gregor, he was always so. Finding people. He found my son Orlando collapsed in a gorse thicket. That was when that sickness of his started. It finished him in a year. Greg brought him home and they were fast friends for . . . for the rest of the time Orlando was here.'

'Hmm. He's a good boy. Did you know his father – a brilliant man . . .'

'But that girl. What a beauty! Gregor should be with such a girl. Strong and laughing, and none of this perfidious English simpering.' Mr Shakespeare unwrapped the parcel and opened the ledger. 'Now, Mr Moxham. Let us see what we can do with my northern property so it doesn't fall into the wrong hands should one of those wild Americans in suits shoot me before I return again.'

Outside the hotel, Shona was still chuckling. 'He was a strange one, that Mr Shakespeare. And where would you get a name like that?'

'He chose it,' said Greg.

'Chose it?'

'He has this long foreign name with zs in it. Came from Russia or somewhere. So he chose a name that would make him fit in.'

'Fit in? He could never do that. I an't seen anybody that'd fit in anywhere less. Why did he choose that one? That name?'

'Because it's the name of a great English poet.'

'Is it now?'

Lauretta was pulling at Greg's coat. 'Where's the bear, where's the bear?'

He laughed and looked up at Shona. 'There was a bear in the market when she came before.'

Shona's eyes widened. 'A bear!'

'Shall we see if he's still there?'

There was no bear, but there was a juggler in ragged red clothes juggling six balls, and a man on stilts with a tall hat. At the far side of the market was a man with a capering monkey on a chain, who danced to wailing music wheezed out by the man on his battered bagpipes.

The four of them stood around watching the show for twenty minutes but Richie was itching to be away. 'It'll be dark soon and I don't fancy those lanes in the pitch dark with that gig. Sure Gil Tait'll have me if I turn it over.'

Greg rode with them right to Gil Tait's stables and jumped down from his horse to talk to Shona while Richie and Lauretta returned the gig.

'So did you enjoy your day out?' he asked.

'I did indeed. I'll go a long way before I'll meet a man like that Mr Shakespeare. I liked him.'

'He liked you, I think. Will you come again?'

'To Priorton?'

He smiled. 'Anywhere. Up to the castle. Out in the country.'

'With you and Lauretta?'

'Richie as well, if he'll deign to.'

She scuffed the toe of her boot in the earth. 'They have to come.'

'Fine. Tomorrow?'

'No, I can't do that. I've to go to church with Biddy. I promised her. And in the afternoon Richie and me are promised to Pat Daley, to go looking for ducks and heron, on the river.'

His lips narrowed. 'Next Saturday then?'

'Can't do that. I'm at the pit. It's only Pay Saturdays I'm off. Once a fortnight.'

He stayed silent.

'Next Sunday,' she said. 'The afternoon, that'd be all right.'

'Yes. We could meet at the castle. At two.'

There was a silence in which it seemed there was nothing to say. Shona searched in her mind. 'Greg, what about Lauretta's mother? Where . . . ?'

'She's gone from us,' he said briskly. 'Oh, here they are!'

He jumped up into the saddle and leaned down to take Lauretta in front of him. 'Now then, pippet, Aida and your grandma'll be shouting for you.'

Shona turned for home, the questions about Lauretta's mother still buzzing in her head. *Lost to us. Gone from us.* Was she dead? The question seemed suddenly important.

* * *

Tommo was waiting for them when they arrived, prowling the kitchen, his head still sore from the afternoon's drinking. Biddy was sitting stitching away at the knitting bag she was making for Margaret McNaughton.

'Where d'ya think you've been, you two, all this time?' growled Tommo.

'Up at Priorton,' said Richie. 'We went to this hotel with Mr McNaughton and met a man.'

'Hotel, is it? Man, is it?' Tommo curled his hands into fists.

Shona grinned at him. 'Such a man, Tommo! You've never seen one like him. He was a gambler like you. He had a purple waistcoat . . .'

'He talked funny, and had just come back from America, and he'd seen the wild men,' Richie butted in.

'You don't go out with that . . . that McNaughton!' Tommo growled. His words were an order.

Shona's gaiety left her. She stood up. 'I go where I like, Tommo.'

He caught her shoulder, his face red. 'You don't! You watch yourself and do as I say.'

Biddy was at his side. 'Calm yourself, Tommo!'

'Ask her what happened when another man took her to see someone! Ask her!'

Biddy looked at Shona.

'I was only little, only twelve . . .' she protested.

'Grandon Seley took her to see His Lordship, Lord Marsteen, who asked her to . . .'

'Take off me clothes. And when I wouldn't, he gave me a slap.'

'The master?'

'No, the man Seley. The master stood by. So I turned and give *him* a right one.' She showed her own curled fist.

Tommo's face showed the faintest of smiles. 'I've felt that meself once or twice. I hope it hurt Seley like it hurt me.'

They were relaxing now, Tommo and Biddy sitting down on chairs and Shona on the bed.

Biddy looked from one to the other. 'And was that it? Nothing happened?'

Tommo looked her in the eye. 'Oh, something happened all right! Our Gerard saw Shona's black eye. His girl had already been hurt when she had her house pulled down about her ears. Well, he went after Marsteen when he was out shooting birds. Trouble was, Gerard hit the keeper, not His Lordship, and got killed himself for his pains.'

'Killed? Yes,' said Biddy slowly. 'The priest said something when he showed me your Auntie Marion's grave. He was a rare one against the landlords too.'

'I saw it meself. Killed like some old sitting pigeon. Now there's a sportsman for you, Lord Marsteen!' Tommo spoke through gritted teeth.

Shona sat up straight. 'So, Tommo. The answer is, I go where I choose. And those who don't like it, or cause me bother, get this.' She showed him her fist again and this time they all laughed together, out loud.

The next day after church Father O'Reilly shook hands very warmly with Biddy. 'Welcome again, Miss O'Farrell – Biddy – and you, Shona. A blessing on you both.'

'The church is busting at the seams, Father,' remarked Biddy.

'Another street of houses finished in the village last week and a whole group of families moved in from Liverpool. The men work in Shotwell but they wanted to be here to live with their own.' He made a drama of looking behind them. 'No Tommo? No little brother – Richie, is it? You must encourage them to come, Biddy. It's their souls you must look to as well as their bodies, me dear.'

'I'm workin' on it, Father, I'm workin' on it,' said Biddy calmly.

'Then I need have no worries, I'm sure.' He turned his attention to another newcomer and they were dismissed.

At home, Shona took off her hat and removed Gil Tait's posy from the brim. The berries were drying now, the carrot-leaves brittle. She shook the posy and it made a faint rattling sound in the air.

She wished she wasn't going duck and heron hunting this afternoon with Tommo and Pat. She wished she had agreed to go to see Greg McNaughton today, though it had been very satisfying in its way, saying no. But now she would have a whole week to wait before she saw him again.

That week her work at the coalscreens was harder than ever. Thoria, Len's cousin, was no match for Mary either as friend or workmate. The week stretched out as long as a sea journey till she would see him again.

She would need a new posy for her bonnet, that was for certain.

'Greg, stop prowling!' Margaret McNaughton looked up from her knitting. 'There must be a book to read. Something useful to do.'

Douglas looked up from his own book, disturbed at the discontent of both his sons, the elder pacing the parlour from end to end, the younger collapsed in an ungainly fashion on a chair by the window. 'There's a book of Mr Wesley's sermons on top of the cabinet there, Greg. The partner to this.'

Greg reached for it without stretching, sat down beside Lauretta, and opened it at page 100.

Lauretta was telling her kitten her own version of the story of the lost sheep from her picture story. 'And the little kitten was lost, d'you see there, Samson? And there's the daddy off out to look for him.'

Lauretta was not allowed to play with her doll on Sundays, but Samson, being a living creature, could not really be forbidden.

Margaret still had her eyes on her son. 'It's not like you to be so restless.'

He held the book closer to his eyes, thinking of flat winter water and ducks and slender herons.

Lauretta's voice fluted on. 'Oh, Samson is a very good boy. So you can have a ride on Richie's little horse. Up, up to the castle, and up, up steps with Shona, and see the world like a bird.'

Stuart swivelled round in his seat. Douglas lowered his paper. Their eyes moved to the child.

Margaret put down her knitting. 'Richie? Shona? What's this, sweetheart?'

Lauretta beamed at her. 'We play with Richie and Cush. And we race with Shona in the castle. And we see the monkey and the man with stick legs.'

Greg guiltily wiped his hand over his face.

'What's this?' said Stuart. 'Where've you seen them?'

'They were at Killock when I went for the ledger. Riding out.'

'Riding out? Irish? On donkeys?'

'The boy works at livery.'

Stuart jabbed his fist against his hand. 'I see! And there in the castle was a *monkey*! Are you sure it wasn't some other old Irish aunt or uncle?'

'Stuart, cease that!' said Douglas. Margaret looked at him timidly. He turned to Greg. 'However, a monkey at the castle does seem somewhat unlikely.'

'We saw them yesterday in Priorton, when we delivered the ledger.'

'By appointment?'

'Yes, in a way. Lauretta likes the boy and his pony.'

Douglas closed his book and turned to Margaret. 'Perhaps you will take the child into the kitchen for some milk and bread.'

She looked desperately at the bell which she sometimes rang for Aida. But it would ring unheeded today, Aida being at home with her grocer from dinnertime on Sunday. She would be gone for good soon. The baby must be just about due. She sighed and stood up rather unsteadily, holding out her hand. 'Come with Grandma, sweetheart. We'll see what's in the kitchen.'

Douglas turned to Greg. 'I can't fathom what you're up to, but it must stop. Whichever way you look at it, these are unsuitable people and . . .'

'That family means trouble,' interrupted Stuart.

'Trouble? Biddy got Ma on better lines than she's been for years. And the younger ones . . .'

'Are Irish, Catholic, and live in a different world to ours, Greg,' said Douglas firmly. 'You will not see them.'

'That girl is a dirty pit-girl. They live in filth,' said Stuart. 'Like swine in muck. You've seen those rows down at New Morven?'

Douglas, unusually, did not dissent. They both stared at him with the same unblinking stare.

Greg stood up. 'I'll see whom I choose,' he said, and walked out of the room and into the kitchen. His mother was sitting on Aida's rocker by the blazing range, Lauretta up to the table with a mug of milk before her.

Margaret looked up at him, black rings under her eyes. 'Did you see Biddy, Greg? Is she coming?'

'Yes. She says she will come soon.'

'Soon? I need to talk to her now. You see, I've remembered and

I need to tell her. Only her. It was the devil I saw, I remember now. The devil. Come for his maiden.'

Chapter Thirteen

Shona tied a blue ribbon in her hair. She had fashioned a new posy from berries and pinned it to her bonnet before she put it on. It was not as cunningly wrought as Gil Tait's, but it would do.

It was a rare fine December day. The hard ground frost had melted and the fields were soft underfoot. She picked her way over the softened grass, with Richie and Cush.

'Ye can ride on if ye like,' offered Richie.

'Ride? After a week standing picking coal at those screens, it's a pleasure to put one foot in front of another, Richie. And how about Cush? Shouldn't he have a holiday too?'

'Cush? Every day is a holiday for him. Every single day!'

She laughed at his gloomy tone. 'And what in the world would you do every day, Richie, if you could choose?'

'Choose? Why, I'd choose a big stable with ten horses. Not to yoke them behind wagons, but to race them against each other. Gil Tait, he tells me about that sometimes.'

'It'd be hard work, Richie.'

'Not as hard as them bluddy furnaces!' He kicked at a stone that stood in his way and yelped as it seemed to kick back.

They walked on towards Killock Common, filing cautiously between bushes and through trees whose branches whipped their faces.

'What's that?' Shona turned her head, her attention drawn by whoops and roars which were emerging from a stone hut deep in a thicket. Smoke curled lazily through broken stone tiles into the still air.

Richie tied Cush's bridle to a hanging branch. The two of them crept across the tufted grass. The door to the hut was tight shut.

One voice shrieked. A different, rumbling voice struck a familiar chord.

'Here!' Shona dragged a log under the high slit of a window. They climbed on and peered in, standing shoulder to shoulder.

At first, all they could see was the log fire burning high in the centre of the room. Then a figure danced through the firelight, followed by another. Astonished, Shona recognised the first figure as Tommo, naked but for an open shirt. The other was a tall figure of a woman, also naked, whose hair glinted right down her long back in the firelight.

They raced around, laughing, until the woman finally allowed herself to be caught in the corner. Tommo kept her there, kissing her face and shoulders, her breasts, her stomach, her tuft of body hair, and finally her feet.

Then she jumped over him and was on his broad back. He reared upwards and she clung there while he raised his muscular arms and swung round and round, trying to dislodge her. Then the pair moved like some single creature to a corner heaped up with yellow straw.

Tommo first knelt, then lay backwards so that Maudie had to loosen her hold and was lying behind him. He turned to face her and the watchers at the window saw the two faces lit with laughter.

'B'Jesus!' breathed Richie.

Shona said nothing, her eyes glued to the narrow space. Her blood was racing and her knees felt weak. She felt she should push Richie away and they should both run, but she couldn't. The thought of Greg McNaughton came into her mind and refused to leave.

Now Tommo was above Maudie, a hand either side of her shoulders, holding himself off her. She was smiling at him, her light brown hair tangled in the straw. Her hands raised themselves to his shoulders and her eyes gleamed up at him. Then he lowered himself slowly on to her. Into her. Her eyes closed and he came away and lowered himself again. And again.

They could hear him groan and see her speak. Still, he moved slowly. Again and again and again, so slowly. Then they could hear the woman's peal of laughter and Tommo's action became quicker. Then Maudie seemed to lift herself from the straw and her head went back and her moans joined his.

Shona finally managed to grab Richie's shoulder and pull him off

130

the log. 'Come on, Richie. We shouldn't!' Her face was bright red, her heart pounding. She shook her head to rid it of the image of Greg McNaughton's narrow face and long slender body.

Richie chortled, 'Isn't our Tommo just the boy?'

'Richie, you shouldn't . . .'

He laughed up at her. 'Shona, you're as red as a night fire! An't you seen that before? I seen it dozens o' times on the boat comin' over here. An' that boy John O'Carrol that brought me here – he could find a girl in every town, every village. He was quicker at it than our Tommo, though. Mebbe had more practice. I seen him with two, once.'

'Richie – oh!'

It was Terry Kennedy, standing there, a sly smile on his face, his hand holding Cush's bridle. 'Ye bluddy little spies,' he rasped, his voice oddly hoarse. 'All alike, your family. Watching that *hooah* with your Tommo! Dirty little buggers.'

He dropped the bridle and caught hold of Shona. 'If ye want to see sommat, I can show you sommat.' His other hand went to his crotch.

She looked down at his hand where it lay. She thought of Mary Challoner and her robust ways of handling the men who harassed her at the pit. 'I'd say, Terry, you'll have a wee worm in there like you've got a big worm in your head.'

'Shona!' warned Richie.

'It's all right, Richie. Just stand there and let's both of us see Mr Kennedy's fine item of manhood. We'll just stand and look in admiration, so we will.'

One hand dropped from her shoulder, the other was raised from his crotch to hit her. She ducked.

'There ye are, Richie,' she mocked, 'a thing the size of my little finger, and he only fit to belt a lass and a wee lad. Pat Daley'll have fun telling the boys down the Cockerel about a feller attacking an Irish girl. Won't he just? Only good for watching other people is this feller, Richie. No use to himself!'

Terry's hands dropped limply by his sides. 'Go and drown in the river, the pair of you. *Hooahs* all of you. That one in there, you, the whole fockin' lot!'

Richie caught Cush's reins and pulled the pony between Terry and Shona and started to plod away through the trees.

'That's it! Get off, the pair of you! Little *hooahs*!'

Terry was still there behind the tree when Tommo and Maudie emerged from the shed, hair and clothes flecked with straw. They were hand in hand; their laughter still pealing out.

'Spies and hooahs, the lot of 'm,' muttered Terry, slipping down the pathway ten yards behind them. 'Spies and bluddy hooahs! They need showin' . . .'

Greg waited outside Killock Castle till twenty-five past two, then he tethered Juvenal to an iron ring at the tumbledown gate and walked the pathway to the great door alone.

Margaret had followed him to the garden gate, Lauretta at her skirts. 'You're riding to see the boy and the girl again, Biddy's people?'

Greg nodded.

'Will you tell them I want to see Biddy?' She looked back at the house. 'I've missed her, Greg. I've things I want to talk to her about.'

His forehead had creased with the words. 'What was that about a devil? There was never any devil, Ma.'

'There was,' she insisted. 'You know there was. You ask that woman, the one you married.'

Lauretta had refused to come. She had clung to Margaret for a week. As her grandmother's spirits swooped down, the child seemed to know it and stayed glued to her side. Even talk of the pony would not entice her.

Greg walked from room to room in the castle, using a lamp to light his way. He stopped in the dining room to set a fire in the hearth and the things he had brought on the table, then made his way out on to the roof through the narrow door.

He looked across the dark landscape with its quiet pit wheels and rearing heaps of spoil. Patches of the burnished green of winter meadow gleamed at him from the dark folds of hedge; the silver thread of the River Gaunt made its way across the countryside, through ruined black and ancient woodland like a blind man seeking an easy way.

He had stood here once with Mary Louisa.

She had called it a spoiled land. She would close her eyes and tell him what she could see through her 'old face'. She had used this

132

term for the occasions when she said she could see through time, to a very distant past before history was written. 'I see woods, Greg. Gnarled old trees as old as time. Broad hedges and buildings of old stone. A timid deer small as a dog and men on horses picking their way through thorns, hounds at their heels. A wild green land with sun on it.'

'And no machines?'

'No machines ravaging the place, no pillaging black smoke nor grinding noise to make your ears ring.'

Mary Louisa had come to visit her brother after caring half a lifetime for her parents who had died. Her brother was the priest in Priorton and New Morven. She had brought deathbed messages from her parents in Dublin and was to stay with him a month or so.

That first day on the train she had started a conversation with Greg, remarking on the exotic painted boxes in his luggage, and he had told her he was on his way home from Russia. Then he had reeled under a torrent of earnest questions as she wrung every last detail out of him, about that land of white wastes and very foreign people.

'And you built them a train?'

'For some of them it might have been a magic dragon, believe me.'

'And you saw the Csar?'

'Very grand. For me *he* could have been a magic dragon.'

Her eyes sparkled. 'I believe you.'

She talked of her brother, who wanted her to go into the church.

'And will you?'

'No. I've neither the wisdom nor the virtue. But he will not believe that.'

Greg had laughed uneasily then, understanding the words but not the meaning.

It was inevitable that they would meet again. They had to make elaborate plans. There was no way, in the normal run of things, their paths would ever cross. So they had met at the castle, had picnics in the rooms and walked the ruined walls. People caught glimpses of them there, people from her community and his. There was resentful muttering but no action because she was the sister of the priest and he was the son of the great Mr McNaughton.

One day she came to him with weals on her arms where Father Peter had tethered her 'for her own good' so she would not go on her unholy wanders to meet Greg. She was to be saved for Mother Church, Father Peter was determined. 'Even when I was small, before he entered the church himself, he was jealous of anything else in my life,' she'd told him. 'He had a kitten taken away, because he said it was diseased. My friend Semilla O'Shea, who came as a maid, he sent her away.'

'You must've choked with all that,' Greg had said with feeling.

Then she laughed. 'Choked? Didn't I think it great, showing that he loved me so?' Her face darkened. 'Then he left me. Back to the seminary and then that was it.'

That had been the first time Greg kissed her, to wipe the dark cloud from the tense narrow face. She responded with a fire and force that shook them both. It was the first time anyone save her brother had kissed her and she told him so. As he kissed her again he knew that he must stay with her for ever. He told her they must be married.

'Then the church'll have to whistle for its nun.'

She'd laughed then, and agreed to it all as though it were a child's game.

So they ran off and were married, and he took her back for the first time to meet his father and mother. He had waited then for the storm to break but it didn't. Mary Louisa was quiet and thoughtful about the house. Her brother seemed to have vanished from her universe. Greg's father soon discovered her talent for drawing and put it to use. And for a time there had been peace.

Then one day her brother had come for her in a lunatic frame of mind, and had been dragged away, gibbering. It was after that everything had started to go wrong.

Now, pulling himself out of his reverie, Greg peered through the wooden shutter then opened it wider. Two figures were making their way down the long road which led to the main gate of Killock. Shona was sitting astride Cush, her legs hanging down, her green hat bobbing with the stately rhythm of the pony's plodding gait.

Greg smiled and waved but there was no response. He pounded down the staircases and met them at the gate. For a reason he couldn't fathom there was an awkward silence between them, which Richie broke.

'No little'n today then?'

'Stayed back with her grandma.' Greg's eyes were on Shona, who blushed bright red at his gaze and looked to one side. 'Her grandma is a bit down now, with only Aida for company. She was asking about Biddy.'

'She's well enough.' Shona's eyes were still looking to one side, away from him. 'She keeps very busy.'

'Too busy!' Richie rolled his eyes. 'Too busy with baths and brooms! Too busy with poss-sticks and smoothing irons.'

Greg laughed at him. 'It shows.'

For some reason this made Shona furious. 'And what might that mean?'

'Nothing, nothing at all!'

He gestured behind him. 'Well, I've a picnic set out for us in the dining room.'

Richie grinned and ran ahead, his sense of direction unerring.

Greg looked down at Shona as they walked along. 'So what's wrong today?'

'Why should there be something wrong?'

'Because you've a face on you like a leek. And you're looking at me like a cat looks at a dog.'

She relaxed just a bit. Her mind was still working furiously to rid itself of the bright sensual images of the happenings in the stone hut.

Greg had a fire of old wood roaring in the hearth. There was bread and apples, an open bottle of wine and dusty glasses on the table.

Richie filled the glasses, his own to the very brim. He swigged it off and smacked his lips. 'That's a drop of good, sir!' He picked up some bread and bit it. 'Well, sir, if it's the same to you, I'll look further in this house.'

They watched him move through the open door. Shona took a sip of the wine and wrinkled her nose.

'You don't like it?' asked Greg.

'It's sour,' she said.

He took a mouthful and rolled it over his tongue. He didn't know how it should taste. There was no alcohol at Garth End Cottage. 'It's sharp.' He drank again. 'But very fresh.'

She tore off a piece of bread and dipped it in the wine and

chewed at it. Watching her, he was irritated. He thought of the dainty way Mary Louisa ate bread, nibbling at it with her neat front teeth.

'You've had someone else here, doing this!' Shona's accusing words pierced his thoughts. Now she could look straight at him; the scene from the hut had faded.

'It's none of your business,' he said coldly, 'but, yes, I used to meet someone here. But there was no wine. I hadn't discovered Mr Shakespeare's cellar then.'

'It was Lauretta's mother. She was here. Where is she now, Greg?'

He stayed silent.

She glared at him and went across to open great double doors connecting with another room which had draped chairs standing like stiff ghosts. And a piano. She pulled off the cloth that was covering it. He came across to the big doors and leaned there, watching her.

Striking one key after another, she found a note which suited her, joined her voice to it and started to sing, softly at first and then in full voice:

> 'The way through the woods
> Was winding and leafy
> My love by my side
> With her heart in my hand.'

She closed her eyes and could see again the leaping firelight in the hut, the wrestling bodies. She wanted this man, the man watching her from the doorway, and was jealous of any woman he'd met here before, might meet here again. She opened her eyes and he saw the passion in them.

He listened as the notes floated delicately in the darkened dusty room, then started towards her.

'Look what I found!' Richie was bustling in behind him, a pair of dusty bottles in each hand. 'Is it all right to take these, sir?'

Shona closed the lid of the piano, her face red. 'No, leave them, Richie. We have to go now.'

'Don't!' Greg pleaded.

'We have to go!' she said firmly, her face closed to him.

'Take the bottles. Take them for Biddy,' he said coolly to Richie. 'Tell her they're good medicine. Keep the cold out. And can you tell Biddy my mother's . . .' he hesitated over the word '. . . longing to see her?' He turned again to Shona.

'She's very busy,' she said.

'Tell her to make it soon will you? You come with her.'

She flashed a look at him.

'Don't worry, I won't be there. I've business in Manchester. Some workers to transport and a manufacturer I have to see.'

'I'll tell her. She intends to come, I know.' She turned to her brother. 'Come on, Richie. Bring those bottles if you must.'

'What's the matter with you? Sourpuss all of a sudden, you are,' he grumbled.

The day was closing in when Greg got home. He met his brother at the door.

'Off away, Stuart?' he said.

'I'm meeting Morry Smith in Priorton. He's got a meeting with Herbert Walton the constable. I thought I'd go with him.'

'What's that about?'

'He has some information about some plot brewing in that Irish pub in New Morven, the Cockerel. To blow up the railway in the Shotwell tunnel.'

It could easily be another of his lies. Greg stood by to let his brother pass. Stuart was always muttering about plots. He saw a shadow behind every tree. When he was little he had been mortally afraid of the dark, always running into Flora's bed. In the early years Greg had felt protective towards Stuart but gradually, as his brother's lies started to lay blame at Greg's door for things he hadn't done, he'd distanced himself, leaving him to his dark imaginings.

Douglas was sitting at the parlour table writing notes by the light of a lamp. He smiled faintly as he looked up. 'You haven't forgotten you're to go to Manchester tomorrow, Greg?'

'No.' He had three mills to visit with drawings and the model of their machine. It was installed in two mills already and was reducing damage to fabric by half. 'I'll be three days, Pa.'

'Three? Should only take two.'

'I have another call to make.'

Douglas put down his pen and looked at him. 'If you must, you must,' he said, picking up his pen again.

Greg stared hard at the top of his father's head. They never talked about what he did in Manchester, yet his father was always accommodating. He was grateful for this but also puzzled, expecting him to be obstructive and questioning.

He went on up to see his mother who was sitting in the dark by her window, with a sleeping Lauretta on her knee. He lifted his daughter in his arms and her head drooped, her sleep continuing.

'You shouldn't be here in the dark, Ma. Father's down in the parlour. You could sit with him.'

She sighed. 'I could feel him wanting me out of the way.'

'I saw Shona.' He enjoyed saying the name. 'She'll tell Biddy for you.'

Her hands came together in a light clap. 'Oh! It must be soon.'

'Nobody approves of it you know, Ma. Us being friends with them. Even Young Jamie in the workshops told me that nothing good would come of mixing with *"them"*.'

'No good came of it before,' she said soberly. Then she smiled and put her hands on the arms of her chair and pulled herself up. 'It's a hard world, son. We have to find friends where we can.'

The main street of New Morven was crowded with people wringing the last ounce of pleasure out of their day off before the descent into work on Monday. It was not difficult, therefore, for Terry Kennedy and Stuart to watch the comings and goings at Maudie Martin's house.

The last person to make his exit was Pat Daley. 'There!' said Terry. 'That's the one. He's the one who's friends with Tommo Farrell. Plotters both.'

Stuart ran his finger along the scar on his cheek, his gift from Maudie on their last meeting.

'I seen 'em both, him and Tommo, out meeting her and others in a stone hut in the woods. She knows what they're up to, I can tell you. You could get evidence for the constable off her.' He paused. 'Squeeze it out of her.'

Stuart started but Terry restrained him. 'Nah. Look!' Two giant ironworkers, frequenters of Showy's bar, hiccuping with drunken laughter, were knocking on Maudie's door. 'They'll be a good half hour with the houah, quick as she is. There's another lass down the bottom end, Bridget Sommers.' He stayed silent a second. He knew his man. 'Nothing wrong with her a good hiding won't cure. Can't we sort out these plotters another day?'

Tommo was sitting in the chair sleeping when Shona and Richie got home. She looked at his slack figure with embarrassed fascination; the last time she had seen him, he was flesh naked.

'He's a good right to sleep!' smirked Richie. 'He must be worn out. Makes too much of a meal of things.'

'Shhh!' Biddy whispered. 'What's that supposed to mean?' She served out two plates of broth from the big pan on the fire.

Richie put the wine bottles with their cork ready loosened on the table 'McNaughton sent it, said it was good for the health.'

She looked at it suspiciously. 'Did you steal them?'

'No!' said Shona. 'There's a cellar in this . . . house he looks after. The house of that queer old man we met the other day. I told you. Well, anything in there he can have, he says. And the wine's in there.'

Richie pulled off the cork with his teeth and poured some into the pot cup which Biddy held out. She swigged some off, pulled a face, then swallowed some more.

'Sure it isn't so bad after all. I'll take some more.' She held out her cup.

'He said . . .' he paused, 'that his mother wanted you there. That she was missing you.'

Biddy frowned. 'I promised to go. I've this bag I've made her for that blessed knitting of hers.' She smiled. 'I'll get across there tomorrow. To be sure I will.'

'Biddy?' said Shona. 'What about the little one's mother? Did she ever tell you?' Shona tried to make the question sound light.

'There was something . . . Something about her being the sister to the priest that was here before Father O'Reilly.'

'Is she dead?'

'Yes, I think so. No, I don't know.' She looked sharply at her niece. 'Do you want me to find out?'

Shona shrugged. 'If you want to. Sure it's nothing to me.'

Tommo stirred and sat up straight. He passed his hand across his

face. His joyous drinking bout with Pat after he had seen Maudie
had left his head like a creaking oak.

'And what trouble have ye two been up to today, then?' he
asked, and fell back down again, snoring.

Chapter Fourteen

The December weather was cutting in very cold. Shona, Tommo and Richie went out to and returned home from work in the pitch dark, though there were so many people around, swinging their lamps, stamping their feet on the hard ground, calling and hailing each other, that it might have been daytime.

Shona never passed Shotwell road junction without thinking of Mary Challoner.

Her replacement, Thoria, came to work with her Uncle Len. She suffered from chilblains on both hands and feet. Those on her feet were not helped by the boots she wore: a pair of her brother's which were a size too small. Her eyes and nose streamed with the cold. She was clumsy too, often dropping coal and sometimes missing obvious stones.

As if to emphasise his lack of favouritism, Len was on at Thoria from morning till night: spluttering attacks which were at odds with his basically kind nature.

At first, because she didn't want to associate with the clumsy girl who had supplanted her friend, Shona colluded with Len's attacks, nodding faintly and ducking her own head away from the girl's mute appeals.

The day after the castle picnic Len was on at her yet again. 'Thoria! Yer bliddy useless, I tell yer! Yer'll be stoppin' the screens at this rate. The tubs are backin' up even now. If it weren't for Shona Farrell . . .' He glanced across to where she was working twice as fast, to make up the short-fall.

Thoria shuddered under the spitting hail of her uncle's temper as he ground on: 'Ye're bliddy useless, I tell yer. Get on with it, I say! If ye canna work nee faster, a's'll have to lay yer off an' set someone quicker on. I'll lay yer off no matter what yer ma says.'

Thoria started to wail, open-mouthed like a small child. Shona put out an arm and pulled her to her side. She put her hand over that of the younger girl, helping her to pick away at the cold rocks with icy hands.

There was muttering along the screen.

'We was better off before, underground,' Meg Tallent called across. 'At least it was bliddy hot down there. Nee bliddy chilblains down there. It's bliddy freezation up here. Freezation!'

'Hot in more ways'n one, so I hear!' Len grinned across genially, his humour restored at making his sullen niece cry.

'No choice, with dirty beasts like your own da down there! And his brother!' retorted Meg.

Thoria started to wail again. Shona picked up the girl's hand. The chilblains were oozing blood.

Shona dropped the hand and folded her own arms. 'Too cold to work down here!' she announced.

Meg looked across at her, then nodded. 'Ye're right there, Shona.' She folded her own arms.

One by one the girls, then the women, stopped. The old men scrambled for a few moments to cover the work, then they too stopped and folded their arms.

Len went across and pulled the lever to stop the screens.

He leaned over the rail. 'What's this? Get on with it, will you? The tubs is backin' up here. Get on with it!'

'We will not,' said Shona. 'We need some heat down here. Aren't our hands droppin' with cold? Sack us and then where'll yo be? Where'll you get experienced pickers like us?'

He looked at the faces turned towards him, the soft made hard and the hard even harder. His own job would be forfeit if there were real trouble.

He shrugged. 'Easy done, lasses. I'll get a bucket and some hot cinders.'

In ten minutes a roaring bucket was standing behind Thoria. The screens started to move again and the pickers started picking. One by one, so the work didn't stop, the women and the old men came to the bin to warm their hands, staying only a minute then returning. The work went faster than ever and Len was satisfied.

He caught Shona on her way out after the shift. She looked at him warily. He put his head on one side. 'For a minute there,

142

lookin' down from the gantry, I thought it wor Mary Challoner down there, her cheeky face lookin' back at us.'

'It could be worse, Len.'

He shook his head. 'Aye, it could be worse, lass. It wor worse for her.'

Thoria walked down the pit road with her. 'T'were nice of you that, Shona,' she mumbled.

'Sure it was nothin', darlin'. You just have to show them sometimes.' Shona tucked her hand into the girl's arm as they walked along. 'Have ye any family down here in Shotwell then?'

'I've five brothers and three sisters, all younger. But they're back up the valley on the farm. Here in Shotwell there's Uncle Len, Aunt May and their lot. But I sleep mostly, so I hardly know them. I wanted to go into service. I like housework and I'm a canny cook. But my ma wanted me here with Uncle Len.'

Shona imagined the clumsy girl let loose in a kitchen and smiled. 'I had this friend, Thoria, who had your job before you. She died.'

'You'll miss her?'

'So I do.'

'Can't I be your friend, Shona?'

She took a little skip. 'So you can, Thoria.'

Handling the knitting bag with great care, Biddy tucked it into her own longhandled bag. She had made it for Margaret McNaughton and was looking forward to giving it to her.

She looked into the smoky mirror and smoothed down the neat lace collar she had bought from a traveller. It shone out against the brown wool dress, a gift from Margaret. Biddy's hair, soft and teased out, looked silver lying up against the brim of her black hat.

She walked round to Gil Tait's to ask him to take her to Shotwell in his trap. 'Now, Gil, I only have threepence for the fare. Twopence there, a penny back,' she warned.

He grinned at her in simple delight. 'Miss O'Farrell, won't it be a pleasure to take you at any price? No finer sight has travelled through the streets of New Morven.' He winked and grimaced at her, touching the brim of his round hat with his whip.

'Tis kind of you to say so, Mr Tait.'

'I do so. Those young'ns, they're lucky to have you for an auntie.'

'Aren't I lucky to have them? Tommo's a good worker, even if he drinks and gambles and spends his money we know not where. And isn't Shona a treat to the eye and the ear? She has the voice of an angel and the spirit of a sharp cat. And Richie . . .'

'Ah, Miss O'Farrell, Richie's the prime one for me, so he is. Did I tell you he was a wonder with the horses?'

'So you did, Mr Tait, so you did.'

They rode along until they could see the chimneys and smoke of Shotwell.

'They do say, Miss O'Farrell, that Shona's walking out with that Protestant, Mr McNaughton. Now I would not say it, but Father O'Reilly . . .'

'Don't say it then,' she interrupted him. She leaned out of the trap to see better the raw brick of the railway streets. Compared with New Morven, there were in the main more curtains at the windows, more children with shoes.

She smiled her pleasure when the familiar neat front of Garth End Cottage came into view. She climbed down and gave Gil twopence. 'Will you be back here in an hour, Mr Tait?'

Gil looked gravely down at her. 'I've a warnin' for you, Miss O'Farrell. Watch yersel' with those Protestants. Too mean to feed the cat and vindictive to boot.' He touched his hat with his whip, clicked his tongue and set his horse down the street at a canter. He was careful to avoid passing the statue of King William, where a crowd of boys customarily sat. Seeing him, they were sure to throw stones and any other missiles which were to hand.

The cottage door opened almost immediately after Biddy's first knock. Aida stood there with no glimmer of recognition on her face. 'What is it?'

'Hello to you, Aida.'

Lauretta tried to rush forward. Aida held the child fast and she started to whimper.

'What is it?' Aida repeated.

'Aren't I here to call on Mrs McNaughton? Greg – Mr McNaughton – sent me a message that I should call.'

'Mr McNaughton sent no such message,' said Aida, through almost clenched teeth. 'He knows well his ma is too ill to have callers. And she's asleep just now.'

144

Biddy moved forward. 'Couldn't I see her for just a minute? I've something here for her. I've something to say.'

Aida stepped back in the face of such determination and Biddy moved forward again.

'What's this?' called a harsh voice behind her. Biddy felt a heavy hand on her shoulder.

She turned to see the sulky face of Greg's brother. 'I'm here to see your mother.'

'I did say Mrs McNaughton was unwell, Stuart!' Aida had her courage back now and was pushing towards her. Biddy found herself sandwiched between two furies. Stuart's hand tightened on her shoulder and turned her round fully to face him, his head too close to hers. 'You'll not see her, madam! My mother has better things to do than to see a scavenging old gypsy like you!' He turned her and slapped her shoulder, pushing her two steps down the path. 'She has her own friends and you're an embarrassment. She told me so this morning. An embarrassment, she said.'

Biddy turned round again and took a step backwards, still looking at them. Her eyes dropped to the whimpering Lauretta. 'Don't you worry, my darlin'. Your Auntie Biddy'll see your grandma, never fear.'

She picked up her skirt and started to walk quickly down the path towards the road. Faster and faster. A clod of earth skimmed her skirt and she looked back to see Stuart wiping his hands and exchanging smiles with Aida.

She hurried on, trying to ignore her ankle, which was throbbing in a way it hadn't for weeks. She looked along the street, but Gil Tait and his trap were nowhere to be seen.

Greg always felt like a country boy in Manchester. Whole new buildings seemed to go up in the centre between each visit he paid. The pattern of high chimneys altered constantly against the skyline. The cabmen always had new stories to tell, of fortunes made and lost.

The shops and thoroughfares were piled with goods and thronged with marketeers. In the offices the fast-talking manufacturers babbled out words and numbers at an extraordinary rate.

Seamus Ogden, who was buying the little gadget that Greg and

Douglas had developed, spent a fruitless time trying to disguise his pleasure at the success of its operation, to force the continuance price down.

After business Ogden insisted on taking Greg to his home for the night. They rode out of the city into the countryside in a fine carriage with two men on top.

The Ogden house was newly built in the fold of a hill, in a place where the chimneys of the city were virtually invisible. Greg met Sarah Jane, Ogden's clever, forceful wife, and his daughters Aurelia and Stephanie. Stephanie took him out to show him the dovecote after dinner and came back to declare to her father in bell-like tones, 'Mr McNaughton is the most interesting man, Papa. Don't you think him clever?'

Mr Ogden did not discourage her enthusiasm, knowing that the McNaughtons were a coming family and that his daughter, though well schooled and most refined, was no beauty.

The carriage which brought Greg on his return journey took him through some of the blackest areas of the city. In one road a cluster of children jumped on to the carriage and rode on it for a mile, oblivious to the cuts of the driver's whip. Sullen women with babies on their hips stood in doorways and stared with stoical indifference as the carriage passed the end of their narrow alley.

Greg was relieved to get back to his lodgings and enjoy the bath that was laid out beside his fire, with fine white towels heaped in a neat pile in the chair.

The day at the Ogdens' grand house had been a trial. He knew that tomorrow his visit to the house of Dr Montague would be even more difficult.

The doctor met him in the hall. 'It's some time since we have seen you, Gregor.'

'I have valued your letters, Dr Montague.'

'I'd have wished that the news was better. Mary Louisa has no pain but is very frail. She is up and well today. Some days she is better than others.'

Mary Louisa was polite enough with Greg. She offered him tea and poured it with great style. She leaned towards him, peering over the pot rather shortsightedly. 'What was it you said your name was? Are you Thomas's son or Patrick's?' She laughed merrily.

'Aren't I the silly woman, with all these nephews and not being able to tell one from another?'

She picked up her own cup. 'Did I tell you about your Uncle Peter – called to the priesthood he was . . .'

He stood up and made as if to go, then cursed himself for cowardice, sat down and finished his tea as meek as any newborn lamb.

Later, on the train, he took a package out of his tailcoat pocket. Pulling the fine paper away, he put his hand over the pink roses, made pale with drying, and tied with a velvet ribbon.

Stephanie Ogden came to mind with her tight mouth and coquettish manner, to be supplanted very quickly by an image of an Irish girl with cheeks the very colour of these fragile flowers.

When Greg got home late on Christmas Eve afternoon Lauretta jumped up to kiss him without her usual smile. He greeted his father who looked up grimly from a letter he was writing.

'Biddy was here,' announced Lauretta.

Greg looked at his mother, smiling. 'Lauretta says Biddy came. That'd please you, Ma.'

She looked at him dully, then her eyes started to clear. 'She came? Biddy?' She stood and leaned down to pick up Lauretta, pulling the small face close to hers. 'Biddy came? When did she come?'

'In the morning after breakfast. Uncle Stuart smacked her.'

'Uncle Stuart did what?'

'Aida shouted and Stuart smacked Biddy and then she went running away. He throwed a stone at her,' she added soberly.

Margaret turned to Greg. 'She came and you turned her away?'

'The child said Stuart,' he growled.

She ignored him. 'I've waited for her for such a long time and she went away again!'

Looking at his mother, it flashed into Greg's mind that she had somehow fallen for Biddy, just as surely as, on that train journey back from Russia, he had fallen for Mary Louisa. That person had to be in your life, no matter what the rights and wrongs of it. No matter what the consequences.

Douglas was suddenly nettled by his wife's intensity. 'For goodness' sake, Margaret, I cannot understand this fuss over that scruffy unsuitable old woman. It is entirely inappropriate. Entirely.'

Lauretta felt her grandmother's distress at his sharp tone and started to cry. Greg came across and took the child from his mother. 'That's enough of this for you, pippet. Let's have you up to bed. I have to tell you about this lovely shop I saw in Manchester and all they had was toys . . .'

Margaret watched them leave the room. 'Unsuitable! Biddy's brother's farm in Waterford was twice as big as my father's. So am *I* unsuitable?' She started to stride up and down the room. 'You should be used to unsuitable. We're used to unsuitable here. *That* woman!'

'Margaret!' He stood up.

'Twenty years older than my Greg. That priest's sister. That priest's whore!'

He reached out and shook her hard, his face like thunder. 'Never. She was not that.'

She faltered slightly but went on, 'You saw that brother of hers. Coming here to the house . . . I never saw such love in a man's eyes. But I wouldn't, would I? He may not have done . . . *it* but he wanted to, didn't he?'

'Margaret!'

'And you all did, didn't you? Greg like a man on drink, Stuart green with jealousy, and *you*! You following her round with that look in your eyes.'

She started to pull away at her hair, scattering her pins on the floor. He closed his eyes tightly a second then went to the door, calling for Aida. As he opened it she fell in.

Margaret turned on the maid. 'And you! You cold bitch. Not a patch on Flora. Not a patch! Fussing and messing around. Too mean to smile, half the time. Not letting me see my friend. No one's good enough for you, is that it? Well, your mother and father weren't too grand to live in a hovel and to throw their rubbish on a heap under the window.'

'Mrs McNaughton, stop! I don't have to . . .'

'Indeed you don't! Get yourself away from here, you mean little bitch. Go to your pennypinching, cheating little grocer.'

'Go? You can be sure I'll go, Mrs McNaughton.' Her eyes slid round to challenge Douglas. 'I've no wish to stay in a house where they let in the sweepings of the streets and goodness knows what goes on.' She rushed out and banged the door.

The look in Douglas's eyes turned from desperation to contempt which intensified as Margaret swept on: 'Unsuitable? They knew it, didn't they? That doll they made of her had white streaks in its hair. Did you see it?'

Three nights running the people had come, carrying the ghastly dolls on a wooden platform. Closing her eyes, Margaret could still hear the terrible clanging noise that seemed to inhabit the night. She could still see the dark figures, faces darkened to anonymity with coal-dust, the men in drooping skirts, the women in breeches; some with sacks over their heads with holes cut in for eyes.

Her voice rose. 'They knew, didn't they? They knew she was an old priest's whore. They knew it was wrong, a young man like Greg and an old whore. They knew it was wrong.' She pulled at the neck of her neat blouse and the buttons flew off into the corners of the room.

Looking at her wild face, Douglas could hear it again now: the unholy clangour, the beating of iron on iron; not the steady heartbeat of the blacksmith's hammer but the random noise of nightmares, of anarchy.

She put out her hands towards him and he put up an arm as though to ward off a blow. 'It wasn't like that, Margaret. It wasn't anything like that!'

Her hands came back and up through her hair, pulling at her front locks until the pins came out and her hair was round her shoulders, leaving a forlorn topknot at the back. 'It was an evil thing she did, creeping in here with her simpering face. Changing my lovely son to an anxious suitor. Making you laugh and smile like you hadn't for years. You loved her!' The challenge was out of her mouth at last.

Now he was shaking her and she was laughing in his face. '*Now* you're holding me. Today's the first time since she came into this house. Four years ago, isn't it? That devil knew. Did you see him out there in front, horns on his head? Taking his great sword and piercing her, smashing her?' She looked up at him, face cunning now. 'Go on! Hit me! You want to, don't you? I welcome it. Any touch. Any feeling . . .'

He flung her to one side and marched from the room. She stared after him, then her wild gaze strayed around the room with its chairs and covers, pictures and plates. 'And this! What's this?' She picked up a plate and threw it at the door after him. For the first time the parrot squawked, lifting his wings and settling down on his perch again.

'This is no home,' she screamed. 'Home is where the heart is! There's no heart here. It's a place of death. A mausoleum of lost souls.' She picked up more plates, books, cushions, to hurl against the door.

She stopped to take breath and could hear the mutter of voices outside the door.

'I hear you, deciding what to do with the poor mad woman! I hear you, deciding to put me on one side. I hear you! I hear you!'

She went across to the window and pulled up the sash.

The parrot squawked again as a blast of cold air swept into the stuffy room. A moment later the room was empty.

Creeping past his quarrelling parents, Greg had gone to look for Stuart. There was a lamp still burning in the works, although they must have closed down at noon on Christmas Eve as usual.

His brother was sitting in the office, with his feet up on Douglas's desk. Before him stood two squat bottles of whisky and three glasses. Sitting on the end of the desk was Morry Smith, Mr Moxham's clerk, and a tall heavy man in a worker's cap who stood up when Greg entered the room.

'Ah, Greg! Just in time to join us in a seasonal toast!' grinned Stuart.

'I want no drink!'

'Friends, my brother is a Puritan, like my father.'

Greg looked at the clerk. 'What are you doing here?'

'I've papers from Mr Moxham. I had to see your brother, so I thought I'd deliver them.'

Greg put out his hand. Smith put his hand to his pocket, then looked dismayed. 'Oh dear! I must have left them at my lodging.'

Greg raised his eyebrows and looked at the third man.

'This is Terry Kennedy,' Smith said, 'a valuable . . . informant of mine.'

'Well, Mr Smith and Mr Kennedy, will you go now? I have to

speak to my brother. Probably knock him down if he's to get his just deserts.'

Stewart stood up. 'They'll stay, Greg. We haven't finished our business.'

Greg looked into his brother's face, saw the hot gleam in his eyes and the faint sheen of sweat on his skin. For the first time he was seeing him with a stranger's eye. Gone was the timid whining child. Here was a cocky, bullying man who thought of no one but himself. His brother.

'You sent Biddy O'Farrell away,' he said quietly. 'Lauretta says you hit her. You should be ashamed of yourself. I've been trying for weeks to get her to come and see Ma.'

Stuart snorted. 'That old gypsy? Dangerous. They all are. Came and cast some gypsy spell on Ma. Anyone could see that.'

'That's just your view. You're full of envy and spite.'

Stuart's lip twisted. 'Why should I be jealous of an old ragbag?'

'You envy the world. That's your problem.'

'You, Greg, you harbour a fancy for the old woman's kin! That's your problem. Always having a fancy for strange papist women. You're hungry for incense, that's your problem.'

Greg kept his temper. He glanced at the gangling figure of Terry Kennedy. 'What's he if he isn't a . . .'

'Ah, I'm no papist, sir. Goodness, no. My father had the misfortune to be born one, but my ma soon knocked that out of him!' He held on to the soft brim of his hat. 'And if I was to give you advice, sir, I'd say keep away from them Farrells, from that Shona Farrell particularly. She's just a common pit-lass and she spells trouble in any language. One brother an assassin killed for his pains, another a troublemaker, friend to plotters and assassins – the boys who plot the downfall of their betters.'

Greg looked from face to face and could see no difference in the gleaming malice in each one. Stuart was more their brother than his.

He went to the coat stand, picked up the pile of coats and threw them on to the desk. He found his father's heavy stick in his hand and raised it slightly higher than the head of Terry Kennedy, who was the tallest.

'Out, the lot of you!' he ordered. 'Do your plotting and drinking elsewhere. This is a place of honourable work.'

Stuart reached under the pile of damp coats for the whisky bottles and stood up. 'We were going anyway. We have business in town. Didn't you say that fight was at eight?'

Morry Smith pulled out his watch. 'So I did, Stuart. So I did.'

When they had gone Greg wiped down the desk with a ball of scrunched up paper, lifting the greasy stains from its shining surface. Then he carefully locked the office door and, in their turn, the great doors of the works.

Aida was standing in the hall of the house when he returned, a large bag clutched to her swelling stomach.

'What are you doing, Aida?'

'Goin' home. For good. Your ma's dismissed me. Your dad said to stay put, but I'm off. I'm not wanted, so I'm not staying!'

'But my mother needs . . .'

'She needs a good hiding. She's run off, you know. She's not right in the head, your ma. I've said it long enough. Tried to make allowances, but . . .' She laughed her coarse laugh. 'Poor Lauretta! Grandma off her head, mother . . . I don't know what. Don't leave much chance for the poor little thing, does it?' She laughed again and stomped out.

Greg looked up to see his father coming down the stairs.

'Where is she?' Greg asked, his voice tight with exhaustion.

'She went . . . mad and ran off. Climbed out of the window.'

Greg gasped. 'Why are you not after her?'

Douglas looked at his son warily. 'There's the child. I thought I'd wait for you.'

Greg took some deep breaths. 'Yes. You stay here, Pa. With Lauretta. Ma'll very likely make her way home again. Someone should be here.' He put his hand on his father's arm and was surprised when it wasn't brushed away. 'Be kind to her when she comes, Pa.'

Douglas coughed. 'Do you doubt it, son?' Then he shook the hand off and went into the parlour to close the window which was still open wide, letting the icy air into the house.

Chapter Fifteen

Faces thrust themselves at her, eyes bulging and nostrils flaring. Her feet were sore with walking. The streets were beaten earth, rendered to a grey dust by hard frosts.

But she knew this was where her friend lived. Her good friend. What was the name? She couldn't quite remember the name . . .

She pulled at her hair to disentangle the dried leaves and rubbed her dusty shoes in a tuft of grass that grew in the middle of the pathway. She had to be neat and tidy for visiting. Her mother had always insisted on that.

'Can I help you, Missis?' A narrow elderly face, none too clean, loomed before her. 'Is it lost you are?'

'Who are you?' She grasped his skinny arm tightly and peered into his face. 'Do you know my friend? I need to see her about it, to tell her. She listened, you see.'

The woman holding the man's other arm scowled at her. The man shook his head and Margaret caught a whiff of sour whisky. 'What friend was this, Missis?'

She frowned. 'I forget it. I forget her name.'

'You'll need more'n that to help you if you're to find her, Missis.'

The other woman pulled at his arm. 'Come away, Mick. Can't yer see the old brew's demented? She'll get you in the spell, so she will!'

They left her there and she followed them and came on a group on a street corner, asking them in turn if they knew her friend.

'Friend? What friend is this?' Suddenly they were pushing her from one to the other, chanting: 'Friend, friend, what's this? Friend, friend, what's-her-name? Friend, friend, what's-her-name?'

The dry creased face of the first woman leered close to hers.

'Friends? You got no friends here, Missis.' She gave Margaret a hard push, then wiped her hand down her apron. 'Protestants! I can smell'm!' she said with satisfaction.

Margaret wandered further along, pursued by hoots and calls and ribald comments. She lifted her head from the dirt path up into the open face of a woman in a green dress.

'Here, Missis, aren't ye too well?' The woman took her arm, kindly this time. 'This is my house here. Come in and get a dish of tea. Ye look as though ye need to get yourself together.'

The room was bright and pretty, and the table at which the woman sat was spread with a cloth. A child was playing on a hooky rug in the corner. She was making a tall structure, using books as building blocks.

The woman poured tea into a china cup. Then she lifted the glittering bottle that stood in the centre of the table. 'And something else in it to set you up? It's a hard old world out there.'

Margaret took a gulp. The liquid stung, then warmed her throat. She looked up into the pretty face. 'I'm looking for my friend but I've forgotten her name.'

'It happens all the time to me, me darlin'. Too many names to remember. Haven't I stopped botherin' about names meself?'

'My friend . . . she was so easy to talk to. I liked her from the minute I saw her.'

The woman lay back in her chair like a stretching cat. 'Ah, a friend is a fine thing, a great thing! Talk to *me*. Why don't you talk to me? It's Christmas after all.'

Margaret gulped more tea and took the woman at her word. She spoke eagerly, the words tumbling out with a blissful ease. 'You see, I wanted to tell her about the night this band came, with iron things for instruments. There was a great clanging and there were the two of them, this woman and my son, up on a wooden board for all the world to see.' She leaned across the table confidentially. 'He shouldn't have married her, you see. She was an *old* woman. And then with child! Can you believe it? And the devil was there. You can be sure the devil was there! It was *he* who did *it* to her. Then killed her with knives. Then burned her. The smoke floated high. So high!' She gulped the last of the tea.

Maudie watched Margaret thoughtfully, then filled her cup

again. The woman must be crazy to the four winds. But she didn't really look it, that was the funny thing.

She sighed. It wasn't often she listened to another woman's confidences. They didn't trust her, the other women. Not the respectable ones, the ones out there in the real world. She had been thinking about Shona, Tommo's sister. She sounded like a good sort. A fighter. A hard little fighter. She would like to talk to her.

'It's a bad dream, me darlin'. What you're thinking is a bad dream. Just put it away and it won't trouble you.'

'No, it happened, I tell you! Men did it to them.'

'Men? They can be the very devil, can't they?' said Maudie, with feeling.

'Now my husband Douglas, he's a *good* man . . .' Margaret's eyes were beginning to droop.

'I tell you what, darlin', why don't you have a little sleep? My Becky here has to go to bed, as I'll have someone callin' soon. Why don't you tuck in with her?'

It was quite a performance to get Margaret to climb the ladder, Maudie urging from below, Becky encouraging from above. Finally, after some heaving and pushing, they got her on to Becky's mattress.

Becky pulled off Margaret's shoes and her soaking silk shawl, and stayed with her until she was fast asleep. 'There, Becky. Cuddle into the nice lady and keep her warm,' Maudie whispered from below. 'You'll both be asleep in no time.'

She stood on the ladder and pulled the hatch over until there was only a slit showing. Then she went down and draped the pretty shawl over the mantel-rail to dry.

She looked at herself in the mirror and threaded a blue ribbon through her hair. She turned up the lamp and opened the curtains. It was too cold to stand outside tonight.

Biddy was limping quite heavily by the time she got home to Stables Street.

Shona helped her in. 'What's this?' she asked anxiously. Biddy's ankle was swollen to twice its normal size. 'Here, sit here on the bed. Put it up.'

'A wet cloth, darlin',' said Biddy. 'A wet cloth'll take it down.'

She told Shona of her adventures in Shotwell.

'That family!' said Shona.

Biddy grinned conspiratorially. 'Sure some of 'em aren't bad. Things'll mend themselves.'

At the end of the table Richie was fiddling with a home-made iron contraption which Tommo had made for above the fire. It was to take the goose that Gil Tait had given to Richie with the words, 'For Shona, for her handsome eyes at Christmas. And y'are not to ask where it come from.' After he got the contraption – which he refused to explain to Shona – in order, he proudly carried the goose in.

'Where did it come from?' said his sister.

Richie squeezed his left eye up in the manner of Gil Tait. '"Sure didn't a kind ge'man, holy drunk, leave it in me trap. I'm sure he had such handsome eyes in mind!"'

Biddy laughed energetically at this, then winced. 'Aw, me blessed foot!' she roared.

Within a couple of hours she had rested the foot and was trying it gingerly on the floor. Just as she was taking her third step from chairback to chairback, there was a great rattle at the door.

The door flew open before Shona could get there. Greg barged in and looked across at Biddy and around the tiny kitchen.

'What is it? What's up with you?' asked Biddy, clinging to the chairback.

'My mother, she's not here?'

'Do you see her? Why should she be here?' said Shona sharply.

'She had a . . . disagreement with my father . . . and she ran off.' Biddy sat down sharply on the bed.

'She'd be feeling guilty,' said Shona. ''Cause Biddy was turned off like some tinker. Too good for us, your family.'

He glared at her. 'My mother was distressed because Biddy *was* turned away. Because they *didn't* let her in. So she went off. Climbed through a window. Without a coat. In thin shoes. She was . . . beside herself.'

'Lord Almighty!' said Biddy standing up again. 'Poor Margaret, wandering out on a Christmas Eve. Now, Richie, hand me me boot! We need to look for her. She'll be out there not knowing her back from her front. Get that pony of yours and I'll ride him.'

Richie kneeled at her feet, laced up her boot and handed her her thick shawl. She lifted a shawl of Shona's off a peg. 'Come on, Greg, will ye? It's a cold night and Margaret has no coat. Didn't ye say so?'

She vanished into the night, Richie at her side.

Greg looked at Shona.

'Sure, I'll stay here, Greg,' she said. 'If your ma's as keen on Biddy as you say, she might still find her way here. I'll wait, in case she comes.'

He caught her hand and kissed it. She looked down, smiling faintly. 'Now then, Greg, you can't be thinking your name's Shakespeare, can you? Get off and find your ma, will you!'

'Greg!' Biddy's voice called from outside.

They had to make their way through the Christmas revellers to search the highways and by-ways of New Morven. They had to ignore bawdy comments about the old woman on the pony and the road to Bethlehem and there being no room at the inn.

Margaret was nowhere to be found.

On their way out of New Morven on the Shotwell road they met Stuart coming towards them with two companions.

'What're you doing here?' demanded Greg.

'What are *you* doing here with this *gang*?'

'I'm looking for Ma. She ran off. We thought she might come searching for . . .'

'The old bog-Irish woman?'

Stuart's companions sniggered.

'She'd have nothing to do with her if she had any sense at all,' Stuart went on. 'But then . . .'

Greg would not be baited. He stood waiting.

'I tell you what, Greg. If I see her at the Puddler's Arms, or at the fight at the Cockerel, I'll bring her home.' His speech was slurred.

'He can say no fairer than that,' Morry Smith chimed in. 'We'll look out for her. You can be sure we'll be very assiduous, Mr McNaughton.'

Greg looked from one to the other. '*Assiduous?*'

'Sure, they're fools and no help at all, Greg,' said Biddy from her perch on the pony. 'We'll get on and find her ourselves.'

Greg glared at his brother as he moved away. 'When this is over, I'll give you such a beating! I'll not forget this, you can be sure!'

* * *

The child was crying and pulling at her. Margaret opened her eyes. She was in some kind of cave or cellar. She peered up at the sloping roof. No, this was a loft.

'It's all right, Lauretta, really it's all right,' she whispered, feeling surer of herself.

Then she sat up straight. Bloodcurdling screams were echoing to the rafters, followed by roars and grunts.

A gleam of light was coming from the floor. The child was pulling her towards it, mumbling and whispering in terror.

Obediently she crept across and peered through the slit. She reached out and cuddled the child to her, putting a gentle palm over her mouth.

In the room down below a man was mercilessly beating a woman with a buckled belt, sending it flying over his head like a dark snake. The woman was tethered somehow to the bedhead and had only one hand free to protect her face.

Moving her head slightly Margaret could just make out a shadowy figure in the doorway.

Suddenly the woman's screams stopped and she sagged against the bed. Now they could hear the distant sounds of revelry outside.

The man in the doorway spoke in a whisper. 'Come away now, sir, there's nothing left in her. Not a thing.'

The man leaned over and wiped the belt on the woman's green skirt before calmly buckling it back around his waist.

Margaret waited for the door to close and scrambled down the ladder, Becky tumbling after her.

She went across and untied the woman and, grunting, lifted her on to the bed. Maudie's face was a mess of cuts from the buckle and pouring with blood. Margaret took the pretty cloth off the table and, making a pad of it, put it against the woman's cheek.

The child tried to scramble on to the bed, but Margaret pulled her away. 'Come away now, Lauretta. Leave the poor lady, leave her. She can rest now. We must get away or the bad man will come back.'

She grabbed a coat and hat from a hook and shoes from under the rumpled bed. 'Here we are. We'll get you wrapped up and go.'

She closed the door carefully behind her and, with the child held tight in her arms, stole along the road. At the corner she bumped into a fair-haired, open-faced man.

That was when she remembered.

'Biddy O'Farrell! That's it, Biddy O'Farrell!'

'What was that, Missis?'

'Can you tell me where Biddy O'Farrell lives? She's my friend.'

'Sure I know nobody better in this town. Let me take the little'n. You look all in, Missis.'

Becky clung closer, her head on Margaret's shoulder.

'No, no. This is my grand-daughter Lauretta. She's very distressed and wants to see her Auntie Biddy.'

'Well, Biddy's wandering the streets herself. Didn't I just see her? Been all the way to Shotwell and back to find a friend of hers. Been at cross-purposes, have you?'

Margaret, brave until now, was crying.

'Now don't you cry, Missis. We'll have you to her in no time. Won't she be that pleased to see you?'

Chapter Sixteen

Greg returned to Stables Street alone. He stood on the threshold, his face pale and drawn, his hands grasping the doorframe.

'She's not out there, Shona. My mother's nowhere to be found. We've been right back up to Shotwell. Richie and Biddy are hunting around New Morven again but I thought maybe she had come here.'

His hands came down to his sides. 'It seems everyone's out there but her, celebrating. No work tomorrow. There's music, people dancing their legs off. But not her.' He closed his eyes tight. 'She could be drowned in the Gaunt, have fallen down some gully . . .'

Shona pulled him into the house and closed the door behind him.

'Shona . . .'

She reached up and put her lips on his. His arms came round her. Once her lips were on him, all his feelings towards her resolved in a crystal clear instant.

He took his lips from hers so he could pull her closer, mould her body to his. Then he lifted her and moved the single step to the bed, sat there so they were the same height and kissed her again and again. His hand was on her face, in her hair, on her thigh where her thick dress covered her leg. Her hands moved from the nape of his neck to his shoulders and hair.

Then she kissed him, her mouth opening slowly so that more could be in contact with him. Her breasts were aching and her stomach churning.

'I want us to do it,' she said, right into his ear.

'Here. How?'

'How?' She laughed at him.

There was a flurry of clothes being dragged up and half off.

The first time he tried, it didn't happen. Shona laughed. 'Sure it isn't possible, there's no place there for it.'

He laughed with her, kissed her and stroked her face. He tried again. For a moment Shona felt herself break apart. There was mind-searing pain, then the wonderment of having him entirely volunteered in her arms as they slipped down on to the bed together.

After minutes when she thought he was asleep, he opened his eyes. He touched her cheek. 'You're white as snow. The roses are gone. I hurt you . . .'

She pulled down her skirt. There was blood on her petticoat, she noticed. 'I wanted it,' she said, faintly smiling. 'But I think we need practice, you and me. Lots of practice. I once spied on Tommo doing it. He took a long, long time. But it looked very good.'

He kissed her slowly, on the mouth, then on the cheek. They could hear the fire falling. Then he sat up, pulling up his breeches. 'What are we doing? My mother!'

'Your mother!' she said guiltily.

A minute later they were turning into the main street when they saw a heartening procession, headed by Pat Daley. He had his arm round the crumpled figure of Margaret McNaughton; Biddy was limping alongside her, grimfaced; behind them, leading Cush, came Richie with a small tear-stained girl in his arms. For a second, Greg thought it was Lauretta, but he sighed in shamed relief when he saw the blonde corkscrew curls.

He followed them into the house and in an instant the little kitchen was filled with people and voices raised in explanation.

Shona prised Becky away from Richie so that he could tether Cush in the yard, lifting the child gently on to her hip. 'Here, sweetheart, you come with your Auntie Shona.'

Greg was talking to his mother. 'What's happening, Ma? Who is this child?' He put his hands on his mother's shoulders and she pulled away from him.

'Leave me alone.' She shook her head wildly. 'That girl said that men were the very devil and they are. You all are. It was a man beat her, pierced her and burned her.' She paused and looked across at Becky. 'But why did they beat that kind woman? Such sweet tea she made. But they punished her, the men. These men are the very devil.' Then Margaret's face became cunning and she reached out to touch Becky. 'But I saved Lauretta from them. Her grandma saved her. I kept her safe! Even if the devil did take your woman, Greg.'

As he stepped back from her Shona came to stand by him, her shoulder to his. Biddy signalled to Pat, who loosened the woman's hand from his arms. She put her arm round Margaret and sat her on the bed.

She smiled. 'I was looking everywhere for you, Biddy. All round this village. I couldn't for the moment remember your name.'

'Now, me darlin', what about this baby? Where did you get her?'

'It's Lauretta, Biddy. Don't you remember, she rescued you from the road? Of course you know her.' She drew Biddy to her until they were nose to nose. 'It's wicked, Biddy, isn't it, to love a father and son in the same way?'

She turned to the child. 'And what about Lauretta here, a wicked gift of love for both father and son. It *is* Lauretta,' she leaned closer, 'isn't it?'

Silence weighed too long in the room. Then Greg thrust both Shona and Becky to one side and made his way across the room to slam his way out of the house.

Biddy turned Margaret to face her and smoothed back the untidy locks from the other woman's sweating face. 'There, sweetheart, don't you take on so. Aren't you babbling like some mad woman? All nonsense it is.'

She looked at Pat, who was standing there uncertainly, staring hard at Becky, her face now revealed in the lamplight. 'Thank you for this help, Pat,' she said. 'You're a good man. We'll keep them here, so you can get on your way. There must be something for you to be doing on a Christmas Eve.'

He shook his head and sat down on a chair, frowning at Becky. 'What about the babe? If it's not the grand-daughter, then the old'n must have stolen her. I've a feeling I've seen her somewhere. D'you see the blood on her dress-sleeves?'

Margaret looked at her blood-spattered sleeves in puzzlement. They all looked at Becky, silent and wide-eyed now, clinging to Shona.

She stroked her face. 'Where do you live, little girl?'

'New Morven.'

'Which house is it you live in?'

The child frowned. 'A house. I live in a house.'

163

'What name have you, child?' said Biddy.

'Becky. Rebecca Maria. And I live in the house with my mama. Her name is Maudie.'

'Jesus wept!' Pat leapt to his feet. 'The babe's mother! I know her.' In a second he was gone.

Tommo had missed Pat at Showy's bar. But the music and the crack were extra good on this Christmas Eve. The ironworkers had half a guinea extra in their Christmas pay, and the Christmas Day off was anticipated with pleasure. There had been whippet racing behind Showy's in the afternoon. And across at the Cockerel there would be dog-fighting tonight, followed by a promising fistfight.

He delayed so as to miss the dog-fight but made his way over in time to watch the boxing.

He squeezed his way through the crowd looking in vain for Pat. Belly Aungers was making his way through the crowd too, taking bets, having a joke here and there.

Tommo watched him exchange jests with the two men whom Pat had called spies the other week. The man with straggling hair was laughing so loudly that even the boisterous people around him looked askance. His face was purplish-red and his eyes were bright, darting here and there.

Tommo turned down Belly's offer of a good price on the challenger. He fingered the money in his pocket and shook his head. 'Haven't I got an old aunt to keep now?' he smiled.

The first fighter into the open space was Jacques Molloy, a great broad man with no hair on top and a long pigtail behind. His challenger was Spain Joss, a dark-skinned man whose back was like a copper barrel.

Terry Kennedy came in, winked at Tommo and made his way across.

'What cheer, Tommo?'

He was surprised at this geniality. 'You seen Pat Daley?'

'Nah. Gone to ground, looks like. I'd'a thought you'd be with your lady-love on a Christmas Eve, eh?' He nudged Tommo with his elbow. 'Or would that be bad for business?'

Tommo turned on him and he was gone. The next time he saw Terry, he was standing just behind the men Pat called spies.

Within a minute of the start Spain Joss had floored his

opponent. There were boos at this, for the lack of blood; then cheers, as Jacques Molloy heaved himself groggily to his feet and caught Spain Joss a glancing blow to the eye which made the blood gush.

Tommo turned away restlessly and fought his way back through the yelling crowd. Something was hammering in his head. Shona?

It wasn't like Pat not to turn out. They had planned a good night. Now he had had a skinful on his own. Drinking on your own had no real pleasure in it.

Maudie's light was on, but her curtains were shut. He knocked on the door and there was no response. He knocked again then started to kick it. Still no response.

He made his way back to Showy's, had one more drink, and came away. He put down his head and set off slowly for home.

When he got there he could hardly get into the kitchen.

'What's this?' He looked round the crowded room. His eye moving from the bedraggled McNaughton woman to Becky Martin.

The child jumped right from Shona's arms into his. 'It was Mama, Tommo. The *bad* man, he hit my mama!'

He frowned darkly and held her to him.

'Who is she?' said Shona.

'Her mother is a woman I . . . her name is Becky Martin.' Then he thrust the child back into Shona's arms and was gone. As he ran through the streets the world seemed to slow down around him. He seemed to be taking elastic, giant steps. The movement, the singing, the raging noise reduced itself to a distant hum. On this journey he was alone in the world.

He fought his way through the crowd of people clustered round Maudie's door and entered the kitchen. His feet crunched on shards of Maudie's pretty china. The ripped remnants of her books were scattered over the floor.

Pat was kneeling on the floor beside the bed where Maudie lay. Her head was on one side, resting against a bloody, embroidered cloth. Her dress was ripped from neck to hem. Her face was clotted with blood from cuts on her brow and cheek. Her hands were bruised, red going to black.

Her eyelids fluttered. 'Tommo.' The words were forced through split lips. 'Becky?'

'Becky's safe, Maudie. Me sister Shona has her safe.'

'Good.' Her eyes closed.

Tommo's eye alighted on a fringed shawl hanging on the mantel-rail. He pulled it down and draped it over her bruised hands and gaping clothes. Then he swept her up into his arms like a wrapped doll and made for the door.

A woman stepped in front of him. 'Ye canna take her. We've sent for the constable. S'murder done here tonight.'

Another woman put a hand on Maudie's shoulder. 'A sad judgement on her, this.'

He elbowed them out of the way, shaking his head. 'Not dead, so no murder,' he growled, and pushed his way through the crowd outside. Then, his heart bursting, he ran with his burden through the streets.

Silence dropped like a sea mist as he walked into the house. Then Becky screamed and fought to get out of Shona's arms. Crossing herself, Biddy pushed Tommo towards the bed. 'Put her here, son. Gently now! Poor lamb. Who is she?' She put Margaret to one side to make space for the woman.

'Her name's Maudie. She's a good friend of mine.'

Becky struggled free at last, and tried to climb on the bed with her mother. Tommo put a hand out to keep her away. 'No, Becky. Not now.'

Margaret bent and picked up the child, holding her close. 'Here, little one, you don't want to be here. Your mama is poorly and your Auntie Biddy is taking good care of her.'

Biddy looked round the room which seemed now to be heaving with bodies. 'Shona, you and Richie take Margaret and the child across to Shotwell. Isn't it time she was home?' She looked at Margaret. 'There'll be room for the little one, won't there?'

Margaret smiled, all calm reassurance. 'Oh, you can be sure there'll be room, Biddy.'

Shona looked at the woman on the bed, her body limp in a too heavy sleep, blood seeping along the long brown hair which was spread across the pillow. The last time she had seen that face it was full of laughter in a little stone hut in a thicket.

The last time she had seen that much blood was when her brother Gerard had been brought home on a gate from Marsteen House. It had taken him two days to die.

She put a hand on Tommo's shoulder. He shrugged it off, looking up at her. 'I thought we'd seen enough of this,' he said.

Then he turned to watch as Biddy tried to pull the embroidered cloth away and replace it with a clean towel.

On their way to the livery Shona and Margaret bumped into Father O'Reilly who was hurrying along muffled in a great scarf, his face shaded by his wide hat. 'Did Tommo bring the woman home?' he said.

'Yes, Father.'

'They say she'll need me?'

'So she will, Father.'

'Is this the daughter?'

'Yes, Father.'

He stood there in the dusty lane and said words of blessing over the child, while Margaret McNaughton averted her face in superstitious fear.

Douglas had waited all this time, sitting on the highbacked chair in the hall of Garth End Cottage. He stood up and watched in silence as Margaret, weighed down by a blonde, curly-haired child, marched past. She was followed by that pert Irish girl, relation to Biddy O'Farrell.

He caught Shona's arm anxiously. 'My wife. She's all right? Greg would say naught.'

She grinned up at him. 'Doesn't she have that much energy I can hardly keep up with her?'

'And who is that? I can't believe she's stolen a child . . .'

'No, no. The child's mother has been injured. And Mrs McNaughton . . . kindly offered to let her sleep with Lauretta.'

'Ah.' His shoulders sagged.

'You just relax yourself, Mr McNaughton. She'll be all right, will the missis.' The certainty in the girl's voice reminded him of Biddy. Biddy . . . He wished she were here.

He returned to the parlour. The parrot glowered at him from her perch, feathers ruffled. The bird must be cold, the window having been open.

There were papers he had to read, but he spent a long time building up the fire. He was surprised what relief he found in the task. He had enjoyed laying the fire in that little house in Carlisle where he and Margaret had lived in those first few months. It seemed a long time ago.

Shona waited a minute, then followed Margaret upstairs. She watched through the open bedroom door as Margaret pulled a clean nightdress on to the naked Becky.

Lauretta was sitting up, bright-eyed. She waved a hand at Shona while Margaret concentrated on fastening the cotton buttons at the neck of the nightie.

Shona walked along the landing to another door which was open a crack. Inside, Greg was throwing things pell-mell into a leather satchel.

She pushed the door wide open. 'Greg?'

He looked up but went on pushing things into the bag.

'What is it, Greg? What are you doing? You're not going off again?'

'I have to go to Manchester.' He had to get away from her, from the temptation. His mother's insane insinuations about Lauretta had brought him to his senses. For a while it had seemed possible to think of starting again, lock Mary Louisa tight in the past and go forward with Shona, but not now.

'You're just back,' said Shona tensely, successfully fighting back tears.

'I'm going back again.' He said it through gritted teeth, avoiding her gaze.

'Why? What's happened to make you do this?'

'I've only been thinking about myself. What Ma said, and seeing that poor girl there tonight, and the motherless child, made me see my duty. It's been too good here with Lauretta . . .' he paused . . . 'here with you. I have to be with Mary Louisa, Lauretta's mother. Stay with her 'til . . . It's too easy to push trouble away.'

What about me? she shouted inside her head. What about how we were . . . just an hour ago? She wanted to say all this, but didn't. Her thigh muscles still ached.

When she spoke, her voice was calm. 'Why is she there, Lauretta's mother?' Her voice was calm.

'She has to be there. She is cared for there . . . She is not herself.'

'You love her.'

'I did, I did. With all my heart. She was enchanting.'

He was ready now. He moved past her rigid figure, the bag in his hand. Then he stopped and put down the bag. He reached into his tailcoat pocket and pulled out a soft paper package. He thrust it into her hand and was gone.

She waited, hearing his steps clatter down the stairs and the front door bang. Then she moved into his bedroom and sat on his bed. The room had his aura, half scent, half objects handled through the years.

Slowly she picked open the package. Inside, skilfully wrought, was a little posy of dried roses. Pale roses tied with a velvet ribbon. She rubbed them against her mouth and her eyes and wondered about the thing she had done today. Then she thought about Tommo and Maudie rolling with joy in the floating hay. And Maudie lying in Stables Street, a broken body waiting at death's door.

She looked up to find Margaret McNaughton staring at her.

'They're asleep?'

Margaret rubbed a hand over her face. 'Lauretta's telling the little one a story. I thought she was Lauretta, do you know? I was mistaken.'

'Sure you weren't quite up to things, Mrs McNaughton.'

'The devil did terrible things to her, that woman.'

'Did you see him, the man that did it?'

She frowned. 'He wore a mask. No, that was the other time. The mask.'

'The other time?'

'That other woman. The one Greg brought.' She leaned towards Shona. 'I knew it couldn't be Douglas. Not him. But don't they say the devil takes many forms? That priest tonight . . .'

'No!' said Shona. 'That was just Father O'Reilly. A dear man.'

Margaret shrugged.

Shona stood up. 'Let me take you to your own bed.'

Margaret showed the way to her pretty bedroom and lay obediently as Shona took off her shoes and covered her with the quilt. Then she took Shona's hand. 'I don't think it was Douglas. Not really. But there was something about him . . .'

Shona looked up, to catch sight of the face of Douglas McNaughton, grey with desperation. He looked angry, standing in the doorway, guilty and helpless. He turned and she heard his feet tramping downstairs.

She followed him down and into the parlour.

'Sit down, tell me!' he said. 'What happened?'

She sat on a chair close to him. 'There was a young woman, badly injured. Becky's mother. Mrs McNaughton was there. But she seems to have her mixed up with someone else.'

He stared at her. 'Miss Farrell . . . ?'

She tried again. 'Mr McNaughton. Seems like our families are proper tangled up. Your missis ran away to our house to see Biddy. On her way she sees this poor woman hurt and takes the child, thinking it's Lauretta. She turns up at our house and upsets your son, whom I thought was my friend. *He* races out and now is off back to Manchester.'

'They run off and get the poor woman, Becky's mother, who turns out to be our Tommo's lady-love. There's no room at our house so we bring back the little one, to share with Lauretta.' She drew a breath.

He smiled faintly and relaxed, his head thrown back in his chair, his body no longer stiff.

'It seems to me,' she carried on, 'no bad thing, your missis letting her hair down. But she does go on a bit. She does get things tangled up.'

He smiled again and from somewhere she caught her courage.

'Mr McNaughton, can't you tell me about the woman? The one your missis calls names? The one she's been mixing up all night with this poor woman? The one that was half killed?'

He sat up. 'It's not an easy thing to say . . .'

She sat up straight and leaned towards him. 'Try,' she said. 'Tell me!'

Chapter Seventeen

'It would be three – no four – years ago now . . .' Douglas faltered into silence.

Shona sat still, searching for anything to say. 'Me, I'd be only twelve then. We still had the farm. Gerard was still alive – he was my eldest brother. And Maire my sister. But wasn't she always frail? She had this bad hand from when she was a baby, and never ate a full meal. And Mammy and Daddy, they were still here.'

He looked at her under dark brows. 'Misfortune for you too?'

It had been a long day. He had done no work, drawn no plans, read no papers. The steady gaze of the dark-haired girl spurred him on. The words came tumbling out. He told her of the time when first the courtship, then the marriage, of Gregor and Mary Louisa had raised the ire of both communities.

The men at the railworks had stopped speaking directly to Greg. Her brother the priest had come and called down the fires of hell on the match, and had to be dragged away through the streets. Groups of Irish boys had waylaid Greg on his journeys, sometimes just riding close, sometimes throwing stones or worse. Once a shot was fired at him. The girl, the woman, Mary Louisa, was pounced upon wherever she went, sometimes by catcalling women, occasionally by children well rehearsed in their abuse.

That was the time Aida started to keep company with her grocer and she relayed the disgust of the village at the McNaughtons being involved in such *bother*. Her tales had worried away at Margaret, blackening the girl, the woman, in her eyes.

Douglas looked at Shona. 'My wife was, *is* a kindly woman and would not have had such bad thoughts without encouragement.' He paused. 'The girl was a degree older than Gregor it is true. But she was gentle and intelligent. It wasn't hard to see what had drawn him to her. She was a threat to no one.' He shook his head sadly.

'She was a talented woman. She drew out designs for me in a way they had not been done before. I still have them.' For some reason he went bright red at this.

'What was so badly resented was her being so much older, and what's more, sister to a priest. Neither the Catholic workers at the ironworks nor our own railway workers liked it.

'That night, it seemed that people from both villages were there, although it was hard to tell individuals. Their faces were blackened with coal-dust; some had hoods on their heads, scarves over their faces. The men were dressed as women and contrariwise. They were banging things, iron on iron. An unholy row.

'They had these scarecrow dolls of Gregor and Mary Louisa, would you believe? Dressed in their own clothes! Aida said Stuart gave them the clothes. *He* said the maid had done it. Mary Louisa gave them both the benefit of the doubt, wanted to believe nothing bad of anyone. She said it was easy enough to steal from the washing.'

They had carried these dolls, tied astride planks. The guy that was Mary Louisa had been a cruel parody, white sheepswool threaded through gingery horsehair making her look ancient.

'The girl was distraught and no wonder.'

Shona wondered why all the time he used the word 'girl' to talk about this woman, apparently so much older than his son.

'On the second night they came, Aida went missing and my wife was in hysteria. And no wonder at that! She was convinced they would murder us at the house. By the third night I was sure of it myself.' He paused. 'The girl was with child. I – we – thought she was in great danger, whatever happened.'

Shona frowned. 'Why not get the constable? The military? In Ireland . . .'

He bit his lip as he looked at her. 'I've asked myself that so many times. There was something of shame, of nightmare in the whole of it. We kept quiet about the first and the second nights, I think we thought if we weakened and called for help they would have won. But on that third night, the racket was unbearable. Unbearable! I was sure now that they had murder on their minds.'

He had given money to Greg who with his wife had crept away like thieves across the fields to Priorton, and on to Manchester.

'Once they were away I began to relax. But the noise came to

172

this great crescendo. I thought they knew of their victory. Then . . .' He stirred restlessly in his seat.

'What happened then?' asked Shona.

Douglas looked down at his carefully folded hands. This he could not tell this child. How a tall man with cow's horns crudely strapped to his brow had stepped forward and grabbed the figure representing Mary Louisa. How he had used it to mime sexual congress before slashing it with a great poker held in two hands. How each action had been accompanied by great roars of approval from the crowd.

'He tore away at her figure, the woman-doll, with a knife,' said Douglas eventually. 'Then they beat both dolls with their iron staves and burnt them both before our eyes. My wife, my wife she . . .' His voice faded away. 'We stood there and watched them, through that very window. Since that time my wife has been consumed completely by that *nervousness* of hers.'

'Mary Louisa, she's there in Manchester now?'

'I believe so.'

'Where does she stay?'

'I do not know. We don't speak of it.'

He thought of the time Greg returned home, a year after these events. During that time Margaret had degenerated into an eccentric combination of the watchful and wild. She had watched him like a cat at a mouse, for any sign of weakness. The more she watched, the more guilty he felt. The more guilty he felt, the more he blamed her for her feyness and eccentricity. The more she wanted him to come close, the more he wanted to stay away. He closed his eyes momentarily.

What a reversal this had been from the early days of their marriage, when for years he had ached for her and she had shunned him, terrified of pregnancies that only ended in death.

He went on: 'Greg brought the little one home with him. She was like her mother. Had great charm. She won us all, even Aida. Even Stuart. Gregor does not speak of the girl now. We are not told.'

Douglas looked at the Irish girl, staring at him with her unfathomable intensity.

'We don't speak of it,' he repeated.

Shona knew there was something else, something in his mind she would not hear. He was not saying.

173

She stood up. 'I thank you for telling me . . . some of it,' she said. She was weary now and without hope. So the woman was there in Manchester. Greg's wife.

He looked at her thoughtfully, grateful that for once in his life he had been allowed to unburden himself. 'You have your aunt's kindness, child. But now you are tired, and I should take you home.'

On the road to Priorton Greg found himself joined at the Shotwell crossroads by Terry Kennedy, who was wearing a caped wool coat. He had silver in his pockets and was riding a fine grey horse. The coat sat ill on him and he rode a horse like a heavy sack of potatoes.

Lanternlight rose to his face as he touched the soft felt rim of his hat. 'Mr McNaughton, isn't it? Brother to Mr Stuart McNaughton? Hard to tell with that hat and scarf. A fine feller, Mr Stuart.'

Greg inclined his head and rode on. He had more to think about than this buffoon. He knew he had let things drag on too long without resolution, saying to himself it was Lauretta he had to think about. But wasn't that what Mary Louisa had said? Ill and sometimes rambling herself, she had insisted he bring Lauretta home out of the foul unhealthy air of Manchester. Well, she was home and healthy now. Now he knew it was up to him to go back and care for her mother.

Greg murmured absently to his horse to urge him on.

In the years since he had been home the only way he had been able to survive was to concentrate on Lauretta and blank out any feeling he had for her mother. Now his passion for Shona had resurrected the ghost of the passion he had had for Maria Louisa and reminded him of the legacy of duty that love brings in its wake. That poor woman dying in Shona's house had somehow finally made that clear.

Terry Kennedy kicked at the grey, which shied to one side then cantered forward to catch up with Greg. 'Seeing we're on the same road, might we not share light, Mr McNaughton?'

Greg grunted. It was true that the road was black-dark and sharing light was a common enough courtesy.

'Look at us, travellers away from home on Christmas Eve,' ventured Terry.

Greg grunted.

'Is it Priorton you're away to, or further afield?'

'I'm to Manchester.'

'That far?' Terry whistled. 'No trains tomorrow, you know, it being Christmas.'

'I'll ride on, then catch a coach further west on Boxing Day.'

For ten minutes the only sound in the cold still night was the creak and jingle of harness and the occasional snort of their horses.

'Bad business down in New Morven tonight,' ventured Terry.

'There's always bad business down there,' said Greg.

'A woman beaten near to death they say.'

'I saw . . . heard about that.'

'The constable was asking questions.'

'He would be.'

'There's a lot of anger down there, though why they should bother about a woman like that, I dinnat knaa. They're saying it was a Shotwell man.'

'They would, wouldn't they?'

'Aye, they would. Bluddy ignorant papists.'

'I'll ride alone, Mr Kennedy.' Greg spurred the horse on to get away from the man, who fouled the air in more ways than one.

Terry called after him, 'What is it? Not good enough for ye, am I? I'd forgot ye was the bluddy papist's friend. Yer brother was on about it . . .'

Terry pulled his horse up and watched the tall figure and the wavering lantern as it faded into the distance. He took off his soft hat and brushed his rough hair hard back under it. Then he clicked his mouth at the grey and turned him round, heading back to New Morven.

He knocked on the narrow door beside the livery stable and looked up as a cross little face stared at him out of the window. 'What is it?' trilled Gil Tait. 'Disturbin' a man on a good Christmas Eve? Haven't I just got to bed?'

'It's me, an' I've come to bring yer horse back. I've no need of it any more.'

Gil came down and opened the great door, muttering complaints as he took the horse.

'An' I'll have me money back, seein' as I'm not usin' it to get to Newcastle no more.'

'Ye'll get no money back off me.'

'I will, no fear, Gil. I'll be back tomorrow and have it out of your hide, else.'

'Half.' Gil reached into his deep pocket.

Terry looked at him. It hadn't been his money anyway, so he was still in vast profit. He jingled the silver in his own pocket. 'Right!'

He counted the silver. 'This feller on the road, he was sayin' he'd passed that McNaughton feller, the one sniffin' after Shona Farrell.'

'Did he now?' said Gil evenly.

'Aye. Runnin' like he had ten tailors after him. They say he did that *huah* down off main street. Half-kilt her.'

'*Kilt*,' said Gil. 'They say she's dead. They had the priest.'

'Get away!' said Terry. 'So he kilt her, you say?'

'Sure, I'm not sayin' that,' said Gil.

'Sounds like you're sayin' that to me,' said Terry. 'Feller's a murderer. No mistake about it! Constables from New Morven and Shotwell is after him. They say he's for hanging.'

Biddy had sewn up Maudie's clothes, cleaned her face with warm water and draped the fine shawl around her.

'Sure she had a gentle face. And it was really kind of her to take in Mrs McNaughton when she was wandering the street.' She fingered the shawl. 'I remember well Mrs McNaughton wearing this very shawl, so there's no doubt she was there. And didn't she save the child from this . . . murderer?'

The priest and the constable, Bob Prest, exchanged glances. It was not the first time they had shared space in a New Morven house with a dead person.

'And did Mrs McNaughton say who it was she saw do this?' said the constable.

'No. She sees nightmare pictures in her head. But it was no one she knows,' said Biddy.

Bob Prest pulled on his gauntlets. He would have to tell the Shotwell constable; word was a Shotwell man might be involved. Then Herbert Walton, their superior at Priorton, would want to be in on the act. This would be in the newspapers, he was sure of it.

He watched coolly as the priest set about his prayers. Like Herbert Walton, he had no time for Irishmen. No time at all.

He looked at Biddy. 'Your nephew Tommo, he's handy with his

fists. He's been in my lock-up more than once. He was out last night drinking and carrying on, they say. On his own.'

She glared at him. 'Tommo's too much of a man to do this. Ye want to look for someone who's not sure of what he is.'

He adjusted his cape. 'Where is he?'

'He went out.'

'I'll be back here to see him, you can be sure of that.'

She watched the door close and listened to his boots clump on the ground.

Tommo let himself down from the loft.

Father O'Reilly watched him calmly. 'Why d'you do that, Tommo? You've nothing to hide.'

'I saw me brother murdered by just such a man.'

'You didn't do this, Tommo,' said Biddy. 'Your brother . . .'

'Makes no difference to them whether you did or didn't.'

'Now, Tommo!' said Father O'Reilly.

His retort was quelled by a blink from Biddy. He went across and took Maudie's cold hand.

'That's it, Tommo. She's gone,' said Father O'Reilly. 'To a better place.'

'A better place?'

The priest nodded. 'Eventually, I'm sure. Look at the kindness she did the Shotwell woman.' He looked at Biddy. 'I must go now. I've the Christmas mass . . .'

Richie, passing him in the street, touched his cap. 'Mornin', Father.'

'And will you be comin' to mass today, Richie?'

'Maybe not today, Father.'

'Then Sunday?'

'Maybe Sunday, Father.'

'Good. You look after your brother, there. He has a great sorrow on him, for that poor dead woman.'

'Dead? So I will, Father.'

Richie avoided looking at the bed and Tommo's rigid figure beside it. 'Shona's getting the goose away over Mrs Kelly's fire,' he announced. 'Mrs Kelly says her young'ns'll have the best Christmas ever.'

'Good,' said Biddy. 'Wouldn't it be a waste leaving it here?' She peered closer at him. 'What is it, Richie? What's wrong?'

'Mr Kelly. He was saying it was all over New Morven. Greg McNaughton's run off to Manchester. They're saying he's done it. This . . .'

'Who's they?'

'Mr Kelly got it from Gil Tait. He says it's all over New Morven. He went ridin' off last night.'

Biddy looked at Tommo, who was gently pulling the heavy silk across Maudie's bruised face. His face came up and she shrank from the wild gleam in his eyes.

'That's it,' he growled. 'Wasn't he always hangin' around after her?'

'Tommo, you've got it wrong! It wasn't Maudie, it was . . .'

He ignored her. 'Yes, always hangin' around, but she was too good for him, she . . .' He was heaving himself into the loft and Biddy could hear him scrabbling about up there.

She shouted up through the hole after him: 'You're crazy, Tommo, crazy! Greg had nothing to do with this poor girl. You're mixing them up . . .' The thuds and bangs continued. Biddy grabbed Richie's arm. 'Go and get Shona,' she whispered fiercely. 'Be quick or there'll be more murder done this day!'

By the time Shona got home Tommo was gone.

'Gone off after Greg,' said Biddy. She put her hand on the bed where Maudie still lay, veiled by the fine shawl. 'He thinks Greg did this.'

'That's rubbish,' said Shona. 'He needs stopping.'

'Sure, it's rubbish, but there's no tellin' him. He's like a wild man. Didn't he just tell us to give the girl a decent funeral and vanish out there into the night?'

Shona sat down hard in a chair. 'We'll do that,' she said grimly. 'And then I'm going after them . . . both.'

PART TWO
MANCHESTER
1850

Chapter Eighteen

Shona turned the blue jug upside down. With an apologetic rattle two farthings dropped into her gloved hand.

'Well, Shona, my girl, that's it,' she whispered to herself. Money saved from more than a year working at the pithead; the broken hands and the cold stones and the bulky silver-black coal; the pride and the independence bought by sixpences and shillings salted away in the blue jug each week.

It was three months since Maudie Martin's murder and Shona's swift pursuit of Greg and the vengeful Tommo. In that time she and Richie, who had insisted on coming with her, had trailed the maze of streets in Manchester, sleeping on the floors of crowded lodging houses, by the beds of instant, sometimes over-boisterous Irish friends.

In that time she had been propositioned by many men, young and old, fat and thin. But sustained by the spirit of Mary Challoner, she had managed to keep on laughing at them and so keep them off her.

The early days of frantic searching sapped her energy and lightened her purse. Each day the city seemed to re-create itself with blind-alleys where pathways had been, buildings where there had been open spaces. Once she found a large building with 'Hospital' carved in stone over the door, but the doorman met her with blank looks when she asked for a Mrs McNaughton. 'Nowt but old men here, Miss,' he said, closing the great door firmly in her face.

As their money went down, Richie said they'd have to stop walking and start working if they were not to starve.

Work was hard to find. Many people in this lodging house were out of work, the familiar blue shadow of hunger on their faces. True, there was some work for grown men in Manchester, digging the latest stages of the railway line, the new tunnels, and making the new roads. But it was hard to get into houses to find work, having no respectable clothes and the English girls teeming in from the country. Shona had been laughed at at many a kitchen door, with her dusty clothes and broken shoes.

Scrubbing floors in the gin shops and places of entertainment had produced pennies for her, occasionally replenishing the contents of the blue jug, but now she had been ill for two whole weeks, cast down with some kind of fever. Her blue jug was finally empty. And this place in a corner under the stinking stairwell on the third floor of Mellor's Yard cost a shilling a week.

She raised herself to the narrow window and held her head at an angle to try to see Richie coming down the narrow alleyway.

He was often away whole days at a time. But this time he had been away two whole days, and she was worried. Without Richie she wouldn't have survived these months. She would have died, as she had seen others die in Ireland and here in Mellor's Yard too. At times the fight for sheer survival made the images of Maudie and Tommo and even of Greg fade in her memory.

Richie ran errands for people, held horses, carried boxes and packages. He pawned his old boots. He brought her the pennies that kept the two of them finally out of the poorhouse or the cemetery.

Sometimes he brought her fruit and vegetables. When these were battered Shona knew he had crawled to retrieve them from under some stall in Studehill Market. Occasionally they were sweet, hard and crisp and she knew they had come by a more direct route, into Richie's capacious pocket while the stallholder was distracted.

She thought it had been from a pie, luscious, tasty, although a bit battered, that the killing fever had come. She had been unconscious for a day, in a sweat for three days, and trembling for a week. For two weeks there was no work for her, no scrubbing or sweeping. No pennies.

The town of Manchester had overwhelmed them from the very beginning. Miles and miles of hard streets. Mountain ranges of buildings, many with the scars of newness on them. Buildings like churches which were not churches; buildings like palaces which were not palaces. People as crowded and frequent as trees in a forest, but moving, always moving.

She and Richie had walked on hard new pavements, like unseen ghosts among people who lived in another world: women in deep-brimmed bonnets which obscured their faces and wide padded skirts which took up the width of the pavement; men in smooth frockcoats with tall shiny hats. These exotic creatures would be tracked by parcel-carrying servants, who might occasionally bestow a look of loathing on the loitering children, which at least made Shona and Richie visible again.

Occasionally Shona would stop a tall top-hatted man, calling him 'Greg', or a broad stocky working man and call him 'Tommo'. Such mistakes would be variously rewarded with a sneer, a hug, a kiss, a slap, or a cuff which would throw her to the ground.

After a time she learned to look only from the side of her eyes and take no action. Her spirits swooped downward. The hard city streets and the harder faces of the people made her wonder sometimes if she would recognise Greg if she saw him. Or, worse, if he would recognise her. All they had had together was a bit of comradely talk and a single painful scramble on a cottage bed when they should have been out after his missing mother. Had that all been so much foolery to him? Or, even worse, had it so sickened him that he had to come racing back to the haven of his wife, a woman of great charm, according to Douglas McNaughton?

Lying there in the shadowy place under the stairs, Shona's mind danced crazily with thoughts of both Greg and Tommo. For two days as she lay tumbled in the fever she thought she saw them both, standing there on the next staircase. She berated them roundly in the old language, for not coming down to see her. Then Greg turned into her old teacher Mr Lynch and beat her soundly for not speaking English.

Now she looked again through the window, smeared with dirt and grease and pearled up by the perpetual rain. At last she could see Richie, cap pulled right down, shoulders hunched against the rain, his bare feet slapping on the pavement. The iron door clanged downstairs and she heard his swift steps. He stood there in a new suit of clothes of brown fustian. His boots, newly mended, dangled over his shoulder, tied together by the laces. He grinned broadly, slid down the wall to sit beside her, and lifted the side of his coat. Bright orange carrots tumbled on to her lap. From his top pocket he pulled out a fresh round loaf, pushed it in her hand and watched with satisfaction as she bit into it.

He took off his round full cap and shook out his rough patch of damp hair. 'I've got a job now, regular, in a tavern. Pot boy,' he announced. 'Worked there two full days, no sleep. But haven't I got an hour off now? So get yer stuff together.'

'Me?'

'I got a loft over the horses. Have to be there all the time, see? For the work?'

'I'm to come? Do they know?'

'Na. Sure, they're all runnin' there like rabbits in a warren. Never notice a little'n.'

The Mitre was a coaching inn in one of the older streets which had once been quite smart. The building was bulky and old itself, with dipping roofs and three windows blocked up on the second floor. It seemed even older than it really was, among the new warehouses shooting up around it.

Shona and Richie arrived at the Mitre with their small bundles and melted into the flurry of activity. Carriages were heaving in and out of the stable yard, decanting passengers and luggage, servants and boxes. Fresh horses were being led in, used horses led away, steaming. No one took the slightest notice of the boy and the slight girl slipping into the space between two stalls and climbing a narrow wooden staircase.

The loft space was quite large and, although there was no window, daylight slipped in between the rooftiles. One corner showed signs of occupation. 'My corner,' said Richie. 'And this is yours.'

He pointed to the other which was heaped with straw and had a horse-rug draped on it. Fresh straw covered the floor and two wooden stools were placed squarely in the centre.

Shona sat down on one of them, grateful for the rest. She smiled up at him. 'Sure it's a great place, Richie. It'll do us fine.'

A voice was bellowing outside.

Richie stood up. 'That's Magga Bell whose place this is. He has the loudest voice in Manchester so they say. I have to go. Why don't you settle down there and have a sleep? Sure you'll be better soon, an' we'll get you a regular job of your own.' Then he was gone.

She looked around. Despite the cold she knew this was a good place. She would get better here and she would get a job. Then perhaps they could write to Biddy and ask her about home, and whether Tommo had come back yet? Or Greg.

Home! Now there was something. Here she was, thinking of New Morven as home. That was a new thing. Home had always been Ireland. The little farmhouse by the stream. When they were all still alive and together. But not now. That was a new thing.

'Come on now, Biddy, cheer up.'

It was a change for Margaret to be cheering Biddy up. In the last few months it had usually been the other way round.

Biddy had settled in very well at Garth End Cottage. She knew her presence helped things here and the fact that she was worried about Shona and Richie and Tommo was a little comfort to Margaret, who had not heard from Greg either.

The undermanager at the ironworks had come to see her a week after Maudie Martin's funeral. Peering round at the neat cottage he had told her she'd have to get out. They had another flush of workers coming in from Liverpool and they would need every space. Now Tommo Farrell wasn't working as a puddler she had no rights to this place. She would be thrown out of the house.

She had sighed. 'I thought it'd get round to this, but not this soon.'

Later that morning she had another visitor, a lumpish ugly girl who sniffed a lot. She was carrying a heavy bundle. She said her name was Thoria. 'I come to ask about Shona?'

'She's away, me darlin', for I don't know how long. And I don't know where.' Then the girl had started to cry and it took Biddy ten minutes to calm her down. With Shona gone, Thoria's work rate had gone right down and her uncle had had to fire her, and had got so mad he had thrown her out of his house too.

She sniffed and looked Biddy in the eye. 'So now I've no job and no home. I'll have to go up the valley back home and I'll get a good hiding off me mam.'

Biddy sighed. 'No good lookin' round here, darlin'. I'm out of here at the end of the week, and I don't know where I'm going meself. You could stay till then.'

She'd set Thoria to cleaning the windows, which cheered her up, and the girl ended up humming as she worked.

There'd been yet a third knock on the door that morning. Peering through the curtains she saw a fine trap behind a familiar black horse. She smoothed her hair and her apron, aware of Thoria's looming presence just behind her.

Douglas McNaughton filled the little doorway. He smiled civilly enough but refused to come in. 'I came to see if you had heard anything from that son of mine or your family?'

He knew of the flight of Biddy's family from Young Jamie MacQuistain, who was always a fount of gossip, usually unwanted. He also knew of some ill-founded suspicions regarding Greg, having had an uncomfortably obsequious visit from Constable Herbert Walton.

'No, not a thing,' she answered him. 'Not from any of them.'

'You'll be here on your own then?'

'Yes. And soon to be thrown out, seeing I'm no great hand at puddling, like young Tommo.'

'Ah. That was why I came.' He paused. 'Garth End's in turmoil. There are the two children. My wife will not countenance the return of Aida. In any case, there is a child there now, I believe. Margaret's trying harder to manage than for many years but she's floundering. In a turmoil herself. It's all such a burden. I wondered whether you'd come to be by her side – not to replace Aida, of course. We'll find someone to do all that. No, just come and calm Margaret down.' He smiled faintly. 'Calm us all down.'

She beamed up at him. 'Won't I be happy to do that, sir? And haven't I got the very helper for you here? A strong young woman who's just looking for some service. She cleans windows like a rare professional, so she does.'

He looked at the red-faced girl and shrugged. 'Do as you please. I must get back to work. Can you come now?'

She looked round. 'There's the house to clear and sort.'

'I'll return for both of you at four-thirty.'

'Right, Mr McNaughton. We'll be ready then, you can be sure of that.'

'Magga Bell needs help in the kitchen,' said Richie, a week after they had moved into the loft. 'He's sacked Janey Smith. He's sacked Digger the other potboy for thieving as well, so they're short-handed.'

They were walking through the streets together in the very early morning. It was mild for March, although the clouds were banking up with their usual damp promise. This was the only time Shona could sneak out with Richie, before the breakfast rush sent him scattering off his feet.

'Janey Smith?'

She had seen the stout little girl hurrying in early, hurrying away late.

'Yes. Says she's getting too fat to squeeze between the tables. Isn't the baby just about due?'

'A baby? Oh, I see.' Shona reddened and thumped him on the arm. For a month she had thought *she* might be pregnant. What would Greg have thought of that? She shook her head. Greg was nowhere to be found and would never have known anyway.

'What's that for?' Richie cocked a belligerent eye at her. 'Anyway I said I had a sister, an' you know what he said?'

'What?'

'He said if you were half as good as me you'd be all right.'

She cuffed him and laughed, then went back and started to gather her things together.

She enjoyed the pantomime of taking her bundle into Magga Bell's parlour as though she had come from many streets away; then being given the job and carting the bundle back up the rickety staircase to the loft.

Magga Bell had said she was a bit thin.

'Easier to get between the tables, sir!' she said.

He laughed at this and told her to stow her things and get back right away to start clearing tables and washing glasses.

The work and the food at the Mitre made her fitter by the day and the blue jug started to jingle again with coppers. The work was easy enough; soft compared with the pit, easy compared with scrubbing down gin houses.

On her second Thursday Magga shouted for them both in his loud voice and they went running to the parlour.

He sat there with his back to the afternoon light, hunched like a great bull terrier, a pipe in one hand, the other holding a black cane. 'I've this special customer comin' with guests every second Thursday. You know, Richie? Mrs – er – Madame *Villeynerve*.'

The boy nodded, a faint grin on his face. 'Sure, the Frenchwoman and her friends.'

'Well, she always has you an' Digger to serve?'

'Yes.'

'Well, Digger not being here, I thought your sister would help.'

'But, sir, she only ever has the boys to serve her. Didn't you tell me?'

'We-ell.' Magga drew on his long pipe. 'I thought we could make a little play for her.' He used the pipe, spittle hanging, to point to a narrow sofa. A boy's suit of brown fustian was draped across it like a limp body.

Shona frowned. 'I'm to wear that? And play the boy?'

'Mmm. Just do the job. Makes no difference. She is an important customer. Brings big people here.'

'Sure, me sister couldn't do that, sir! Wear that,' said Richie.

Shona stared at the clean suit and then at her own battered dress. 'I can keep the suit, sir?' she said.

He looked at her, surprised at her compliance. 'Yes. You keep the suit,' he said, surprised now at his own compliance.

'I'll need a hat.'

He lifted the jacket with his stick. A round hat lay squashed underneath.

'And more pins for my hair.'

With two fingers he felt in his waistcoat pocket and produced a shiny sixpence.

'Right, sir, I'll do it.'

'Shona, you're not to!'

'Not to? Richie, me darlin', it won't be the first time I've worn breeches and it's an easier thing to do here than at the pit.'

Magga laughed a great bellowing laugh at this and thrust the sixpence into her hand. 'Now go and make the transformation, dearie. The coaches'll be here by five.'

Magga Bell profited greatly from these evenings of Madame Villeneuve's, whose insistence on boys to serve stemmed from her desire to have no female distraction from herself as the centre of attention. She always booked two rooms on the third floor of the inn: a smaller room with a large bed and sofas and a warm fire, and a larger room with a huge sideboard groaning with food, as was the table set for eight. For her he put out his best velvet cloths and his finest crystal, bought from a man at Liverpool docks, no questions asked.

In this room every fortnight Marianne Villeneuve held a party for one or two friends and select newcomers to the town. These newcomers recommended by friends were eager for some light entertainment after a hard day's business in the humming town.

From the kitchen, Shona listened to the commotion as the carriages arrived. In five minutes a bell tinkled and Magga came bustling in with two foaming jugs of ale and two jugs of wine in each hand.

He looked over his great belly at Shona. 'Ha!' he said grinning his blacktoothed delight at the slender figure before him. 'A fine lad yer make! What happened to all that hair? Cut it, did yer?'

Shona took off her cap to reveal four tightly wound plaits pinned close to her head.

He laughed. 'Good yer didn't cut it. Wouldn't 'ave liked that. Oh, no!'

He thrust the ale at Richie and the wine at Shona. 'The glasses are beside the plates, just fill each customer one of each and come back down here to get'm filled again. Then go and stand just inside the door.'

The bell rang again and they raced upstairs, Richie first and Shona following. The room was flooded with bright light from lamps which covered every surface. A tall woman, wearing a fine green hat and a dress which showed plump white breasts almost to the nipple, was presiding over a table of men wearing high collars and dark suits.

Theatrically she held up a plump white hand. 'Ah, gentlemen, here is the wine. We may start!'

Her voice was light and the sound emerged from her red lips as though squeezed through a lemon: fine, tart, and very foreign.

Shona swallowed a smile. Life was looking up. Now this would be something to write to Biddy about to be sure!

Chapter Nineteen

After two hours of running up and down the stairs with jugs of wine and extra food, Shona's legs were aching. She had never seen so much food consumed so quickly. The sideboard groaned, in passing, with hams and poultry, roast beef and venison, fruit and cheeses. The memory of recent days surviving on scraps under the corner of a leaky staircase ticked away in a section of her mind, as did a more distant one of the high shriek of hunger heard in the remnants of an Irish cabin in Clare.

When the mouths finally stopped chewing Shona and Richie were ordered by Madame Villeneuve to clear the table of everything except the glasses.

Shona had taken little notice of the conversation, concentrating on her aching legs and the replenishment of plates and the glasses. But now she pressed her aching back surreptitiously against the wall and opened her ears.

'. . . And in France we have the greatest theatre, the greatest writer, Monsieur Voltaire.'

'Greater than Mr Shakespeare? Surely not, Madame?' The tall elderly man beside her smiled indulgently, his eyes cool.

'Greater indeed than your Mr Shakespeare. Now listen . . .' Madam Villeneuve stood up and, trammelled by her very wide skirts, needed help from the man to climb up on her chair. The others laughed and applauded.

She stood up straight, put her head back and looked around to command absolute attention. Then she struck a pose and started to declaim in her own language.

The sound washed over Shona just as English had washed over her when she had first heard it, before being forced to tackle its ugly quacking sounds in the village school. A year later she had been awarded a basket of peaches from the gardens of Marsteen

House for being the best English speaker in the class.

She thought on, of Greg's Mr Shakespeare with his dyed black hair, snapping black eyes and dusty castle. He was a nice man but no poet, she thought. But he liked Greg. You could tell that. She closed her eyes and could see Greg, tall and fair, as he had been that day in the sitting room of the Gaunt Hotel in Priorton.

Her eyes snapped open. Cheers and applause were ringing out again as the woman finished. As she climbed down from the chair, she fell very slightly against the man called Marcus, who helped her down.

She tapped him on the shoulder. 'Now you, dear Marcus.'

Mr Marcus Hodgkiss simply stood up, held his coat lapels and started to declaim: '"This day is called the feast of Crispian . . ."'

As he finished, Madame led the applause and offered him her hand, which he kissed. 'That is an excellent speech, M'sieur, most excellent. In which of Mr Shakespeare's plays does it appear?'

A younger heavy-set man shouted from the end of the table, 'It's the one, Ma'am, where the King of England gets ready to trounce the French. The battle of Agincourt.'

The company laughed in unison at this.

Madame held up her hand, the shadow of a frown marring her smooth brow. 'Pah! Fairytales! All fairytales. I think we stop the boring 'istories. We 'ave more fun. Now push the chairs back! Push, push!'

In seconds she had cleared a miniature stage before the curtains. Shona gasped as Madame swiftly stepped out of her full skirt which she stood up by itself in the corner. She took a bow in her long red pantaloons. This time the applause was unrestrained. The men banged their glasses on the table.

Madame looked across at the startled Shona. 'Boy, you go into that room there and on the *bed* . . .' there was more applause '. . . you will see a brown box. Go, boy! But first, put your eyes back in your 'ead!'

Shona found the long flat box in the bedroom and brought it in, holding it cautiously towards Madame.

'Open it!'

She pulled off the lid to reveal six red balls lying on black satin. Madame pushed up her sleeves and picked up two of them. She threw them into the air one by one and in a second had them circling. 'Now, boy, you give me them, one by one as I ask for them. Now! Now! Now! Now!'

The six balls danced in the air, gleaming in the bright lamplight. She threw them two and three at a time; she juggled them behind her back, under her knees; she lay on the floor and juggled them through her raised legs.

There were roars of laugher and appreciation at each stage of the performance.

Finally, one by one, the balls thudded back into the wooden box in Shona's hands and the applause raised itself to a crescendo.

The elderly man kissed her hand very tenderly and led her round the room to have her hand kissed by each and every man. There was much laughter.

Shona carefully replaced the lid, put the box on the sideboard, then went to stand again by the door.

Richie, familiar with these scenes, was grinning into her startled face.

Madame replaced her skirt in a businesslike fashion and looked round at the merry flushed faces. 'Now! What next?' She looked with artful innocence around the room, examining each face.

'Cartwheel, cartwheel . . .' The chant was started by the brawny young man at the end of the table.

She put her head to one side. 'Per'aps . . . per'aps so.'

'Yes! Yes!'

Now they were banging the table again.

'I need more space!'

There was a great clatter while the table and chairs were pushed even further back.

This time she lifted her dress at the front and tucked it in her sash. Then with a great swishing sound she accomplished ten cartwheels in succession, walking back with each movement to make space again. She executed it so quickly that the swirling scarlet skirts did indeed resemble a cartwheel with her legs and arms as the spokes. This time Shona joined the roars of delight with her own hearty applause.

Madame was sitting in her chair, arms akimbo and knees spread out peasant fashion, regaining her breath. Her glace fell on the still applauding Shona.

'Ah!' she said. 'The boy also thinks I am wonderful.' She paused and her eyes twinkled even more. 'Now your turn to do the cartwheel. Cartwheel, young man!'

Shona shook her head.

'Now come on,' the woman's voice cooed, coaxed. 'I will show you how.'

Shona still shook her head and a silence dropped into the room. A gauntlet had been thrown. They were all looking at her with clinical interest.

Richie broke the silence. 'Sh— he can sing a good song, Madame, a pretty song.'

'Sing?' The woman clapped her hands. 'Ah! Come 'ere, boy, and sing while *pauvre Madame* regains her breath.'

Shona was pulled forward by the elderly man and placed on the spot which had just recently been the centre of Madame's cartwheel.

She closed her eyes to wipe out the sight of the shiny over-heated faces and sang:

> 'Through the night and through the day
> We will ride, we will ride,
> Away from grave embraces
> We will ride my love and I.
> Away from sweet mem'rie
> We will ride, we will ride.'

Shona opened her eyes wide to sing the chorus:

> 'Across the dark blue water
> There is a brighter sky
> Shining down on little houses
> Where mothers needn't cry . . .'

By the time she reached the last verse, the room had stilled to perfect silence. Some of the men were mopping their brows. Others were looking at the floor. Marcus Hodgkiss looked uneasily at his hostess.

Then Madame led the applause which was enthusiastic but restrained. 'Thank you, boy. You 'ave a very sweet voice.' She stood up and looked round at her guests. 'I think, gentlemen, our evening is just about at an end. Mr Bell the innkeeper will 'ave your 'ats and cloaks ready downstairs. I will bid you good night.'

As they left, each man shook hands with her, murmuring words of appreciation. The elderly man stood by his chair, obviously intent on staying.

Madame turned to Shona and Richie. 'You boys, you are to clear all this . . .' she looked round the room '. . . muddle. And tell Mr Bell that Mr Hodgkiss and I wish for 'ot chocolate. And you, songbird, are to bring it.'

Then she took the arm of the elderly man and walked gracefully into the next room.

'Richie, why didn't you tell me?' muttered Shona, manoeuvring a loaded tray through the door.

Her brother grinned. 'Your face, Shona! You should see it. She's not a flying dragon, you know.'

The dining room, when Shona finally returned with the jug of hot chocolate, was still empty. She knocked timidly on the connecting door and obeyed the instruction to enter.

Madame was sitting by a great table littered with boxes and bottles. She was wearing a loose silk wrap fastened only at the waist. Her nut brown hair had been unpinned and was loose down her back. The man, fully dressed, was brushing it with a silver-backed brush.

'Here!' With a broad sweep of her hand, Madame made space on the table for the tray.

Shona placed it carefully in the cleared space and then jumped as her wrist was caught in Madame's small vicelike grip.

'What is it we have here, Marcus? Is it a songbird? A songboy?'

The man chuckled and settled in an overstuffed chair by the fire as if to watch another performance.

Madame's other hand flew upwards and swept the round cap from Shona's head. 'Ah. Another kind of songbird! One who doesn't think I know girl from boy?' She chuckled. 'It is my business, *ma p'tite*.' She stood up and plonked Shona into the chair she had just vacated. 'Here, sit!'

The Frenchwoman's hands were pulling out Shona's hairpins. Then those same hands were brushing out the plaits. Her head felt sore with relief from constraint.

'There Marcus, see, such beautiful black hair! What a pity to pin it up in those ugly braids.'

The man laughed. The sound was strident, unpleasant. Shona turned to look at him. His arms were reaching out to encompass both her and the Frenchwoman. She wrenched her head away and fled the room, pursued by their laughter.

The next morning Shona was woken by a great roar in the stable yard. Richie's corner was empty and the light trickling in betrayed a much later hour than her usual rising time.

Magga Bell met her at the bottom of the steps. 'Ye're to go to Madame Villeyneuve dead quick,' he said, pipe still in mouth.

'Would there be something wrong, Mr Bell?'

'Dunno that. Ye'll soon know when you see her. The food was fine, she said. Fussy about the food is Madame.'

The French woman was sitting at the long table with papers in front of her, a pen in one hand. 'Ah, the songbird. I see you are a girl this morning!'

She was wearing a well-cut dress in brown wool, a rope of gleaming pearls dropping over her bosom. Her hair was simply dressed and her face was free from powder and paint. She looked older and at the same time more innocent.

Shona darted a glance at the connecting door.

'Mr Hodgkiss went well before dawn, songbird, so we are alone.'

Shona waited for the onslaught. Hadn't Richie said the woman would only be served by boys? There would be trouble here for sure.

'Do you see this?'

The Frenchwoman tipped a pile of golden sovereigns on to the table from a canvas bag. They glittered in the morning light.

'Yes, Ma'am,' said Shona warily.

'This we earned last night. You, me and the little one. My friend Mr Hodgkiss says the labourer is worthy of his hire. One guinea from each man and two guineas from Mr Hodgkiss, who is always so generous.' She used the pen to separate out a single guinea. 'There, that is for you and your young comrade. He is thin but he has a merry face.'

'He's my brother.'

'Is he? Ah. The sister and the little brother.' Her tone of voice had lost its exaggeration, its excess. 'Go on, take this!'

Shona reached out, put it in her apron pocket and bobbed a curtsy. 'Thank you, Madame. Most kind you are.'

'Ah, you are *incy mincy* as a girl, songbird. In breeches you were much more bold.'

Shona smiled openly. 'I wore breeches in a place I worked before, Madame. At a colliery. A coalmine.'

Madame shrieked. 'You went under the earth? Into one of those black holes?'

'No. Just at the top. But it was dirty work even there. One woman I knew, she'd worked underground. But she died. And her babies too.' She examined the woman before her, not much older than Mary Challoner but as different as a gaudy velvet glove from a string gauntlet.

'Ah, yes.' Madame returned the gaze, eyes narrowing shrewdly. 'Always the hard life. But is it so much better here, clearing slops in this dirty old inn?'

Shona's resentment grew. 'Before this, Madame, I was lying starving in a stinking attic, with no money for food. It's much better here than that.' She waited grimly. The guinea was burning a hole in her pocket. Despite her animosity, one part of her mind was picturing Richie's face when she showed him.

'Ah, yes. I like Manchester. So much energy. In the men, always making, making things; in the streets, always going, going. But, songbird, it's such a black place. What made you come here, to this other black place, from your coalmine?'

'I came looking for my older brother and my friend . . .'

'Friend? Is he your lover?'

Shona blinked at the directness, then thought of the one time with Greg and smiled lightly at how clumsy it had all been, between them. 'I don't know that, Ma'am. I thought so. But . . . anyway, I haven't found them yet, my brother and my friend. And then Richie and me used up our money. Now, with working, I've no time to look for them, the boys.'

Madame stacked up the golden guineas in a careful pile. 'Ah! Inspiration strikes. Do you know, songbird, I am to have a house! Mr Hodgkiss, who builds houses and factories and many other things, is very rich and has too much money – he wants to give me a house he has built not far from the railway station. I think he sometimes worries about places where I choose to show my . . . cartwheels. And the guineas from the other men. I have said no for many months now, but now I think I will say yes.' She touched the shining pile before her. 'I am tired of always finding a place to give the entertainment.'

Shona looked round the room, its dinginess overlaid by smooth cloths and bright crystal. 'I thought this place no place for such grand . . .'

Madame's glance followed hers round the room. 'They are not all grand, songbird. And those who are? They get a *frisson* from such places – being, how you say, cheek by jowl with the poor and the very bad.' She straightened her papers and put her pen in a neat line beside them. 'And now I will have this house and I am inspired that you and your little brother will come and help me. I want no stiff English maid. You can help me! You can live with me and you will have time to look for your lover and your brother, I promise.' The words were being squeezed out of that pursed mouth so fast they were hard to understand.

'What? Beg your pardon, Missis?'

'Yes, I say it again. You will come with me to the house by the station. You would like it, no?'

The woman was mad, that was it. Shona frowned at her, then thought again of Richie's grinning delight at Madame's antics. And the long hours of heavy work at the Mitre. 'Yes'm,' she said slowly, 'it'd be no bad thing. P'raps Richie could take care of your horse? He's a wonder with horses. Ask anyone at home.' She paused. 'If you'll answer one question, ma'am?'

'Anything, songbird, anything.' Madame opened her eyes wide.

'Why're you helping us? What'll we have to do?'

'I liked the way you laughed and clapped last night. You are a little brother and sister, left as I was with my little brother. My little brother . . . he was killed in Paris in 'forty-eight. Like your friend from the mine, who died.' One soft hand touched Shona's. 'Don't worry, songbird, you will help me at the house, that is all . . . and sometimes sing your little songs for my guests. Only a few guests now, when I choose. And you will wear the breeches. I do not like the stiff English maid.'

She rubbed her forehead with the back of her hand with a tired gesture. Shona had watched Mary Challoner make that same gesture, in the last fatal months of her pregnancy. It was the familiarity of it that led Shona finally to know in her heart she could trust the Frenchwoman.

In the fourth month of their stay in Manchester, Shona and Richie packed up their bundles once more and went to live in Madame Villeneuve's new-built villa near Manchester station. Shona was to take care of the house with the help of two Italian girls hired by Madame; Richie to care for the horse, carry coal up four flights of stairs and run errands.

Shona was to wear breeches and jacket; brown during the day and black in the evening, much to the amusement of the Italian girls. Three afternoons a week, dressed in a proper skirt, with her bonnet and shawl, it was agreed that she could walk the streets of Manchester to continue her search for Greg and Tommo.

At the end of her first week she wrote a letter to Biddy on Madame's paper, headed 'Versay Villa'.

Dear Biddy,

Richie and me are safe here you will be pleased at last to know. We have jobs working in a house for a lady from France. The pay is good so I can save. I look all the time, every afternoon, for Tommo and Greg McNaughton but haven't caught sight of them. But I still keep looking.

This is so great a town you would not believe it. Big factories and roads and you can't get across the street for wagons and carriages.

I hope you are well and they are letting you stay in the house. Do you get to Garth End Cottage at all? I was worrying about Lauretta and how she is without her daddy. And there is the little girl of the poor dead woman. Do they know where Greg can be? If they do, will you let me know so I can seek him out?

Madame is very kind here, if a bit strange. But I miss you. Funny after such a short time knowing you. Richie has two fine horses to care for here but he misses Cush and says would you go round to Gil Tait and see how Cush is doing?

Best wishes from your niece
Shona Farrell

Pat Daley picked out Garth End Cottage easily. It was set back at the end of the row and had a strip of garden at the front and side. In the neatly laid out side-garden an old man was setting about a large shrub with clippers.

Pat leaned across the hedge. 'That's a nice wee garden you've got there, sir.'

Old Jamie MacQuistain looked across his neatly dug patch. He had cloches over the vegetable beds to warm them ready for planting and over the sprouting strawberries so that they would fruit early. He had dug out the last of the overwintered vegetables and pruned the apple tree and the pear. Now he was busy with the butterfly bush, reducing to sticks what would, much later that year, grow into a froth of deep purple attended by its crop of butterflies.

'Aye,' he said slowly, 'it's been hard to get out, between the hard frosts and these legs. But it an't my garden. It's Mr McNaughton's. It's him I work it for.' He turned back to his pruning.

Biddy answered the door at Pat's ring. She smiled broadly and stepped back. 'Come in, won't you, Pat? Isn't it nice to see you?'

Taking off his cap, he followed her through to the kitchen. The scullery door was open and a thickset girl, clattering pans in there, looked up as he came into the kitchen. Two children were sitting up to the table playing with pastry.

Biddy pointed to a chair pulled up to the glowing iron range. 'Sit yourself down, Pat. Now what is it you want?'

He held out the letter. 'It's this, with your name on it. The undermanager at the works brought it to me, he not knowing where you were.'

She took the letter from him. They all looked on with interest as she turned it over, then opened it and peered at its contents.

She shrugged helplessly. 'Do you read, Pat?'

He shook his head, then stood up clutching his cap as a slim fragile-looking woman came into the kitchen with a box in her hands. He hardly recognised her for the one he had found on Christmas Eve, dementedly wandering the streets of New Morven.

Biddy held out the letter to her, smiling. 'Margaret, me darlin', here's Pat Daley who's brought me a letter from the post. An', ignorant as we are, there's neither of us can read it.'

Margaret smiled. 'Good morning to you, Mr Daley.' She gave the button box to Lauretta who immediately rooted amongst its contents, giving chosen specimens to Becky who started to make patterns with them in the pastry.

Margaret turned the letter over. 'It's from Shona. The address is Versay Villa, Manchester.'

Thoria came to stand at the scullery door, rubbing her hands on a dry cloth.

Margaret read the letter out to them in her clear Cumbrian voice.

'A Frenchwoman!' said Biddy.

'No Tommo!' said Pat glumly.

'No Greg?' said Margaret sadly.

'Shona an' Richie sound as if they've done all right, though,' said Thoria.

After a pause Margaret said, 'Do you want me to write back to her for you, Biddy?'

'Yes, yes. You can tell her I'm safe across here with you, and Thoria's helping.'

'Tell her to watch herself,' said Pat Daley. 'And tell Richie that Cush is all right. I just seen him yesterday with Gil Tait. An' tell her to keep lookin' for Tommo. He's a big miss.'

Pat had never believed the rumours, which now had the status of common knowledge in the pubs, that Tommo had slaughtered Maudie Martin, in some plot with the Shotwell Protestant, the one who had disgraced the sister of the priest.

'An' tell her to keep lookin' for Greg,' said Biddy, glancing at the girls, seemingly engrossed in their button-game.

'An' tell her that Thoria is asking after her,' she called from the scullery door.

'Grandma, Becky and me want to make a marzipan man! Can we make one?'

Margaret laughed. 'I can see this will have to be a long letter.' She put it in her apron pocket. 'I'll write it tonight when these two little puzzlepots are tucked up in bed.'

That night after supper she went up to Douglas's workroom where he was sitting at the large table, papers before him.

He put down his pen as she came in.

'You're working hard, Douglas.'

'There's more to do now, Greg being away.'

'Isn't Stuart helping?'

'Yes, surprisingly enough. He's been covering more of Greg's work while he's been away. He did the monthly check for Mr Moxham up at Killock Castle today. But he's no good on the engineering.'

Apart from one incident, Stuart had been remarkably affable with Margaret since Greg had been gone.

The incident happened the week after Greg's disappearance. She was in the garden with her stick, poking at the frozen plants and the wandering autumn shoots of the apple tree.

Stuart had come across to her. 'Is everything all right, Ma?'

She had looked at him blankly, then smiled at him faintly. 'Nothing is all right. My son has gone. His daughter is crying in there for her daddy, alongside the daughter of a poor dead woman, this child crying for her mother. The devil is overwatching this house, making sure it'll fall to pieces.'

He had laughed uneasily. 'That's all silly, Ma. I'm here. I'm your son, aren't I? The only bad thing in this house is that child. A street-walker's child has no place here.'

She frowned. 'Her mother was a good woman. She saved me.'

'You don't need her child. I'm here for you. I'm your son. You love me.'

It had been a question, not a statement. She'd looked at him in the darkening afternoon light and something stirred in her. She lifted the stick and started to beat him about the shoulders. He stood there, his arms up to protect himself, and did nothing.

Douglas had hurried across the grass and wrested the stick from her. 'Margaret! Stop this!'

He led her into the house. She was sobbing.

'What is it, Margaret, what is it?'

'I thought I saw him, Douglas. The devil.'

He held her to him for a second. 'Would it help if I went for Biddy?' he said gently.

So that night Biddy had come to Garth End. Since she had been here the whole household had calmed down around her.

She brought a girl who was very silent but who worked harder than Aida or even Flora had ever done. Margaret was allowed into her own kitchen for the first time for a decade. Douglas was more approachable than he had been for years. Even Stuart, after that first incident, was affable, almost obsequious, to everyone, even to Biddy.

But she did miss Greg.

'What was that, Margaret?' Douglas was still looking up quite patiently from his work table.

'Biddy's had a letter from her niece Shona. She seems quite safe. I'm to write a reply for her. She's been searching for Greg and for her brother, to no avail.'

He stirred uneasily. 'I've wanted to write to men I know in Manchester to enquire for Greg. But then I thought he'd not like that, to be pursued.'

Margaret knew Douglas was right. 'But I miss him, Douglas. I want him here.'

'So do I.' He picked up his pen and she turned to go. 'Perhaps the young woman will find him and bring him home, Margaret?' He was thinking, suddenly, of a bunch of violets he had bought for his wife once at Carlisle market and tucked into her hat. She was so innocent then, and even now had that quality about her.

Her smile as she turned to him reminded him of that young Margaret, all those years before. 'Yes, Douglas. I'll tell Shona what I – that is, what both of us are hoping.'

Chapter Twenty

Shona and Richie settled down in slightly bemused comfort in the tall brick villa which Marcus Hodgkiss had given to Madame Marianne Villeneuve.

The villa was different from others on the neat new-laid road. Unlike its neighbours, the elaborate façade had no door. The main door was at the side, down a narrow entry, so that visitors could alight from their carriages unseen. It was different also in that in the long drawing room, opposite the centre fireplace, was a raised area: a dais or small stage.

The first week at Versay Villa was a flurry of activity as Madame, keeping a sometimes resentful Shona always by her side like a talisman, bought furniture and curtains, appointed the two Italian sisters to housekeep and a gardener to tame the wild field which was to be the garden.

The house belonged to Madame by deed of gift. She showed the deed to Shona on her second day.

'See here, songbird,' she said, her voice echoing in the bare hallway. She rustled the heavy parchment. 'See what it says? *By deed of gift.* That means it belongs entirely to me.'

Tentatively, Shona fingered the heavy vellum.

'Now,' went on Madame, 'if that skinny wife of Marcus tugs on his reins, or if he finds himself another acrobat, then I still have my villa –' she fingered the pearls at her throat '– and my jewels.'

'You were an acrobat, Madame? In a circus?'

She shrugged. 'In the circus, in the theatre, wherever the men wished to see a woman tumbling around. I was very good!' She smiled complacently. 'When one is good, one always has very good friends.'

'Why come here, Madame, to this black town?'

'I do not know. Maybe the devil himself drive me here. The time before Mr Hodgkiss, I choose not such a good friend. A working man, a blacksmith, a friend of my brother. But so 'andsome, a wonderful lover! The three of us, we used to laugh when I told him about the great *milords* who had the pricks the size of your little toe!' She sighed. 'Like you, songbird, I had a brother and a lover. But my lover, he was shot beside my little brother in the uprising. And then they came for me and I had to run.'

'Me own brother, Madame, he was shot by the military. The English that was.'

Madame kissed her extravagantly on both cheeks. 'I knew it, songbird, when I saw you smiling at me in your little brown suit! That you too had suffered.'

Shona pulled away slightly. 'So what about Mr Hodgkiss, Madame?'

'Ah, I met Mr Hodgkiss on the boat coming from France. In a minute he was my slave. He had worked hard all his life – his nose, as he says, to the grindstone. Do you know, songbird, he did not know how to laugh? I teach him how. And when he say he came from Manchester, I knew Manchester was my fate. And Mr Hodgkiss! And all this gold he makes from building, building, always building!'

Madame took Shona on outings through new streets, into showrooms and echoing warehouses which she had never seen before. Despite her determination not to be charmed by her, Shona relished the fragrant butterfly presence of the French-woman and the witty way she handled the dour tradesmen, whose haughty manners at dealing with this strange pair melted when they saw the size of her order and the glitter of her gold.

Shona's apprentice delight at these procedures was compounded by the opportunity to prowl into new areas where Greg or Tommo might just turn up. Despite the giddy excitement of life at Versay Villa, they were always in her thoughts.

Madame sensed her distraction. One day, returning yet again in a laden carriage, she turned to Shona who was peering intently out of the window. 'Songbird! I see you always watching, watching, watching. Is it the police? Are you pursued?'

'I told you, Madame. I have to look for my brother and my friend.'

Madame clapped her hand on her forehead. 'Ah, I forget. I am the selfish beast. The pursuit of the lover! You must persist, songbird, you must persist!'

For a minute Shona could have slapped her for her theatricality, her selfishness. She closed her eyes and tried again to bring Greg's image before them. There was an ache, a deadness inside her which would not come alive again until she saw him, touched him again.

She opened her eyes. 'Sure it's the thought of finding him – them – that's keepin' me going at all, Madame,' she said, grimly ignoring Madame's wide-eyed appeal.

The Frenchwoman shrugged and turned away from Shona to stare out of the carriage window into the crowded street.

The second week was taken up with dressmakers (English for the dresses, French for lingerie), who were to replenish Madame's wardrobe.

Madame made Shona stand up on the little portable dais to be measured for dresses and skirts, shifts and pantaloons. 'These are for you. For fun, for seeking out the lover.'

'But for the working and for the evening – a tailor!' She laughed. 'I will have no mincing maids around me in the evening. I do not like the English maid.'

She sent Richie off to buy a horse and he returned with a lugubrious Lancastrian who did not believe the boy's tales about the woman who would pay for his fine horse. Richie had chosen a grey which he called Boru, and a smart trap which he polished lovingly before it had taken them on a single journey.

'Now a reception!' said Madame. 'I have had urgent notes from Monsieur Hodgkiss who is longing to see me but I said: "Two weeks! Give me two weeks!" Now on Saturday we will have a reception. Just a few old friends and a *leetle* entertainment.'

On Saturday Shona dusted the heavy furniture in the dining room and polished the brand new silver. Madame spent the day harassing the Italian women. There were shrieks and cries from the kitchen but during the afternoon the buffet gradually filled with exquisite food.

In the evening Shona and Richie got into their matching black wool suits and white gloves. They laughed as they looked at themselves in the large mirror which seemed to cover one wall in Madame's room.

'Do not laugh! You look very smart. Two little blackbirds. Now what about the hair, songbird?'

'Is it the plaits, Madame?'

'No. You will not play that game again. Perhaps just a ribbon.' She opened one of the many drawers in a vast cabinet which nearly covered one wall, and plucked out a pink ribbon. 'Come here, we will tie it back. Just a *leetle* bow at the back, so! Very neat.'

She turned to Richie. 'You will help with the juggling, little one? Tonight I juggle with the boxes and the balls.'

'Sure it'll be good to know what the hell's happening this time!'

She laughed at this. 'And you, Shona, I want three songs. One that'll amuse them at the start. Then one after the tumbling, so I can get my breath back. And one at the end, to send them all to their beds. Do you know three songs?'

'Three?' said Shona. 'Don't I know a hundred?'

The three men Marcus Hodgkiss brought to Madame's reception were obviously old friends. She kissed each of them on one cheek, having kissed Marcus on both. Two of the men were slightly younger and fatter than Marcus, and wore the sombre coats of business, slightly creased over their rising stomachs. The third man was younger still, not much older than Madame herself. He had bright yellow hair brushed straight back, wore a frockcoat in an elaborate check and a yellow silk necktie which nearly reached his ears.

'Jonnie! What a *surprise*!' After kissing him she turned to Shona. 'This is one of my great friends. I performed at his hall when I first came to Manchester and –' she glanced at Marcus Hodgkiss '– was still a woman of independence.'

The men stared openly at Shona and Richie.

'You are curious, gentlemen? These two young people are to assist the performance and help us to enjoy ourselves. Master

Richie will assist with the juggling and Miss Shona will sing. And – I see the light in your eyes – that is *all* she will do. The child has the voice of a bird.'

'Ah, so *she* is the one!' said the man called Jonnie. 'Marcus was entranced.'

The evening was more restrained than that at Magga Bell's inn. The men here were more clearly guests. On her own territory Madame had less need to please.

They had supper in the dining room, Shona and Richie helping with the pouring and fetching and carrying, just as they had at the inn.

After dinner, the clearing was left to the Italian girls and the rest of them trooped into the drawing room which was set up for the performance, with chairs and couches arranged to face the dais on which stood an upright piano draped with one of Madame's shawls.

She stood Shona in the centre of the space. 'Now Shona will sing her song.'

She sang a Gaelic lullaby first, one which her grandmother and her mother had sung to them all at bedtime when they were very little.

Waiting for the enthusiastic applause to die down, Marcus Hodgkiss stood up and took his turn declaiming a poem about Horatius at the Bridge. He bowed to more applause and turned to Madame. 'Dear Marianne, it is you we come to see. We await your artistry with bated breath.'

She smiled, inclined her head, then rose and made a deep curtsy to the company which showed off her white shoulders and the rise of her breasts above her rather plain brown dress. Then, with the familiar neat movement, she stepped out of her dress and handed it to Shona. Underneath she was wearing a brief yellow knitted top and pale yellow pantaloons to her knee, with white stockings held up by garters of yellow flowers.

She bowed to acknowledge the patter of applause for this transformation. Then, elegantly putting one leg forward and her arms out for balance, she sank slowly into a perfect splits. Still slowly, she put back her head and reached behind her to hold her foot, moving her front foot round to join it. Somehow she managed to make a perfect O which rocked forward and back, then forward and over, so that she ended upside down, crab-like, on her hands and feet. Then her feet shot into the air and she was walking on her hands, right around the room, on and off the dais, in and out of the chairs and sofas as her visitors chuckled in appreciation. Then, still on her hands, she walked back into the central space where she did a back somersault and landed on her feet just beside Marcus Hodgkiss's chair. He stood up to applaud, as did the others, and she laughed with delight and kissed him on both cheeks.

'Now a *leetle* lemonade,' she said, slightly breathless. 'Then the songbird.'

Shona was glad not to have to follow such a performance straight away. When they were all settled down – Madame, still in acrobat's gear sitting on the arm of Mr Hodgkiss's chair – she stood centre stage again.

'These are two little songs which I will sing in English,' she said. 'The first is about the mountains and valleys of a lovely country and the longing a young boy feels to return. The second is about a wee man who has had a drop too much poteen one night and teases one of the little people, who banishes him to another world where all drink tastes of vinegar.'

She sang without drama, with her hands quietly by her sides. When she sang the first song she had them all in tears of sorrow; when she sang the second one she had them in tears of laughter. The applause for her was as great as that given to Madame.

The man called Jonnie stood up, still clapping. 'Come and sing in my hall, Miss Shona. Come and sing for me.'

Madame's eyes narrowed; her mouth was sulky. 'Shhh, Jonnie,' she said, standing up. 'The show is not over. Richie! The boxes and the balls if you please.'

First she juggled with the balls again, including two small sharp knives in the performance. Then she juggled with five boxes of different sizes, keeping them in the air with amazingly dexterous skill. All the time the movements she made showed off the graceful lines and the suppleness of her body.

Shona, who had seen the scowl and contemplated the incredible thought that Madame might be jealous, led the applause, admiring everything about this magical woman whom she would surely never match as a performer.

Madame threw her a smile as she pulled a long green cloak round her. 'And now, my songbird will give an extra song. She will sing us all her lullaby, to send us safely to our beds.'

Shona sang her final song and the excitement in the room turned to warmth and satisfaction at an evening well spent. She watched her audience's bright eager faces as they clapped, and felt very satisfied.

The man called Jonnie stood up, his yellow hair bouncing. 'Another song, just one more song.'

Shona glanced at Madame, who looked back at her then smiled and nodded.

'Well, this is one that my brother's friend Pat Daley made up for me. It's called "My Wild Irish Rose".

> 'There on a hillside my rose is a-blooming
> Kissed by the sun and washed by the rain
> Her cheeks they are pink and her eyes they are
>   golden
> I fear 'tis my fate not to see her again.'

This time they were on their feet as they applauded and she bowed low from the waist as was suited by her man's garb.

While Madame was seeing off her guests, Shona and Richie pushed and pulled the chairs and sofas into position round the tables.

Richie yawned. 'A funny old night, that. She's a strange woman, Madame.'

Shona looked at him, frowning. 'Richie, is it all right for you here?'

'It's all right, I suppose. The woman's mad as a stoat but she's a heart in her. But I could've cried meself tonight, like them old men, when you sang of the mountains and the green. And the Wild Irish Rose. I keep wondering about Cush . . .'

She put her hand on his shoulder. For once he didn't pull away. 'Soon as we have the money, Richie, you'll go back to Cush. And there's Biddy for you to look to as well. Can't I find them two men meself? I'm better placed for it now.' She gave him a little push. 'Get yourself away up to bed. Ye're as tired as an owl. Too much old fun here for you altogether!'

He had gone when Madame came back in from the hallway, followed by Marcus Hodgkiss. They were arm in arm, laughing quite loudly.

'Well, songbird, I've had three offers for you, including one from Jonnie insisting that you sing in his hall . . . don't glare, *p'tite*. I told them to go to France with their offers. You need no protector. I take care of you.' She turned to Marcus. '*We* take care of you. You find your lover – and *pouf*! You will take care of each other.'

'I can take care of meself.'

'I say stop scowling!' Madame steered Marcus towards the door. 'Now would you please get the chocolate from the kitchen? It will be keeping hot on the range. Those girls must be in bed, there is no sound of them quarrelling . . . And the chocolate, bring it to my room. Ah! I forget. A letter for you was brought this afternoon. It has been on the dressing table all day. You may collect it when you bring the chocolate.'

Then, in her long green cloak, she made her way slowly upstairs, attended by the ever faithful Marcus Hodgkiss who carried her brown dress over his arm.

Shona raced to get the tray and take it upstairs. When she got there Mr Hodgkiss was already in his braces. Madame, without troubling to tease, handed over the letter and Shona flew up into her own little room.

She turned up her lamp and lifted the letter nearer to read it. It was in a neat looping hand.

Dear Shona Farrell,

I am writing this for your Aunt Biddy as she is unable. Everyone here is very well, Biddy is with me as the company would not let her stay in the house. She brought your friend Thoria who is wonderful at housework and what's more very quiet.

Did you know that Aida had a child? A girl, I believe, though I don't see her.

Biddy is good company. She and I have long talks about things. Lauretta and little Becky, the daughter of that woman, are quite good friends now and play together with only a few quarrels.

Rumours about the death of Mrs Maudie Martin are rife in both villages. According to Pat Daley there is much talk of either your brother or my son Greg being responsible. The constable has been back to ask both Biddy and me lots of questions. We have urged him to keep looking closer to home. She and I both agree that these suspicions are nonsense but feel it a pity they are not here to defend themselves.

My son Stuart drops all sorts of dark hints but he was never reliable in his judgement of people. I will ask Mr McNaughton to enquire among his Manchester acquaintances about Greg. He may not be pleased at our persistence but I miss him too much to please him just at the moment. If we find out where he is I will let you know. Then you can bring him home.

Yours faithfully,
Margaret McNaughton

Shona sat at the little table and looked at herself in the pretty little mirror Madame had insisted they buy. The girl who stared back at her, above the black jacket and the neat white shirt, was sleeker and cleaner than at any time since she had been in Manchester. Than any time since she had been at the farm by the water. What would Greg think at such a sight? Laugh or scowl? He might not even recognise her. The first time he'd seen her she'd been in her pit-breeches, making scones with blackened hands.

Her mind moved then to their frantic love-making the night his mother went missing. Her hands went down to push at her thighs where they had ached so much for two whole days. There had been such a mutual feeling of surrender and peace afterwards.

She drifted across and lay on the little narrow bed, staring upwards at the wall through the iron filigree bedhead. Slowly she stripped off the clothes which had been her uniform for the evening and kicked them to the floor. She shivered. The fire had died down in the little fireplace and the room was chilly.

In one movement she leapt under the bedclothes and rolled from one side to the other until the icy sheets were warm. Her hand went down between her thighs to where Greg had been. There was space. It was possible. How could something be so terrible then in the end so good? Her hand stayed there as she thought of the games that Tommo had played with Maudie in the stone hut. She wanted, she ached, to play them with Greg. She closed her eyes and saw the staircase of Killock Castle. There in the dusty rooms at Killock they would play those games. The ache became unbearable and she had to rub it until it went away.

She awoke in the dark an hour later and searched the bed for her nightgown, struggled into it and lay back. Her mind was clear now. She knew what she would do.

She would look even harder for Greg. He would probably be preoccupied with his wife but even so she would look for him, urge him to return home and show them he had not done that awful thing.

Her heart sank lower. What if he shook her off, refused even to talk to her? What if he were filled with contempt for her because she had invited his intimacy on that last night?

She pulled the blankets right up under her chin. In that case it was even more important to get paid work. She needed to work, to build up some money of her own, not be here playing games with Madame, even if she was turning out to be a jolly companion. She would get enough money to send Richie back to Biddy and Cush.

What work would pay enough for that?

She frowned into the darkness, trying to remember the name of the man who said he had a hall, and that she should sing for him. He would pay her. That would do it.

It was only when she was finally dropping off to sleep again that she realised that all her thoughts had been for Greg, not Tommo. Greg'll help me find Tommo, she thought, forgetting

214

her earlier doubts as she drifted into a dream of castles and music and exotic acrobats, all of whom had Greg's fair handsome looks.

Chapter Twenty-one

Shona dodged to one side, just avoiding a second hairbrush thrown with vicious force.

This attack was the consequence of trying to tell Madame that she had decided to sing in Jonnie's hall.

'But you've just arrived here, songbird!' The Frenchwoman shrieked. 'You and Richie have just come to be the little brother and sister in my house!'

Shona ducked under a flying scent bottle. 'But I can still be here, Madame, if you want me. *Being* the little sister – it's not right to be paid for that. And the little room is payment enough. Richie, he's doing the driving, so that's all right. I'll work in the hall of that man Jonnie, sing and be paid, *and* help you here. I liked it when I worked at the pit. Earning me own pay was right for me, I told you that. Not mincing round a house – like you say.'

'That hall is a place of bad people. Bad women and bad men. They will eat you alive!'

Shona caught a round glass powderbowl. 'Sure that hall of Mr Jonnie's, it can't be worse than the pit where they bury you alive!' She caught at a floating scarf which Madame threw at her and folded it neatly. 'Tommo never wanted me to work. Never. He earned enough for us at the ironworks. But I wanted to work.'

Madame began to tear at her hair. 'You are *méchante*! I find you in a slum with not a coat to your name, sleeping on straw and I give you a sweet little bed. I find you in rags and I put you in fine suits of clothes. I find you alone and I 'elp you find your lover . . .'

'Isn't that all very fine of you, Madame? I'll work and I'll pay you for all that. I'll pay for the bed and the clothes. And to be sure I'll find what you call my lover. But I'll not be your . . . thing . . . your toy songbird.' She paused. 'If you let me and Richie stay, Madame,

I'll pay my way and Richie will do the horse. I'll be your friend, then. We can still be the brother and sister.'

The commotion stopped. Madame leaned over to pick up a brush and slowly started to pull it through her tangled hair. The fine clock with its lovebirds and cupids, its fruit and flowers, ticked away on the mantelpiece.

'Will you not wear the suits?' she said sorrowfully.

Shona started to smile. 'I tell you this, I like the suits, Madame. Perhaps I will sing in Mr Jonnie's hall in the suits.' She looked at the scrubbed clean, surprisingly innocent face before her. 'But only when I choose, Madame,' she said gently.

With a graceful gesture, the Frenchwoman lifted up her arms to pin up her hair. 'Well, I will make sure for you the hall is no danger. And if I am to be your big sister, songbird, you must call me Marianne.' She smiled a bright smile. 'And I will call you Shona. That is a lovely name, but strange. My name is of a saint, but Shona . . .'

'It means the woman from the sea, Madame, in my language.'

'Marianne!' admonished the Frenchwoman, standing up now, slipping her brown dress over her shift and clipping her pearls round her neck with her accustomed efficiency. 'Well, dear Shona, we must get underway if we are to see Jonnie this morning.' She caught a look in Shona's eye then smote her head with her hand. 'Oh, I tell you again! I make the orders.'

Shona laughed out loud. 'Yes, *Marianne*, to be sure we'll do that. It's kind of you to help.'

Jonnie Forster's hall lurked in a narrow backstreet behind the inn which he had bought and renamed Forster's Hotel. At ten o'clock in the morning there were only a few customers at the tables and the staff did not have quite enough to do.

Jonnie Forster was more dishevelled this morning. He had abandoned his mimicry of a gentleman's demeanour with his evening clothes. Still, he smiled and rubbed his hands together when he saw them. He was unsurprised when Madame introduced Shona as the songbird. 'I spotted it last evening, Madame.' He gave Shona a knowing wink and she stared coldly back at him.

He took Madame's elbow and led the way through two rooms

which smelled faintly of dust and old cigars under a shallow gallery, and into a large curtained room with tables packed closely in long rows.

Jonnie pulled a long curtain to one side. Bright spring light shot through one of the high narrow windows and danced on the dust fifteen feet up.

Shona looked around with interest. This was different from the public houses in New Morven. It was different from the Mitre.

In the centre of the wall on one of the long sides was a table with three chairs behind it, set out like a judge's bench. In the far corner was an extended dais which was not quite a stage.

Jonnie swept his hand around the room. 'This is my singing hall. Made from the alleyway between the hotel and the house behind. We put a roof over the space and we had our hall. That is, your Mr Hodgkiss's builders did, Madame! Built it in no time. Good rates, of course. I always get good rates from Mr Hodgkiss. He has control over his lads – not like some. And I've had a house full to the doors every night for two years.'

'I'd be standing here if I sang?' Shona jumped up on to the platform. Dust rose at her feet and she could smell old perfume.

'Yes. And I'll sit here.' He walked across and sat down behind the table in the centre chair.

'And you'll pay me every time I sing?'

'I'll pay you the first night. Then if they like you, I'll pay you every time.'

'Now sing, Shona. See how the sound works in here,' Marianne urged. 'Sing that last one, "The Wild Irish Rose".'

Jonnie banged a wooden hammer that lay on the table and as he shouted his voice echoed loudly in the long empty hall. 'And now, ladies and gentlemen, all the way from Ireland it is our great fortune to have the Wild Irish Rose herself – Miss Shona . . . *something*.'

'Farrell it is, sir.'

She started to sing, her voice echoing thinly in the big hall and fading into stillness on the second line.

Marianne bustled with clicking steps to the very back of the room and vanished. She reappeared on the shallow balcony.

'Now, Shona,' she called. 'Take a deep, deep breath and sing right to me. Lift your head, look at me and sing!'

Shona took a deep breath and started to sing. She kept her face on Marianne, who put her hands on her heart and cast them out in wide arcs again and again as Shona sang the sentimental lines. This made Shona's head go up and as it did the music began to fill the space, becoming not so much louder, as clearer and clearer by the second.

When the last echo had died down, Marianne clapped her hands and was still clapping as she ran down the hall. 'Bravo, songbird, for that is what you are. *Vraiment!* Bravo!'

Jonnie Forster put his cigar in his mouth to join the applause, then scraped back his chair and came and stood close to her. 'I knew it! Marcus knew it too. We have something here.' He put his hand on Shona's forearm.

She looked down at the hand and it was as though the power of her gaze forced it back to his side. He reddened. She smiled at him sweetly. ''Tis kind you are, Mr Forster. Marianne did tell me that you were a man to be trusted. Didn't I ask her particularly?'

In the trap on the way home Madame recalled approvingly the neat way Shona had dealt with Jonnie Forster. 'You will have that to do many times. The men, they think you are there, so you are theirs. Dolts! *Idiots!* But the women, they have to deal with the way men are. In Jonnie Forster's singing hall you'll see many women, songbird, who deal with it by putting a price on themselves. With some it is a wedding ring. More fool them! With some it is the guineas. Or the shillings. Or the pennies. A bad thing this, because you cannot sell the same *thing* time and time again. What 'appens? It becomes old and tattered. A nasty *thing*.'

'So what do you do, Marianne?' Shona wondered where the Frenchwoman put herself in this equation.

'The value, songbird, is in what you *do*. You sell what you *do*, not what you *are*. That is how the men deal with it. It is the proper way to be.'

'So what about . . .'

'Me? What I *do* is cartwheels and great acrobatics. What I do is juggling and a *leetle* bit of magic. What I do is teach people to play, to know themselves. Like in the theatre. A labourer is worthy of his hire, doesn't Monsieur Hodgkiss say so?' She took Shona's hand. 'And you can do the same. Sing your songs, make them laugh and cry. Make them feel the guilt, the great guilt. Make them feel the great joy. But don't give yourself, give your song. And make them pay! And soon, like me, you will have your own house. And, *mon Dieu*, you can have your own coalmine, and then go and dig in it to your heart's content!'

Shona roared with laughter at the thought. Marianne joined in and Richie called back for them to stop the screams or wouldn't they frighten the horse?

Shona stood in the narrow space behind the stage in her black broadcloth boy's suit with her hair tied back with a wide pink ribbon.

The hall was heaving with customers: mainly men, most of them working types, with a sprinkling of visibly more well-dressed men, what Jonnie Forster called 'toffs', a word Shona had never heard before.

At one or two tables working women sat with their husbands. At others were prostitutes in brighter and more gaudy dress. Madame had warned her of this, the unrefundable price some women paid for survival.

There was a constant ripple of movement. Men moved in and out of a side door to relieve themselves in the back lane outside. People at the tables laughed and talked, came and went, as the waiters squeezed between them to deliver great jugs of beer. The lamps set high around the room could barely pierce the pall of pipe-smoke that rose to the ceiling.

Shona stood and watched two turns before she climbed on the dais: the first was an acrobat who walked up and down red stepladders on his hands; the second was an opera singer in a faded black suit who changed key in surprising places. Each of these was awarded silent attention for just the first minute of their performance, but after that the noise washed back into the hall like the tide, swamping the silence, then drowning the sounds and the sights coming from the stage.

As Jonnie Forster announced Shona with a great rattle of his gavel, she looked up desperately at the balcony. There, standing dead centre among the dark shadowy figures, was Marianne

Villeneuve gleaming in overdecorated cream silk. She was standing with her hands placed dramatically over her heart.

A ripple of interest raked through the hall as Shona climbed on to the dais to sing. Into the capsule of silence produced by Jonnie's gavel and his romantic introduction of her as the Irish Rose, Shona threw her voice:

> 'There on a hillside
> My white rose is blooming . . .'

Her eyes fixed desperately on Madame, Shona waited for the restless sounds to well up again, the clashing and banging to start.

But the attentive silence persisted. The audience maintained concentration until the end of her song when there was a storm of applause, the banging of glasses on tables and the piercing shriek of whistles.

Shona looked around with delight. She smiled into the crowd and started to pick out individual faces. She could sell her songs to these people, to be sure she could. This was what she could *do*. What she would do.

She put up a hand. There was silence. 'This next song,' she called, 'is a lullaby which my mother used to sing when we were very small.'

Tommo pulled at the tall man's arm, wrenching him half round before he saw the red hair under the hat and realised the man wasn't Greg McNaughton.

'What's this, what d'you think you're doing?' The man shook Tommo off, throwing him into the running water of the gutter. A month before Tommo would have stood his ground, but the weeks of hunger and snatches of sleep in doorways had weakened him and he stayed where he lay. Hurrying workers walked round him with barely a glance as he closed his eyes and waited for his strength to return so he could haul himself to his feet.

In the past weeks Tommo had been circling around Shona in the teeming city centre, being missed by her as she accompanied Marianne in their fruitful searches for objects and items with which to fill Versay Villa. He had often been in the centre of the town in his search for Greg McNaughton, the murderer, he was sure, of

Maudie Martin. Some of the women in the city centre reminded him of Maudie – very slight things like their way of standing hand on hip or the tilt of their head. Some of these women responded to his interest, but soon cooled down when they realised he had no money.

In all these weeks he hadn't bothered about whether he ate or what he wore, relying on his great strength to keep him going. Sometimes, at night when he closed his eyes, he would see Maudie, eyes a-dance, her mouth slightly open, glossy with invitation. Sometimes he would see Shona standing before him, with her deep-set, strangely light eyes, her strong mouth and her hair springing from a centre parting in its own particular way. As the days went on he was not quite sure whether it was his lover or his sister he was seeing.

Each morning he would find his way through the bustling streets to the gateways of some great engineering works where Greg McNaughton might have found employment. Each night, at home time, he would wait at a different gateway.

On the thirtieth day he had finally found yet another works, Watson's, and leaned up against the wall outside. As always other men were there too, waiting in an agony of hopelessness for the offer of a day-rate job or a turn on the nightshift. In any loitering group Tommo might not be the tallest but he was often the broadest, and even after these weeks, the fittest.

He watched the workers as they left, faces showing white with weariness under the dirt. Their steps were lighter on the outward journey because home, whether it be room or cellar or dark tenement, was beckoning.

Tommo learned to scan closely those men with cleaner faces, lighter clothes and finer boots. He kept his eye out for the slight tall figure and fair good looks of the McNaughton fellow. One glance, just one in that face, and he would know whether it was the last Maudie had seen on this earth.

The men walked past, hats pulled down, coats complemented by heavy capes and squeaking boots. Short, tall; fat, thin; men with faces the colour of porridge or of plums – not one with the fine elongation of McNaughton.

Something drew him to wait a second night at Watson's gate; that was the night he found himself in the gutter. As he struggled to pick himself up a tall stout man caught him by the shoulder, his voice kindly. 'I've seen thee two nights at the gate here, Mister. Art thou waitin' for work, like? Thour't at wrong end of shift if thee is.'

'No, sir, it's not work I'm after. Isn't it a man I'm seeking, that I'll know when I see him? He's a tall fair feller . . .' As he spoke, the image of Maudie's face floated before him. Then Shona's. 'My sister . . .' He slid to the floor as a warm flood of air seemed to pluck him out of the cold. Then there was blackness.

As he fell into the void he heard a voice saying: 'I'd leave him alone, Mister, if I were you. Just another drunken bloody Irishman.'

He woke up on a couch in a high narrow room where a bright fire blazed in the hearth. A fine glass-fronted cabinet stood against one wall and there was a long strip of carpet on the polished wooden floor.

Tommo lifted his head and put his hand to his neck at the sudden shooting pain in it. 'Ouch!'

An old man was sitting in a chair opposite. 'Thou banged thy head on the wall, it seems,' he said. 'As thou came down in a dead faint.'

Even sitting down, the man was tall, with grizzled hair. He wore a collarless shirt and a great leather belt holding up breeches which were too big for him.

Tommo sat up straighter and rubbed his neck. 'Who're you?'

'My son brought thee. 'E's doin' a job for the Statistical Society at Watson's. Out now, seekin' vittles.'

Tommo looked round. This was a grander room than any he had ever been in, save the rent room at Marsteen House. He felt a shiver run down his back. You couldn't trust such as these. None of them.

The old man thrust a pot mug into his hands. 'Here, drink this. We don't take alcohol but I'm told brandy has wonderful reviving qualities.'

Tommo tasted the sweet brew, some hot concoction of milk, spices and alcohol. He gulped it down, feeling the heat forge through to his skin almost immediately and lie there, burning.

The door rattled and the younger stouter version of the old

man barged in, a tray in his hands. 'Ah, awake now, is he?' He pulled a small table up in front of Tommo and plonked down a plate of bread and cheese. 'Plain hunger, I think, rendered thee faint, but a hard crack on thy head rendered thee dead to the world.'

Tommo looked round. 'Where am I? Did I walk here?'

'Nay. I hired a cab and my dear father helped me lump thee upstairs.' The younger man bowed to the elder, who bowed back.

'It's grand lodging you've got here.' Tommo, realising his hunger, started to wolf down the bread and cheese.

The younger man smiled. 'Just rooms we rent from a distant cousin who is a banker here, and a far grander citizen than we.' He smiled at the older man, who smiled back. 'This is my father, Septimus Granter, and I am Matthew. We believe we should help our brothers.' He put out a hand.

'We have ventures in hand to alleviate the dreadful conditions of this city,' said the father, holding out his hand in turn.

'A bluddy venture! Is that what I am?' said Tommo bitterly, then stopped as he saw the hands drop and identical expressions of alarm and hurt crossing the two homely faces. He smiled then, and stood up shakily, brushing the crumbs off his jacket and then taking both men heartily by the hand. 'I'm an ungrateful donkey, so I am. Thank you for your kindness, gentlemen. Sure I hadn't realised I was so hungry but there are thousands in an equal state here. Why pick on me?'

''Tis true there's too much hunger in Manchester today, sir. Our little ventures are just a drop in a very wide ocean,' said the old man. 'It's a disgrace, with fortunes heaping on more wily heads by the minute.'

'We're agreed on that,' said Matthew Granter earnestly, bowing again to his father. He held on to Tommo's hand. 'And you are here because I tripped over you on my way out of Watson's. It seemed to me that God's hand was in evidence then. And you are?'

'My name is Farrell, Tommo Farrell. And I'm in this devilish city looking for a man . . .'

'Farrell? Something Irish about that. Now, where did I read that name?' Old Septimus Granter reached for the newspaper. 'Somebody called Farrell . . . Farrell . . .'

But Tommo heard no more as the void reached out to suck him in yet again.

Chapter Twenty-two

Shona enjoyed great success at Forster's singing hall. Paradoxically, the sweeter and more innocent her songs, the more the wild drinking, swearing and gambling crowd loved her.

The phenomenon was discussed at length in one of the town's newspapers, using pious overtones to express a similar relish.

A PLATFORM FOR INNOCENCE

Your correspondent has expressed before his concern regarding the threat to moral and physical safety engendered by the new singing halls which are springing up like rank toadstools overnight in various parts of Manchester and surrounding towns. The threat to life and limb, in the compression of so many people into such flimsy inflammable structures, has been much discussed in these pages. The debilitating moral atmosphere of such places, with drunkenness being a declared aim of all those attending, and further vices available on the premises, has been much deplored. Your correspondent, therefore, at the urging of a colleague, visited such a place last Saturday night. He was intrigued to find, in such a den (the Hall of Mr Forster), a performer whose appeal seemed to neutralise the venal atmosphere of that place. The savage breast was indeed soothed. Miss Shona Farrell, from Ireland, performing for the first half in male attire and the second half in a simple dress, sang songs of the hearth and home, of love and longing, with such sweetness, that for a moment the black torment of life in this great growing town was stilled. One must regret that in order to be thus entertained, one must run such a gauntlet of squalor and vice. We would call again for the creation of places of entertainment where drink, and therefore drunkenness, plays no part. Then such pure and healing performances as your correspondent witnessed on Thursday night would be available for all, even the most respectable people.

Marianne roared with laughter as she read this out to Shona. 'Hypocrites! They are all hypocrites. That man, the one who calls himself *Spectre*, is always in those places, always consuming the whisky he so much despises, always chaffing with the girls at the tables.'

Shona frowned at the report. 'He must have been there on Saturday.'

'And another thousand! Jonnie Forster is packing twice as many in now. You are bringing extra customers in. He says the house has never been so full.'

Marianne had been there that Saturday with Marcus Hodgkiss and several other gentlemen in tow, eager to show off her protégée. Shona had joined them for supper at Versay Villa afterwards and been inveigled into singing one song on the little stage in the drawing room.

Looking around as she sang, at the fleshy, prosperous faces, she had realised that, as an audience, she preferred the roaring crowd of Forster's.

As Marianne read the paper, they were sitting in her small upstairs sitting room, indulging in their new custom of a tray of coffee at ten-thirty before embarking on a trip to Market Street to find some new item which Marianne desperately needed. Today it was lace to trim a light green dress.

Richie drove them the short distance and waited for them in a sidestreet as they dawdled from shop to shop.

Coming out of the third hat shop, Shona bumped into Marcus Hodgkiss.

'Hello!' She smiled up at him.

He looked down at her with a blank unseeing gaze. His eye never lighted at all on Marianne, who was at Shona's side. The elderly woman standing next to Marcus glared at Shona and barged past, pulling her wide grey skirts to one side as though they would be tainted by Shona's plum-coloured velvet.

The incident was over in a second but as the two friends walked on, it left a strained atmosphere between them. Marianne marched to the trap and shouted for Richie, who was holding the head of Boru, whispering into his grey ear.

The Frenchwoman climbed in, straight-backed, and sat stiffly beside Shona as the big horse delicately picked his way through the heavy mid-day traffic up towards the railway station.

Shona respected the cue for silence, but in the house she followed Marianne up to the bedroom and sat on a small overstuffed chair. She watched as her new friend ripped off her soft doeskin gloves, as she took off her great feathered hat, jammed the amber pins viciously into its crown and threw it on to the bed. Then she started to prowl up and down the long room.

'Marianne, I'm sorry,' began Shona.

The other woman looked at her in surprise, as though she didn't realise she was there. 'Sorry? Is it you who should be sorry, songbird? *Non!* It is I. The thing I have with this man – here at Versay Villa, it is everything to him. He is my slave. Out there, in Market Street, it is nothing. I am the dirt beneath his feet. And you, songbird. And you,' she went on sorrowfully, 'I tell you to sell what you do, not what you are. So what am I? Can I be forever turning cartwheels like some demented windmill?'

Shona laughed at this, the joyful sound reaching out of the bedroom right through the house so that Tonetta, the younger Italian sister, cocked her head and listened a while before she went on with scrubbing the step.

Marianne scowled at the sound, then slowly a rueful smile softened her expression.

Shona stood up. 'Come here, Marianne, let's practise it. See who's better at sweeping their skirts away like the lovely Mrs Hodgkiss.' She put her head down to mimic double chins then minced around the room, bumped into Marianne and swept away her skirt with chilly hauteur. Then Marianne did the same to her. They went through this mime several times before, laughing, they collapsed on the bed.

Marianne reached out and took her hand. 'Never, songbird, have I had a friend who was a girl. Only the little brother and the lovers, all men. I think per'aps this is more precious.'

Shona sat up. 'I had a friend when I worked at the colliery. The one who died.'

Marianne sat up beside her. 'Well, she was a good teacher for friendship. Now shoo away, songbird. You have to rest so you can be all simpering, singing innocence tonight. And I have to consider what the naughty Marcus should do to make amends.'

Shona stood up. 'Oh, you're a bad'n, Marianne.'

She smiled up. 'Always, always, songbird, that's what I am.'

After the next Saturday's performance Jonnie Forster came into the dressing room he had had made for Shona by getting builders to dig into an old wall at the back of the inn.

She was in her street clothes, just about to put on her hat, and looked at him askance in the mirror.

'Another big impression you made there, Shona. More customers, more good-paying customers.' He pushed a small leather pouch into her hand. She didn't count it. It was part of Jonnie's expansive style to be generous. Her savings had long overflowed the blue jug into a large tin.

She smiled at him. 'If it suits you, Jonnie, it suits me.'

'There is something . . . There're some people here. Toffs. Desperate for you to sing to them privately.' He was eyeing her warily.

She pulled down her veil. 'Where? When?'

'Well, now. There's a visitor from abroad somewhere, a big toff, and he's off to foreign parts tomorrow.'

'Where?'

'It's a big place, just on the edge of town. About twenty minutes. They're good payers. Put five sovereigns in there just for you.' He nodded at the purse. 'And there'll be more. Twenty, the big toff said.'

'You'll come?'

He shrugged his shoulders.

'You come and I'll give you a quarter of whatever I get. And we go there with Richie, not with them.'

Richie whistled. 'Some place, this!'

Lights were blazing from every window, from great open double doors, and flooding down a broad flight of stone steps.

Shona and Jonnie climbed out of the trap.

'Richie,' she said, 'don't move from here. Stay right here.'

They left him arguing with a superior footman who wanted him to move the offending vehicle round to the stables.

A tall butler, who reminded her of the manager of the Gaunt Valley Hotel, showed them into the brightly lit drawing room whose long windows looked straight out on to the lawns. She resisted the instinct to peer out and see if Richie had won the battle to stay out front.

A table near the door was laid with food and drink. Beside it stood a young footman, eyes straight ahead, motionless as a stone lion. Four men were sitting at another table set out for cards.

Only one of them stood up as they entered the room. He was balding, had a wide fleshy mouth and was wearing an ill-cut jacket.

'Ah, our Irish Rose,' he drawled. 'Will you take a chair, Miss Farrell? Booker'll take your coat and hat.' He watched as she settled on a high upholstered chair then lifted his gaze to Jonnie. 'Forster, you've troubled to come! So kind of you to come out of your way. Would you care for some refreshment?'

Jonnie fingered his hat. 'Kind of you, Sir Robert.'

The man turned to the hovering butler. 'Booker, be so kind as to take . . . Mr . . . Forster to the kitchen for some refreshment.'

He watched the butler usher the hesitant Jonnie away, then turned to the men at the table. 'Come, gentlemen, won't you take a seat so we can enjoy to the full the talents of this wonderful young . . . lady.'

Shona watched the men as, with murmurs of laughter, they took seats by the fire. Her gaze was caught by an older man with thinning hair, either yellow or grey, it was hard to tell which.

'Now, my dear,' said Sir Robert, 'tell us about yourself. Are you long in England?'

'Two years it is now, sir.'

'Which part of Ireland do you come from, child?' The pale-haired man by the fire spoke and her heart jumped at the familiar tone to the voice. She raised her eyes and those she met watched her keenly, though without recognition.

'Far to the west, sir,' she said steadily. 'Sure, you wouldn't know it.'

The other men laughed at this. Sir Robert smiled a foxy smile. 'His Lordship knows Ireland very well . . . owns great tracts of it, to be true, as well as much of Lancashire. He's off across there tomorrow to deal with some unruly fellows.'

She glared at him. 'He'll not know my part, my place in Ireland. It is invisible to him.' She paused deliberately. 'Sir.'

'And what do you think of the traitors and assassins who still run wild as animals in Ireland in these days?'

'There are assassins of every colour in my country, sir. My own brother was victim of one such.'

There was a still silence in the room. Then Sir Robert reached into his pocket and trickled ten sovereigns on to the table beside her. 'Your songs, miss. We will have your songs,' he said in a chilly voice.

She repeated the programme that had gained her such acclaim earlier that evening in Forster's hall. Here too there was appreciative applause at each offering. After her last song she curtsied and looked around. 'That is my programme, gentlemen.'

Sir Robert, still clapping, stood up, came across and put an arm around her, which she shook off. He reached into his pocket and trickled five more sovereigns on to the pile beside her.

'Well, gentlemen, that is my offering for this fine Irish maiden. Forton!' He lifted his gaze to the wooden-faced footman by the buffet table. 'You may gather the gentlemen's bids.'

Obediently the footman took a silver tray around and brought back the heap of money.

'Now, Forton, tuck it all safely into the young lady's bag.'

He did this, his eyes on Shona's face. As he did so he was transformed from wooden servant to a boy, not much older than Richie. She heard him mutter one fierce word: 'Window!'

She grasped the edge of the chair.

The host took her hand and gently pulled her to her feet. 'Now, my dear young lady, which of these fine gentlemen will you choose?'

Mesmerised, she looked round the faces which were now suffused with veiled eagerness.

Clutching her bag she walked over to the yellow-haired man by the fire. 'I choose Lord Marsteen,' she said. 'No assassin, but the master of assassins.'

He stood up before her, smiling, and she spat into his narrow, high-nosed face. He laughed and grasped at her. She twisted away from him. The others chuckled, entertained by the struggle before them. They were not near enough to stop her as she landed an almighty kick on Marsteen's upper leg, twisted away out of his narrow grasping hand, then raced to the long window. It was, as Forton had hinted, open.

She clambered through, yelling at the top of her voice, 'Richie! Richie!' as she dropped lightly on to the grass outside.

Boru came careering across the shaven grass, dragging the trap behind him, Richie clinging on for dear life. He had barely halted the great horse, for her to climb in, before he was off again towards the great gates.

The tumult behind them faded away very quickly and they were soon in the ill-lit outskirts of Manchester. Richie pulled Boru back to a sharp trot, adjusted the reins in his hands and glanced at his sister. 'So where's old Forster?'

Shona lay back against the cushions, still gasping for breath. 'In the kitchens back there, feeding for tomorrow, I should think.'

'So why the chase? Was it the silver or the crystal you stole?'

'No, Richie, they were after stealing off me.'

'And they didn't?'

'They didn't.' She paused. 'D'you know who it was with them back there, Richie? The great visitor from abroad? Lord Marsteen! He was the one going to do the stealing.'

Richie directed a gob of spit neatly over Boru's back and into the swimming gutter. 'And what was it you did to him?'

'I spat at him. And gave him such a kick! I only wish I'd had my pit boots on.'

'You're a good'n, Shona.'

She smiled up at him with great fondness. 'Richie, I think it's time you went home. Back to New Morven. Back to Biddy.'

'Leave you here in this place, Shona? I could never do that.'

'Sure I can take care of myself now. Haven't I shown it?' She lifted her bag to feel the weight of the coins. 'Richie, how would you like to buy a share in Gil Tait's stables? Be equal partners with him?'

Richie walked past the house in Stables Street on his way to see Gil Tait. He peered in at the window and two ginger-haired children leapt up to face him, putting their fingers in their ears and waggling them. He put out his tongue at them and went on his way.

He had always liked that house right from when he first arrived, carried on the back of the man from Clare. He recalled tumbling down from that broad back into the arms of Shona, whom he had remembered more by the bushiness of her black hair than by anything else. He recalled the feel of Tommo's large hand on his head, pushing the lank hair away from his face.

Memories of the times before that, the awful days, were fading now. Sometimes he couldn't recall them at all. He knew about them as though someone else had told him. As though it was someone else who had lived through it all. It no longer hurt like a pressed bruise to think of it.

Gil Tait was busy sweeping out the stable yard when Richie entered the wide gates.

He stood in a patch of June sunlight and leaned his chin on the broom handle. 'By Jesus, if it's not the young feller,' he cackled, grimacing and winking in the familiar way. 'And aren't you the big feller now? Must've grown six inches. Look fifteen years if a day. Do they feed you on carrots in that town now?'

'Big dinners, Gil. It was big dinners.' Richie looked around. 'Sure this place hasn't changed a bit.'

'Well, truth is I miss yer *impident* face. I've had other lads here but can I stand'm? No good with the horses. Allus makin' faces behind me back and thinkin' I'll not see. So I boot 'em out and then there's more work for me. Hardly ever in Showy's now. Workin' here by lamplight.'

'Plenty o' work?'

'Too much if you want to know, with all these new people comin' in. Clerks and draughtsmen as well as pitmen and ironworkers. All wantin' a ride here or there, or a horse to make on to their neighbours they're bigger than what they are. Here, where you goin'?' He scurried after Richie who was working his way through the stables, rummaging in corners, peering through doors. 'What is it? What is it you want?'

Richie jumped up to sit on a wooden divider and grinned down at him. 'See it's like this, Gil. Here you have four empty stalls full of the grandfathers of spiders, not occupied for twelve month. How'd it be if I bought me two nice cobs and maybe a nice little trap, and you and me could share a little bit of that extra business that's comin' your way?'

Gil scowled at him. 'Ye're tellin' me yer want to rent them stalls?'

Richie jumped down. 'No. Look!' He dragged Gil to the big doors which had 'Tait Livery' painted on them in green and gold. 'What if it were "Tait and Farrell"?'

'Partners?' Gil Tait laughed merrily. 'Doesn't a man need a deal of money to become another man's partner?'

'Look here, Gil.' Richie opened his coat and pulled open the top of his capacious inside pocket, which was full of twinkling gold sovereigns.

'Is it robbing banks you've been, across in Manchester?'

Richie shook his head seriously. 'Indeed no, Gil. All honest come by, you can be sure. I saved some. Shona give me the rest. She's singing at concerts across there. Feller pays her a deal o' money.'

Gil peered back into his stable and looked down into the boy's eager face. 'If the money's right, it's a bargain. But no name on the door for twelve month.'

He spat in his palm and held it out. Richie spat in his and they shook heartily.

Richie looked around. 'Is Cush here?'

'He's down the field, by Bolan Common, son. Been out loose for two weeks now.'

'Can I borrow the bay, then? I need to see my auntie down in Shotwell, an' I'll collect Cush as I go.'

'Will ye be staying down there in Shotwell?'

'Nah. New Morven's my place. Thought I'd bed down here in the loft. Seein' I've an interest now.'

Gil grinned and laughed and shook hands again before he set about the yard with his broom, this time whistling a jig.

When Richie arrived at Garth End Cottage Biddy and Margaret were sitting on chairs in the sunshine, sewing opposite ends of a long sheet. Beside them, on a patch of rough grass, Becky and Lauretta were playing with a pale grey rabbit.

Lauretta spotted him first. 'Richie! Here's Richie with a big horse and the little one.' She flew towards him. Becky stood back, clutching the rabbit to her chest. The two women put down their sewing and stood up.

Richie jumped down, put Lauretta on Cush's back and led the two horses down the path.

'Richie, I'd hardly have known you,' said Biddy. 'Haven't you grown a foot in each direction? You look more like Tommo than himself.' She hugged him to her until he had to draw away.

'I didn't come all the way home, Biddy, to get suffocated,' he laughed. 'Good afternoon to you, Mrs McNaughton.' He took off his cap.

She smiled and shook his hand, trying not to look down the street to see if Greg were following.

Richie shook his head. 'We still haven't found Greg or Tommo, but Shona never gives it up. Always looking she is. Every single day.' He looked round. 'Your letter said the constable had been about those two and the mur—'

'No, no,' she interrupted hurriedly. 'The constable realises all that was evil rumour. Everything's quietened down now.'

Becky was staring up at Richie, tears rolling down her face into her tight curls.

He dropped the halter and picked her up, rabbit and all. 'And would the rabbit like a ride on the big horse?' He put the child up on the broad back of the bay and stood there with her until the tears stopped and the hand grasping the rabbit's fur stopped trembling. 'And what name has the rabbit?'

'Her name is Maudie.'

He shot a glance at Biddy, who shrugged. 'We called it Fluff, but she insists on that name.'

'Richie! I fall off!' said Lauretta, in reality safely ensconced on Cush, whose back was as broad as a church bench.

Margaret smiled from one to the other. 'Let's have everybody off the horses and we'll go and have some of Thoria's scones. And then Richie can tell us all about Shona and Manchester.'

After an hour at Garth End, being treated like the returned prodigal, Richie made his way back to New Morven across the fields. Not far from the road, he heard squealing and whimpering noises in a thicket. He pushed his way through to investigate and found a dog, a spaniel bitch, tethered to a low bush. She was on her side and blood was still running from knife cuts recently inflicted. He counted eighteen of them.

The dog whimpered, her eyes almost blind with pain, reacting to his presence. He looked around desperately, then took the saddle off the bay and used its blanket to smother the dog in a few seconds, with an efficiency that frightened him.

When he rode on, after untethering the body and pulling it deeper into the thicket under leaves, he was so angry that tears stood in his eyes.

Half a mile further on, on the road into New Morven, he came upon Terry Kennedy with the long-haired man who was Greg's brother. They were giggling and chattering and there was a silver flask in Stuart's hand.

Terry squinted up at him. 'Well, if it isn't the Farrell brat come up in the world. Ridin' one horse and pullin' another.'

'Probably stolen them,' said Stuart. 'Can't see a horse without stealing it, the Irish.'

And the two men roared with laughter that was too high and loud to be sane.

Richie knew they had done it. He wanted to kill them both the way they had killed the dog, with a knife. But he squeezed his knees, urging the bay to hurry away from their laughter, towards the kindness and refuge of Gil Tait and his stable.

As he rode along, tears came to his eyes for the second time. This time it was at the unbidden thought of the little girl who called her pet rabbit after her mother, Maudie.

Chapter Twenty-three

To Shona's surprise the only repercussion from her assault on Lord Marsteen was a long discussion with Jonnie Forster about the state of his feet, after walking back into Manchester at the dead of night. Even then, his sense of injury was against his host rather than her.

He had brought her a bunch of white roses before the performance.

'*Toffs!*' he said. 'You can never trust'm. They think we're a different breed, like some kind of dog or racehorse. Give me a gambler or a builder any day. Gets his money by honest cheatin' and you know where you are with him. And he knows his pa's no better than yours nor anyone's.'

She stroked the petals of the white flowers, still slightly damp to the touch.

He looked at her with faint anxiety. 'You are all right, songbird, ain't yer? That servant feller Forton told me you gave some old goat an almighty kick and jumped out of the window like a steeplechaser. He'd never seen anything move so fast.' He paused. 'He's seen it when the girl didn't get away too.'

She laughed into his face. 'Feeling guilty, are we, Jonnie?'

'Well, to tell the truth, yes.'

'It's over. Just leave it. But that's the last private party I do. The very last.' She pointed her hairbrush accusingly at him.

He backed out of the tiny room. 'Yes. Yes, right, Shona. You just get yourself ready for out there. It's a full house.'

Making his way through the crowded hall, he relished his relief. What a mistake it would have been to kill off the goose which was busy laying all these golden eggs.

He stood at the back and watched the turmoil of customers and waiters thronging the hall. He had to stand to one side to let two more customers squeeze in at the back. They were an unmatched pair: a tall stout young man in a heavy, good quality suit of old-fashioned cut, and a shorter broader man in working clothes, a shock of black hair under his round cap.

The hall stilled as the chairman, deputising for Jonnie, called for silence for the Irish Rose. Then there she was, on the stage in her suit of boy's clothes, bowing to massive applause.

Immediately, the pair beside him started to talk excitedly. He hushed them, telling them sternly it was his hall and he allowed no noise during Miss Farrell's performance.

At the end of her cycle of songs of lost loves and lost homes, of travel and longing, Shona left the platform to a storm of applause and her place was taken by an indifferent fiddler.

In the ensuing hubbub the taller man turned to Jonnie. 'Would it be possible, sir, for my friend and I to see the young lady?'

Jonnie rubbed his chin. 'And who might you be? I must tell you I allow no private performances.'

'I am Matthew Granter, from Manchester. And this is Tommo Farrell, an acquaintance of mine.'

'Farrell?' Jonnie looked closer at the shorter man.

Tommo took off his cap. 'Your singer is my sister, sir.'

'Dost thou see why we wish to meet the young lady?' asked Matthew.

Another storm of applause heralded the reappearance of Shona, this time wearing a green silk dress with a high neck and a narrow white collar.

Jonnie could feel the restlessness of the pair beside him as the performance proceeded, even though they applauded as vigor-ously as anyone. At last the singing, including two encores, was over. The hall returned to its normal noisy, drunken anarchy.

The three men threaded their way through to the front, aiming for the narrow passageway beside the stage. Matthew Granter looked around him with interest; Tommo was impatient at each small delay, each person blocking their tortuous route.

Jonnie bade them stay at the end of the narrow corridor and knocked on Shona's door. He put his head round. 'I've a man here says he's a friend of yours, Shona.'

Greg instantly in her mind, she jumped up in a turmoil of pleasure. So, instead of her finding him, he had found her!

She raced down the corridor and faltered as she saw the tall bulk of Matthew Granter. Then she spotted Tommo in the deep shadow of a rotting wooden buttress which had once stood on the outside of the old inn.

'Tommo!' She flung herself into his arms. Clasped together, they rocked to and fro and part of the ache that had remained inside her in these last months started to melt.

He pulled away. 'We saw you sing, Shona. Our father sang those songs. Hadn't I forgotten every one of them?'

'"The Wild Irish Rose" – Pat Daley wrote that one, remember?'

'Thou'rt a sweet singer,' put in Matthew enthusiastically.

She looked up at the portly young man, a faint frown on her face.

Tommo took her arm. 'This is Matt Granter, Shona, a Manchester man. Sure he's all right, despite being a Protestant and a man given to "ventures". It's him who found that you were here. I couldn't believe it. Thought you safe back in New Morven.'

She looked from one to the other.

'To be accurate, Miss Shona, it were my dear father who discovered the presence of another Farrell in Manchester, and being concerned for the health of our new friend, Mr Tommo here, we thought a sister might be of help.'

She looked at Tommo. 'You were ill?'

'Three weeks in a fever in my father's house, Miss Shona. But as bright and strong as ever now, I think.'

'They said I couldn't come 'til I was proper on my feet. Sure you never saw better nurses than those two.'

Matthew turned to Jonnie. 'Wouldst show me thy hall, sir? There was an interesting article in the *Guardian* suggesting new ways of improving these places of entertainment.'

They went off together, an odd pair in the smoky darkness of the corridor.

Shona and Tommo sat knee to knee in her small cubbyhole, just staring at each other for a few minutes.

Then she remembered his mission. 'Did you find Greg McNaughton?' She feared his answer even as she spoke.

'Nah. Didn't I stand outside every engineering works in Manchester? Neither sight nor sound of him, the murderer!'

Shona sighed with relief. 'I'm sorry about all that, Tommo. That Maudie Martin, she . . . she seemed a pretty, jolly girl.'

He glanced at her sharply. 'How would you know? You only saw her wrecked, spoiled by that maniac.'

She frowned. 'No, I did see her . . .' She blushed. 'Oh, I remember! Me and Richie saw the pair of you in a hut by the old wood.'

Now Tommo was red. 'You saw us doing . . . ?' Then he smiled broadly. He could see Maudie now, and her glorious body, teasing him and leaping about in that little hut. In all these weeks he had been seeing only the grey face of death and her bloody broken body. 'You're right, Shona, she was a jolly girl.'

She pursed her lips. 'That shed, Tommo! I'm thinking Terry Kennedy had been peeping too. He called Maudie foul names. He was horrible to us . . .' A supposition was forming in her mind as she spoke.

'Maudie didn't like him,' said Tommo slowly.

'And Greg? What reason would Greg McNaughton have to kill her, Tommo?' said Shona gently.

'Well, they said in the village it was him . . .'

'Tales set round by Kennedy, you can be sure. A bad man, that.' Now she was convincing herself.

He jumped up. 'Kennedy! That's it! Maudie loathed him and wouldn't let him across her step.'

Shona put a hand on his arm and looked up at him. 'He's bad though, Tommo.'

'Nothing to me. Easy enough to squeeze it out of him.'

She clasped his arm tighter. 'Come home with me and meet my friend, Madame Villeneuve, Tommo. She started all this for me. Then tomorrow you can get a train most of the way home and set the constable after Terry Kennedy, if you really think he's the one.'

They said their goodbyes to Jonnie and Matthew Granter, who were still deep in conversation at the back of the hall, then hired a cab at the rank and rode home.

The cabby appraised the unlikely pairing, of this workman and the very smart woman in the velvet cloak, and shook his head. He snapped the reins to move his horse along, pondering on the sights you were likely to see on the streets of Manchester nowadays. As he observed to his missis when he got home at two o'clock the next morning, nothing surprised you in the end.

Shona put Tommo to bed in the room recently vacated by Richie. The next morning she tapped on the door of Marianne's sitting room and asked if she might bring someone to join them for coffee.

Her friend touched her hair and sat up straighter. 'Have you a friend here? But of course.'

Shona pulled Tommo in behind her. 'This is my brother, Tommo. He came to Forster's Hall and found me. This is Madame Marianne Villeneuve, Tommo.'

Marianne held out her hand gracefully and he shook it in a hearty, bonecrushing grip.

'So you are the big brother! Shona, she has looked every day for you. Every afternoon, month in, month out, for you and the other. Greg, is it?'

Tommo shot a glance at Shona who laughed.

'Didn't I have to stop you chasing him and murdering him for something he didn't do? Then you'd be hung and I'd have the pair of you on my conscience.'

Marianne poured the coffee, eyeing Tommo up and down. 'He is beautiful, Shona. Just like my *pauvre* Jean.'

Tommo took the fine cup from her, his cheeks bright red. 'Thank you, Ma'am,' he mumbled.

Shona grinned at him. 'Madame's first sweetheart was killed at the barricades in 1848. A sad thing. He was a blacksmith, worked with iron too.'

Tommo looked round the opulent, overfilled room and sat back in silence. This was too hard to take in. Too hard by far.

'Tommo's going home,' Shona told their hostess. 'He's things to see to.'

'Oh, Shona, always sending the brothers home. Next it will be you and I will be all alone again.'

But Marianne was smiling, fingering an emerald necklace which was beautifully offset by a dress of the finest pale brown cashmere. Marcus Hodgkiss had paid dearly for his public slight of her.

Shona went with Tommo to the station, loath to lose him now but somehow lighter in heart than she had been since she had first come to Manchester. They walked along together and inspected the engine, joining an admiring crowd of people who were watching it build up steam.

'Seems to me you've changed, Shona, livin' here,' Tommo said awkwardly.

'And is that a bad thing?' she said fiercely. 'Changing?'

'Indeed it isn't!' He laughed and leaned down and kissed her on the cheek. 'I'm pleased to be going back, though. I think you're right – the answer's there. I'll get him. You can be sure I'll get him.'

'Go to the constable!' said Shona. 'And mind yourself now!'

He looked round at the station, and further away to the town. 'And you mind yourself. This is a hard place.' He laughed. 'But then, seeing as you've grown up so much, you'll be all right to be sure.'

Coming out of the station, Shona turned round a corner of a building and caught a glimpse of a fair head high above the crowd around him, making steady progress down the street. It was too much to think both could be returned to her in the same week.

'Greg!' Her desperate shout was lost in the noise of the traffic and the bustling crowds. She pushed and pulled her way through what seemed like a wall of people, to reach the spot where she had seen him. He was no longer there.

It had been Greg, she was certain of it. He could have gone in any one of three directions. She paced each of the streets several times but there was no sign of him. Her air of desperation and her patrolling up and down drew glances in her direction which she ignored. She had been there two hours before she abandoned her search and trailed wearily home, near to tears.

The house was empty except for the Italian girls whom she could hear talking in the kitchen. On the silver tray in the hall was a note in Marianne's flourishing hand.

Songbird,
    Marcus has come to take me to ride in the country. We will be at Forster's tonight to see you sing and have supper here afterwards.
    Affectionately,
    Marianne

Her friend had put Marcus's insult of the other week behind her.

A bounty having been paid for it, it was as though it had never happened. There was something unpleasantly calculating about it all, Shona felt, looking round the pretty hall – also paid for at a price. She sighed. She had received kindnesses from Marianne and almost in spite of herself she liked her. But she must be wary. Was the little sister role she found herself playing the price she must pay for those kindnesses?

She was dead tired, but there was only time to wash and change and send Anna to find a cab to take her to Forster's.

That night as she sang in the crowded hall she examined the audience's faces anxiously one by one, seeking one in particular. In the middle of the third song the words came out more and more slowly and finally stopped. Her mind was blank.

There was an uneasy rustling in the hall. Jonnie, from his place at the chairman's bench, was glaring at her.

Then a voice from the middle shouted, 'Come on, get on with it!' The shout was taken up and some people started to bang on the tables with fists and glasses. Individual voices became a multiple roar.

Jonnie stood up and started to walk towards her. A fight started in one corner and another in the middle of the hall. A large man upturned a table at the back, upsetting a lamp. Immediately large tongues of flame leapt up the dusty curtains into the dark roof-space. Suddenly the whole of one side of the room was on fire and Forster's Hall, used to noise, was now filled with shouts and screams of terror.

Still Shona stood rooted to the spot.

Finally Jonnie reached her and grabbed her by the shoulders, heaving her off the platform. He pushed her towards the narrow corridor. 'Your dressing room!' he said. 'The door!'

Then he turned back to see what he could do about the inferno which had once been his singing hall.

Shona stumbled to her cubbyhole, grabbed her coat and hat and let herself out by the little door. She stood in the narrow alley and breathed hard. As the clean air rushed into her lungs common sense returned to her.

Fastening the coat round her tightly, she dashed back into the hall. The whole of the far end was a sheet of flame. She looked upwards. The fragile balcony, where Marianne should have been, had already crashed down and there was a great gaping hole in the roof. Jonnie was nowhere to be seen.

She grabbed the man nearest to her. 'Another way out,' she shouted. 'There's another way out!'

She showed him the way, then between them they grabbed people and pushed them through the little room to the outside alley. In ten minutes it was too hot to return.

Now the alleyway was full of crying, moaning people. Walking round two streets, Shona found her way to the front of the hall where more moaning people thronged. Jonnie was there, his face black, his hands burnt.

'Marianne?' she shouted above the noise. 'Was she there?'

He shook his head. 'No, thank God. Poor devils on that balcony had no chance.'

The house was in darkness when Shona returned. She went into the kitchen, and ladling still-warm water from the boiler into the sink, stripped to the waist and washed off the soot and dirt with kitchen soap.

She was at the bottom of the stairs when Marianne dashed in, followed by Marcus. Marianne drew Shona to her and hugged her until she could hardly breathe.

'We took the coach to get you at Forster's and the place had vanished! It was gone! The singing hall, the hotel, everything! The doctors and the firetenders were there, but all it was was a black hole in the street. And I thought you had gone, songbird. I thought I had lost my little sister!' Her face blotched with tears. 'But then we found dear Jonnie, and he told us you were safe.'

'Marianne, it was my fault! I forgot the words and the place was in uproar and a lamp was overturned and . . .'

Marianne's own tears flowed freely. 'Nonsense, songbird! The place is a deathtrap, always has been. Oh, that I should lose you!'

Marcus coughed and patted Marianne's shoulder. She smiled tearfully at him over Shona's head. 'And we had had such a day. Do you know, dear Marcus showed me the sweetest little house in a wood which he wants me to have.' She looked round the hall. 'But I don't know that I could do without dear Versay Villa!' She smiled up again at him bravely through her tears, well aware that some scheme was afoot. Probably to uproot her from town and bury her in the country. Well, he'd have to think twice about that!

'I thought you were on the balcony,' said Shona, trying to free her waist from her friend's clasp. 'That went first.'

'*Mon Dieu!*' Marianne crossed herself, a thing Shona had never seen before. 'Saved by the little house in the country. It has served its purpose, don't you think, dear Marcus?' She put her hand to her head. 'Oh, I forget! A letter for you from the postman as I went out.'

She lifted her reticule daintily, bringing out a small envelope covered with vaguely familiar handwriting.

Shona clasped it and said quite calmly, 'Well, Marianne, I'll go up now if you don't need me? I'm so tired after all this business.'

'And so brave! Jonnie told us you saved many lives. Yes, yes, go to bed, my dear one.' She raised bright watchful eyes to Marcus. 'I do so need a wash after my dusty journey. Marcus will help me, I think.'

He raised her hand to his lips, a gesture of pure defeat. 'With pleasure, my dear.'

They were oblivious of Shona as she plodded on up to her room on the third floor.

Hurriedly she turned up the lamp and peered at the letter. It was in Margaret McNaughton's writing. Richie had arrived safely and it was a joy for Biddy to see him, apparently. He was now in some kind of partnership with Gil Tait and working at the stables full-time. The girls were well. Mr McNaughton was well too although missing Gregor sorely in the business.

And finally may I ask you a favour, Miss Farrell? My husband has been trying for some weeks to locate Gregor in Manchester. Now, finally, he has an address from an acquaintance. Would you kindly seek him there and assure him of our continued good feeling, and tell him that Lauretta is well?

Underneath, neatly written, was a town centre address for the Chambers Commercial Hotel.

Shona put the paper to her face and for the first time in that long hard day, for the first time in her long hard stay in Manchester, she started to cry. The flood of tears made the ink run and later that night, when she had washed her face again and put on her nightdress, the letter was almost unreadable. The only thing that stood out was the address of the Chambers Commercial Hotel, Chadwell Street, Manchester.

Chapter Twenty-four

Tonetta Cellini jumped as Shona appeared in the kitchen at seven o'clock the next morning, dressed to go out.

'Ho, Miss Shona, an early bird this morning? You wanting tea? Bread?'

'I've a very early errand this morning.' She looked round. 'Where's Anna?'

Tonetta's sallow, delicate face registered subdued panic.

'Is she ill, Tonetta?'

'No. Miss Shona. She is out at our father's home and will be here soon. Very soon.'

Shona frowned at the fear in the other girl's face. In the previous months she had become used to acting as go-between between the two girls and Marianne who, bored with playing the chatelaine, was now running the house on a very distant rein.

Tonetta grasped her arm. 'She comes soon, Miss Shona. Our Papa is ill. The beautiful tiling he had to do was finished and so his job went. Our house went too. Now he's in a cellar – a horrible-smelling place – and he has a fever.'

Shona thought of her own early lodging in the stews of Manchester, under the stairwell. 'Is all your family there, Tonetta?'

'No. Papa and Pietro only. Mamma died before we came from Italy, in the troubles there.'

With swift abstraction Tonetta was making a pot of tea and a plate of bread and butter and placing them at the corner of the table on a white napkin.

'Is Pietro any good with horses, Tonetta?' Marianne had told her only yesterday to sort out the problem of a lad for the horses and get Boru back out of livery.

Hope flared a second in Tonetta's eyes, then died. 'Pietro knows nothing of horses,' she said sadly. 'We are too poor since we are in

England for the horse. Now Papa, he tells so many tales about taking care of his father's horses. Even now he knows the names.'

Shona, suddenly hungry, sat down and set about breakfast with a will. She spoke with her mouth full. 'When Anna gets here, Tonetta, send her back for Papa and Pietro. They can stay in that tackroom over the stable. There's a stove in there. You can warm it up. Then Papa can get better and then show Pietro what to do with the horse.'

Her own brighter times had started with a room over a stable. Now here she was in a fine house wearing fine clothes with a tin box full of sovereigns upstairs and a letter in her pocket with Greg McNaughton's address on it. Things were brightening up.

'Madame?' said Tonetta uncertainly.

'I'll explain to her. I'll leave a note as I'll be out most of the morning.'

Even at seven o'clock the narrow streets were thronged with people of every degree of life, setting about their day in the shops, offices, banks and business premises that dominated the centre of this great town. The only group absent were workers from the humming factories and mills, who had been at their benches and looms more than an hour already.

Shona made her way through the blackened streets, looking down the narrow alleyways and raising her eyes above street level to the steep pitched roofs which gave way here and there to the high grim palaces of the great warehouses and mills.

The letter in her pocket made her think of riding through the green fields to Killock Castle to meet Greg that first time. New Morven might be a slum. The countryside might be littered with pitheads and spoilheaps. But at least up there you could see green round every corner, and trees and hedgerows showing the change of every season.

In this town the variation was between new brick and blackened older brick; new stone and blackened older stone; tall buildings and low buildings. No trees. No stretches of grass anywhere. Shona felt hungry for a stretch of green.

She frowned. There had of course been the shaved lawns of the suburban mansion of Lord Marsteen's friend. She shuddered. But that did not count. It couldn't count. Never.

She loitered by a cab rank at the end of Chadwell Street, realising suddenly she did not know what she should do. She was afraid of

Greg's reaction. Should she burst in on him? Would the woman be there? In all these months she had thought only of finding him, not what she should do when that happened.

The Chambers Commercial Hotel was a neat narrow building with a dark red door and three shallow steps leading up to it.

She drew breath sharply as Greg came down the steps, carrying some kind of small case. He looked even taller. His face was thinner. She put her hand towards him, framed her mouth to shout, but no sound came out. He set off, walking quickly down the crowded street, and all she could do was follow him at a distance. Twice she could have called him but each time something stopped her. She shadowed him over half a mile like this, more cautious as the crowds thinned out. But he was striding on, oblivious to anything round him.

He stopped and turned in through the gate of a double-fronted house with a front garden filled with glossy evergreens. He rang the bell and was let in by a stout, aproned maid.

Shona hung about outside the house for half an hour but Greg failed to reappear so she walked past the house and noted the brass plaque which read: Dr A. Montague. She walked down to the end of the street and checked its name: Charleston Street.

Then, after waiting ten more minutes, it started raining, first in a drizzle then in torrents. As Shona grew wetter and wetter, her hopes of seeing Greg and talking to him faded. Wanting to get back on to familiar territory she set off to return in what she thought was the direction of Versay Villa. At the third junction she realised she was lost. She looked up above the houses, noted the denser, darker part of the town which was the centre and set off again.

In forty minutes she found herself in familiar Peter Street in front of St Peter's Church. She sighed with relief. She had traversed streets she did not recognise and walked down alleyways where barefoot children had thrown pebbles at her skirt and men, morning-drunk, had shouted after her. It was good to be back on more familiar territory.

She looked up at the church, and, unbidden, Father O'Reilly came to mind. It was many months since she had been to confession or even inside a church.

She went inside, crossed herself and kneeled inside a pew at the back. Looking down the shaded interior of the church towards the altar and the cross, she said a Hail Mary and an Our Father and waited in vain for the feeling inside which would tell her what to say next.

A bustling clerical figure came towards her out of the distant shadows and she fled.

Almost without her realising it her feet led her towards Forster's Hotel.

Jonnie Forster was standing in the drizzle looking at the jagged blackened ruins which had been his hotel and hall. He stared with great concentration as though, just by looking, he could recreate what had for him been his masterpiece. Beside him was a tall burly figure which Shona recognised as that of Tommo's rescuer, Matthew Granter.

He was talking urgently to Jonnie, gesticulating to lend his words added emphasis. The two men turned at Shona's approach.

'Shona!' said Jonnie, almost in tears. 'Look at it! Ashes and stinking cinders. All my hopes and all my fortune.'

Matthew removed his hat and bowed. 'Good morning, Miss Farrell. I'm relieved to see thee fit and well. My dear father read me the dreadful news in the paper, and bade me return to see neither thou or thy brother were injured. Now Mr Forster here tells me that thou hast saved many lives by your action last night.'

She looked at Jonnie. 'Some people died?'

He shook his head. 'Eleven. And fifteen injured at the hospital, some crushed by others in the rush to the door. The papers are full of it.' He laughed mirthlessly. 'Some are saying it was an Irish plot.'

'Thou'rt lucky it were not more deaths, more tragedy,' said Matthew. 'I was telling Mr Forster he should build a new hall, good and sturdy, not thrown up by one of these gimcrack builders. And dedicate it to entertainment only. No hotel. No drinking. No gambling.'

Jonnie groaned.

'I tell thee there would be many patrons. This town is teeming with such-minded people. Working men and their wives and their families would come to see good entertainment of the lighter kind. Thou couldst serve food and light cordials.'

'Sounds all right to me,' said Shona. 'It sounds good.'

Matthew bowed gratefully in her direction. 'There! The entertainer *par excellence* gives her judgement.'

Jonnie lifted his head a little. 'But all my money is gone with this.'

Matthew laughed. 'Today in Manchester, my dear Mr Forster, for the right cause money is no problem at all. My dear papa has a banker for a brother, and then there are the Friends.'

'Where would I build it?'

'Here, on this spot! You could call it the Grand Phoenix Music Hall.'

'It would take time. A building like that would take months to build . . .'

'Use another place in the meantime. Experiment with this Temperance idea. My papa, a cotton man in the old days, has a mill a little way down the Thirlwell. It was in the country then, but is surrounded by houses now. It's a sound building. It would only take a week or so to fit out.'

Jonnie stroked his chin, finally interested.

'Why do you take this interest, Mr Granter?' asked Shona quite sharply.

He looked at her with his open smile. 'My father and I are interested in the welfare of the ordinary people of this place, Miss Farrell, on whose backs the wealth of this great town has been amassed. We've been helping to get a great public library here in Manchester, open to all. That scheme is near to fruition now.

'And now the singing halls. We were told these places were dens of iniquity and vice, and, never having been inside them, we believed it.' He laughed. 'From the inside of Mr Forster's hall, to be honest, one might believe the judgement accurate. However, I was charmed by thy performance the other night. And, dear lady, noticed the island of calm reflection thy performance brought into the lives of your audience.'

Shona made a slight curtsy.

'I talked of this to my dear father and we concluded that, as ever, the vice was not in the desire to entertain, but in the corruption of drink which releases the beast in all men, of high or low estate. So we believe what is needed is the calming and uplifting effect of entertainment without the demoralising effect of drink. Ergo a Temperance Hall of Entertainment. It is a simple idea and not original. I believe it is being taken up elsewhere.' He put his head on one side and looked at her. 'Don't you think it a grand idea? Would you sing in such a place?'

She laughed, her humiliating pursuit of Greg driven from her mind for a moment. 'Just wonderful, Mr Granter. Just wonderful. And, yes, I would sing there.'

He rubbed his hands together. 'Well, all we need now is the people to contribute the capital and help with the planning.'

'I know one person who is very well suited,' said Shona. 'Why don't we go and see her now? I see you're hanging on to a cab. Can we use that?'

At Versay Villa Shona showed the gentlemen into the drawing room, told Tonetta to give them coffee and some little sugar cakes she had made, and flew up to Marianne's sitting room.

She had the curtains drawn and a damp muslin cloth on her head. Last night with Marcus had been a disaster. He had fallen asleep halfway through their supposed lovemaking and she had looked at his old body and wondered why it made her feel old too.

Shona knew that with Marianne boredom manifested itself in physical symptoms. 'Is it you? Where have you been?' she said in a sad small voice. 'And what is this about Italians in our stables?'

Shona strode across and opened the window, allowing in a shaft of the peculiarly grey Manchester light. 'Marianne, Marianne, sit up! Jonnie Forster is here and a friend. Well, a friend of Tommo's really, and they have a wonderful idea . . .'

Marianne sat up, the muslin cloth falling into her lap. 'Be still, songbird!' she commanded. 'Tell me slowly. A friend of Tommo's? Another Irish?'

'No, no. The Manchester man who helped him. A queer one this one! But rich, I think. A Quaker who uses funny speech. But he has this wonderful idea which I think you . . .'

Marianne was on her feet, putting her hand flat on Shona's mouth. 'Sit down, take a deep breath and tell me ve-ery, ve-ry slowly.' She was smiling now. This day after all would not be drenched in that debilitating *ennui* which had always been her greatest enemy.

When Shona had finished Marianne pulled her back to her feet. 'Now, Shona, you go and take care of our guests. I'll be with you in five minutes.' She put her hand over Shona's mouth. 'Five minutes!'

Marianne made her entrance twenty minutes later. She was wearing a fine navy linen dress which fitted her perfectly above the waist and fell in simple pleats to the ground. Its only decoration was a delicate lace collar with eight points, two of which lay over her firm breasts. She wore a single pearl ring and her hair was pulled straight off her face into a heavy bun which showed a promising weight. Her face was practically without powder and her lips seemed naturally red, without any artifice.

She held out her hand to Matthew Granter who bowed low over it, his lips hovering twelve inches away.

'Madame,' he said in a whisper.

Shona, her own lips twitching with amusement, almost applauded the performance. She knew the deal was almost sealed there and then, before a word was spoken. As she watched, her mind went back to the house visited by Greg. The doctor's house. There, she was sure, she would find the solution to the mystery of Mary Louisa.

Tommo waited for Pat Daley to come out of the ironworks at the end of the shift. The weary men clumped past him, many of them nodding some kind of greeting. Other heads were down, carefully examining the contents of their paypackets. Some men averted their faces from him in a manner which puzzled him.

Pat greeted him with comforting delight, clapping him on the back and laughing loudly. 'Bejasus, I thought I'd never see yer again, Tommo. Thought you'd dropped over the edge of the world.'

Men were flowing round them like a parting sea, their glances still leaving Tommo prickling with unease. 'And what would be the matter with these fellers, Pat? You'd think they'd seen a ghost.'

Pat pulled his arm. 'Come on, Tommo. Won't you come down Showy's and have a pint, and tell us what yer've been up to?'

Showy brought the pints across to them and shook his hand, refusing their money. Pat watched him waddle back to the bar, and shook his head in turn. 'History made, that is! History made! Free beer off Showy.'

'Now what is it, Pat? Why are they looking at me like that?'

'Your Shona'll've told you, Tommo. They think you did it.'

'Did what?'

'Maudie.'

Tommo leaped to his feet with a wordless bellow. The after-work buzz stilled all around them. Pat desperately pulled him down beside him, muttering, 'No, no, Tommo. Won't it just make them think they're right? You and your temper.'

'Why? Why d'they think that?'

'Well, Terry let slip a couple of things . . .'

'Terry Kennedy?' This time he stood up on his feet slowly and calmly, saying: 'He's the one sent me careerin' after the McNaughton feller. And didn't Shona say she saw him spying on Maudie and me in the woods? Didn't I know when I heard that, that he was the one? I knew it! Where is he, Pat? Where is the *bastard*?'

Pat was standing beside him, equally grim. 'He'll be over at the works collecting his pay. Doesn't work in the loading bay now. Always out and about running errands. Bosses' man to his fingernails. What'll you do, Tommo?'

'Kill him.'

Pat shook his head. 'No,' he said urgently. 'You don't know for sure. Take him to the constable and let him know what you know.'

Tommo shook his head to try and dislodge the yearning for revenge inside it. 'An Irishman against a bosses' man? Police hate us too, y'know.'

'Look,' whispered Pat fiercely, 'let's just get him across to that Missis McNaughton. Didn't she see it happen? Went off her head after but she's all right now. She can say.'

Still shaking his head, Tommo allowed himself to be hustled out of the bar by Pat.

Showy went across and picked up their glasses. 'Anyone like these pints? Part used, a ha'penny a pint.'

Tommo and Pat went across to the stables to collect the delighted Richie, who was very satisfied at Tommo's reaction to his increased size and new status.

They explained their errand and he nodded vigorously.

'We'll take me own trap and the grey,' he said proudly.

They watched him back the big grey into the shafts.

'What's he called?' asked Tommo, picking up a hank of rope which was hanging neatly on a hook.

'Boru the Second,' answered Richie. 'He's a fine feller.'

They met Terry Kennedy on the deserted road coming away from the works. He hailed them uneasily and then drew his hands up in front of him like a boxer as Tommo and Pat jumped down from the

256

trap and blocked his way forward and back. Richie manoeuvred the trap to prevent him escaping on the other side.

Tommo started to punch his shoulder. 'You did it,' he shouted, 'you killed Maudie.'

'Who says?' Terry was flinching and ducking away from them. 'Word round here is that *you* did it, Tommo Farrell. Or that McNaughton feller who ran away. Or both of you.'

'Only your word,' said Pat, pushing him one way.

'Only your filthy word,' said Tommo, pushing him the other.

Terry was flung against the shafts of the trap and the horse reared up, whinnying. Richie muttered soothingly.

Terry closed his eyes. 'Don't kill me, lads! Don't kill me over some little *hooah*.' Tommo's fist smashed into his face and he lay curled whimpering on the ground, almost under the feet of the horse.

Pat pulled Tommo away and shoved him against the trap. 'Get up, Tommo! Get up beside Richie!' He almost lifted Tommo into his seat. 'Richie, pass me that rope.'

They pulled Terry behind the trap for the whole three miles between New Morven and Shotwell. Occasionally he shrieked as he lost his footing and Richie would patiently pull Boru the Second to a halt. Once Terry regained his balance they would set off again at a slow trot.

Biddy's pleasure at seeing Tommo was dampened when she realised his errand. She lifted the lamp to get a closer look at the bulky man tethered to the cart. 'Well, Tommo, Mrs McNaughton is in the house. Let me explain to her before she sees him.'

She went up to the workroom to get Douglas. 'Mr McNaughton, I've to explain something terrible to Margaret. About that tragedy when the poor woman died. I need your help.'

He stood up immediately and looked down at Stuart whose head was bent over a great ledger. 'Time to finish anyway, Stuart. Will you turn out the lights when you leave?'

His son nodded without raising his head.

Margaret came out into the road quite calmly, between Douglas and Biddy. They brought her closer to Terry and she thrust her face forward to study him closely.

She lifted her hand. 'You wicked, wicked man! May the Lord

have mercy on your soul.' Then she fell against Biddy and her voice dropped. 'Wicked, wicked, wicked, wicked. The poor woman was kind. And so pretty. She saved me. And such a pretty house. She saved me. A kind . . . wicked, wicked!'

'I'll take her in,' said Biddy, and raised her eyes to Douglas. 'Perhaps if you take this man in to Priorton to the constable, Mr McNaughton, he'll believe you. You heard what Margaret said. You and Pat take him in.'

Douglas turned on his heel and returned in a second in his greatcoat and hat. He looked at Pat. 'We need him up on the trap, Mr Daley. Will you help me?'

Tommo walked along the path behind the two women. In the wide hallway he touched the shoulder of his aunt, who was fussing over the mumbling Margaret. 'Is the little girl here, Biddy. The one called Becky?'

She smiled at him. 'A lovely little thing she is, Tommo. Upstairs, second on the right.'

There were two heads on the large white bolster, but he would have recognised anywhere Becky's mop of blonde curls. He picked up a single curl in his fingers.

She opened her eyes wide, instantly awake, in the way of children. She beamed and sat up. 'Tommo!' she said. 'Did Mama come too?'

His tears dropped on to her curls, melting the last of the leaden lump of revenge that had been lodged in his head for months. He put his finger to his lips, glancing at the other small still head on the bolster. 'No, she isn't here, me sweetheart, but do you know what? Didn't she send me to you 'specially to take care of you?'

Downstairs, Biddy was sitting beside Margaret, patting her hand. 'It's all right now, they have him, the wicked feller. He's away now. You're all right now, Margaret.'

She shook her head hard from side to side, in the manner of a child. 'No, Biddy, no! He stood in the shadows, that one. Where's the other? The one with the belt? Have they caught him? Have they caught him?'

The front door slammed and her head went up 'Who's that? Who's that?'

Biddy went to look. 'There's no one there at all, Margaret. Not a soul.'

Chapter Twenty-five

The next day Shona was standing in the rain beside St Peter's Church at ten o'clock. She identified the road that had brought her there on her odyssey from Charleston Street and set out to return there.

She had woken up that morning with the sure conviction that she had to see Mary Louisa before she saw Greg. Only after seeing her would she know what to do.

It took her two hours to find her way to Charleston Street and her feet, in their new elastic-sided boots, were sore when she reached Dr Montague's house. She took a deep breath and rattled at the lion-shaped brass knocker. The sour maid looked at her impassively from under a starched cap.

'I've come to see Mrs McNaughton.'

The maid looked at her blankly.

'Hasn't Mrs McNaughton – that is, the old Mrs McNaughton – asked me to call because she's concerned about her?'

The hard face was softening. 'Mr McNaughton was here earlier. He didn't say . . .'

'I'm just arrived last night and Mr McNaughton is at his business this morning.'

Now the maid was opening the door wider, a smile transforming her severe face. 'Well, dear, the doctor's making his calls, but sure it'll do no harm for you to take a little peep.'

Shona stepped inside, smiling broadly. 'You're from Ireland.'

'So I am, County Kerry.'

'I'm from Clare.' Shona reached out and shook her hand heartily. 'My name's Shona Farrell.'

The woman looked guiltily around the empty echoing hall. 'I'm Molly McCaughey,' she whispered, pulling her hand back to her side very quickly. She stepped back. 'You need to be up the stairs,' she said in a louder voice. 'Mrs McNaughton's on the first floor.'

The bedroom was large enough, and brightly lit by eight lamps. It was comparatively bare and stiflingly hot from the blazing fire which was piled high in the grate. Two highbacked chairs were positioned beside tall windows which looked out on a narrow sooty garden.

'It's very bright in here.'

'The doctor insists. He says she lives in her own dark world and must be pulled into the light.'

The woman was propped up on pillows in the bed, eyes closed. Her face was pale and its bones were prominent. Her hair, snow white, had been carefully brushed and came down over both shoulders in thick plaits. On the table beside the bed, next to the water-jug, was a wrought iron crucifix and rosary beads.

Molly went across and adjusted the pillows behind the fragile patient. 'Now then, Mary Louisa, we have another visitor for you. A young woman from Clare, not fifty miles from where we were born, you and me.'

She pulled one of the chairs so that it was beside the bed and whispered, 'Sit here, Shona. She might speak to you. She comes and goes, so she does. Can I get you some tea? And I'll take that coat and dry it off a bit.'

Shona smiled at her. 'Tea'd be manna from heaven, Molly,' she whispered.

She stared hard at the woman in the bed and struggled with a sense that she had made a mistake. This woman looked so fragile, so old: older even than Biddy. She was too old to be the mother of little Lauretta. How could she be Greg's wife?

After ten minutes the woman started to stir and her eyes opened. She blinked, then wonderful liquid brown eyes were glaring at Shona. 'Here again, are you? Never away. Nagging, nagging, nagging. You never stop! I tell you, there's nothing. Nothing I can tell you!'

Then she closed her eyes and Shona could see the fragile blue-veined lids. Timidly she reached out and grasped the hand that was lying on the coverlet. It turned and clutched hers with frightening strength.

This was different. The hands were those of a young woman, soft and strong. The nails were gleaming and well kept. Shona turned the hand over and winced as she saw the ugly scars, old and new, on the inside of the wrist.

After twenty minutes Molly McCaughey came back. 'Anything?'

'She spoke a bit. But it doesn't make sense.'

Molly shrugged. 'Sometimes she makes a lot of sense. Sometimes she might be on the moon.'

Shona unclasped her hand from the woman's tight grip and stood up. 'I suppose I'll have to go.'

Molly said, 'Would you like a bit of a warm and more tea? The cook's just gone off to the market and'll be a good hour.'

Sitting in front of the blazing range beside her steaming coat which was hanging on a clothes horse, they talked of Ireland at first.

Molly had come from Kerry ten years before with Dr Montague. She had sent money home for her family until there was no need, them all dying in the hunger.

Shona let that story take its course then said, 'And what about the poor soul upstairs?'

'Oh, she's had hard times, poor lamb. She's been here three years now. Dr Montague calls her self-destructive. It's an illness, he says, but I've never been nearer anyone who was under a curse.' She crossed herself.

'What happened to her?'

Molly narrowed her eyes. 'Just why is it you're so interested then?'

Shona took a deep breath then took a risk. She told Molly just about everything, except the swift, disappointing lovemaking the day Greg's mother went missing. She even admitted Greg knew nothing of her presence here. 'So, d'you see, I need to know about her, and what it is that makes him so miserable?'

Molly shook her head. 'Ah, it's a terrible thing, loving someone so. It's a cross that's hard to bear and I honour the confidence. That Greg, he's a nice boy. I take to him, so I do.' She poured herself some more tea. 'I only know the last bit of it. They were living here in Manchester and she had this baby. Dr Montague delivered her. I saw her once or twice. A lovely little thing, hair like cobwebs.

'Well, it seemed Mary Louisa hurt the little thing, so Mr McNaughton couldn't leave her alone. Then she hurt herself. First

261

smashing her hands through windows, then using knives on herself. They suggested an asylum, but he wouldn't hear of it. Then she jumped out of a window. Not too far, just enough to break her arm. The doctor had her here to recuperate and she seemed much calmer away from her husband and the baby. When she was well enough to go home with her husband, she fought to stay. So she's been here ever since.'

Shona looked round the roomy kitchen. 'It must cost some money, to keep her here?'

'Seems while he was here, the boy invented some little valve or something for the dyeing machines. He signed the – what is it? Royalties? – over to the doctor. I've heard him say many times he got the best of the bargain.' Molly grinned. 'Sure I'm not supposed to know any of this, but what you learn in service is that even if you're told to be deaf as a post, you're not.'

Shona thought of Forton, the servant who had told her of the open window.

'And why did he go away?' she persisted.

'She got worse by the day. If he brought the baby, she would crawl up the walls or try to strangle it. Sometimes she'd leap on him. Other times she'd be as sweet as pie, talk as nice as you like. She'd say her prayers with me and talk about when she was a little girl, and her brother Peter. Then for weeks she wouldn't say a word. Or else talk jumbled rubbish, backside first words and things.' Molly shuddered and crossed herself.

'So why did he go? Why did he leave her?'

'Well, the little girl was ill from the cold for a month. We had her here. The Manchester air is poison itself for the lungs, the doctor says. Then one day he took the boy into his surgery, and glaring right at me, locked the door – maybe he doesn't think I'm deaf as a post after all! Anyway there was shouting in there, and then the boy came and got the baby and went. And then he would come once a month on his own to see her. Then he came back to Manchester to stay again without the child, a few months ago.'

Shona stood up and pulled her shawl more closely around her. 'But why did she go strange like that?'

'The doctor said it was the baby, some women go like that after one. Me, I think it was a curse. She goes on sometimes abut the devil, then we say our prayers together. Sometimes the priest comes, which is a big thing for the doctor, seeing he's a heathen himself and believes in nothing.'

Molly followed her to the door. Shona turned to face her.

'Can I come again? I'd like to listen to her, just listen. But as a secret. I don't want to bother Mr McNaughton.'

Slowly Molly nodded. 'You can do no harm. And if you come after eleven, they'll both be out.'

It was one o'clock when Shona finally got home. Marianne waylaid her. 'Ah, here is the little stranger. Sit! Sit! Now tell me first why you run away today and leave me in this chaos? Then I will tell you all my news.'

Shona couldn't tell her the whole truth. 'I've found out where my . . . friend Greg is.'

Immediately Marianne's demeanour softened. 'Ah, the lover! An assignation! I will ask no more.' She paused to enhance the drama of her own news. 'Well, I have been surrounded by wailing Italians all day. The papa *you* put in the stables is failing, so we 'ave to 'ave him in the house and get the doctor. The boy does not know one end of the horse from another, so I take him to the livery and tell them to teach him. There is no lunch from the wailing girls so I make the giant omelette for everyone. Mr Hodgkiss calls and I introduce him to the amusing Mr Granter and Jonnie and we are all to build this peculiar music hall *sans bière*. And I decide I will sell the emeralds and buy my own share. And Mr Granter has given me a special task. I am to find lots of charmers like you to perform in this great hall!'

'Won't he mind? Marcus? About the emeralds?'

Marianne flicked her fingers. '*Pouf!* How will he know? I have the best copier in England to make me a replacement.' Her face became cunning. 'Like the rest.'

'Are they all copies?'

'But of course! All turned into gold. Gold is best. Always remember, songbird, gold to invest. Already my pearls have made twice their value.'

'So you'll find the artistes?'

Marianne sighed, a smile twitching the corners of her mouth. 'Yes, it will be so-o hard, going to all the shows and finding all these songbirds and jugglers. I think they will have to reward me well for my work.'

'You are a bad'n, Marianne!'

'So you keep telling me. Also, Jonnie was sad to miss you and says you are to sing at his stopgap hall on Saturday. He will send a cab.'

'Right.' Saturday seemed a long way off.

'And I am to meet Granter *père* for the English tea this afternoon. He sounds such a fascinating man, if one listens to that charming son of his.' Marianne adjusted her velvet sash. 'According to Jonnie, they are very very rich, the Granters.'

Shona watched as Mary Louisa opened her eyes and put up a hand to shade them from the bright light. Their gazes met and Shona leaned forward anxiously from her chair at the side of the bed.

'Hello there! And who might you be?' Her voice was light and strong. Unlike the meandering aggressive whine which Shona had listened to for the last three mornings.

'My name's Shona Farrell and I'm here to visit you.'

Mary Louisa closed her eyes, opened them again, then struggled to sit up. Shona rushed forward to help.

The other woman shook her off. 'Well, Shona Farrell, will you open a window a bit? Molly's a darlin' but she will keep this place like a waitin' room for hell.' She adjusted the creased collar of her nightgown. 'So why is it you're visiting a woman you don't know? And a woman who has no idea who you are?'

Shona was struggling with a stiff catch.

'Oh, leave it, Miss Shona. Molly'll have twenty fits if you do open it. Now come over here and tell me all about yourself.' She patted the bed beside her. 'Isn't it a treat to see a new face?'

Her own pale face was animated; the woman seemed to have shed twenty years in a second. Shona, mesmerised by the bright interest in the liquid brown eyes, found herself telling the story of her life since she had come from Ireland. Then she paused for breath.

Mary Louisa smiled. 'How enchanting to be so young, so full of mouthwatering life. I was like that myself a few weeks ago, before this wretched illness. Peter always said I was full of the sap of life, bursting with God-given energy.'

Shona chattered on, delighted finally to be talking properly to her. Mary Louisa held up a hand. 'Did you say New Morven?'

Shona nodded.

Mary Louisa laughed. 'Now isn't that funny? My brother Peter is a priest in the nearby town. Priorton?'

Shona nodded again.

'I only visited him briefly.' A frown marred the translucent brow. 'But he had changed. His thoughts were . . . sinful.' Her hand reached out for the rosary which she enclosed entirely in her hand. She smiled. 'I met this boy, Greg. Do you know, he had been to Russia? He's a brilliant engineer. The best in England. I would love to go to Russia. I will when I get better. Anthony – Dr Montague – has promised me.' She carefully restored the rosary to its position on the table beside the bed.

'Did you marry him? Greg?' said Shona, carefully.

The patient frowned again, 'Yes, I think I did. He was so eager, so keen, you see. But my brother wanted me for the church. No, really for him. He wanted me for him. So I married the boy.'

'And you were happy?'

Mary Louisa laughed. 'Who wouldn't be? He was perfect . . . but always remember, Miss Shona, we're not supposed to be happy. We're supposed to suffer.'

'How did you suffer?'

Mary Louisa closed her eyes and Shona thought she was asleep. She tried to loosen her hand, but it was held tight.

Mary Louisa's eyes opened wide. 'I knew it when I saw the other one, Greg's father. The terrible mistake I'd made. It was as though, as some kind of jest, some fallen angel had fashioned us one for another. Douglas knew it. I knew it. Douglas thought the baby was a punishment for our sin.' She leaned forward. 'But you see, Shona, I thought if Heaven had made a mistake then that was no one's fault.'

'I can't see the fault in it, Mary Louisa.' She frowned, confused by these references to Douglas, and to sin.

'The devil came. Then I knew I would be punished. He came and we had to flee, me and Greg.' She leaned forward even closer and looked straight into Shona's eyes. 'You love Greg, don't you?'

Shona took a deep breath. 'Yes.'

'Then you must have him. That'll bring the thing in balance and end my torment.'

Shona sat quiet.

'That devil . . . He made me punish myself, you know. He made me kill the baby. Douglas's baby.'

'The baby's not dead, Mary Louisa! I've seen her. She's lovely. Has a head of lovely fair hair. She's a little sunshine, and she makes the people around her smile. She makes Douglas smile.'

'Does she? Does she?' Mary Louisa picked up her hand and kissed it, and Shona turned scarlet. 'Look after her, won't you? And Greg? And my dear Douglas? Promise?'

'I promise.'

'But the devil, he won't let you. He'll stop you!' The fine eyes were suddenly full of terror.

'I'll stop him, Mary Louisa,' said Shona urgently. 'Believe me, I'll stop him.'

The woman dropped her hand and turned her face away. 'I thought that, but Peter saw to it that I couldn't do it. And yet it started with his sin. He was wrong to love me like . . . forgive, forgive!' Her voice went up a pitch and lost its measured tones. 'Why is she here, with her sly questions? Send her away . . . she hurts me . . . I am not worthy . . . Lord, I am not worthy . . .'

The door opened and Molly bustled in. 'Time for you to go, Shona. Me and Mary Louisa'll say our prayers now and she'll get some sleep.'

'She talked,' said Shona.

Molly smiled gently. 'Yes, I heard. She's a fine woman, a sweet woman. No wonder all these men saw the magic in her.'

Shona allowed herself to feel happier as she walked down Charleston Street. No matter how strange the situation, she and Mary Louisa had really talked today. Somewhere in her confused mind Mary Louisa had recognised Shona's feelings, given her a kind of permission. Shona finally understood that Greg had treated his wife with honour.

She found her feet almost making their own way through the town and into the Chambers Commercial Hotel. The porter showed her into a small sitting room which also served as an office. She told the severe woman sitting at the desk that she had come from Dublin and wished to see her cousin, Mr McNaughton, whom she believed was staying here.

The woman looked her up and down but could find nothing to take exception to in the neat dress and jacket and the discreet bonnet. 'I am not certain that he's in, Miss. He is often out at business in the afternoons. Jenkins will show you to the sitting room and go and call Mr McNaughton.'

In the dark stuffy sitting room she stood by the window and looked down at the traffic fighting for passage in the street below. She heard the door behind her click but didn't turn round.

Greg caught her elbow and turned her round, his face lit by a broad smile. 'Shona!'

Her arms went out. Groaning, he almost fell into them. He hugged and hugged her until she had to pull away protesting. Then she kissed him on one cheek and then the other. His lips touched hers. The pain of months disappeared and she pressed her body into his for a second, then pulled away. She drew him towards a mean narrow couch and pulled him down beside her.

He put his head on one side and looked at her. 'You seem different.'

'I *am* different. I've been months out of your sight. I've done a million things. Been down a million alleyways looking for you.'

'How did you find me?'

'That's a long story and it'll wait. Greg, I've seen Mary Louisa.'

Now when she looked at him she could see the shadows under his eyes, the new sharpness in his features. He sought for words and couldn't find them.

'She's a lovely woman, Greg.'

He smiled faintly. 'She was magical. She brought lightness and joy with her, spilling on to everyone.'

'She told me . . .'

'She talked to you?'

'Yes. Twice when I went, she just rambled. But today she talked.'

'You went four times? Did Dr Montague . . . ?'

'The doctor didn't know. Molly helped me. Did you know she was from Kerry?'

'Mary Louisa talked?'

'She told me a lot. She made a good deal of sense. She told me I was to have you, to take care of you, then she could rest.'

Greg put his elbows on his knees and his face in his hands. 'I don't know what to do, Shona. All this has been so hard. I don't know what to do.'

Her wide petticoats rustled as she kneeled before him, took his hands away from his damp face and, smiling, stroked back the fair hair. 'Don't worry, my dear Greg. Haven't I got this brilliant plan to make it all better?'

Douglas could see and smell the acrid smoke from Old Jamie MacQuistain's pipe before he turned the corner, so the hunched figure of the man on the iron seat before his cottage was no surprise. He was sitting with his head back against the stone wall, his eyes squeezed tight against the bright rays of the evening sunshine.

Jamie opened his eyes as Douglas sank down beside him on the iron seat. They sat in silence for a while.

'I remember you making this seat,' said Douglas, 'those last weeks in Scotland. A present for your Dora.'

'Ye were gettin' a rare hand with the bellows then, tho' still a wee'en.' Jamie raked in his pocket and brought out his pouch. 'Will ye share a pipe?'

Douglas shook his head. 'I never took to the pipe, you know that.'

Jamie drew hard on the newly packed tobacco, coughed and spat. 'Yer daddy now, he liked a good pipe o' tobacco.'

'He did, didn't he?' Douglas paused. 'I missed you at the works today, Jamie.'

The morning had had the sudden darkness of late August, as indication that the summer was fading. He had been turning over some new castings in the blacksmith's shop with half an ear for Jamie's early morning shuffling gait. All day long, as he had worked on some new drawings, gone through some figures with Stuart, dealt with a self-important official of the company, supervised some trials of a new engine – all the time the thought of Jamie had been niggling. The unease could only be resolved by his strolling down here to Dairy Terrace to seek out the old man.

Jamie watched the new tobacco glow and smiled. 'Well, Douglas, I found it a bit hard getting out of bed this morning.'

He said no more about it, and Douglas had to take his cue from the old man, who went on to ask about Margaret. 'She's looking a sight better than she used to. Gets into the garden, talkin' about the plants like she did in the early days when you were first wed.'

Douglas smiled. 'I was just thinking abut that. How you set the garden at Garth End Cottage for us, after you came from Scotland.'

'Aye, and working full-time in the blacksmith's shop as well. She watched every spadeful, Margaret. Even did some diggin' too, when my back was turned.'

'She loved – loves – the garden.'

'She seems to flourish with all those papists around,' said Jamie carefully. She had in fact asked him if he wanted Pat Daley to do the back-end digging, clearing up after the summer vegetables. To his own amazement he had agreed with only a little bad grace.

'It certainly looks like that,' said Douglas with equal care. 'She hasn't been so lively in years.'

Pat now helped quite a bit with the garden, and the boy Richie came regularly to give the two little girls rides on his pony and to take Biddy and the little Martin girl to the Catholic church in New Morven on Sunday in his pony and trap.

Margaret had stopped watching Douglas with her soul-destroying despair and would instead rush to tell him breathlessly of her busy day, just as she had as a young bride.

'If they help her to feel well again,' he said shortly, 'they're welcome.'

'Welcome in the works as well, I hear?'

Douglas had just taken on fifteen new men, sent by a Liverpool agent, to work on the building of a new machine shop.

'They're workers and human beings. I have no objections to them.'

'The men don't like it.'

'It's not for them to like or dislike.'

Jamie nodded in reluctant agreement. Douglas had succeeded so well because he made up his own mind about everything, listened to no doubting Thomases. 'Ye're right, but there's a lot of rumbling down there, ye'll need to watch it.'

Douglas stood up. 'I'll have to get in for my supper. Will I see you at work tomorrow, Jamie?'

'Och, Douglas, it's gettin' rare hard to get up in the morning now.'

He leaned down and put a hand on the old man's shoulder. 'Watch out now, Jamie, I'll be down to see you soon.'

'Aye.'

Jamie sat back, pipe in mouth, and closed his eyes against the sun, which was now a gleaming red ball on the horizon.

Douglas found Margaret reading on the couch in the parlour. The house was unusually quiet. 'Where is everyone?'

She smiled. 'Biddy's putting the girls to bed. Lauretta says, will you go to see her when you get in? Would you like some supper first?'

He sat down beside her. 'In a moment. I saw Jamie. He seems tired.'

'He's a very old man, Douglas.' Timidly she reached out and took his hand. When he didn't reject her, she held on fast. 'You are very fond of him.'

'He's part of my childhood, Margaret. I owe him so much.' To his horror there were tears in his eyes.

Screwing up all her courage, she put an arm around him and drew him to her, hiding his head on her shoulder until the tears had ceased.

Biddy, finding them like this, stole away.

Later Douglas went into the girls' bedroom and found them tumbling about on the counterpane. He told them sternly to get into bed, which they did with alacrity.

Lauretta screwed up her mouth and closed her eyes. 'Kiss, Grandpa!'

He obeyed, amazed as always at his own delight in this small creature.

'Now Becky.'

She looked up at him, her bright eyes uncertain, then smiled as he bent to do further grandfatherly duty.

He thought of that fellow Kennedy, still locked up while Herbert Walton went through plodding investigations to see if he really had killed Becky's mother. Herbert had told Douglas he had found various bloody items of clothing at Kennedy's lodging. However the prisoner was claiming it was the blood of rabbits he had killed and skinned for his landlady's pot.

Loosening his necktie, Douglas walked along the landing, knocked on Margaret's door and went in. 'May I come in?'

She was sitting up in bed reading, a lace nightcap over her plaited hair. She leaned over and pulled back the coverlet. 'Of course, Douglas. You know I want you here.' Her face was pink but her eyes were quite calm.

Chapter Twenty-six

Marianne stamped her small crêpe slipper with displeasure at Shona's plans to leave Versay Villa.

Shona merely smiled at her. The fonder of the Frenchwoman she became, the more she realised how different they were. But some things she had learned. Useful things. 'It's your own fault, Marianne. Didn't I see how you do things and learn a lesson or two? Before I met you I wouldn't have thought of this at all.'

'Oh, yes, everything is my fault,' said Marianne gloomily. 'Listening to Monsieur Marcus Hodgkiss, you would think that the burning down of Forster's Hall was my fault!'

'When that's clearly my fault! Is Mr Hodgkiss kicking up a fuss then?' asked Shona, settling down to listen to her friend's troubles. As always, Marianne was the centre of her own particular universe and thought everyone should sympathise with her.

'My dear Shona, he's jealous of the Quaker and I think will not help with the new no-beer hall. He says it is bad business: insufficient profit.'

Shona peered closely at her. 'But *you* are not worried!'

Marianne shrugged. 'There is more to life than profit.'

'What?' Shona grinned her delight. 'Aren't we changing the colour of our coat now?'

'Monsieur Granter now, he talks a great deal with me. He has great enthusiasm for his cause.'

'And he'll give some money?'

Marianne smiled primly.' A great deal of it. For the cause. For saving people from drunkenness, which leads to poverty and bad acts. He says it's drink which makes stews like Angel Meadow and those places round Shudehill Market an insoluble problem.'

Shona said grimly, 'The problem with Angel Meadow is people with no jobs, no money, no hope. Even the poorhouse won't tak'em. A penn'orth of gin is a warm coat for an hour or two.' Then she laughed. 'Madame Villeneuve, you like him! You like the prim Quaker!'

Marianne laughed out loud. 'Just so. I like all his thee-ings and thou-ings. It makes me think of home. We call it *tutoyer* – only for the most intimate of friends.'

'Then the world is his intimate friend.'

'Just so. Is that not very sweet?'

'And . . .'

'And he's a bachelor. No troublesome wife to kick one into the gutter; no one to call every other kind of woman a prostitute. And . . .'

'And he is very rich?'

'Shona, how could you? Would that sway me? *Non!* And now here you are, about to leave me.'

'You have Tonetta and Anna . . .'

'And Pietro whom the horse kicked yesterday, and the father who is recovering miraculously and has the appetite of a lion.'

'And what does all that tell us about you? You're a magician! You changed our lives, me and Richie. I'd'a been lying dead in an alley near Shudehill Market if Richie hadn't found his way to that greasy inn and to you. And here you are changing *their* lives, the Italians.'

'Huh! It will be *Saint* Marianne next! And you may cease to use that wheedling Irish charm on me. You're leaving me. You can't change the colour of that, miss.'

'Ah, to be sure, I'll be down here seeing you most days.'

'And you will sing on Saturday night for Jonnie at this warehouse?'

'I'll be there.'

'Then you must watch this wonderful young man I've found, who 'angs upside down by a rope from the rafters and escapes from chains, while 'is friend chops away at the rope with an axe.'

'Of course I will. Now, Marianne, where would you recommend for my . . . meeting?'

'Try the Tricorne. It is in a little turning off Market Street. I stay there when I am first in Manchester. Very grand in a small way. And very discreet. The *patronne* is French but you would not know it. She calls herself Mrs Smith.' She hesitated. 'Songbird, are you sure? You are so young, and the men, no matter how nice they seem, are

274

'not to be trusted. You could stay here. He could visit you here.'

'Isn't it me who's decided on it, not him? And I do not want to see him here because those who dislike you would call it by another name.' Shona paused. 'And nobody's ever young again who's watched their mother and father die from want, and had to walk right out of their own land. Nobody young ever watched their friend die of hard work and having children.' She smiled gently. 'And nobody young has faced a full house at Forster's Hall and survived!'

Late in the afternoon Shona hired a one-horse closed carriage.

Unlike the bleaker Chambers Commercial Hotel, the Tricorne had a desk in its wide reception hall. Shona was attended by Mrs Smith, a brisk slight woman all in black who didn't blink an eye when Shona requested a bedroom and sitting room. She nodded cordially as she was told that the young woman's husband, just back from business in Russia, should arrive sometime in the evening.

A maid hurried upstairs to light the fires and Shona followed with the porter, a red-faced, whippet-bodied elderly man, at a more leisurely pace. He put the bulky bags down at the open door and ushered her in before him. He went through the connecting door and put them in the bedroom.

She put sixpence in his hand and he touched his cap. 'Beggin' pardon, Ma'am, but I seen you sing, and admired it.'

'Thank you, Mr . . .'

'Tom, Ma'am.'

'Thank you, Tom.'

'It's a pity about the Forster's old hall firing up like that.'

'They're going to build a brand new one.'

His face beamed. 'New? Then I'll come there to watch you, Ma'am. And my wife, who's from Ireland herself and loves your songs.'

She felt guilty about wishing he would go, but stood there silently smiling until he left.

She peered into the bedroom where the maid was carefully hanging up her clothes. The bed loomed embarrassingly large. She closed the door quickly.

She sat by the window and pretended to look out. In the darkening panes she imagined she saw the scenes in the stone hut in the woods, with Maudie and Tommo playing their games with such sheer pleasure. Slowly she nodded her head. That was how it should be.

'Will you dine here, Ma'am, or in the dining room?' The little maid was standing beside her.

'Oh.' She thought of the embarrassingly large bed. 'The dining room, I think.'

The maid closed the curtains against the gathering dusk, lit more lamps, bobbed a curtsy and left.

Shona took off her jacket and went into the bedroom. Eyes averted from the bed, she hung it up in the vast wardrobe. She poured out some water and washed her face, then brushed some of the water into her hair to make it frizz out. She took out some powder, a parting gift from Marianne, dabbed it on, then brushed down her face with the soft brush which had accompanied the box. Peering into the round mirror, she saw a stranger looking out.

Closing the bedroom door behind her, she went across to the sitting-room window and pulled a gap in the curtain to peer out into the street. Men and women, carriages, barrows and carts, packed the road, making their way to and from the throng of Market Street which seemed never to be quiet.

'Shona!' She turned round guiltily.

He was standing by the door, his bags at his feet. She ran across to him and into his arms and he swung her round and round until he was giddy, finally dropping on to a wide couch and pulling her on to his knee.

'I can't believe this is true. Are we here?' he said. 'Is this us?'

He pressed his face into her shoulder then kissed her neck and face, his hands in her hair, scrabbling at her pins. Her hair came down and spread out in great black wings either side of her face, and he was kissing that too.

He rolled free of her and was kneeling at her feet and taking off her soft boots, kissing the arch of her foot.

She laughed and his head came up. 'It seems you're pleased to see me then?'

Drawing him to her, she kissed him again, then loosened his necktie. Her hands felt their way inside his shirt, feeling the smooth muscles of his shoulders.

'My turn.'

He loosened the demure bow at her neck and his hands, helped by hers, tackled the interminable row of buttons down the front. He pulled the top of the dress off until it was draped round her waist, loosened the ribbons on her shift and pushed it down over her shoulders with soft, wandering hands.

She sat up straight and looked down at him, one hand loosely over her naked breast, feeling her nipple harden against her own wrist.

He leaned up and kissed one breast and moved to the other. Her hand went to his head to keep him there as he kissed, licked and tugged gently with his teeth.

Her stomach contracted, and her knees gripped him hard.

He groaned and his hands were under her gown, pushing it back so he could see the green ribbon garters and kiss the soft inner thigh above the white stocking. His hand parted her legs a little wider, and his mouth was there, at first gently kissing then flicking across the soft areas with his tongue, then teasing her other lips wide with softly nipping teeth.

Now it was her turn to groan and he laughed with delight. Then his tongue worked away at a single spot, gently at first then harder and harder. Then his hands were there, one hand continuing the work on the single spot, the other deep inside her, pressing and releasing in a gentle rhythm.

Now he was watching her. Her head was up and her eyes half-closed with pleasure. He leaned up to kiss her and she could taste her own salt on her opening lips.

Her back arched and she groaned and down below he could feel her body liquid shoot over his fingers and into the palm of his hand. He groaned too, sharing her pleasure and stifled for this moment his own hard desire.

They were still for a moment and when he drew back he saw her face was deadly white and beads of sweat were standing on her forehead. He withdrew his hand, rearranged her skirts and said with anxious concern, 'Are you all right, my dear dear sweetheart, my beautiful girl?'

She smiled slightly. 'I think I might have seen heaven or somewhere like it.'

'Now . . .'

'Now,' she said. 'Can I do something like that for you?'

He pulled her to the rug by the fire and her hands were busy on him, one separate part of her mind contemplating that something this size could and would do the work of his fingers inside her.

He came very quickly, his body heating up and his voice pleading and groaning at the same time. 'Oh, Shona!'

They lay in the quietly flickering firelight for a few moments and she thought he was asleep. Her body was ringing, resounding from their coming together. She felt alive to her fingertips, to her eyelids, to her toes.

There was a loud knock on the door and she jumped. His fingers were on her lips. He coughed. 'Yes! What is it?'

'Dinner, sir. Ready in ten minutes in the dining room.' It was the porter's voice.

'Thank you.'

They listened to the footsteps fade away, then Shona sat up and started to laugh.

Greg stood, pulling up his breeches. He went for the washbowl from the bedroom, brought it in with the white towel and knelt down to hold it for her.

He grinned down at her as she washed. 'So how do you think this practice is going?'

'Wasn't I thinking I need a good deal more practice at all to make me perfect?' she said softly.

'Perfect! You *are* perfect. You were perfect that first day I saw you when you were making scones with those strong hands, black with coal-dust. I bless the day Biddy was knocked down by that cart!'

He pulled her to her feet and raised her hand to his lips. He kissed the palm and turned it over to look at the back, now smooth and soft, the nails buffed and manicured.

'You're the same, Shona. I love you now as I loved you then. But how you've changed! What on earth has been happening here?'

'Where can I begin? Help me up. Won't there be time to tell it all while we eat?'

At five o'clock on that same Friday Stuart McNaughton decided he had finished work for the day. He was the only one in the office and for once the decision was his. He had no responsibilities outside this office. The draughtsmen just got on with their task and Douglas always left Young Jamie MacQuistain with detailed instructions for the works. Stuart laughed. He wouldn't have known what to do if he got down on to the workshop floor anyway. Greg had been the boy for that, never away from the dirty place.

He peered through the glass partition into the drawing office. They all had their heads down over their boards. He stood up to reach into the back of the bought ledger cupboard for his silver flask.

He unscrewed the top and took a welcome draught. The liquor bit his throat and he grimaced, then smiled. Juggling with figures was thirsty work.

He wandered across to his father's table and sat in the big chair. He enjoyed these afternoons when his father went off to dispense justice at the court in Priorton. He often thought then about the money. The humming noise of all that work in the shop outside was spinning money that would eventually be his. He would probably get all of it now, Greg running off like that. Good riddance to him.

A knock sounded on the partition door. He thrust the flask into his tailcoat pocket and grunted, 'Come in.'

Three men stumped in, caps in hand. The brick dust on their clothes told him they were from the building work rather than the machine shop. He looked at them coldly.

'Yes?'

He recognised the taller, heavier man who took a slight step forward to speak. He was the leader of the men who worked on building; Stuart had seen him speak for them before, to his father.

The man coughed. 'Well, Mr Stuart, we wondered if we could see Mr McNaughton, like. Ah'm Tad Pinkney and me and these lads work round the site on the new buildin's.'

'Mr McNaughton's in court today.' Stuart sat up to his full height, which left him still half a head shorter than his father. 'You can deal with me.'

He didn't invite them to sit, although there were seats in the office for that purpose.

'Why, it's like this, sir,' said Pinkney. 'It's aboot those Irish yeh've set on.'

'My father set them on.' Stuart had been furious about it, and had let his father know it, in the hearing of that Irishwoman and the child of the dead Irish whore.

Pinkney caught his wandering eye. 'Why, sir, the lads isn't happy with them. Them Irish dinnat ken the job, like. They slow it down. And they jabber away amongst themselves. Yeh canna get a word they say. Plottin' half the time. 'Tisn't right. There's plenty of canny

Durham lads needin' work here. And now word is them Irish're takin' a lower rate for the jobs.'

It was true. At least Stuart had made one breakthrough with Douglas, and argued the economics of setting the Irish men on at the lower rate, 'until they learn the job'.

'If they're on a lower rate it's no business of yours. That's my father's decision.'

Pinkney grasped his hat harder. 'Aal the lads say it is our business. Them Irish comin' in is undercuttin'. Our own wages'll get cut next.'

Stuart was suddenly suffused with fury at the insolence of this scruffy, dusty man. He fingered his father's long pen with its newfangled nib. 'What we pay any worker here is no business of your friends or you, Mr Pinkney. If my father chose to fill the works with Irish and throw you into the workhouse, you can do nothing about it.'

The men muttered among themselves and Pinkney's hands curled up into fists. Stuart began to sweat as a thrill of fear shot down his spine.

Now he could play the other card. He would be boss himself here one day after all. He gave Pinkney what he intended to be a reassuring smile. 'Look, Mr Pinkney, nobody could agree with you more. I tried to persuade my father against this idea of replacing the force with Irish. If . . . when . . . I'm in charge . . .'

The men were looking at him in astonishment. 'When I run this place they'll not get jobs here. They're stupid and lazy and no earthly use. I've told my father many times to get rid of them and that we'll need no more. But he's a soft spot for them. Has an Irishwoman living in his own house, and an Irishman digging his garden. So what can I do? I'll urge him on your behalf, you can be sure.' He paused. 'In the meantime, I believe there're things you can do to show them you don't care for them? And perhaps show my father that you are not happy with his decision?' He dipped the pen in the inkwell. 'And now, perhaps I could have your names? You must've lost half an hour up here. It's a small matter to take the time off your wages.'

'I wouldn't try that, Mr Stuart,' said Tad Pinkney.

The other men exchanged glances and slowly backed out of the office. Their leader glanced back at Stuart with narrowed eyes. Tad Pinkney was an intelligent man. He was perhaps the only one apart from Stuart really to understand what had gone on, and how unusual had been the quiet sulky son's betrayal of his father.

On their way along the gantry and down the stairs they passed a thin bearded man in dark clothes who brushed past them as though they didn't exist.

Morry Smith came into the office without knocking. Stuart looked up at him sullenly. 'It's good manners to knock, you know.'

Morry looked round. 'Can't see any gentlemen here, Stuart. I saw your father in court this afternoon so I knew he wouldn't be here.' He sat down in the most comfortable chair.

'What might a lawyer be doing in Shotwell?'

'I was at Priorton police house this morning, talking to Herbert Walton the constable. I thought he needed to see how useful Kennedy's been to him, with his information. Stands to reason the Irish killed their own whore. When they're in drink there's no holding them. Stands to reason. I told him Tommo Farrell's back down in New Morven, large as life. He'll be goin' down to see him.' He looked blandly across at Stuart. 'See what I do for you? As well as that, I talked to Terry Kennedy.'

Stuart looked at him sharply. 'What about Kennedy?'

'He told me he was waiting for help from certain quarters. And if none was forthcoming he'd have to help himself. Tell some stories, he said. Apparently he's been paid for telling stories before.'

'I gave him the whore's ill-gotten gains, from her box.' Stuart felt in his pocket for the flask. 'What will you do?'

'What'll *I* do? Nothing to do with me, dear boy. I'd finished with her. Saw nothing.'

Stuart jerked forward, his eyes wide; fear and threat coiled there together like twin snakes.

Morry held up his hand. 'Well, dear boy. There's money! You'll need money to get someone to tell lies about Kennedy and where he was that night. But fellows are none too keen to do it, either here or down in New Morven. Not a popular fellow, this Terry Kennedy. Liked him well enough myself. A useful kind of fellow.'

'Get strangers to say . . .'

'I'm working on it. I need money.'

'Well . . .' Stuart shrugged. He stood up, only staggering slightly, and knelt before the floor safe. Using a key fastened to his watch chain, he opened the safe and counted coins out of a large full

281

tin. He stood up, locked the safe, and poured the gold into the pocket held out by Morry Smith's helpful hand.

Morry smiled slowly at him. 'Stuart?'

'What?'

'What did it feel like, when you did it? Did you feel good? Were you . . . excited?'

Stuart looked blandly into his eyes. 'I don't know what you're talking about. I did nothing.'

Morry shook his head slowly. 'Anyway, friend, I've Moxham's carriage here at the gate. I thought you might like a ride across up to Priorton, get a bite to eat in the White Ox. And we'll see what sport Priorton has to offer on a Friday night.'

Stuart hustled to lock the drawers and cupboards. He pocketed the keys and turned round, grinning, his face young and untroubled. 'Priorton can be very lively on Friday nights. There's whores needing a lesson standing on every corner down in little London.'

Morry Smith followed his friend out of the noisy factory and wondered just what he had unleashed when he had picked the boy up at the first boxing match. He reflected that each time now he got more entertainment than he bargained for. But it had its satisfaction, pushing the boy further and further. A few years or so and he'd be in line for this prosperous business, this flourishing works. And now he was sitting nicely under Morry's thumb.

The small dining room was busy, the large table in the centre occupied by various men of business: travellers, engineers, men of commerce.

Some smaller tables were occupied individually by three older men, one a red-faced farmer. At another table was a stout mother and her young daughter and son. Nearby was an elderly man with what might or might not have been his grand-daughter.

The murmur of conversation lulled as Shona and Greg entered, then restarted as Mrs Smith settled them at a corner table, almost masked from the room by an ancient plant with stringy leaves.

There was no choice of menu, she said. It was to be fish soup, venison and fruit tart. At Greg's request, she brought a dusty bottle of madeira and two glittering crystal glasses.

The fish soup was delicious, tasting slightly of aniseed. They ate in silence, Greg watching Shona as though she might vanish any second.

The maid took the soup dishes away and Shona sat back.

'Now tell me what's happening. Do you know how they are at home? How long have you been here?'

She told him how he had come under suspicion for Maudie Martin's murder. How he had been pursued both by Tommo and Shona herself, and had virtually vanished.

He laughed ruefully. 'This is a big town, teeming with people. It would be easy to miss anyone here, a thousand times. I'm pleased anyway that Tommo's found another quarry. He's too big for me to take on.'

'It was funny you racing away like that.'

He shrugged. 'I told you. Maudie dying like that on Christmas Eve, and mother's raving, made me think of Mary Louisa more than I had in many months. And with us so close . . . suddenly I felt guilty, I suppose.'

'So what is it you've been doing here? Oh, I know you've been seeing Mary Louisa, but neither your mother nor your father heard from you for long enough. It's only this week your mother sent me news of where you were living.'

'I've been in the workshops of the dye-company, developing this valve I made for them. Then Mr Montague introduced me to a man who wanted a transport system inside his manufactory, to transport goods to a railhead. So I supervised that. Then I met a man called Ogden known to both my father and myself at the Exchange. He wanted me to visit him.' He laughed. 'I think he had his eye on me for one of his daughters. Anyway, I let him know where I was staying before he mentioned my father had been in touch with him.'

'Why did you hide? What was it you feared?'

Greg shook his head. 'I felt guilty because I had all but forgotten Mary Louisa. And she was my wife. Lauretta! How's Lauretta! And Biddy?'

'Seems Biddy's there with your ma, who's much improved. Lauretta's basking in too much attention, and has as playmate the little girl left by Maudie Martin.'

They paused as they were served with venison, which lapped

over the edge of the great plates, dishes of vegetables and potatoes, and a silver jug of gravy.

Shona looked at the table and shook her head.

'What's the matter?'

'When I was first in Manchester, this would have done me and Richie for a month.'

'Does it trouble you? Should I take it out for some street urchin?' He stood up and lifted his plate.

Mrs Smith started to walk towards them.

'Sit down, will you, Greg!' said Shona, through gritted teeth.

He smiled. 'Well, just eat it now, and think you're eating it for months ahead. Were you really so hungry?'

'I nearly died, of hunger and a kind of fever. Others in the same yard did die. Richie kept me going. He stole from Shudehill Market, bartered, fetched and carried for people. How he did that, with other lads his age starving in alleyways or lying stupefied with gin, there's no saying.'

'He's a fine lad, and from now on my best friend,' said Greg, biting into the succulent venison. 'Now, eat up!'

He finished his food first and watched her struggle through hers. He leaned forward. 'I like your hair,' he whispered. 'Like a blackbird's wing.'

She laughed and spluttered and put her knife and fork to rest, looking regretfully at the plate, still half full.

The plates were cleared and the waitress brought them fine tarts, covered with apple slices, edges set against each other in circles.

'A pretty tart,' said Shona looking at him.

'A pretty girl.' He put out one hand to touch hers and she shivered, thinking again of his gentle skilful hands.

They ate in silence, their eyes on each other.

Greg brushed the last crumbs from his lips. 'And how have you survived here, this place being such a sink for the poor? How do you come to be here in that nice dress which makes your eyes look so blue?' He turned her hand over. 'And with such soft hands.'

'I have a friend.'

He dropped her hand and looked at her hard.

'Richie worked a bit for her at the inn. She's from France, and doesn't like having English around her. So at first I helped her, in the house.'

He was still puzzled. 'What kind of woman is she?'

'I don't know what you would call her. She is a kind of entertainer. Started out in a circus. She does cartwheels.'

'What?' His voice was loud. The other diners turned openly to stare.

Mrs Smith was coming over with a heavy silver tray. On it was a bottle in a silver pail and two crystal glasses. And a platter of oysters.

'These have been sent here by Madame Villeneuve. She wishes you to have them.'

Shona looked at the woman and saw the slightest glimmer of amusement in her eyes.

'Sure, that's a lovely thing to do. Thank you, Madame.'

They watched her place the platter carefully in the centre of their table, and pour them two glasses of sparkling white wine.

'Now,' said Shona, looking Greg hard in the eye, 'how on earth do you eat these?'

'I had them once at a reception in St Petersburg. You just tip them in.' He showed her and then laughed at her efforts and grimaces as she copied him, washing down the slippery, chewy oysters with great draughts of the white wine.

He dabbed his mouth again when he had finished. 'It's supposed to be good for your energies.'

'Energies?'

'You'll see.'

There was a pause as their table was cleared and a small bowl of flowers placed in the centre.

Mrs Smith stood beside them. 'Is there anything else, sir? Would you care for cognac?'

Greg shook his head and they were left alone. He hesitated. 'I must go and see Mary Louisa tomorrow.'

Shona nodded. 'Yes. I want to come with you. That's the plan.'

'Come with me?'

She nodded again. 'She'll want it, I know she will. To see you are . . . that someone loves you. I know it.'

He grasped her hand hard. 'I loved her, Shona. I loved her so much. She was a new world for me.'

Despite her firm plan to keep the oddness of the situation under control, she wriggled to escape his grasp but he held on tight. 'And

I love you totally, you fill my mind and heart. But somehow, underneath and around it, there is still this feeling for Mary Louisa that I know will never go. She's part of my growing up and will always be part of me, whoever I am.'

Her hand relaxed in his. 'Like I said, I'm coming with you, tomorrow and all the other days.' Then she sat up straight. 'Tomorrow! What day is it?'

'Saturday.'

'Oh, I've to sing tomorrow night! On Jonnie Forster's new stage.'

'Stage?' he said, puzzled. 'The theatre?'

'No, no! It's a hall – no, it was a hall, then it burned down. Jonnie's got a warehouse for the time being, they're hoping to build . . .'

He dropped her hand and stood up as the meaning of her words sank in 'A *singing hall*? You!' The words rang out through the dining room and this time people twisted round to see and the woman with the children got up to go.

Mrs Smith came across. 'M'sieur, I beg your discretion,' she said grimly. 'My clients . . .'

'Come on!' he whispered fiercely to Shona, who stood up and passed him, making for the door at high speed.

He caught her on the first landing. 'Stop!'

She kept walking and he hurried up beside her.

'A singing hall, a singing hall! You know what that means, Shona? The kind of women they say . . . this Frenchwoman, what kind of woman is she? Tell me. Tell me! You're not to go to any singing hall. I won't let you!'

She turned on him before their door. 'You won't *let* me?'

She marched through to the bedroom and locked the door behind her. Then carefully, slowly, she stripped to the skin and washed herself all over. All the time she ignored the urgent knocking at the door, the frantic whispers at the other side. She took down her hair and brushed it until she could see the sparks emanating from it. Then she pulled on a plain linen nightdress, caught in slightly at the waist with an embroidered sash.

The knocking had finally subsided and there was silence in the other room. She decided Greg must have lain down on the sitting-room couch.

286

She turned the lamps right down and climbed into bed. After five minutes of staring blankly at the ceiling, she climbed out again and padded to the door. Holding her breath in the darkness, she silently turned the key. Then she went back to bed, lay down, closed her eyes, and almost instantly drifted into slumber.

She was woken by kisses on her neck and brow. She could feel the heat of him and make out his shape as he bent over her. She put out one hand and it passed down his naked body. Then her other arm went up and she pulled him in with her.

He kissed her. 'Was I wrong? I was wrong, wasn't I? I didn't mean . . .'

She put a finger to his lips. 'Tomorrow's soon enough to talk about all that.'

He pulled at the neck of her gown, then the sash. She kneeled up and he kneeled with her to help her take it off, and they stayed there, kissing until Greg toppled sideways and took her with him.

She laughed. 'Now what?' she whispered.

'The same as before with a different ending.' He kissed her on every part of her body before focusing his attention. She held his head to her as he aroused her and shivered again as he came up to kiss her, leaving his fingers down there to stroke and tease her.

When her head started to fall back his hands came up and he placed them one either side of her head and himself between her legs. She arched her back and his erection found easy passage into her. Gently he pushed his way right into her. She kissed him desperately, trying to hold on to the feeling that was suffusing her, the merging of pleasure and pain, the feeling they were in reality one body.

Then his thrusting became harder, stronger. Threading through it was some of the anger he had felt with her earlier. Now she could hold on to nothing and had to let herself go, in a swirl of feeling that made her part of the universe. Greg cried out, became furnace hot, and she could feel him losing, then the tight lock inside her loosening. And they were both still.

He came out of her and lay to one side, his face close to hers. He pulled over a lock of her hair to blot their tears. 'Whatever happens tomorrow or the next day or the next, Shona, I can't lose you. Not now. Not ever.'

Chapter Twenty-seven

The next morning Shona and Greg sat down demurely to a large breakfast under Mrs Smith's benevolent eye. Occasionally their glances would meet and Shona would blush slightly at the thought of their night-time contact.

She was thinking carefully about it. She knew about the closeness between men and women. First from Mary Challoner, who had stood beside her at the coalscreens and whispered to her of voracious men and the dreadful consequences of their baser appetites. Then from Marianne Villeneuve who seemed more in charge, taking the lead when she was with any man, despite the fact that women of her calling were usually seen as being used by men. And now Shona knew everything from the promptings of her own body, which seemed to lead her in pathways entirely unknown before.

She felt a nudge on her foot. 'Come back, daydreamer,' said Greg. 'I said, are you sure you wish to come with me to see Mary Louisa?'

She nodded. 'I'm sure. I do want to come.' She hesitated. 'Will you come to the singing hall with me tonight? We'd have to go to Versay Villa, Marianne's house, first.'

He frowned and her heart sank. She prepared for the battle ahead, feeling the seeds of resentment growing within her.

Then he shrugged. 'I can see I'll have to meet this woman who saved you.'

'Sure I'll show you first where we were before, me and Richie. And then you'll know what it was out there we faced. That we faced each day before we got to Versay Villa.'

When they arrived at the room in Dr Montague's house, Mary Louisa was lying back on her pillows, pale with exhaustion. She lifted a hand towards Greg. 'You came? Did you get my note? No? I was going to send a note and I forgot. Russia? How was Russia. You have to meet Peter, my brother. He's a priest, you know. He said I was for the church . . .'

Greg pulled the chairs across to the bed and sat on the one nearest to her. Shona sat on the other. Mary Louisa's eye lighted on her. She frowned, then smiled. 'And you're here too! I told you about him. Didn't I tell you about the boy going to Russia?'

Shona nodded.

'Come here.'

Shona squeezed past Greg and put her face close to that of the other woman. Mary Louisa caught hold of Shona's ruffled collar; as she brought her even nearer Shona could smell the sweet-sour breath of illness. 'I loved the father,' she whispered. 'That was the greatest sin. The devil knew that. The punishment is just.'

Shona kissed the pale cheek which was so close to hers. 'Sure, there's no punishment, dear lady. You're sick that's all.' Yet, despite herself, some stern words of a priest back at home echoed in her mind and she shivered.

Mary Louisa's hand dropped and her head sagged to one side. The eyes were blank in her pale face.

They stayed another hour, Greg holding his wife's unresisting hand. She ignored them both, blank eyes focused on the silky fringe of a lamp that burned steadily by her side. Occasionally she blew the fringe so that it fluttered, but apart from that there was no movement in the room.

It was a relief to get outside again. Greg handed Shona up into the cab and said nothing as she directed the cabby to take them to Shudehill. As they lurched along the noisy streets, he reached out and took her gloved hand. 'What did she say to you?'

'She told me how wonderful you were. That you were so clever.'

'What else?'

'That the devil had punished her for being so wicked.'

'It was no devil. They were guised up, people from New Morven and Shotwell. New Morven had lost their priest, her brother, and Shotwell people hated her because she was Catholic. And all of them had been raving on because she was so much older than me, it struck a common chord. So they dressed up, guised themselves and came to rout us, to drum us out of Shotwell. Jamie MacQuistain said it was *old ways* to do that. Old ways. They did it in Scotland apparently.'

'So it was just a show?'

'No. More than that. I swear to you, with them all joined together there was evil there. I was terrified myself and more terrified for her. It was a relief to run.'

'You came here?'

'Yes, I got some work in a machine tool shop in Chorlton Street and my father gave us money.'

'So it was all right here?'

'Yes. Mary Louisa was better. More her old self; funny, so full of life. Then she had Lauretta and the whole nightmare came back.' He swallowed. 'She . . .'

Shona put her other hand on top of their joined hands. 'I know. Molly told me.'

'Shudehill!' The cabby called from on top.

The market lining the street was in full swing. Some of the market sellers had stalls, some had tables, some just had their goods heaped on the ground. A thin man in a filthy jacket pinned together at the neck stood before a begging cap, juggling stones. One stall was covered with bloody meat; the stallholder had a child by the ear and was kicking him soundly in the backside with blood-blackened boots. Dark-faced children, equally hungry, looked on silently.

One much cleaner stall displayed poultry; its owner in a whitish apron attended a stout woman in greenish-black, with a man's cap on her head. She was holding up a scraggy hen and shaking her head derisively while he laughed and offered her a plumper specimen.

Two boys were scrabbling behind a vegetable stall, picking up rotting cabbages and carrots.

'That's how Richie got us food,' muttered Shona in Greg's ear.

She pulled him down a back alley and they stumbled over two men sprawled there, the stink of gin mixing with the general odour of decay emanating from the market.

They bumped against a woman with a baby lurking in the doorway, a bag or sack at her feet. She held out a hand, slightly cupped. Shona thrust sixpence into it and marched on, feeling angrier and angrier all the time, part of her anger spilling over on to the man beside her.

'You shouldn't do that,' said Greg. 'It'll only go on gin. These people . . .'

Coldly she drew her hand out of his arm and went forward on her own. She ducked her head under the arch to get into Mellor's Yard. There was mud under their feet and an unbearable stench from the overflowing single privy at the back of the yard.

Greg looked at the grim four-storey buildings that crowded in on three sides. 'You had a room here?'

'We didn't quite have a room.'

He looked bewildered and she softened, caught his hand and walked towards number six. Two men emerged and stopped to watch them. One called across, politely enough, 'Can I help you, sir?'

Greg shook his head and bustled past them into the building, gagging at yet worse smells.

Shona took him up on to the third landing and showed him the corner under the staircase where she had endured three weeks of fever.

The little window was blocked right up with rag; there was a sack of stinking straw there and signs of recent occupation.

'You stayed *here*?'

'Yes. Me and Richie, until he found himself a place waiting at an alehouse, and then me a place too. And then Madame found us and things looked up.'

He put an arm round her waist and pulled her to him. 'Come on, come on. Let's get out of this vile place. Whatever you're trying to tell me, I believe you.' He was walking fast, almost dragging her out. 'I've been here months and I didn't know about this. There's the workhouse, there are the soup-kitchens. There are great charities. You read about them, the poor – the deserving and the undeserving . . .'

He only stopped muttering and hustling her when they reached the only slightly fresher air of Shudehill.

'Now!' She smiled up at him. 'Sure it seems terrible after looking at all this. But don't you worry yourself. Me and Richie, we're out of it now. We'll go back to the Tricorne for luncheon and then go and see Marianne this afternoon. I'll send the cabby with a note to tell her.'

* * *

Marianne had company to tea. Two men stood up as Anna showed Greg and Shona into the long drawing room.

Matt and Septimus Granter came forward and shook them heartily by the hand.

Shona had already met Matthew at Forster's Hall but looked at his father, an older, more grizzled version, with interest. He was dressed in heavy old-fashioned clothes, smelling of the cupboard, stiff from lack of wear; his face was ruddy, his eyes needle-sharp.

As Anna served them small cakes and tea, Marianne looked around with pride. 'Now isn't this nice? Dear Matthew brought his father, and now dear Shona has brought her . . . friend.'

Greg wriggled in his chair, his face reddening, wondering how a pair so otherworldly as these Quakers had come to be in the company of such a woman.

Matthew beamed at him, reading his thoughts. 'My father and I have long looked for a charity that would make a real difference to the lives of the poor, Mr McNaughton. Of course, like all decent Manchester men we contribute to the provision of soup-kitchens and night-refuges. But Madame's scheme for a music hall – where there are all the joys of good entertainment and fellowship, and none of the degradation of drink – has the strongest appeal. In this way we catch people with wholesome entertainment before drink drags them into the gutter.'

Marianne's eyebrows flickered slightly as she looked at Shona. The Quaker's modesty in crediting *his* great idea to her was the least of his wiles. In the last week she had felt herself becoming the object and item of his tide of goodness. Not only would he save his portion of the poor of Manchester, he would save the Frenchwoman from her fallen ways and sweep her into a virtuous life.

Marcus Hodgkiss had been almost rigid with fury at the impertinence of the man. He could smell marriage in the air like a taint. Marianne smiled faintly at the thought. There was no outrage like the offended morality of an immoral man. The price she would pay with these Quakers would be marrying the pair of them, the quaint son and the eccentric father. They came in a pair, like gloves.

'. . . and so for tonight, Mr McNaughton, Madame has collected for us musicians and clowns, jugglers, a teller of tales. And Miss Farrell here as the songbird, reminding the weary of their innocence.' He bowed deeply to Shona and Septimus clapped his hands. 'And our audience will be content with Adam's ale.'

Marianne smiled sweetly across at him. 'Matthew my dear, you will save the world with your eloquence.' She turned to the startled Greg who, preparing to dislike them all, was instead bewildered. 'Don't you think your friend Miss Farrell has the sweetest voice?'

He smiled at Shona. 'I only heard it once, Madame, the very first day I saw her. Then only from a distance.'

'Ah, songbird, you must sing! Your friend Mr McNaughton and dear Mr Septimus Granter, neither has had the pleasure.' She walked to the piano on the low stage at the end of the room, willing Shona with her eyes to follow her. The songbird's innocence might just feather the fly with the father. The son, she knew, was well hooked on her line.

Shona felt the plea. She stood up, removed her hat, pressed her hands to her sides to cool them, and followed Marianne. With a swish of her skirts the Frenchwoman sat at the piano and waited, ready to follow the path of Shona's song with a few graceful notes and a seductive lift of the hands.

Shona folded her own hands and stood looking down at the three faces. Greg, watching uncertainly, now her profound love. Matthew, benevolent but sharp-eyed and no fool. The old man beaming already, nodding to some unseen rhythm.

She looked past them to the window as she sang the verse:

> 'I wish I were back
> in those rolling green meadows
> Where great rocks of stone
> Tumble down to the sea
> There mothers all smile
> And children play sweetly
> and the rain it falls gentle
> on my love and me.'

Then, looking at Greg, she sang the chorus:

> 'A distant land beckons
> My love comes to me
> The land of the mountains
> Is all memory.'

She stopped then, and let Marianne's tingling piano echo the tune.

Matthew applauded heartily. 'Just the tone we want to make in our people's hall of music. So many will share the gentle sentiments, Miss Farrell, it will soften all hearts!'

'Hear, hear!' called Septimus.

Greg did not applaud, but stood up and watched Shona as she made her way back to the chair beside him. He bowed, and she could not make out whether he was pleased or displeased.

'Isn't she wonderful, Mr McNaughton?' said Marianne. 'Doesn't she pull at your heartstrings?'

'Yes, Madame. I thought I knew Miss Farrell, but I learn new things all the time. Wonderful indeed.' His tone was neutral, even cold.

Madame decided that Shona should go on ahead to the new makeshift theatre with Jonnie Forster, who had come in his cab to seek her, and with 'dear Matthew' who would want to see the fruits of the first instalment of his money.

The cabbie, on Jonnie Forster's orders, stopped by the site of the burnt-out Forster's Hotel and the old singing hall. They all leaned out to peer at the blackened gap in the street. The burnt debris had already been removed and they could see rain glittering in the channels where the new foundations had been dug. Piles of bricks and wood filled one corner.

'New place'll be up in two months,' said Jonnie. 'I've had a gang of Irishmen on there all week, clearin' and diggin'. Worked like soldiers.' He winked at Shona. 'You'd'a been proud of them, Miss Shona.'

'Sure, they'd be pleased of the work, Jonnie,' she said in a dry tone.

Matthew pulled down the blind against the driving rain. 'Bills, Mr Forster? Thou'lt see we have all the bills neat and trim? My dear father and I, we will need the bills for our accounting.'

'Bills, Mr Granter?' said Jonnie. 'I assure you, everything will be absolutely trim, absolutely above board.'

Shona wondered how they would ever know that, with the subtle way Jonnie always dealt with things. Then her mind went back to Greg and the cool way he had received her singing. If that offended him, what would he think of her singing in a hall for hundreds of people?

The smell of newly cut wood pervaded the inside of the warehouse, which had hastily been painted a plain cream. The tables, as at Forster's Hotel, were set in long rows leading away from the stage, which was larger here. Two women were still sewing the hems of great curtains which hung before it. Always before, the artistes had walked on to an uncurtained stage.

Shona climbed the steps and stood on the stage in front of the curtains. 'The hall's longer,' she called down to Jonnie, her voice echoing slightly.

'Try it!'

As she did so she stopped several times to take a deep breath and modify her voice downwards to compensate for the echo. In ten minutes she had it right.

'You'll finish the first half after the man on stilts, and start the second,' called Jonnie. 'And save one song for the Finale. You'll need to go through your songs with the feller with the flute.' A man fiddling with sheet music in the small orchestra space bowed in her direction.

Jonnie took Matthew over to the chairman's table, where he and his cronies would sit that night. It was set before the orchestra space, looking out over the rows of tables and the tightly packed chairs.

'Thou'rt expecting many people, Mr Forster. Would that be so, on this first night?' asked Matthew.

'Well, Mr Granter, people are curious. Tonight they'll come just to see what it's about. You see, my lads've pasted posters everywhere but on the moving trains, telling'm all about it. In respectable places. Stressing it's family entertainment: "Three-pence entrance and free refreshments. Come early. First come first served." There'll be no profit from beer, so we need to pack the people in.'

'Refreshments?'

'Lemonade. Pies. Never fear, Mr Granter. Your money, your rules. You can be sure of that.'

The hall was full by half-past six. The partitioned spaces behind the stage were humming with people getting ready for their performances. A man heaving great stilts around was complaining loudly about the height of the roof. The dancers with painted faces were trying full point in their drooping skirts. A clown wearing a red pom-pom hat was carrying a great hoop over his head. A man and woman wrestled with three yapping dogs. A giant of a man with a child's cap on his head and a jacket that was far too small for him was practising crying on top of the steps leading up from backstage. A muscular man was up on a rafter, fiddling with a thick snake-like rope.

Shona pushed through to an even smaller area where three female violinists fought for space in front of a cracked mirror which she recognised from the old place.

The eldest, a tall thin girl, made space for her. 'Have you ever heard anything like it, dearie? A singing hall with no gin. Never heard the likes!'

Shona set about the awkward task, in such a crowded space, of getting out of her rather smart blue dress into the boy's suit of black wool.

The tall girl whistled. 'You go on in boy's gear, dearie?'

'In the first half, yes. In the second half a dress.'

'They'll like that, girls and boys both.' The tall girl leaned over and kissed her on the cheek. 'Best of luck to you, dearie.'

When Shona glanced in the dusty mirror she saw the stain of rouge from the woman's lips which she vigorously rubbed off.

As soon as she was ready she went out on to the stage to join others who were taking turns to peer through a cunning crack in the curtains, designed so they could see out without their curiosity drawing attention.

The hall was packed and the noise formidable. Unusually, the voices of women were more prominent in tonight's audience.

Shona scanned the tables until she found what she sought. At a table not far from Jonnie's chairman's table sat Marianne, resplendent in rust-coloured damask, holding court between Matthew and his beaming father. Marcus Hodgkiss was sitting grim-faced beside the old man. Slightly behind Marianne, towering above her, was Greg, looking around with open interest and wonder.

Shona warmed at the sight of him and crossed her fingers, wondering what he would think of her when he saw her in boy's clothes, singing her tales of fantasy and fairy in Ireland.

A fourth great furnace had been built at New Morven and Tommo, with his reputation and experience, was set on again at the ironworks. Being a single man he did not get back into Stable Street but took a mattress in a corner in Pat Daley's crowded house. Pat watched him like a mother hen, but made no comment on his life which had degenerated into a sullen round of work, bed and Showy's bar. They still went there for a session after work and Tommo would drink steadily, without enjoyment or excess. The fact that Terry Kennedy had not yet been brought to trial was not mentioned between them.

On the Saturday when, unknown to him, Shona was making her debut in the makeshift music hall, Tommo and Pat had spent a long afternoon payday session in Showy's, drinking and gambling on scratch dog-racing in the field behind the pub. There was never any trouble around Tommo now; men kept a respectful distance. They kept from him the talk that Terry Kennedy was coming out of the cells, because all they could find to prove Tommo's certainty that he had done it was the word of some old Protestant woman who was known to be mad as a hatter anyway.

The two friends had to take the longer way back to Pat's house. Tommo never walked past Maudie's little place which was now dark and grimy, like the other houses in the row.

They walked in silence. Pat turned as they reached the door. 'I've a great idea, Tommo. It's a fine day and it's a while since I've been rabbiting. Now won't you come along?'

Tommo shrugged, not showing his keenness. Though his bones were aching and his head was fuzzy from the beer, the last thing he wanted was an afternoon half-sleeping in Pat's noisy household. So he nodded. 'Sure there's nothing else to do.'

'Wait here.'

In five minutes Pat was back with a sacking bundle and one pocket bulging with a wriggling ferret.

They walked out of the village towards the woods.

'So what's this?' Tommo flicked his hand towards the sacking bundle.

Pat moved the sacking to show the gleam of a gun barrel. 'Don't I keep it in good nick for I know not what? It might as well pay for its keep with a rabbit for the pot.' He laughed. 'There, I'm a poet! Sure

I should get back to writing the songs. Though it's not the same without Shona to write them for.'

'Its a lunatic thing, keeping guns. Keep one and you'll use one. If they find it on you, you'll end in the cells alongside Kennedy. They'll say you stole it and send you off in a prison ship, like all those other Irishmen.'

'It's not to use. A few of the boys has them, and this came my way from the brother of a feller I know that died. So I cleaned it up. I'll get some money for it, so I will. There's those boys going back home with a pocket of money. They'll buy.'

They tramped along in silence. Pat coughed. 'I see her now and then, Maudie's little girl.'

Tommo cocked an eyebrow.

'I saw her myself. She looks well.'

They walked on.

'And how is it you see her?' Tommo enquired presently.

'I've helped dig the garden, times. There was an old man there did it whose legs is gone now. Nice old codger, even if a Scot.'

'Does she speak of her mother, little Becky?'

'Not that I've heard. And Biddy says the same.'

'They want nothing in that house, Becky nor Biddy! Nor you. What do the boys at the Cockerel think o' you, gettin' on with Protestants like that?'

'They're not sorry. Well placed for information. House of a magistrate, see?'

'And would ye give such information?'

'Such as would hurt no one.'

'No such information, I tell you, Pat. All information hurts in one way or another.'

Tommo said no more about it. At least Becky had plenty of people watching for her, what with Pat and Biddy and Richie who was up in Shotwell most days on errands for Gil Tait.

'Well,' he said, 'if this ferret of yours is any good at putting up rabbits, Pat, sixpence says I can finish'm with my hands faster than you can with that gun.'

Almost sorrowfully Pat set his ferret to work. His head ached. He wished something would happen over all this business. It was as if the whole world was holding its breath, waiting for he knew not what to happen.

* * *

The first thing that did happen was a visit from the constable that night. He knocked on the door of Pat's teeming cottage and called the pair of them into the dark yard.

'We've been talking to Kennedy,' he began.

'We know that,' interrupted Pat. 'Didn't we deliver him to you like a trussed chicken?'

'Well, he's not having it. Says he wasn't there.'

'It was him, and he needs hanging,' growled Tommo.

'Well, Mrs McNaughton, the magistrate's wife, said she saw him. But he was at the side. It was another man did it, so she said.'

It had taken three visits to the magistrate's house to squeeze that out of her, with that Irishwoman sitting like some guard-dog beside her. Herbert Walton sniffed. What a magistrate's wife had been doing in the house of a whore was a question never asked.

'So what brings you creeping down here?'

'Kennedy says you were her . . . that you were going with her.'

Tommo stood up straight. 'That's right.'

'Asking for trouble, going with a . . .'

Tommo lunged to take a swing at him but Pat held him off.

Walton looked at Pat. 'Kennedy says you have guns here.'

'That's not true, sir,' Pat gasped, still hanging on to a struggling Tommo. He cocked an ear at the hubbub that was coming from inside the house. 'Of course you could root around in there and find out. If they let you.'

Walton pulled his cloak round him. 'Not necessary just now, Mr Daley. But you watch it, the pair of you. This thing hasn't finished. You're part of it, I know it.'

Pat waited until Walton had pulled the gate to behind him and spat contemptuously in the road outside, before he loosened his hold on Tommo.

He pushed him back into the house. 'Leave it. Things'll sort themselves out. You watch.'

Chapter Twenty-eight

Greg McNaughton viewed the swelling crowd in Forster's new music hall, his astonishment turning to dismay. The people looked noisy and none too clean and there was an air of pandemonium about the place.

Having no experience of Forster's original hall, he could not appreciate the difference between the two enterprises. Here, in the roughly converted warehouse, there was nothing wild or threatening in the laughter and it was mere noisy good humour which rippled from table to table. There was no stench of alcohol in the air. This crowd was not rowdy or drunken. Here, there was a much greater preponderance of working women and younger working people from the mills, laughing and joshing in a way familiar to them from work.

The prostitutes confined themselves to a couple of tables in the corner, out to enjoy themselves for once. Jonnie had filtered out those who were dressed for work and sent them home to find more respectable hats and shawls to cover the lewder garments.

With Matthew Granter looking on, Jonnie had assured the girls that, respectably dressed, they were welcome to come and enjoy the entertainment for its own sake. They and he knew that their business would come later in the public houses of nearby streets.

Greg felt a hand on his arm. Madame Villeneuve – he had privately determined not to call her Marianne – was leaning towards him.

'You look forward to seeing our songbird sing?' she asked, her eyes shrewd.

He laughed shortly. 'To be honest, I cannot say so, Madame. I'm not yet used to the idea. In my walk of life this would be seen to be a very . . . forward way for a woman to disport herself. And yet

301

I know Shona does it in all innocence.' His eyes accused her of being the corrupter, the change-maker.

She took her hand from his arm and shrugged. 'Well, Monsieur Greg, she tells me that, when you met, she was *disporting* herself in a coalmine. Black from morning 'til night.' She paused. 'And with neither the time nor the inclination to sing, and pauper's pennies earned at the end of ten hours.'

He held her gaze. 'Shona makes her own way. That is her character.'

The hand was back on his arm. 'That is why we love her. And would we change her?'

His determination to hate and despise the woman who lived – nay, profited – by her charm, faltered. He had worried about her influence on Shona. Watching her now, as she wavered between the options of life in the pay of a doting Hodgkiss or an official liaison with the virtuous Granter, he was overtaken by a reluctant admiration. He had seen business deals fail for lack of such subtlety.

Marianne sensed his reluctant admiration and beamed. 'There, Mr McNaughton. Truly we're on the same side. We wish the songbird well,' she whispered. 'At present she sings for Jonnie's money and for these good people here. Oh, I know, performing on the stage will condemn her to be seen as less than a lady. But which lady sorts dirty coal? Which lady clears slops at a dirty inn? Ah, here!'

The little orchestra was wheezing to a start. Despite himself, Greg had enjoyed the magic acts, the clowns and the skilful stilt-walker. In his mind's eye he could see Lauretta enjoying all this too.

Then the curtains closed on the stilt-walker and the applause faded. The flautist stood up and played the first notes of a plaintive air. The crowd hushed into silence. The curtains swished back and a handsome boy stood with one foot up on a low stool and began to sing about a man who was sadly tricked by the little people as he came home from the inn.

The blood pounded in Greg's ears and his face burned. The voice and the hair – thick, black and tied back with a ribbon – were entirely familiar. Despite this the Shona up there on stage was a stranger, a girl dressed in boy's clothes, a coquette who knew just how to handle the eager audience with her pastiche of innocence. He endured the whole song, then stood up as the applause and shouts of appreciation rippled out across the big hall.

He leaned across to the Frenchwoman. 'I have to go, Madame. Would you tell Shona I will see her at the Tricorne?'

And he was gone.

Shona was angry when, from the stage, she saw the space beside Marianne. However, if anything her anger put more fire in her performance, to the delight of the crowd.

Afterwards she refused Marianne's invitation to a celebratory supper at Versay Villa.

The Frenchwoman took her firmly by the arm and led her to one side. 'Let the boy cool his heels. Teach him that you must . . .'

Shona shook her head. 'That may be your way, Marianne.' She nodded towards the two men, Marcus Hodgkiss, glowering in great bad humour, and Matthew Granter beaming across, oblivious of any ill feeling, delighted at the success of his charitable project and the elegance of Marianne herself. 'But I will do things my way. I will be direct.'

Marianne patted her shoulder. 'You are right, *ma p'tite*. The horse for the course.' She leaned closer and whispered so that her breath tickled Shona's ear, 'He is very 'andsome, your Greg. I'd wager he's the artist in bed.'

Shona's temper faded and she laughed. 'Isn't it you who are the artist, Madame?' And she curtsied, to be offered an even deeper curtsy in return, while the men looked on in a bemused fashion.

In the little sitting room at the Tricorne, the fire was blazing and the small table by the window was set with a cold supper of beef and relish. A jug of coffee simmered over a candle heater, filling the room with its fragrance.

Greg stood up from his chair as she came in. They looked at each other.

Shona dropped her glance, pulled off her hat and coat and laid them on the wide couch. 'Sure, I must have put in a terrible performance to send you running away like that.' She sat down at the table, served herself some beef and started to eat. 'You've had your supper?'

'How could you do it? Stand up there, dressed like that?' The edge of his voice was roughened almost to tears.

'I could do it for money. For me own money. To have money beyond the next meal or even next week. I could do it 'cause I like it, the pleasure that people take, hearing the applause. I could do it 'cause it's the work I choose.'

'But you don't have to, now. I'm here for you, with you.'

She wiped her mouth vigorously with the Irish linen napkin and stood up, holding on to the table. 'Me father and me mother and me sister and brother, they were there for me. But they were taken. Tommo was there, but he went. Being there is nothing. It's not about the week after next. Or the year after next.'

'I'll be there. We'll be married.'

'That's a terrible thing to say. There's Mary Louisa.'

'She's fading.'

She found herself, after many months, crossing herself. 'What are you saying? Wishing death on . . .'

Now he had her by the elbows. 'I loved her. The world began and ended with her. I thought I had the keys to the kingdom. But the poor soul on that bed is not my lovely Mary Louisa. She's long gone.'

'But don't we betray the poor soul with all this talk?' She looked him hard in the eye, blushing. 'And with what we do?'

He threw himself on to the chair and groaned. 'You're right. And equally we . . . I . . . betray *you* by what we do, how we show our love. Though I've come to like your patroness, you're no Marianne. You are no light lover.'

'Well then, we shouldn't show it like that,' she said, her firmness belying her own despair. 'We will not show it.'

'Until we may . . .'

'Don't speak of it!' She put up her hand. 'And before we finish this, I tell you, if there were ever a day even a thousand days from now when we could be wed, I would – will – still choose to work at what I may. I've learned that at least from my life here and from my patroness.'

'Then I can't marry you.'

'That may be your choice.' She picked up her coat and her hat from the couch and rearranged the cushions to make a pillow. 'I'll bring a blanket.'

Later that night as she lay there stiffly she could hear him stirring in the next room, padding around from time to time. It took all the strength she had achieved from the hard times in Ireland, from her life in New Morven and her survival of near death here in Manchester, not to call him to her and tell him she would do anything just to be with him.

Richie relished his partnership with Gil Tait in the running of the stables. Gil was scrupulous. During the day they took the fares turn and turn about, pooled the takings and split them three ways. One share for Gil. One share for Richie. And one share for the Tait and Farrell Fund.

The Fund had existed before Richie came, as the Tait Fund. Gil had always saved; the accumulation of sometimes tiny amounts would one day buy him further stables and horses which would run for the joy of it. The joy of winning. This seemed liked an excellent scheme to Richie, who was happy to join in.

He got a good deal of extra work at night. Gil was now back enjoying his sessions with the music in Showy's bar. This meant that Richie worked from the minute he got up from his straw mattress in the loft, until the moment he went to bed. But he was quite happy.

On the same Saturday that his sister was giving her first performance at the new music hall, and that Tommo was hunting rabbits with Pat, Richie was sitting in Gil's cubbyhole polishing horse brasses while he waited for fares.

'Gent wants a cab at the Queen's.' The narrow face of a lad no more than six stared out at him from under a ragged cap.

'Right.' He jumped up. 'Want a ride, charver?'

The pinched face broke into a grin and Richie had company on the way.

Two men were leaning against the wall in the shadow of the overhang of the public house's roof. Seeing the cab, one helped the other to stand up straight.

'Here we are, Stuart, our chariot awaits.' They got in with much bumping and lurching.

'Hey, mister, I want my penny!' the urchin cried from the road.

'Shotwell, if you will, driver.'

Richie waited.

Stuart barely looked at him. 'I said Shotwell! The Drover's Arms.'

'Doesn't the young'n need his penny, sir? Or you'd have no cab at all.'

'Give it to him, Morry,' came the slurred voice of Stuart McNaughton. 'They're all in league. All lazy scoundrels. Every last one of'm.'

A penny came out of the window of the cab and landed in a muddy puddle in the dirt path. Richie waited until the child had scrambled to pick it up and then gently set the horse away.

Morry Smith jumped out to help Stuart down outside the Drover's Arms. 'You'll be all right now, Stuart. No, I can't come! Just see who it was you wanted to see, have a glass of whisky to warm you up, and get back home. I'll send the cab back to wait for you.'

He jumped back in and told Richie briskly to take him on to Priorton. Unlike Stuart he was careful not to get drunk.

After the twenty-minute ride, Richie dropped the clerk outside the Gaunt Hotel and waited for his fare. 'Ah, driver! You're to return to the Drover's in Shotwell. Wait for that same gentleman and take him home. Calculate what's due and he'll pay.'

Richie made sure he got a good look at the man as he strode away. He turned the cab round in the wide road. It wouldn't be the first time he'd had to pursue individuals for unpaid fares.

He waited for half an hour outside the Drover's for his fare. At last the man whom he knew to be Stuart McNaughton came out, accompanied by a plump young woman. He had his arm round her shoulders and, giggling, she helped him into the carriage.

The man's voice was slurred. 'The Gaunt Hotel, Priorton.'

'Gent said the fare was in Shotwell, sir.'

'Do as you're told, driver.'

Richie turned his weary horse again and set off. He ignored the giggling and the bumping inside the coach as he calmly drove along. This was a not unusual service required by some who called themselves gentlemen.

'Gaunt Hotel,' he finally called down.

There was silence inside.

'Gaunt Hotel,' he repeated.

'Shotwell, driver.'

The night was getting colder. He pulled up his rug, shrugged, and turned the horse yet again.

There were more bumps and groans inside. They were halfway to Shotwell when he heard high-pitched screams. Then, as he slowed at a corner, the door was flung open and the carriage lurched forward, much lighter now.

Richie pulled up and climbed down.

Only Stuart McNaughton was inside. His face was red and he was breathing heavily. Gold glittered in his proffered hand. 'Shotwell. Drive on!'

'Where's the lady?'

'What lady? There was no lady in this cab. You must be imagining things.'

Richie leaned over and plucked a coin from his palm. 'Thank you, sir. That'll do for the fare. Now get out.'

'What?'

Richie deepened his voice. He liked to think he looked big in his driver's coat. He knew also that the McNaughton fellow had not recognised him. 'Get out. There's a lady back there I need to pick up and I don't want you in the cab when I do.'

'Drive on,' Stuart snarled.

'Get out or I'll boot you out.'

The door opened. Richie jumped back up and swung the rig round fast, so that his surly passenger was flung with a thump into a nearby hedge.

He found the girl lying face down in the road, sobbing. He turned her over. There were bruises on one side of her face. Blood was dribbling from a small nick in her neck. Her dress was open from neck to waist and there were flecks of blood on her hands.

He half-dragged, half-lifted her to the cab and pushed her in. He got the oiled rug from the front and drew it awkwardly over her.

'Now, Miss, what's your name? Can I take you to your home?'

'I'm called Ruth Pinkney,' she mumbled through bruised lips. 'An' I live in Low Row, up from the railway works. Me father works there. That feller's father works there too, funny enough.' A thread of bitter irony wove itself into her pain and weariness. 'An' I daren't tell me da or he'll give me as big a hidin' as that one there did. Just tek me home, there's a good lad.' She struggled with clumsy fingers to fasten the front of her dress. 'Just tek me home.'

Chapter Twenty-nine

During the two weeks following their disagreement Greg never returned to their shared bed. They did go together to see Mary Louisa every day, however. In the atmosphere of tense restraint between them, these times were moments of truce.

Mary Louisa had brief moments of lucidity but was more often than not muttering wordlessly or asleep. Molly welcomed Shona to the house now with sisterly warmth. Often Shona stayed in the kitchen drinking tea with her, so that Greg had some time with Mary Louisa on his own.

On the Thursday of the second week she found him sitting there, his face white with misery. Mary Louisa's head had dropped sideways across the pillow; her mouth sagged open, her white hand uncurled loosely on the quilt.

Shona came up behind him and, only to comfort, put her hand on his shoulder. His hand came up to clasp hers tightly and when he looked up his eyes were full of tears. She kept his hand in hers and sat close to him for the rest of the fruitless visit.

The mood of dull misery engendered by Mary Louisa's helplessness lasted right out into the street. They walked the pavement silently in the rain, Shona sheltering under Greg's umbrella.

She cast her mind around to find something to say. 'I was thinking about Lauretta, Greg. She's a cheery little thing, but won't she be missing you by now?'

He frowned down at her. 'I can't do anything about it at the moment, Shona. She's secure with Biddy and my mother.'

'What about a present, a little gift for her? Something to show her you're still here in the world? You could send it in the post.'

He stared at her, his heart lightening by the second. The very thought of Lauretta with her small round head and fine white hair made him smile. 'Yes.' He looked around. 'Now where would I find something?'

'There's a shop on Red House Lane. Marianne buys trinkets there.'

She led him down a side street and into a narrow alley parallel with Market Street. The sign on the door said in green lettering 'Mersten Fine Jeweller'. In every other way the place looked like a private house.

At a desk in the corner sat an old man, who half-nodded, half-bowed to them and went on with his writing. In the centre of the room was a table dressed with a large black velvet cloth, densely covered with items in silver and gold.

Among the filigree ornaments and heavy pearl necklaces they found a little silver charm bracelet with a single bell hanging from it.

Greg held it up. 'I wish to buy this for my daughter. How much are you asking for it?'

'Three guineas only. And I can engrave the bell for you,' Mr Mersten said from the corner, his pen poised. He looked at Shona. 'Your initials on one side and your little girl's on the other.'

Shona could feel Greg freeze beside her. She smiled at Mr Mersten. 'Could you just make that ML for Mary Louisa on one side, and L for Lauretta on the other?'

The old man nodded. 'Beautiful names indeed.'

'So they are.'

'It will be ready by four this afternoon, I promise you.'

They were making their way through the curtained door when Shona stopped and turned round. 'Do you have another bracelet, just the same?'

The old man nodded, finally standing up and reaching to a shelf behind him.

She looked up at Greg. 'One for the other little one, Becky – Rebecca. We can't leave her out. With Maudie's name on the back.'

Greg handed her the umbrella. 'You get back out of this rain. I'll see to this. Then I have to get out to Chorley Street to check a winding engine. We could dine at five. Before you go . . . out.'

That evening over dinner they were easier with each other than they had been for days. The dining room was empty and Mrs Smith served them herself.

The tiny bracelets lay glittering in the lamplight on the table between them.

Greg ate his beef and potatoes absently, watching the neat way Shona ate, as though she had never been hungry.

'I want to know everything about you,' he said suddenly.

She paused, a fork halfway to her mouth. 'And what might that mean?'

'What you were like when you were as small as Lauretta? What you played at? And did you have friends? And were your parents kind to you? Did they give you presents, that you should think of a present for Lauretta?'

She put down her fork. 'Now it's a long story you're wanting.'

'I want it.'

'Well,' she laughed, 'as a little girl, they said I was a handful. Always wandering off out of the village. They once found me right by the sea, more than a mile away. I was poking in the sand, nose to the water, bottom in the air.

'My mother, she was the mild one, but strong in her body. She could work in the house and in the fields from rising to sleeping, and never flag. And I never heard her shouting, like some mammies did who were neighbours.

'My daddy, he was strong like Tommo. He had the fields but he was a blacksmith too. They said he knew magic but I saw none of it.'

Her voice faded away. Greg was looking at her, his own eyes bright.

'Go on,' he urged.

'Tommo, from a small child, loved the iron; to be by the big fire; to help with the bellows. Daddy gave him little jobs and he would do them fine. He followed Daddy, thought he was a king. When he died, Tommo cried, a thing I thought I'd never see.'

'Go on. You had a sister?'

'I had four. Three died and the one who stayed alive was Maire. She was as lovely as a spider's web. So fine, so neat. But always poorly. Coughing. And she had this little hand which didn't grow. She was everyone's love, never a complaint. Always a hot interest in what we were up to.' She smiled at the thought.

311

'She died?'

'In the first season when the potatoes were bad. A wet autumn, she just caught a worse cold than usual and had no strength to fight it.'

'You loved her.'

She looked at him. 'I loved them all.'

He was silent. She went on without prompting: 'And Gerard was the shining one. Everyone loved him. The room looked bright when he came in. Narrow, even elegant like Mammy, and with Daddy's fine temper. And he could dance and play the whistle. But he didn't like the early mornings; like a sore-headed dog in the morning.

'And then Lord Marsteen started the clearances – one after another turfed out. You see, he had tax to pay on each house, whether he got rent or not. So the houses were tumbled. Gerard's sweetheart was hurt as a roof came down, then His Lordship gave me a black eye for not wanting his attention. So Gerard went after Lord Marsteen with a gun and killed a keeper by mistake. So he in turn was killed, by an Englishman's bullet.' She paused. 'He wasn't the only one. The landlords are hated in Ireland.'

'And Tommo. Is he like that? Full of revenge?'

She shook her head. 'Funny enough, he wants none of it. He looks forward, not back. Wants to get on with things, forget it. All the dying sickened him. There was no vengeance in him.'

'Vengeance in many others, from what I read in the papers.'

She looked him in the eye. 'Some justice in it.'

He shook his head. A year ago he would have been certain. Sorry for the Irish but blaming them for their own misery, in spite of Mary Louisa. Now that, like many things, had changed.

He put his hand to an inner pocket and brought out a small package. 'I thought if I could buy a present to remind Lauretta that I was still here, then I could buy a present to remind you also that I'm still here.' He paused. 'And always will be.'

She teased the soft paper away from a small gold ring which had three garnets in a setting of roses finely wrought in gold. She turned it this way and that and peered closer at the inside, which was engraved: *Shona, love always, GM*.

His hand came out and he slipped the ring quickly on to her little finger. 'He said his father had made it, in Russia where they came from, and he had never wanted to sell it. We talked a bit about Russia.' She moved to pull it off but he closed both their hands over it. 'We'll say nothing now, make no plans, strike no bargains.'

'I love you, Greg,' she said quietly. 'I don't know if I can stand this.'

'It's too hard. I've been thinking – can you stay with Marianne? We could see Mary Louisa and dine together. But the rest . . . It's too hard.'

She nodded sombrely, then smiled. 'Are you tellin' me you can't get a decent night's sleep on that wee couch then?'

Marianne welcomed her with open arms. 'Those Italian girls, they have no conversation!' She pushed Shona away from her, to study her closely. 'So the true love with the handsome Scotchman, it fades?'

'No, Marianne. It's too complicated. The true love goes on but the rest is complicated.'

'Ah! He is married! I know the problem.'

'Yes, he is, but it's not like that.'

Marianne put her head on one side. 'Ah, songbird. They all say that.'

Shona gave up. 'What about you? How is Mr Hodgkiss and his elegant missis?'

'Dear Marcus. He vanished from the scene, very angry and suddenly very grand. Now I am – how did he put it? – no better than any other of my kind.' She laughed uproariously. 'I have had the letter from the lawyer telling me to return the house, but I have the official papers and will not budge. The labourer is worthy of his hire – Marcus's own words.' Her tone softened. 'Now dear clumsy Matthew gallops to the rescue like Saint George.'

'What did he do?'

'He buys another house from Marcus, to give him some profit and keep him happy. He will rent it to someone. A respectable clerk with a large family. And Marcus has the rent for the first year.'

'Sure, he's very kind.'

'My dear, he's in love. And . . .' she drew Shona to the couch and sat close to her '. . . I am to be respectable.'

'Respectable?'

'We are to marry.'

Shona hugged her.

'Ah! It is no bad thing to be unmarried and your own mistress. I did not say yes for many ... hours. Only with special arrangements will we be married.'

'And what might those be, then?'

'We will be married like the Quakers. And, as I said to the dear man, he cannot leave his father. They are too close. There is no question.

'So he will stay in his house and I will stay in mine. The perfect arrangement.' She laughed. 'Love in the afternoon, always my favourite. He is longing to love me. And I say yes, when I have the certificate. I am to be respectable. I have had many adventures in my life, but the adventure of respectability is new to me.'

Shona realised how much she had missed this lightness, this gossamer way of seeing the world.

'Were you always like this, Marianne, always so knowing about what to do?'

She stroked Shona's hand. 'There have been difficulties in my life, *ma p'tite*. And in the circus you are always seen as the delicacy on other people's plate. You jump, you die, and still they applaud. They buy you with the ticket. But my dear Jean, he taught me this must not be so. No one can buy you with a ticket. That was what our great revolution has taught us and people forget. You belong to yourself. Even unto death, as he did, he belonged to himself and sought that for others. He judged the danger and took his own chance.'

Shona thought of the little brother who had died at the barricades with Jean but said nothing.

'Now, dear Shona, will you come and see me and Matthew married? On Saturday?'

Shona smiled. 'Indeed I will. And I'll try to get me friend to come. A historic event! And you've to come to hear me sing tonight. I've three new songs that the flute player found. Did I tell you he was a Connemara man?'

Tad Pinkney was glad of his dinner break, short as it was. His mind had not been on his work this morning, a dangerous thing for a roofer.

His mind had been on other things. Like the new Irish workers, getting into that row of new houses in Shotwell. The other men, some living two families to a house still, had been nagging on at him about that for days.

Then there was the fact hinted to him by Stuart McNaughton, and repeated elsewhere, that all the building work would be handed right over to the Irish, who would work for a much cheaper rate.

Then, underneath it all was his daughter Ruth, who had been sick in the drain every morning this week and finally admitted to her condition. She had babbled on about its not being her fault, not her fault. When he had finally beaten the name of the man out of her, he didn't know whether to be pleased or the opposite.

He put his remaining bread back into his sack and set off decisively for the main building. From his viewpoint on the roof, he had seen Douglas McNaughton enter not forty minutes before.

Douglas was alone in the office. Taking out his watch to check the time, he asked Tad to take a seat.

'That needn't worry. It's me bait time.'

'Sensible of you, Mr Pinkney.'

'There's a few things on me mind, like.'

'Spit'm out.'

Douglas had had these sessions before with Tad who usually spoke for the builders around the works. Sometimes they were useful.

'I seed your lad about first one, the thing about the Irish.'

'He never said.'

'Why the lads is resentful like, all these Irish comin' in to tek their jobs.'

'There's work for everybody.'

'But for how long? They're driving down the rate for the jobs. And the works has always been chapel, anyway.' Pinkney was a lay preacher, a stalwart of Shotwell Wesleyan Chapel. 'Not papist.'

'What I pay and to whom is my business.' Douglas regretted now letting Stuart persuade him about the rate of pay. This trouble would not be worth the money saved.

'And there's word that in time all the builders'll be replaced by cheap Irish.'

'Nonsense! It's not true.'

'But wi' respect, like, you would say that, wouldn't yer?'

Douglas retained an aloof silence.

Tad drove on, 'And now it seems they're in that new row of houses. And the lads, some of 'em is two, maybe three families to a house. It's not right. Durham lads should get houses.'

'The houses are built, Mr Pinkney, for the people at the works, whoever they are. And these Durham lads, as you call them, come from all over: Scotland, Wales, Cornwall. So none of your romantic nonsense about Durham lads if you please.' He looked at his watch again.

Tad Pinkney put up a hand. 'But the main thing is this, Mr McNaughton. Me daughter's fallen wrong, like. Now we're a Godfearin' family, not used to shame like this. So I give her a good hidin' and finally she tells us the lad's that one of yours, Stuart . . .'

Douglas sat in silence, absorbing this. Stuart meant little more to him than a neat set of books and a whining, complaining voice at the supper table. He worked long hours alongside his father but apart from that was never in the house.

Douglas stood up and coughed. 'You are sure of this, Mr Pinkney?'

Tad stood up himself. 'The lass is ower scared o' me to tell a lie.'

'I'll check on this. If it's the truth, then you can be sure that honour will be served.'

Tad climbed down the gantry steps, not displeased with the interview. He had expected that return on the Irish. It'd take more than a mild suggestion to get McNaughton to change his mind. Didn't he have a houseful of Irish himself, one way or another? The lads'd have to deal with that in their way. But first he had wanted the business of Ruth sorted. And that had gone down not so bad. Not so bad at all.

Douglas confronted Stuart at Garth End Cottage, in the workroom after supper.

'Pinkney? Ruth Pinkney? I've never heard of her.' Stuart toned down his anger and made his voice soft and sweet. 'Here, Pa, get a Bible, get a stack of Bibles. I'll swear that I never knew a Ruth Pinkney.' Douglas duly got the Bible, and as Stuart was mumbling the words he speculated on the facts. Technically it was true. He'd met Ruths and Joans and Pegs and Jills, but as Morry said, why bother to ask their last name? They were hardly ladies.

'It's that Tad Pinkney getting too big for his boots, Pa,' he said.

'Did I tell you he came in, whining that we couldn't set our own rate for the job, our own workers on? Sent him away with a flea in his ear, I can tell you! Now, Pa, can I get on with these figures? We won't be finished by ten at this rate.'

Douglas sent for Pinkney the next day. Stuart was sitting meekly at his desk.

'Mr Pinkney, I have discussed this matter with my son and have ascertained that there is no truth whatsoever in your tale. And I would tell you that if you spread this tale further than this room, your work here is at an end.'

'It's true. I swear to God it's true!' Pinkney lunged towards Stuart and caught him by the throat. 'Ye bliddy liar, bliddy fornicator! Keen on beatin' girls, she said. You cut her. The lass's dress was torn to ribbons. She showed me.'

Douglas leapt towards him, dragged him off the cowering Stuart and heaved him through the door. 'That's enough, Pinkney. You can get away home and don't bother to come back. There's no job for you here.'

Douglas watched him stamp along the gantry and flinched as he turned back and yelled in his bellowing chapel voice: 'Closet papists that's aal yehs are. Evil fornicators. Unnatural demons. Yeh day'll come, yeh can count on it.'

The roaring sounded even above the sound of hammers and workmen looked up to see what was happening. When he got to the bottom of the stairs a small group of men clustered round him and looked back up to Douglas.

'You men, back to work,' he bellowed. 'Get back to work or all your jobs'll be forfeit!'

Stuart smiled gratefully as he came back into the office. 'Thanks, Pa. That'll show them who's boss, won't it?'

Douglas looked at his younger son thoughtfully, almost as though he was seeing him for the first time.

'I'm taking your word on this, mind, Stuart. I'm trusting you.'

Stuart put his hand on his heart. 'Pa,' he paused, 'you can trust me till kingdom come.'

Chapter Thirty

Septimus Granter looked on critically as the tailor brushed a last imaginary speck from his son's coat. 'A new coat! Thy mother would have relished this day, Matthew.'

He smiled his cherubic smile. 'And doth thou cherish the day, dear Pa?'

'Indeed I do. I had grave fears – grave fears, dear boy, that thou wouldst die in the bachelor state. And now here you are to be wed. And to a fine woman, in my view.'

Matthew nodded to the tailor, who picked up his bag, bowed and left.

He turned to his father. 'I note Mr Hodgkiss paid you a visit yesterday, Pa.'

The old man smiled up at him. 'Indeed he did. A very forward-looking man. A dynamic builder of Manchester in his time, although others are overtaking him now.'

'He had business with you, Pa?'

'Well, he is a client of thy uncle's bank. But, dear boy, I believe he came to share his pleasure at thy forthcoming nuptials.'

'Ah. He's acquainted with dear Madame Villeneuve.'

'So it seems. He was kind enough to tell me that her family was involved quite deeply in those troubles in France a year or so ago.'

'That's true indeed, Pa. Her brother and her intended were killed at the barricades.'

'Well, as I said to him, even though violence is anathema, Friends know what it is to battle for a principle close to the heart. And in the end Mr Hodgkiss agreed with me that Manchester seems full of people from many countries fleeing from the events of that fateful year. People of talent and acumen.'

Matthew sat beside his father and smiled fondly at him.

'And, Matthew, thou'lt be pleased to know that he thinks you have captured a great beauty. A beauty that improves with age. As I said to him, thine own blessed mother was indeed beautiful when she gave birth to thee in her forty-sixth year.'

'And then he went?'

'Yes. He seemed to have a very urgent appointment. He was in such a hurry I almost forgot to tell him that the bank was very happy to extend his loan, at an appropriately adjusted interest, for a further six months.'

Matthew laughed heartily at this and bowed to his father, who bowed back.

Septimus did not attend the simple ceremony, but was there, ensconced in the biggest chair, being tended by Tonetta and Anna who wore fine lace aprons and velvet roses in their upswept hair, when the wedding party returned to Versay Villa.

He beamed from one to the other. 'Matthew, I have never seen a smarter wedding party!'

Everyone's cheeks were red from the unseasonable cold. Marianne was wearing a very becoming pale green dress with a white lace collar; on her head she had a bonnet in the same material, whose deep brim was lined with a very flattering peach silk.

Shona was wearing a cream silk dress with narrow blue velvet collar and sash, and a simple pale blue bonnet. Greg was wearing his business coat, well brushed, and Jonnie was wearing a fine rust wool jacket and checked waistcoat in yellow to match his old-fashioned brushed back hair.

Matthew came across and bowed to his father. Septimus, helped by Anna, struggled to his feet. 'Father, may I present my wife, Mrs Matthew Granter?'

Marianne swept downwards in a deep curtsy; Septimus bowed from the waist. Then, taking Marianne's soft hand, he drew her to her feet and pressed her hand with both his. 'A great pleasure, my dear. I know you will make my son happy or he would not have chosen you to be my daughter. I know he will make you happy, as he has made me happy all these years.'

Marianne leaned and kissed the old cheeks, first left, then right. '*Merci, mon père*. I am captured by both the father and the son. I surrender.'

Everyone laughed and applauded at this and Anna and Tonetta served lemonade and fine French wine, followed by dainty Italian and French cakes.

Greg allowed himself to enjoy the spectacle without really participating. He stayed close to Shona and whispered in her ear, 'Did you enjoy the ceremony?'

'Sure, it was that simple! Hard to believe they're married at all.'

'Look at them!'

Marianne was sitting on the long couch, her arm through that of Granter *père* on one side, Granter *fils* on the other.

Shona leaned across to Greg to whisper, 'I think she may have met her match. A marriage made in heaven.'

'Shona, you look beautiful.'

'Shhh.'

'I want to make love to you.'

'Greg, won't you behave yourself?' She laughed, unable to be stern.

Then she had to stand up, as there were calls for her to sing for the happy couple. Smilingly, she agreed, searching her mind for a special song. She remembered one that Pat had written for the wedding of a workmate in the first May she and Tommo had spent in New Morven:

> 'May all your joys be like the sun
> And shine on each and every one.
> All your sorrows like the rain
> To wet the earth and dry again.
> May all your troubles be confined
> To things which don't rob peace of mind.
> The way you love be ever sweet
> Until the gates of heav'n you greet.'

Septimus beamed and everyone, even Greg, applauded.

Jonnie stood up and bowed to the bride and groom. 'And now, further entertainment.' He signalled to Tonetta who opened the door, red-faced.

In tumbled the clown from the music hall, followed by the flautist and the accordionist, then the acrobats and the stilt-walker, with large boots but no stilts.

In the ensuing commotion, Greg dragged Shona into the hall. 'I have to go to see Mary Louisa. You stay here with your friends.'

She heard the music strike up, then shook her head. 'No. I'll come with you.'

While Greg went off to find a cab, Shona whispered a message for Marianne into the ear of Anna, who was passing with another tray. Then she picked up her pale blue wool shawl from the hall table and arranged her hair against her bonnet.

Inside the coach, he picked up her hand and kissed it and kept it against his face. 'I want to make love to you now! Now!' he said urgently.

She looked out of the window at the busy Saturday morning traffic and laughed. 'Sure that would stop the traffic now, wouldn't it?'

'Come back to the Tricorne with me. Before we go to the doctor's house.'

'There's no time. If we're not there by noon, Molly will wonder about us.'

'Please. On this day. You can't sit there so much who and what you are, and say no.'

A combination of the agony in his voice, and the thought of Marianne there on the sofa between the two men to whom she was now married, made Shona relent.

As Greg shouted the changed instructions to the driver, she allowed herself to look forward to it, the breaching of the dam of these last few weeks, when she was certain that her agony of restraint had quite matched his.

At the Tricorne, Mrs Smith raised no eyebrows when she saw her, although she had not seen 'young Mrs McNaughton' for many days.

Greg locked the door behind them, lifted Shona up into his arms and swept her through to the bedroom. He laid her on the bed, carefully removed her bonnet, and equally carefully took the pins from her hair. She reached to take off her boots but he shook his head. He kissed every part of her face, then, over her silk dress and her kid shoes, every part of her body. With every kiss she ached more for the resolution of flesh on flesh.

She brought his head up and kissed his face, bringing her tongue out a little to tickle the skin. She took his hand and kissed it all over, then guided it down to the hem of her dress which rustled as they ruched it up to her waist. Then she left his hand there while she concentrated with one part of her mind on kissing him and with the other on his caressing hand. In a minute he was over her and entering through the mountains of petticoat and silk. In seconds they were touching heaven together. After only a few minutes they were lying side by side.

Shona breathed hard, her senses still reeling, her mind whirling. She turned to look at him. His eyes were closed. She thumped him on the arm. 'Is it an insufferable bore that I am, then, that it's over too quickly and I send you to sleep?'

He opened his eyes and laughed. 'Exquisite. You are exquisite. And it was you who made it quick. You did it on purpose.'

She sat up and smoothed down her skirts. 'Yes. We've to go and see Mary Louisa.' She looked over the rumpled bed and sighed. 'And really, really we shouldn't . . .'

'Don't say that.' He was standing, pulling down his waistcoat. 'The Mary Louisa who's there is not the woman I married. I wish, I wish that today it was we . . .'

She put her finger on his lips. 'Don't wish, or you may get your wish.'

As they left the Tricorne, Mrs Smith's eye lingered for an extra second on Shona's crumpled dress and wispy hair, now not quite contained by her bonnet, but she smiled amiably enough as she murmured good day.

Molly's grave face hit them like a cold shower as she opened the door.

'Thanks be to God that you're here,' she said, taking Greg's hat and umbrella. 'We thought we'd lost her in the night. And then again this morning. But the dear one has hung on for you. The priest and the doctor are with her. Though how they can be in the same room, sure I don't know. At each other's throats all the time. Can't bear the sight of each other.'

Shona sat on a chair in the broad hall and watched Molly shepherd Greg upstairs, talking away. After five minutes she came back downstairs, escorting a priest this time: a youngish man with iron grey hair sticking out in all directions like coiled wire.

'This is Miss Shona Farrell, Father.'

He shook her by the hand. 'How de do, Miss Farrell? And what do you think of a priest thrown out of the sickroom?'

'Sure that's not so, Father,' protested Molly. 'The doctor just wanted the wee thing's husband to have her to himself for a minute.'

The priest peered more closely at Shona. She felt he could see in her eyes just what she had been up to in the last two hours.

'And when were you last at mass?' he said.

She went bright red. 'I was in a church a few weeks ago, Father. But before that, it would be in the winter. Before I went away.'

He shook his head gravely. 'We both know that won't do, Miss Farrell. Won't do at all.'

'Yes, Father.'

'Now get up there to see your friend before she goes on her longest journey. Dr Montague, cursed atheist though he be, is a brilliant doctor, but now she's ready to go.'

'She was asking for you last night,' put in Molly. 'Said she wanted to see the wee girl from Clare.'

She passed the stout figure of the doctor on the landing and went into the little end room. Greg was cradling the fragile form of Mary Louisa in his arms. He nodded his head. Shona came near and touched the thin hand which was clutching the rosary.

Mary Louisa's fine lids struggled to open. At first her eyes were clouded then they cleared and a faint smile crossed her lips. 'The girl! You two, you two together. The little one – didn't harm her – thought I did. But I didn't. So Father says the next journey will not be so long.' Painfully she lifted Shona's hand in hers and put it into Greg's. 'You two together,' she repeated. 'Take care of my baby.' Exhausted, she closed her eyes for a second. Then she opened them and looked just at Shona. 'Give him my love. And tell Greg about him . . . tell . . . ?'

She seemed to choke and fell back awkwardly against Greg who laid her on the pillows and put her hands and the rosary together on the coverlet. His lips were trembling.

Shona fell to her knees and started to say prayers she thought she had forgotten and Greg walked slowly to the door and beckoned across the banister for the priest.

Montague had arrangements in hand for the funeral – arrangements which Mary Louisa had insisted that he write out

324

and they both sign. Her body was to be taken back to Kerry to the village where she was born. The funeral was to be in the little church where she'd said her first confession and she was to be buried alongside her mother and sisters. The doctor, so fond of Mary Louisa, was prepared to pay for the journey out of his own pocket and to send Molly to make sure it was done correctly.

Greg however would not hear of it. 'I have to go myself,' he told Shona soberly two days later as they sat in Marianne's little sitting room. 'I'll take her home.'

'Do you want me with you?' she said hesitantly.

To her relief he refused. 'Molly's coming. "To see the dear girl right", as she says.'

'Oh,' Shona said dully. Talking to him in these last days had been like talking to a stranger. He seemed more absorbed in the dead Mary Louisa than he had ever been when she was alive. He had been at the doctor's house two whole days and evenings, talking, talking to Molly and the doctor about the Mary Louisa they all knew well, and of whom Shona had had only the briefest glimpse.

He was cutting her out again, as he had when he had fled New Morven, as he had when he had hated the thought of her on stage. There was still unfinished business with Mary Louisa.

She bit her lip to force back the tears. She felt shut out. But wasn't it right that she should be here suffering on the outside? Hadn't she betrayed the woman? Hadn't he?

The silence between them had gone on too long. Greg looked around. 'You'll stay here while I'm away?'

'How long will you be?'

'I can't say.'

She looked around the room and shook her head slowly. 'No. I think I'll go home.'

He frowned. 'Home?'

She laughed wanly. 'A funny thing to say about that dirty old place, New Morven. For how long have I called Ireland home? And in one bit of me heart it'll always be so. But I want to go back to Richie and Tommo. Seeing that happen to Mary Louisa, being there, made me think of my sisters and my mother. And Gerard.' The tears started to flow in earnest. 'I want to be with Richie and Tommo. I'll go tomorrow.'

He patted her hand awkwardly as though she were a stranger, and stood to go. She stayed where she was.

'I will take you to the station.'

'Matthew is taking me in his uncle's carriage.'

'Well . . .'

She didn't go to the door with him to see him out. Tonetta looked in on her and returned five minutes later with a little tray of tea. 'Good for the nerves,' she announced, pouring the liquid into a pale cup. 'You look very un-beautiful, Miss Shona, when you are sad. Your nose is very red and your eyes wet. And the hair – it might be seaweed.'

'I don't think I can take it, Tonetta, I don't think I can.'

'Yes, you can, Miss Shona. The women, they are built to take it.'

The next morning Matthew Granter came to pick up Shona and Marianne to take them to the station. Shona admired the smart coach which had a uniformed driver and a glossy black horse to pull it.

'His uncle the banker has it and says Matthew and Pa must use it, but they take no notice and ride in dirty cabs,' announced Marianne. 'But now!'

'But now,' put in Matthew, 'we have a lady to transport and it becomes significant.'

Marianne and Matthew melted into each other's arms and Shona turned to ask Pietro to bring her luggage.

Greg was at the station when they arrived. He walked along silently beside Shona to the platform where her train was steaming up. Matthew Granter gave Shona a brotherly hug and lifted her cases and boxes on to the train.

Marianne hung on her neck. 'What will I do without you? Without my little songbird? You must write, write me a letter every day. And I will visit you. Yes, I have seen little of England yet. I will visit you.'

Matthew bowed. 'And I earnestly hope, Miss Shona, that the music hall will continue to succeed without thy special contribution, although I gravely doubt it. And perhaps thou'lt give thy brother my felicitations? A fine man. A fine man indeed. And what is more, the mysterious cause of my present happiness.' So saying Matthew led his new wife tenderly away through the swirling steam.

Shona smiled weakly at the thought of those same elegant skirts trailing the mud of New Morven.

When she could wait no longer, she turned to Greg. He kissed her chastely on the forehead, and for a moment she felt as young as Lauretta. 'Shall I send a message for you to be met?'

'No. I have money. I'll take a trap.' She looked around her and thought of the way she had arrived, with a small bundle and a blue jug filled with sixpences. 'Have a good journey to Ireland,' she said stiffly.

'I must do it, Shona.'

'I know. I see that.'

'Give my love to Lauretta and regards to my parents.'

'Sure I'll do that.'

'I wanted to ask you – what was it Mary Louisa told you to tell me, at the end? What was it?'

She smiled woodenly and turned to get on to the train. 'It was nothing much. I'll tell you when next I see you.'

Settling down in her seat, she knew that what she wanted most of all now was to see Richie and Tommo, to have them within reach, to hear their voices in her ear.

Looking out of the window she watched Greg's tall straight figure depart without a backward glance. He was a stranger again.

PART THREE
COUNTY DURHAM
AGAIN

Chapter Thirty-one

'Margaret! I've a rare visitor here!'

Douglas finally found his wife in the dining room. A stout man with silver moustaches bustled in after him.

Margaret was sitting up to the dining table, a little girl either side of her and wooden alphabet blocks before her on the chenille tablecloth. She stood up to shake hands, recognising the man she had met briefly some years ago, when he drew up her will for her.

'Mr Moxham! How kind of you to call.'

'I'm rarely out of my office, Madam. I would have been denied this pleasure had not my clerk let me down yet again. He is a new man and is proving most unsatisfactory, most unreliable.'

'Grandpa, see my bracelet!' Lauretta was holding up a podgy wrist from which hung a little bell attached to a silver chain. 'My daddy sent it. It has my letters on and my mammy's letters on. See!'

'And mine!' Becky put up her own more fragile wrist.

'Greg sent them both bracelets, wasn't that nice? And he says he is very well. See, we got out the blocks to show them how the letters made their names.' Margaret smiled at him.

'See, Grandpa. See!'

One line of blocks on the table spelt M.A.R.Y. L.O.U.I.S.A., the other spelt M.A.U.D.I.E.

'Ah, the wonder of Mother – or in this case Grandmother – as teacher,' said Mr Moxham. He turned briskly to Douglas, who dragged his gaze away from Mary Louisa's name and observed with some surprise the calm demeanour of his wife.

'Mr Moxham came to the works on urgent business, Margaret. Perhaps you'd join us in the parlour?'

She stood up and jumbled up the letters on the table. 'There, girls, see if you can make the names again.'

Mr Moxham was standing as far away from Irma the parrot as was polite, having refused a chair. 'You know, Mr McNaughton, how I like to get on? And standing up for business is the best way to get on with it.'

'Well, if you don't mind, I'll sit down.' Margaret smiled up at him. 'I find I like to be comfortable.'

Mr Moxham glanced at Douglas, who nodded. 'Mrs McNaughton, I am here on most confidential business. I've a client, a Mr Shakespeare, who is at the moment in America pursuing some – er – business. Now he is an enterprising but somewhat – er – eccentric gentleman. To put no finer point on it, he is a gambler who likes, and has profited from, a gambler's risks.'

'He's the fellow who has Killock Castle,' put in Douglas.

'I remember there was a boy, Orlando,' said Margaret. 'One of Greg's waifs and strays. Didn't he die, poor soul?'

'Stuart checks on Killock Castle for Mr Moxham each month. A task Gregor used to undertake,' said Douglas.

'And here we get to the substance of the matter,' Mr Moxham bustled on. 'I've received, in a package from Mr Shakespeare, a copy of his will, which names Gregor and mentions gratitude for the friendship with his son. It also names another young person whom I, and indeed Mr Shakespeare, met but once and who is named in the will as "the gypsy girl called Shona Farrells".'

'Good grief!' said Margaret.

'Indeed,' said Mr Moxham. 'Now I must say the papers are all in order, drawn up with scrupulous care by a lawyer in New York. There's some query about the spelling of the name, but I have letters permitting me to correct it if necessary.'

'It's just Farrell, I think,' said Margaret. 'Her aunt lives here in this house.'

'Her aunt lives here? Ah! She is respectable!'

'My son's not the only one who indulges in lame ducks,' said Douglas dryly.

'Although in my case,' rejoined Margaret gently, 'it is I who am the lame one. Yes, Mr Moxham, she *is* respectable, as is her family. They are not gypsies. Mr Shakespeare is mistaken. The younger brother has a good business as a horsekeeper. And the older's a hardworking man, I believe.'

'The epithet "gypsy" was, I believe, a flattering one in Mr

332

Shakespeare's usage. And should she be a gypsy, there is no difference. These American papers are absolutely sound. The young woman?' Moxham looked round the room. 'She lives close? This is why I am here. I need an address.'

'No. She is at present in Manchester. In touch with our son, I believe now. I have the address.' She sorted through her writing box and held out the letter. 'See, she has a fine, schooled hand.'

'So I see.'

Carefully, she copied the Versay Villa address on to some clean paper.

Mr Moxham put on his spectacles to read it. 'Good, good. This is what I need. She is in touch with your son, you say? Mr Shakespeare and I saw them together. They made an interesting . . .' He removed his glasses and looked at them both. 'I need not tell either of you good people that what I have divulged is private and confidential. Absolutely.'

They nodded.

'Well I will take my leave, Madam. Please to continue teaching your grandchildren. It is in the education of the young that civilisation is sustained.'

Douglas saw him to the door and came back into the dining room. The girls were still playing at the table and Margaret was standing with her back to the fire. He noticed her hair was smooth, and she was wearing a cameo brooch at the neck of her pale yellow blouse. The lame duck was, indeed, walking again.

'That was an odd thing,' she said. 'Biddy's niece in a rich man's will.'

'These are odd times, Margaret. Plain men make fortunes and grandees suffer losses.'

'Grandpa, see! I've made the little name.' Lauretta had pulled together two worn blocks to make the initials ML.

'What a clever girl,' said Margaret.

Douglas stared at the letters and thought of a drawing, signed with those same initials, deep in one of his drawers upstairs.

'I have to go back to the office,' he said abruptly. He turned, then turned round again. 'It would be kinder, nay, more sensible if you don't mention this to Biddy, Margaret. We've no idea of what it really means and whether anything will really come of it. Moxham did say the man was eccentric.'

Later, at supper, Douglas was quite genial. Biddy being there, Moxham's visit was not mentioned. They talked about the silver bracelets and the cleverness of both children in their spelling, Margaret noting that, if anything, Becky was quicker than Lauretta.

After supper, Biddy helped Thoria to clear the dining room and went off with her to chat in the kitchen.

As was his recent habit, Douglas sat with Margaret in the parlour for five minutes before he went up to his workroom to get on with his letters.

He cleared his throat. 'Margaret, I want you to tell me about Stuart.'

She frowned at him. 'He came and got changed and went off for an appointment at Priorton. He's often straight out in the evening these days. What about him?'

'It just occurred to me that I hardly notice him. It is as though he makes himself invisible, even in the office. I noticed Greg when he was here . . .'

She took her knitting out of the bag stitched by Biddy and pulled the ball of wool off the needles, ready to knit. 'He's always been an odd boy. Hard to reckon. I missed so much of him when he was little. He's your son too, Douglas. What do you know about him?'

He cleared his throat. 'Would you say he was unprincipled, violent?'

Carefully she inserted her needle into the first stitch. Her hand shook as she pulled the wool over to make the stitch, but her voice was quite even. 'Being our son, we should be sure of his principles, that they should mirror our own. But he's so secretive, it's hard to know what his principles are. He has strong views about some things; he and Gregor had quarrels – about his intolerance, I suppose. And he tells lies sometimes. I've discovered that through the years. Violent?'

She thought of how he had attacked and kicked her when he was eleven, when Flora left. And incidents since with cats and birds, all hidden from Douglas because of her own fear of his wrath.

'Violent?' she repeated determinedly. 'Yes, perhaps. Why do you want to know?'

'A fellow at the works has accused him of violence and . . . immoral action towards his daughter.'

'And what does Stuart say?'

'He denies it.'

'But,' she said slowly, 'he would deny it, wouldn't he?'

They sat in silence for a minute. Then he shrugged. 'Leave it. I've burdened you enough already. It helps to talk to you.' He stood up. 'I must get some work done. Will you bring up a warm drink as you go to bed?'

She nodded calmly and bent her head down over her knitting, trying not to show how delighted she was about the way things now were between them.

Upstairs in the workroom, he went straight to his document cabinet and rooted out an exquisite drawing from the bottom drawer. He held it towards his face so he could breathe in her scent, almost imperceptible now. He passed his fingers over the initials at the bottom. Then, holding it over the fire, he slowly tore it into very narrow strips which curled and twisted on their way into the flames.

In the kitchen Thoria was showing Biddy some 'finds'. Thoria was a magpie, collecting any odd throwaway items from the household which she kept in a washed out flourbag in her attic room. These were always for her mother or her brothers when she eventually went 'back home' up the valley.

'I found these. I was givin' the coal-hole a good swill out and these were at the back, behind the last of the coal.' She laid out a small black wooden box painted with faded colours, and a leather belt, all twisted and misshapen.

'Ah wor wonderin', Biddy, if I could mebbe have 'em? Clean them up, like. The box ud go for one of me sisters and that belt is good leather. It'd do for one of me brothers. A bit of a wash'd mek world o' difference. See all this black round the buckle? Like I say, a good wash'd mek a world o' difference.'

'Sure, nobody would miss an old belt or a dirty old box, Thoria. Wasn't it thrown away in the first place?'

Pleased, Thoria went and held them under the pump which was neatly ensconced in one corner of the scullery. She brought back the box and placed it on the windowsill to dry. Then she went back to start on the belt.

'Hey, come here, Biddy. See this.'

The water was running a sludgy grey but as they watched it was gradually becoming a rusty brown.

Biddy knew with dull reasonableness that this was blood, and that the belt had been used violently to hurt someone or something. In her mind's eye she could see the blows coming down, the buckle hitting and cutting.

She removed it from Thoria's grasp. 'You want nothing with this belt, me darlin'. Nothing at all.' She patted it dry with one teatowel and wrapped it in another. 'I'll put it away. I can't see how it could be any use to anyone. Not at all.'

The box, pretty as it was, stayed on the windowsill.

Later that night, on her way to bed, Biddy found Margaret in her little upstairs sitting room, looking out of the dark window in the old way.

Biddy put a hand on her shoulder. 'What is it, me darlin'? Is there somethin' troubling you?'

'I've been sitting here thinking, Biddy. Douglas . . . No, not about Douglas. He told me something about Stuart. Biddy, I'm sure Stuart's done something terrible. Horrible. I just feel it.'

Biddy leaned on the windowsill, and faced Margaret. 'Now what is it? What's happened?'

Terry Kennedy was already in the White Buck when Stuart and Morry arrived. He was tucked into a dark corner table with an empty glass in front of him. Stuart ordered more drinks from the hovering landlord and then sat down beside Morry.

Terry grinned across at Stuart. 'Good thing for you I'm out.'

'Bound to happen,' said Morry. 'No real proof. No one's that interested in the death of some whore, months ago.'

Terry nodded vigorously. 'Aye. Like I said, Stuart. Lucky for you. I might just have been tempted . . .'

'You got money,' said Stuart sulkily. 'I sent money with Morry here.'

'Aye, but it's gonna be hard to pick up work now, and a place to stay. No one'll put me up any more. I need to get out, get away. Newcastle mebbe.'

They all thought of the last time he had 'got away' when they had convinced him he would be blamed; only to come back with the gleeful news that he didn't have to take the blame – Greg McNaughton was running off. Just as likely he had done it, wasn't it?

'This time, though, you stay away,' said Stuart fiercely.

Terry put both hands up mockingly. 'Aal right, marrah! Aal right, *Mr* McNaughton! I seen what you can do when roused. I dinnat want none of that.'

Morry watched how Stuart handled this, always interested in other people's reactions. He noted the hand under the table, opening and closing in quick succession.

Morry put in his own bid. 'And to be frank I am in need of money as well, Stuart,' he said smoothly. 'It's time I was on my way. Old Moxham is getting a certain look in his eye, and I want to leave while I can squeeze a reference out of the old fool.'

Stuart looked from one to the other, their faces glowing palely in the dark corner. They looked as though they were about to eat him. He wriggled in his chair.

'I need a favour. There's a woman who's harassing me. Her father is harassing me, rather. I need someone to talk to her, persuade her to stop.'

He told them his own version of his encounter with Ruth Pinkney. 'So you see, she needs to be persuaded to tell them it was all a mistake.'

They were both shaking their heads.

'I wouldn't do it, not after last time,' said Terry. 'Do your own dirty work.'

'Well, at least can you get her somewhere quiet, really quiet, so I can see her? I can tell her the big mistake she's making. Persuade her myself.'

Terry stroked his chin. 'I could do that right enough. You'd need a carriage or sommat.'

'Easy.'

'An' it'll cost yer.'

'I've no money.'

'I imagine you obtain money for the wages from the bank?' said Morry.

'Yes, I do that. Every other Thursday.'

'Well, that should furnish both myself and Mr Kennedy with ample means of departure. And a little over.'

337

'I can't steal it from myself.'

'No need,' said Terry. 'Just tell us when it'll be in the safe, give us a lend of the key and we'll *furnish* oursels wi' the money.'

'No. You'd have to break into the safe. Otherwise I would be suspected. I can tell you how to get into the office.' He paused. 'But I must have my favour first.'

Their heads close together they made their plans. Much to his surprise, the landlord, coming across for further orders, was waved away.

On Thursday before supper Biddy and Margaret were in the upstairs sitting room looking out at Lauretta and Becky who were in the garden playing with the rabbit, Maudie.

'Supper'll be a little later tonight,' said Margaret. 'Douglas is visiting old Jamie.'

She and Biddy had been there together in the afternoon and sat by the old man's bed. He had come to life just once, to ask Margaret if that Irish feller had got the lettuce and carrot seed in, then drifted away.

Pat Daley had come straight from work and, after consuming one of Thoria's huge delicious pies, was now removing the warming cloches and planting seeds of lettuce, radish, spring onions and carrots in careful rows.

They looked along the street and past the works at a neat carriage which was making its careful way round potholes in the street, and watched with interest as its driver brought it to a halt at the gate of Garth End Cottage.

A woman in a pale blue bonnet alighted and spoke to the driver who touched his cap and nodded his head, then settled back to wait. They watched as Pat went across and hugged the lady thoroughly. The children ran across and Lauretta was lifted up and swung round shoulder-high so that she showed her bloomers.

'Heaven be praised,' said Biddy, 'isn't it Shona, home like some bird of paradise?'

'Good grief,' said Margaret, hurrying to the door. 'I'd never have recognised her. Not in a thousand years. Come on, Biddy.'

338

Chapter Thirty-two

On her arrival at Priorton Station. Shona had made a deal with the coach driver. She needed to make two or three stops on the way to her destination, but didn't wish to pay waiting time. Business being slack at this time on a Thursday evening, he was happy to agree.

Her first stop had been the little presbytery beside the new Catholic church in Priorton. She had to use all her charm to get past the severe housekeeper, who insisted that the fathers were at supper, and poor hardworking souls shouldn't be disturbed.

'Sure it's only Father O'Reilly I want, Ma'am. I have great need of him, but just for a few minutes.'

The housekeeper sighed. Everybody's need was just as great as this, and nobody needed more than a couple of minutes. And her special meat pie would go cold yet again.

At first Father O'Reilly didn't recognise Shona; then he did and smiled, quickly veiling the doubt in his eyes. What had the child been doing to make such a transformation in her means and demeanour in such a short time? Three or four months, wasn't it?

She told him something of her life since she had left New Morven.

'Singing?'

'Singing. And that's all, Father. And now it's finished. It was a means to an end.'

'Ah, I always said you sang like an angel. Perhaps the good Lord has made that your salvation in a trying time. Now, while it's wonderful to see you here, Shona, I have to tell you, people don't come to see me like this, save they want something. What is it you want?'

'A few things, Father. There was a woman I met in Manchester, such a lovely woman. She was sister to the last priest here, Father Peter . . .'

'Ah, yes, Father Peter.'

It had taken Father O'Reilly some time to find out, from his flock and from his superiors, that his predecessor had broken down in health here in Priorton and was at present being cared for in a closed order west of the Pennines. And from the local sources he knew now the special connection between Father Peter and the Protestant household in Shotwell.

'She was fond of her brother and troubled about him, really troubled,' Shona went on.

'Was?' he interrupted.

'She died, Father, just last Saturday.' Less than a week and it seemed like a year. 'Sure it would be a good thing if you could say a mass for her, in her brother's church? Her name was Mary Louisa. Mary Louisa McNaughton. And a mass for him, the brother, wherever he is.'

He stood up, gathering his soutane to him. 'Would you like to come now into the church and join me in a little prayer for them?'

She hesitated.

'It will help you when you think of her,' he said. 'You can be sure of that.'

As they walked the short distance to the church he turned to her. 'And it might help also if you made your own confession, Shona. Have you been in church since you left home?'

'I sat in the back of a Protestant church once, but no. Not in the real way, Father.'

Later, she felt a warmth, a satisfaction as she heard Mary Louisa's name spoken by the priest in this church, bedded down in an old Latin which had its own mysterious stream of comfort. Then she went through the ritual of her own confession, using the conventional words and phrases made to cover the whole of human activity, approved and disapproved. The priest's voice, as he advised the appropriate penances, was reassuringly neutral.

He waited in the back of the dimly lit church for her to finish and walked with her to the waiting coach. 'Is there anything else, Shona? I feel there's something. I feel it.'

She shook her head. The little church had felt comfortable, right. She'd longed to ask him then about a marriage. A marriage to an outsider. But there was no certainty in her heart. It seemed that with her death, all Greg's early love for Mary Louisa had come flooding back, leaving no room at all for Shona. Perhaps that was to be her greatest penance.

At the livery stables in New Morven, Gil Tait jumped up and down at the sight of her, sweeping his hat off, winking and twitching, finally gaining enough control to yell for Richie.

He shook her hand heartily and, after a token resistance, submitted to a hug and a kiss on each cheek. 'Are ye back, Shona? Or just visiting?' he asked.

'I'm back. I like this place. Ye could see it all from the train: it's all rolling green, even with the pit wheels and the dirty little villages. I'm sick of streets and streets and streets. And high buildings.'

'What'll you do? Can't sing for money anywhere here, 'less I take the hat round for you in Showy's bar.'

'No fear of that. There'll be something. I might rent a little shop in Priorton, sell some trinkets. And I can always go back to the pit.'

'You want nothing doing that again.'

'Wasn't bad. I liked the coal itself. And see how it warms the world.'

'Ye're a lunatic, I'll say that for ye, Shona.'

'Ye're right, Richie. That's just what I am. Anyway, what about Tommo? Where's he?'

'He's bedding in with Pat's crew. There must be nineteen in that house now.'

'What happened with Terry Kennedy?'

'They say he's out of the cells. There's to be no trial.'

'We were sure, Tommo and I . . .'

'They say there's to be no trial, whether he did it or no.'

In the end they went along to Showy's bar and Shona waited outside while Richie went in to rake Tommo out.

After enjoying his first bear hug, Shona stood back to look into Tommo's eyes, dulled by too much drink, with dark circles underneath from lack of sleep.

'Sure, Tommo, you look like death.'

'S'nothing, Shona.' His speech was slurred. 'Aren't I as lively as a cricket?'

She glanced towards the bar. 'Where's Pat?'

'Where's Pat? Isn't he across New Morven, digging like a good Irishman for those Protestants you and Biddy love so much?

341

There's talk about him round here, now. Changing sides, they say. The boys down the Cockerel won't even speak to him. Might catch him in the dark one night.'

'Come on, Tommo,' said Richie quietly. 'Let's get you home.'

'Home? Home, he says. Home to a fleapit where you take turns . . .' Tommo mumbled on while they poured him into the coach; he was still mumbling when they deposited him on the doorstep of Pat's house and pushed him through the door.

Shona had tears in her eyes as she turned to Richie. 'He was never like that before. All those hard times in Ireland and since.'

Richie shrugged. 'Nothing to be done for him.'

'We'll see about that!' The tears dried up entirely. 'Now I'm away to see Biddy, as I've got something to tell the McNaughtons. I don't know what'll happen there.' She paused. 'Anyway, you meet Tommo out of work tomorrow, before he starts to drink, and get him across to the McNaughtons'. I'll meet you there. We need to talk together about what we all have to do now. But,' she put her hand on Richie's arm, 'we'll do it together. We're not separating any more. It's not good for any of us.'

Richie grinned at her. 'I'm all right, Shona.'

'So you are, Richie. Sure, you're quite exceptional.'

At Garth End Cottage Thoria was the only one who was not startled at the change in Shona. For her, Shona had always been rather exotic. A few pounds in weight, the extra gloss on her hair and brighter, prettier clothes made little difference.

Shona found herself chuckling at the open amazement of Biddy, who kept harping on the changes. 'Each time I look at you, Shona, I think I'm seein' a vision. Indeed Richie did say you were managing, but said nothing about this.'

They were up in Margaret's little sitting room. Shona was relishing tea and Thoria's scones, having eaten and drunk little since she had left Manchester.

She laughed. 'A few clothes, Biddy – presents from the lady who took us in to work for her, and a hat bought from my own earnings! That's all it is.'

'You sang for money, Shona?' said Margaret, watching her with that combination of doubt and speculation which had shown itself already on Father O'Reilly's face.

'That was all I could do there, Mrs McNaughton. Sure, I couldn't find any coal to pick. And the singing hall I worked the most in was a new kind of place. For families. A temperance place. No drink at all.'

'And they paid you money for that?'

'I was well taken care of and well paid. I enjoyed the singing, but they were just a few simple old songs. I wouldn't do it for ever.' She stood up. 'I'll have to get on.'

'Where'll you stay?' said Margaret.

'There'll be somewhere down in New Morven. Even here in Shotwell.'

'Well,' said Biddy doubtfully, 'Richie's in a hayloft and Tommo's staying at Pat's with I don't know how many thousands of others.'

'I know. I've just seen them.'

'You can stay here,' said Margaret, suddenly eager. 'There's Douglas's dressing room; he uses it very little now.'

'Sure I can't do that, Mrs McNaughton.'

'There's a spare bed in the attic by me,' said Thoria, standing by the door taking it all in.

They all looked across at her, surprised that she was listening so closely. Then Shona remembered the first night she and Richie had waited on Marianne and the wooden-faced footman who had saved her from rape or worse by Lord Marsteen and his friends.

She glanced at Margaret. 'That would be fine. If you . . .'

'Yes, fine, fine.' Margaret nodded vigorously. But she was somehow dissatisfied. She wanted Shona this side of the invisible line which divided masters from servants even in this modest household.

Shona had the carrier bring her considerable luggage into Garth End. While he was unloading she talked to Pat, who had his tools by him and was ready to go.

'To tell the truth, Shona, I can't keep up with Tommo these days. He drinks so fast and's less company than a stoat. Then the old boy who does the garden here was so sick I just did some jobs for him. And now he's in bed. And then that Thoria there, I've never met cooking like it. Sure she's a homely kind of girl, but kind too.' Then Pat shook his head apologetically. 'Sure I couldn't keep up with Tommo at all, Shona. I'd end up more miserable than him and fit to slit me own throat.'

She grinned. 'Well, I'm back now, Pat. All he wants is a good kick. You watch me sort him out.'

She paid off the driver, telling him to drop Mr Daley in New Morven on his way back to Priorton. Much to the driver's relief, Pat, in his dirty ironworker's clothes, climbed up to sit on the driver's seat beside him, and not inside his nice clean coach.

Douglas had watched his younger son closely under the hard routine of the working day.

Stuart was out of the office a good deal on Thursdays, checking work sheets with Young Jamie MacQuistain, ready to put up the pays on Saturday morning. Today he looked at the figures with cold fear, knowing that this week they were some kind of fiction.

Once, when he came back in the office, he found his father, pen down, staring at him.

'Did you want something, Pa?'

'Are those paysheets ready?'

'They will be by tomorrow morning. Like they always are every Friday.'

That was true. Douglas knew Stuart was meticulous, absolutely reliable, with his paperwork.

'You know, I do appreciate the fact that you work hard here, Stuart. I see how you dedicate yourself to your job.'

Stuart's heart lurched. He longed to throw himself on his father shouting: 'Too late, too late!' Instead he managed to say coolly, ''Course I know that, Pa. We can't all go off with bleeding hearts.' And put down his head again over his books.

Later that day, after sorting out some work schedules with Young Jamie, Douglas asked after his father.

Young Jamie shook his head. 'He's fading, the old man. Tranquil enough, though. Maybe it's worse for us that watch. My wife is sore troubled by it.'

'I'll walk back with you tonight to have a word with him, Jamie.'

'Right, sir. He would like that, I'm sure.'

'Now then, what about that batch of wagons we're doing for Wilson's pit?'

When they arrived at Young Jamie's house that night, the old man was fast asleep under a quilt in his son's front room.

He stirred, awoke and smiled a gap-toothed smile at Douglas. 'Hello Mester Douglas. And how is the lady now?'

'She's well, Jamie. Better than ever.'

'That's good. And how's the garden? Is it set yet?'

'Aye, Jamie. The feller that was helping you's doing a fair job.'

'Aye. Not bad for an Irishman.' His eyes closed, then opened. 'You'll need to watch your back a while yet, Master. The old ways is nearly finished but not quite.'

They watched as he drifted off again into a light sleep.

Douglas looked at Young Jamie. 'What did he mean?'

Jamie shrugged. 'He wanders. He's a highlander and a blacksmith and some of the things he says might hold a shred of meaning. Both of these things give a man the sight. But he's an old man on the edge of infinity and he wanders.'

That night Shona sat down to supper with the McNaughtons under the proud beam of Biddy's gaze and the dark malevolence of Stuart's. He had glared at her sourly when Margaret reminded him of who she was, and had not returned her greeting.

The meal started quite decorously. Margaret asked Douglas about Jamie, and shared his sadness at the old man's fading state. She smiled faintly. 'You won't be able to call his son Young Jamie any more, will you?'

'It was getting ridiculous anyway,' he said shortly. 'The man must be forty if he's a day.'

When he had finished his soup, he turned to Shona. 'So you had contact with our son, Miss Farrell? Is he well?'

'Yes, very well. Seems to be flying around doing all kinds of work for some toolmakers. And he'd invented some kind of valve for some dyers, I think.'

Douglas paused. 'And the reason for his disappearance to Manchester? What of that?'

The rattle of cutlery on plates stopped. The very walls seemed to be listening.

Shona's clear voice went on steadily. 'I think he was there to tend to his wife, who was ill. But she died on Friday and he has gone to take her home to Ireland.'

'Ha!' said Stuart, almost grinning. 'I –'

But whatever he was about to say was silenced by a thunderous look from his father. Looking at him, it finally dawned on Shona that it was he, not Greg, whom Mary Louisa had loved. And that he had loved her in return. Her mind went back to Mary Louisa's words on her sick bed. The words which had so puzzled her.

'Had she been very ill, poor soul?' said Biddy quickly, conscious of Margaret McNaughton sitting rigid beside her.

'I fear so, Biddy. She asked that we take care of the little girl. She talked a great deal of Lauretta.'

Stuart looked with loathing at this young Irishwoman with her fine dress, her airs and graces, her simpering manner, being listened to with more attention than had ever been given him.

He stood up abruptly. 'I have to go. I've an appointment.'

'So soon, Stuart?' said Margaret absently. 'You're always rushing away.'

He glared at her. 'What does it matter? You don't care a damn whether I'm here or away. You never have. That rabbit in the hutch is mothered more by a whore's brat than ever I was by you.'

Her head went up. 'That's not true, Stuart. It was . . .'

Douglas interrupted her. 'Apologise to your mother, Stuart. That was disgraceful language in front of ladies.'

'Ladies!' Stuart sneered. 'You call these ladies?'

Douglas's chair scraped back as he leaped to his feet and lunged at his son. Margaret put out a hand. 'Don't, please, Douglas . . .'

He paused and Stuart stamped out of the room.

They all froze until they heard the front door slam, then Margaret collapsed back into her chair and started to cry. Douglas came round the table to her. 'Come, Margaret.'

She stopped crying and looked at him, her eyes quite clear. 'No, Douglas. Biddy can help me upstairs. You stay and talk to Miss Farrell. She'll have much to tell you about . . . Greg.'

Douglas and Shona sat there for a few minutes, their eyes on the table, the remains of the meal between them. Then she lifted her eyes to his.

'Did she suffer very much?' His need for some fact, some detail, was naked.

'Well, I don't know what the illness was, Mr McNaughton. Something about having the baby and not being over it. Or something more. Whatever the illness was, it made her forget a

346

good deal. Sure, in a way you might say that was a blessing. She was taken care of by these beautiful people. A doctor with a lovely Kerry woman there, a maid who loved Mary Louisa like a daughter. Greg went to see her every day. I did too, when I found them.'

He was staring at her, wanting more.

'She was clear sometimes. Clear as a bell. You could see how lovely she had been. She said I was to tell you that she loved you.'

His hand went up and covered his eyes.

'And she said that Greg and me, we were to take care of Lauretta.'

'Did – does Greg know about it all?' The words were muffled by the enclosing hand.

'I don't think so. And I say to myself, what good would it do if he did?' She leaned over, quite timidly, and touched his hand which still remained on the table. 'I would never say it to him, Mr McNaughton, because it would hurt him. And it would hurt the little girl.'

'But it's the truth, and the truth cleanses and purifies, they say.'

'But a fire, doesn't it burn the most delicate of things to nothing? They vanish. Mary Louisa wouldn't want to leave a son without a father and a father without a son. Now would she? She wouldn't want Greg's love for you burnt away by this truth you talk about, now would she?'

His face came from behind his hand. He drew out a white handkerchief – washed by Thoria, ironed by Biddy, and laid out lovingly for him by Margaret – and mopped his face and blew his nose.

'I don't know whether it's the voice of an angel you use, or the voice of Eve, Miss Farrell. But your words sound sweet.' He blew his nose again, as if to dismiss his unusual sentimentality. 'So thank you, Miss Farrell. I appreciate your role as messenger.'

He stood up, 'Now if you'll excuse me, I'll see how Mrs McNaughton is. She'd been so well lately. Stuart can be thoughtless and cruel . . . But my heartfelt thanks to you, Miss Farrell.'

She smiled at him. 'Mr McNaughton, I can't recognise this Miss Farrell person you keep talking to. Would it be too hard for you to call me Shona?'

He smiled at her before he turned his back. The tall figure, the fair hair: it might have been Greg standing there. Her heart ached.

Thoria came straight into the room with her tray. 'Why, Shona, I thought they'd never gan away. They can talk underwater, these folk. Now, gi'us a hand with these pots and tell us what it's like singing there for a hundred folks.'

'Sure, it would be four hundred. Five hundred sometimes, Thoria.'

'Gerraway! I canna believe that, niver in a thousand years.'

They worked on harmoniously, their talk fading into a companionable silence as they sat with their feet up on the fender before the hot iron range.

Then Thoria's heavy face turned from the flames to look her shrewdly in the eye. 'What is it, Shona? What's up? Yeh've got a funny look on yeh.'

'Sure I was just thinkin', me darlin', what short memories these men have. Love ye one day and leave ye the next.'

Upstairs, Biddy slipped out of the bedroom as Douglas came in.

Margaret was sitting up in the bed against the white pillows, her little lace cap on her head and her hair combed over her shoulders.

He sat on the bed beside her. 'Do you know what I was thinking about, Meg? About that time in Carlisle market when we saw the dancing bear. And I bought the violets and I . . .'

'Tucked them in my hat,' she said, smiling, her hand reaching out.

Chapter Thirty-three

Stuart pulled up his horse a little distance from the White Buck and composed himself. The lights were on but there was no glow from the windows because of the deceptive half-light of the early evening. He threw a penny at some children who were hanging around the doorway of the inn and thrust the reins into the hands of the one who scrambled to it first.

Morry Smith and Terry were in the corner of the sitting room, heads together, as though they had not moved since the other night.

Morry smiled when he saw Stuart and beckoned him over, shouting, 'Here, landlord, get my friend a gill of your best.'

They waited until the landlord had finally vanished into the public bar.

'Did you fix it?' Stuart asked anxiously.

'She'll be there at eight o'clock. I telt her you'd have some money for her. To help her,' said Terry.

'There? Where will I find her?'

'I'll tell you where, when you tell us about gettin' into the works. Into your place.'

'You can get into the works by breaking the lock on the big gates. It's years old. I'm going for the money tomorrow. My father shouldn't go back to the office on a Friday night.' Stuart put three keys on the table. 'The bigger ones are for the outer and the inner office. The steel key does the safe. Break the glass in the doors as you go through the office. Make it look real. The safe's low on the wall behind my father's desk. The big desk. You can smash that lock after you get into the safe. Now . . .'

The other two exchanged glances. Then Morry nodded. 'Right. We'll have to trust you, Stuart.'

Terry thrust his legs straight out before him. 'She'll be on the back road between Old Morven Pit and the road down from Shotwell. Just where the road parts there's a stile. There at eight o'clock. Shouldn't be anybody around.'

Stuart looked at Morry. 'Money! You said I'd give her money. I've no money with me.'

Reluctantly Morry put his hand to his pocket and pulled out a handful of sovereigns. Terry's eyes widened and he whistled.

Morry gave a gratified smirk. 'Foresight, don't you see? The best enterprises depend on planning. I took the precaution of – obtaining this earlier. A favour from a friend.'

Stuart grabbed it and stuffed the money into his pocket without counting it. 'Yes, yes! You'll get a hundred times that tomorrow night. Leave it 'til late, and be quiet. I swear my father can hear right from the house even if an extra breath of the wind goes through the forge. Be quiet or he'll be over there.'

Stuart bolted from the room, forgetful of his glass of beer. He jumped on his horse and clattered away, knocking over his young horseholder in the process.

Out in the main road, he calmed down and forced himself to proceed at a more sedate pace. He knew he had a good twenty minutes to get there and he didn't want to be early.

A woman was waiting at the stile. He barely recognised her. She was in drab working clothes rather than tawdry finery, a fresh bruise on one side of her face.

'Hello, then, Ruth,' he said, forcing a benevolent tone into his voice.

She stood up and bobbed a curtsy. 'Hello to you, Mr McNaughton. Terry Kennedy said you'd be along.'

'Yes. Well, we've things to talk about.' He leaned over and hooked his arm. 'Here, catch hold. We'll take a little ride. Go to a quieter place to talk.'

She hung back suspiciously. 'We talk here.'

He looked around. 'You don't want dirty miners knowing your business, do you?' He dipped into his pocket. 'Here, see this gold? I've brought it for you. That's the very least of our settlement. Come on!'

She linked her arm through his and he heaved her on to the horse in front of him. He set the horse on, turning into a narrow black pathway round behind the pit head.

He spoke into her ear. 'There now, pretty Ruth, we can get to a quieter place and talk about this properly.'

'You gatta look after me, sir, I tell you . . .'

But her words were lost on the night breeze as he spurred the horse into a faster pace, urging it further up towards Killock fell.

He finally stopped by ruined buildings of a worked-out mine. Tying the horse to a gateway he pulled her along into a shed with a stone-tiled roof. The ride had shaken Ruth and she only offered a murmuring token resistance.

Their feet shuffled through the remains of an old fire in the centre of the floor. He lifted her and sat her on an upturned barrel in one corner.

Reaching into his pocket he took out all the money that Morry had given him, lining up the coins on the ledge of the window, through which the last of the evening light filtered. She looked sideways at them, a gleam of hope in her eyes.

'Now there's no question of me marrying a whore like you, is there, Ruth?'

She scowled at him.

'Is there?'

'If you say not.'

'And I mean it. With a whore like you, who knows whose this brat is?'

'It was only . . . I was only ever out that night . . .'

'Who knows?'

'I know. It's yours,' she said defiantly.

His hand came out to strike her and she ducked. He came across and she flinched as he lifted her, quite gently, off the barrel.

'I tell you what, Ruth, either I'll marry you or you can have that pile of money there. Which do you choose?'

She took a sidelong glance at the money and thought of this man whose hands were harder than her father's, and whose head was wilder.

'I'll have the money,' she said. 'Ye're a bliddy maniac, you. I pity the lass that takes up with you.'

'There!' he crowed. 'Whore! I told you, that's just what you are. A penny'd buy you!'

She turned to reach out for the money and he caught her hand. 'You're a wicked girl, do you know that?' He leaned forward and kissed her, laughing into her mouth as she struggled. 'Oh no you don't! You'll earn the money, whore, like you did last time.'

He had her on the floor, squirming around in the ashes of the old fire. She lay back and let him do it, closing her eyes to shut out the sight of the laughing mouth.

When he had finished he stood up. He reached down and ripped her skirt right off her. Then he went to the window ledge and tipped the coins back into his pocket.

'That's mine!' she wailed.

He went to the gaping door then looked back. 'I'll be back. And if you move about the lanes like that they'll know you for the whore you are.'

It took him twenty minutes to find what he wanted, and then he went back to get her.

On Friday Douglas suggested that Shona should go into Priorton to take a note to Mr Moxham. He told her it was something to do with Mr Shakespeare. He believed that she had met him?

She laughed. 'Sure he's the one who has the castle, isn't he? He was a strange man. He made me laugh. He had hair the colour of fireblack and had a soft spot for Greg, I think.'

In the end they all went: Margaret and Biddy, the two little girls and Thoria, whose glum looks at being deserted had aroused Margaret's pity. It was a full carriage that bumped its way to Priorton.

They filled the little outer office and Morry Smith had to struggle through the visitors to go and inform Mr Moxham. Coming through the door, the old man's eyes popped as he saw the crowd of females on his quiet premises. He shook hands with them all, even Lauretta and Becky. Then, telling Morry to find chairs for the other ladies, he swept Shona through to his inner office.

Morry found chairs for Margaret, Biddy and Thoria and went back to stand at his desk and continue his copying.

Margaret leaned sideways to look at him more closely. 'I think we must have met, Mr Smith.'

'I have an acquaintance with your son, Mr Stuart McNaughton. A fine man.'

352

'Yes, I think I remember. Yes.' She sat back uneasily and could think of nothing else to say.

Inside the larger chairless office Mr Moxham had read the letter which Shona had brought from Douglas and was looking the Farrell girl up and down. This was the same girl, but where were the boots and the red stockings, the shawl and the comic hat with its wild flower trim? This girl looked two or three years older; she was a beauty who would grace most respectable drawing rooms, if one could tone down the colours just a touch.

'Is there some way I can help you, sir?' Shona was at a loss to know what was happening. 'Did Mr McNaughton wish me to help you?'

'No, not really. It is perhaps a little impolite of me. But Mr Shakespeare, whom you met briefly, has mentioned you in a . . . letter that he sent me from America. And Mr McNaughton knew I was curious to remind myself of your . . . identity.'

She grinned widely, though she was still puzzled. 'Sure it's an honour to be mentioned in a letter that's come all the way across the oceans!' She curtsied to him. 'And now, sir, the ladies out there are aching to visit the shops here, though I have to say now they are not a patch on the establishments in Manchester.'

He bowed his head and laughed. 'You take me to task for keeping you here on half an errand when you have better things to do. I stand corrected, miss.' He reached out to shake her hand. 'It has been a pleasure to meet you. I am sure we will meet again.'

He watched the swirl of her wide skirts as she swept through the door and thought that she would do. She would definitely do. He waited for the rattle and chatter of the women in the outer office to fade away and called for his clerk. There was this matter of the unsatisfactory attitude of the man. His work was neat, well executed. But Smith was often late, and vanished at odd times. He would have to be dealt with, an unpleasant business, and Mr Moxham hated unpleasantness.

A moment later, Morry Smith stood before him, smiling slightly. 'Mr Moxham, I was just about to ask for a moment of your time. I've had a letter from my uncle in London, offering me a marvellous position in the offices of a lawyer there. It would mean, I'm afraid, that you would have to release me from my commitment here . . .'

Mr Moxham, relieved, put up a hand. 'Mr Smith, that is satisfactory. You must take up such a marvellous opportunity.'

Morry Smith allowed his slight smile to broaden. 'That's very gentlemanly of you, sir. I wonder if you would be so kind as to write a few lines for me to take to this lawyer, as to the quality of my work?'

It would be a week before Mr Moxham needed to check the tin box in the back of the great safe, behind the scrolls and documents, and would discover the absence of forty-eight gold sovereigns. By that time Morry knew he would be well ensconced in an office in Leeds, busy making another good impression, happy at the growing foundation of his fortune.

'What in heaven have yer been doin' with yerself?' said Biddy.

Richie had brought Tommo across to Garth End Cottage after work. He had insisted on going back to Pat's house first to swill his face and change his scorched and patched breeches, but Biddy was still surveying him with a mixture of pleasure and puzzlement.

'What have yer been doin' to yerself?' she repeated.

'Sure, I've been working me guts out.'

'And drinkin' them rotten, looks like.'

'Nothing else to do. No room at Pat's to do anything but sleep. The constables have let that Terry Kennedy go. Pat has had word there were two other men drinkin' with Kennedy that night, a man in a green coat and another. So it's not so clear.'

The kitchen door opened and Lauretta peeped round the door and then ran in and jumped up on to Richie's back. Becky followed more slowly. She looked up at Tommo and her lip trembled.

He picked her up and swung her round. 'Little Becky. Sure aren't you the princess now?'

She smiled weakly then looked behind him, across at Shona and Biddy, and then behind them.

'No Mammy,' she said sadly.

Tommo looked desperately at Shona who came and put her arms round both of them. 'Your mammy's in a better place, sweetheart. But didn't she tell Tommo and me and Biddy to take care of you? Don't worry. We will.'

354

Lauretta tumbled from Richie's back, came across and climbed up on Tommo's knee so that he was holding both children. 'And Lauretta,' she said. 'Lauretta take care. And Greg.'

Thoria came and, using a cloth to protect her hand, opened the iron door of the oven, releasing the smell of yeast and hot spice.

'Tea-cakes!' She put them on the table, reached for the butter and beamed at the children. 'Ah thought they might be ready. An't they your favourite, youse two? Sit here nice and you can have them hot.'

Tommo relinquished his burden with some relief and watched as Becky tucked into the buttery tea-cakes. 'She looks all right. They're treating her well, Shona?'

She nodded, smiling.

'And what about you and that McNaughton feller?'

'He's in Ireland, taking his dead wife home.'

'An' you think he'll be back?'

'I think so.' She was blushing, aware of her own uncertainty.

His eye wandered across to the windowsill. 'What's that?' He picked up the painted box.

'I found it,' said Thoria. 'In the coal-hole. Chucked away.'

He turned it over.

'Do you know it?' asked Biddy, watching him keenly.

'I do. It belonged to M . . . to the wee'n's mother. She kept her money in it.'

The children's noisy chewing was the only sound to be heard.

'It's just an old box,' said Shona gently.

'It's hers,' said Tommo grimly. He glared at Biddy. 'What else was there? Was there anything?'

She went to a press drawer, brought out the tea-towel, brown-stained itself now, and opened it to reveal the twisted buckled belt. She looked up at him. They both imagined the flailing buckle coming down on a face . . .

'I think the belt belonged to Stuart,' she said. 'Stuart McNaughton.'

Tommo stuffed the box and the belt into his jacket and looked towards the door. 'Where is he?'

Biddy put up a hand. 'He's not here. Came in and went out again,' she lied. 'He was goin' up to Priorton.'

Richie stood away from the wall. 'Time we was away, Tommo.'

355

'Where're you going?' said Shona.

'Down New Morven to collect a thing Pat has.' He paused. 'Then across to Priorton.'

'Not in my rig yer ain't, you're not collectin' any *thing*,' said Richie, who knew exactly what Tommo wanted to collect from Pat's. 'Gil Tait has a fare for me in twenty minutes.'

'Aren't I tellin' yer . . .'

The women breathed a sigh of relief as the door closed behind the quarrelling brothers.

Thoria spoke their thoughts. 'Now what's gonna happen about that? What's that daft Stuart done?'

Biddy looked purposefully at Becky and shook her head. 'Sure, it's nothing. Nothing we can talk about here.'

Later they watched Stuart closely at the supper table, but nothing seemed amiss. If anything he was more affable about everything, complimenting Thoria on her fish pie and telling his mother she was looking very well these days. He even chucked the two little girls under their chins.

Surprisingly he didn't go out at all that evening but lounged around in the parlour with the week's papers until it was bed-time.

As was now her custom, Biddy had a word with Margaret on her way to bed. 'Sure, Stuart seemed perky tonight.'

Margaret smiled. 'He seems to have recovered from his fit of the miseries, doesn't he? Douglas was just asking me the other day if . . . there was some business over a girl. But I can't think so. He's so . . . normal.'

Biddy bit back the comment that that was unusual in itself and went to bed.

In their attic Shona was reminding Thoria of the death of Maudie Martin and she was shaking her head at the sheer impossibility of Stuart McNaughton doing such a thing. 'Word in Shotwell was that it was some drunken Irishman,' she insisted.

Shona rolled over and faced the wall and thought about Greg.

Douglas went across to the works very early as usual on the Saturday morning. He was annoyed to find the great gates unlocked. Someone must have left them open. He would give whoever it was a good talking to.

Not for the first time in these months, he missed the shuffling gait of Old Jamie. He sighed. He knew he wouldn't hear those steps here again. That made him feel old himself. As a child he had thought big Jamie MacQuistain as eternal as the mountains.

He picked his way through the machine shops and the wagon shops and down to the forge, handling a tool here, touching the hard cold wall of a wagon there. For once, the perfect concentration, the perfect focus, wouldn't come.

Mary Louisa was in his mind. In her time in his house she had torn through the dull fabric of his life like a fine rapier; making him feel young and alive again; making him reaffirm his pride in his own work through the admiration in her shining eyes and the enthusiasm of her generous heart.

Of course the rapier, as well as letting in life and light, had cut and wounded Margaret, leaving him with a legacy of guilt which had soured his view of his gentle wife, making him turn from her reproach and hate the touch of her hand. And somehow that same rapier had turned on Mary Louisa herself and finally cut her down.

But now the time which had rolled on, banishing Old Jamie from the works, had somehow healed the ragged tear between him and Margaret, putting Mary Louisa back into time as a sweet and harmless memory.

Later that morning, still down in the works, Douglas was walking towards the wagon shops when Tad Pinkney stepped in front of him.

'What is it, Mr Pinkney?' said Douglas stiffly.

'Ah come to say to forget it. Forget what our Ruth said. Ah know it to be the truth, like. Ah'd tell it on the Bible. But forget it. The cow's gone missing now. No reckoning her. Ah've worked here five years now. Aal ah want is me job back. Ah'll mek no trouble. Me family needs it. I need it. There'll be no job round here for wuh now you've laid wur' off.'

Douglas believed him; believed what he'd said about Ruth; believed his earnest promise of no trouble.

'I'm sorry, Mr Pinkney,' he said gently. 'You know it'd be impossible after this. I have to believe my son. I can give you a reference as a good worker, though.' He put his hand in his waistcoat pocket and drew out the guinea he always kept there. 'Perhaps this will help you 'til you get your next job?' He pushed it into the man's hand and walked on. He did not see Tad Pinkney

357

spit on the ground behind his back. If he had, he might not have blamed him.

Young Jamie MacQuistain, at the door of the machine shops, had watched the episode. 'There's a bit of bad feelin' among the men, Mr McNaughton.'

Douglas shrugged. 'It happens from time to time, Jamie. Like the tide. We just ride the top of it. Now come on to the office. I want you to see the new designs for a company in France. Best yet.'

'Father!' They looked up. Stuart was crashing down the iron steps from the gantry. 'The money's gone! The money I brought from the bank for the pays, it's gone!'

They raced up the steps and Douglas surveyed the smashed door and the empty safe. He brought himself round to face Stuart who was a picture of innocence.

'How did this happen?'

'I don't know! I don't know! I came in ready to put up the pays and this is what I've found.' Suddenly Stuart was holding his mouth trying to stop himself from being sick. He staggered back against the desk, his face a ghastly white.

Douglas turned to Jamie. 'Take Stuart across to the house, then get on to the constable.' He put his hand on Jamie's arm. 'And say nothing to the men. They've got their work to do, and there'll be no pay for them today.'

'Nothing?'

'Not 'til Monday at the earliest.'

'They won't like it, Mr McNaughton. They'll have their bills to pay.'

'Neither do I, Jamie. Neither do I. And this is a bill I'll have to pay twice.'

Chapter Thirty-four

Tad Pinkney made his way up to the fell, restraining his old cross-breed dog with its rope noose. He had come home that afternoon with a headache, having disposed of most of McNaughton's sovereign in the pub, sharing out the largesse with those who were both without credit and without pay. His complaints about Stuart McNaughton and then of the papist-loving McNaughton clan had fallen on sympathetic ears.

His wife, a fat woman who was normally very timid, had met him at the door and insisted that he went to look for Ruth. She was sure that the girl had not gone off nor intended to run away. Something must have happened to her.

To his own surprise, Tad had not winged his wife one for being pushy, but had tied the rope halter on the dog and set her away to search for Ruth.

It took twenty minutes to reach the fell where the lurcher started to pull more vigorously. After sniffing backwards and forwards he started to scrabble around the edge of a large hole which had one or two boards thrown casually across but was by no means secure.

Tad pulled two boards away, got on to his hands and knees, and peered down. He moved crab-wise around the hole to get a better look.

'Yer bugger in hell!' His eye caught the gleam of a white blouse and a thrown-back arm and he jerked backwards and fell over. Scrambling to his feet, he tied the dog to one of the boards, told it to stay, and raced back the way he had come.

It was getting towards dusk when Greg finally arrived back at Shotwell, walking wearily from the station. The main street, usually full of noisy goodwill on a Pay Saturday, was thronged with men standing in groups, talking and gesticulating. Greg greeted one or two men well known to him and was puzzled by their surly response.

He had been journeying for five full days to and from a place which seemed like a foreign country to him. He had fulfilled his purpose of delivering Mary Louisa into the hands of the priest of her home parish in Kerry.

His journey had led him through beautiful mountains, and through scenes of the abject poverty which was the residue of the still-threatening famine. He had ridden alongside glittering lakes and by the side of beautiful rearing gorges into half-empty villages where he had given coppers to beggars.

He had seen the sea, the wide Atlantic, in which Shona had played as a baby.

It was only on his journey back that he began to realise that some of these must be the pathways she and Tommo had taken with their things in the little donkey cart, with neither the comfort of coaches nor the magic of rail to help them. Young Richie had done it on foot, without even the donkey cart.

He warmed with admiration at the thought of them, and longed to see them to tell them so. He had seen the mountains, seen the villages. He longed to see Shona and talk to her about the priest who had spoken lovingly of Mary Louisa.

'Watch out, will you?'

He had turned a corner and walked slap into Young Jamie MacQuistain.

'Sorry, Jamie, I was miles away.'

'Gregor! Best place for you, miles away.'

Greg looked around more carefully. 'What is it? I've had more grunts than greetings.'

'The pay was stolen. Constables in the works all day asking questions, and the men not paid 'til Monday. So there's no drinking tonight, no bills paid, and only them with good credit gets food for the bairns.'

'Oh . . .'

'And there's another thing, Greg. Tad Pinkney was at the works. Seems he's accused your Stuart of attacking his daughter . . . and worse. Now they're saying he's had his dog up on the fells and they've found her down an old working. Dead as Christmas. They came back for ropes. I was comin' back to the works to tell your pa.' He stroked his short beard. 'And another thing. Trouble comes in threes, so they say. My old man, he died this afternoon. Thought your pa would want to know.'

'I'm sorry, Jamie.'

'Aye, he was a fine man. Ye'll tell your pa he mentioned him, just at the end?'

Greg nodded. 'Yes, yes, I'd better get up there. Quickly.'

Margaret had come out to find an ashen-faced Stuart leaning on the doorjamb. 'What is it, Stuart?'

He clutched his stomach. 'Something's wrong, Ma.'

She took his arm. 'Come on, Stuart, let's get you to bed. You'll feel better there.' She led him tenderly to his room and tucked him up in bed. 'There. Now I'll find you some soda water.'

He waited anxiously for her return and sat up obediently and sipped at the glass. As she sat there with him, his feeling of sickness receded. She put the glass on the night table.

'There now. Lie back.' She smoothed down the covers.

'Ma, will you stay? It was a nightmare and . . .'

'Just lie back. I'll be here.'

She held his hand until he was fast asleep and then crept away. He slept right through the day but when she was finishing off the table for supper with Biddy, a great roar from his bedroom made them both jump. Biddy set out for the staircase but Margaret held her back. 'I'll go. He'll be sick again.' She went into the kitchen for a bowl.

Stuart looked at her piteously from the bed. 'It was a nightmare, Ma. I want to be sick but I can't be.'

She sat by him and held his head, but it was no use. She persuaded him to lie back.

He held on to her hand when she tried to leave. She sat there quietly as he seemed to drift off to sleep.

Suddenly his eyes flew open. 'You know I never was happy, Ma. Even when Flora was here. I wanted you and she was keeping me away from you. I wanted *you*.' Tears were falling down his cheeks and his hand clutched harder. She looked at the tears and the hand and realised that she didn't like him, she didn't like him at all. Sitting here, holding his hand, was a thing she must do but it was not done from love. There was something in him which didn't quite

361

connect. And was that her fault? Because when he was a child she was mourning the lost babies before him and minding the sickly baby that came after? His unhappiness made him more unattractive, not less. She had injured him, somehow done him irreparable damage. Was it hard to love what you yourself have injured? Was that when Douglas stopped loving her, when somehow he thought he had injured her?

'I've done bad things, Ma.'

'Shhh, Stuart.'

'There are bad women, you know. Really bad women, Ma, not like you. This dream . . . awful dream. The bad woman needs to know . . .'

She snatched her hand away from him. 'What have you done?' she demanded, aghast. 'What have you done?'

He grabbed her hand again. 'Bad things, Ma. Really bad. The woman, that whore . . .'

She remembered the hand, the belt buckle rising and falling. Then she saw the face, for the first time since it had happened. She said quite calmly, 'I saw you. I saw you do it.'

'You saw it, Ma! Didn't you see *her*?' His lip curled. 'She was a bad woman.'

She wrenched her hand away and started to slap him hard where he lay; harder and harder, her hand came down on his face and shoulders. He lay there absorbing every blow, welcoming the contact, the passion.

'You wicked, evil . . . That poor girl!'

He caught the hand, wanting more. 'There was another girl, yesterday,' he said, almost eagerly. 'Another scheming, bad girl.'

'What did you do?'

'Don't worry, Ma, they won't find her.'

She started to shriek then curled her fists up and began to punch him, gaining strength from a rage deep inside her which had little to do with Stuart and the evil things he had done.

Downstairs Biddy heard the commotion and bustled the girls into the kitchen. Shona put a hand on her arm. 'You keep them here, Biddy. I'll see what's happening up there.'

Margaret's voice was almost unrecognisable. 'Get out of this house! You cur! You dog! Get out! You get out and tell that father of yours what you've done. Then you get down on your bended

362

knees and ask God to look at what you've done, because he can't forgive you. You've hurt those girls and every blow on them is a crucifixion for me.'

He grasped her wrists and held them from him. He flung his legs out of the bed, sick no longer, then collected two narrow wrists into one hand and brought his fist back to strike her.

At that moment Shona came through the door. In an instant she picked up the tin bowl and started to hit him with it. He turned towards her and she banged and clattered it against the bedpost. The great noise rang through the house and Stuart's fists dropped.

Margaret pulled at Shona's elbow. 'Come out of here. You don't want to be in here with . . . *him*.' She turned on Stuart. 'Get out of this house! I don't want to see you again, ever. Get out.'

Minutes later, from Margaret's sitting room, they heard the doors crash as Stuart left.

'What will you do?' Shona turned to Margaret.

'I'll wait until Douglas gets back.' She leaned into her soft chair. 'He's late. He'll be here soon. He'll know what to do.'

They heard Lauretta shriek and raced downstairs, their hearts pounding. But it wasn't Stuart, it was Greg holding the two little girls high, one on each side of him. Biddy was beaming up at him and Thoria was standing in the kitchen passage looking on with interest.

He turned towards Margaret, put the girls down then came and kissed her on the cheek. Then he kissed Shona soundly on the mouth while the girls looked on with great interest.

'Greg!' said his mother. 'The children!'

He kept his arm round Shona. 'I wished to embrace Shona, Ma, because I love her more than life. There's things to do here, but when they're done, I want to ask her to do me the honour of becoming my wife.'

'A very public declaration,' Margaret said speculatively.

Shona took one step away from him. 'Sure, your man is quite certain of himself!'

'No. No,' he said, 'I presume nothing.'

'Lauretta,' Biddy said, 'why don't you take your daddy into the dining room, and Thoria and I'll warm up some dinner for him.'

Greg looked across at Shona. 'You too? I've things to tell you.'

'And we have things to tell you,' said Margaret grimly.

'I know,' he said, looking around. 'Where's Stuart?'

Margaret put her hand on his arm. 'Greg, it was him I saw doing that awful thing to . . .' She glanced at Becky. 'And there is another girl. He said he hurt another girl. Yesterday.'

'Young Jamie said something about a girl being found out on the fell. And something about Stuart. Her father has found her.'

She looked behind him, suddenly abstracted. 'And your father not back yet.'

'Money – the pays – were taken from the works. He'll be there still dealing with it. I'll go across when I get my breath back.'

'Money?' she said. 'Stuart never mentioned a word about robbery, Greg. What has he been doing? He came home very sick, didn't he, Shona? And then he became wild, past himself, and ran off.'

Shona shook her head soberly. 'He was in a strange way, Greg. But to think he's done such terrible things!' She shuddered, thinking of her own encounter with Sir Robert at his mansion on the outskirts of Manchester, and the leering attention of Lord Marsteen and the other guests.

Greg was staring at her, trim in a dark blue dress with soft shoes on her feet, and at his mother, disturbed but not defeated by the events of the day.

'What is it, Greg?' said Margaret sharply.

'I missed you, both of you,' he said abruptly. 'I'll go across to the works now. Then I'll go out and look for Stuart.'

'I'll come with you,' said Shona, not wanting him out of her sight.

The works office seemed to be full of policemen.

Douglas was listening to Herbert Walton. His white, strained face broke into a slight smile when he saw Greg, then he glanced closely at Shona. Not since Mary Louisa had a woman been in the works. 'Good to see you, son. You've been much missed. You know about all this?'

Greg nodded. 'Jamie told me.'

'Well, there's more to it. The Priorton constable has picked up a man called Terry Kennedy with much of my gold on him. Caught spending it, before he made his way I know not where.'

Herbert Walton coughed. 'And Kennedy tells us – in fact he was boasting about it in the Buck, Mr McNaughton – that your brother lent him and another feller the keys for this robbery. And that what's more, your brother was the one who beat the Priorton prostitute to death. And now there's a Shotwell girl gone the same way.'

Shona's hand reached out to touch Greg's.

Douglas said grimly, 'I should have listened to her father. He told me and I didn't listen.' He stood up. 'We'll have to take the constables across there. What your mother will . . .'

'My mother knows it was Stuart, Pa. She finally remembered that she saw him on that night. She was there, if you recall? Now it seems he's run off, I don't know where. We told Ma we'd look for him.'

'We'll find him, Mr McNaughton,' said Herbert Walton. 'You can be sure of that. Now you should be careful. There's a deal of bad feeling about these events in both villages. Muttering here about there being no pay, and the poor lass that was kilt, and now the rumours about the other girl down in New Morven. I'd not venture out tonight at all if I were you or any of your family. Trouble, I can feel it in me bones.'

Nevertheless Greg and Shona left the policemen with Douglas and began to comb the streets of Shotwell. They were treated to sullen looks from people on the pavements, and some men whom Greg greeted averted their gaze. But no one stood in their way.

In the end they found Stuart at a livery at the very edge of Shotwell, bargaining with a narrow-faced man for a horse, trickling gold coins into his hand. He looked round as they entered and gave one of his strange barking laughs. 'Ah, the young lovers. So you've come to retrieve the bad boy?'

'What do you think you've done, Stuart?'

'What do I *think*? What do I *think*? I *think* that bad women get just what they deserve. But not all of them. Some get away with it. And, brother, on quite another matter, I *think* I know more than you do.' He winked knowingly at Shona. 'I've been *thinking* that our father is not so much the plaster saint . . .'

'Stuart, hold your peace,' said Shona urgently.

Greg looked from one to the other. 'What is it, Stuart?'

The livery man led the horse out. Stuart flung himself up on to the horse before he spoke. 'The child, the one you call daughter, has our blood but not our mother's.'

Greg frowned. 'What? What are you saying?' he suddenly roared. He made a lunge for Stuart as he guided the horse past him, then gave chase down the street. 'What are you saying?' he screamed after him.

Shona winced as she heard the stinging slap of Stuart's whip. To her relief Greg gave up and she watched him make his way back to her. 'What was he saying?' he said much more softly, shaking his head in angry bewilderment.

Shona put her arm through his and her head sideways to see him properly past the wide bonnet brim. 'D'you see, Greg. He loved Mary Louisa like you did and she loved him like she loved you. No, more.'

'Who, Stuart?' He was avoiding the inevitable.

'No, sweetheart, you know I don't mean Stuart. I mean Douglas.'

They walked along in a silence that Shona thought would never end. Finally Greg stopped and faced her. She looked up into his eyes. 'I think I knew, Shona, underneath it all, I think I knew. I loved it that he liked her, but it surprised me too. Now I'm not surprised.' He paused. 'My poor mother.'

'Just think, Greg. Isn't she happier now than you've seen her for years? She says it and shows it in everything she does. Have you seen them together? They might just have met.'

They started walking again, then he stopped and turned her to him. 'More? You said more?'

'He was a grown man, Greg. And she was a grown woman. Like we are now.'

He laughed shortly. '*We?* You're younger than I was when I went to Russia.'

'But older in experience, Greg. Women are always older.'

He kissed her on the cheek. Whistles and cat-calls pierced the air around them. Clods of earth thudded around them. 'I do love you more. More than anyone at any time. Now for Heaven's sake let's get back to the house, before these people lynch us like they do in Shakespeare's beloved America.'

Chapter Thirty-five

That night Pat handed over the gun to Tommo and they joined the usual Saturday night crowd in Showy's bar.

Pat was uneasy, but not too uneasy, about giving Tommo the gun. He had seen the boys carrying guns before, more often out of bravado than any real intention of acting.

Richie, unusually for him, joined them in the bar. Their recent disagreement over the gun uppermost in their minds, he and Tommo glowered at each other and spoke little. Pat's insouciant remarks glided over the silence like thin shoes over ice.

Gil Tait shouted across in their direction, 'What's it with you, Richie? Is there no horse business tonight, no leather to rub, no brasses to shine?'

He grinned. 'The flash fellers can do without their rides for one night, Gil.'

He knew there was no real rancour on the part of the little man. Richie did duty at the stable every night and Gil's working life had never been as relaxed as since he had gone into partnership with the boy.

Showy brought them their jug of beer and turned to Tommo. 'I see they've got Terry Kennedy back in the cells in Priorton.'

Tommo lifted his head. 'For Maudie?' he asked.

'Sure I don't think that's the case. They say he was stopped, rolling drunk and spewing bile, outside the Buck at Priorton. So when the constable got him inside, didn't they look in his old satchel? And inside the satchel, wasn't there more money than you'd ever dreamed?'

'He'd robbed it?' said Richie.

'Right first time,' Gil called across. 'The pay boxes over at the railway works in Shotwell were robbed. Cleaned out.'

'Hmm,' Tommo said in satisfaction. 'Can't wriggle out of that one. Still . . .'

'And there's word now,' went on Gil, almost too blandly, savouring the spice of news, 'That they've found a girl, beaten just like Maudie, at the bottom of some pit-hole on Killock Common. This time they know the feller. No doubt at all. Son of that heathen family where the money was robbed, where yer own auntie stays. Not the tall feller, the other one. The penpusher that was in here a couple o' times. One of that pair that Showy took care of, sucklin' 'em like a cow in milk.' He paused, relishing the attention of the quietening room. 'If he did that girl like that, then you can be sure he did for Maudie. Sure as one day chicks.'

The chatter in the pub had faded into silence.

'That one was in my cab once, beating on a woman. Usin' a knife on her too. I tipped him out,' said Richie laconically.

Tommo reached under his seat for the sacking parcel and stood up. 'I knew it anyway. Isn't he the feller I'm goin' for?'

A murmur of approval swelled in the room; everyone knew the contents of the package.

Pat stood up beside Tommo and Richie glared at them both. 'Are ye crazy, the pair of ye?' Pat shrugged his shoulders helplessly, but still followed his friend through the narrow door.

Richie sat on for a whole, supping his pot of ale and puffing his pipe. The buzz around him intensified into a hubbub. Men who had both used and despised Maudie Martin when she was alive had finally, in their talk, transformed her killing into a devilish onslaught on the entire New Morven community.

Gil Tait walked over to the fireplace, put one hand into the chimney then lifted it and stroked it down his face from brow to chin. He picked up the iron fire bleazer and the poker, and rattled one against the other. Richie could not recognise the soot-black warrior who emerged for the merry little man who had been his idol since he had lived in New Morven.

Cautiously Richie stood up unnoticed by the crowd, where one man after another was following Gil's example with the soot, beginning to bang their sticks on his bleazer and boast just what *they* would do when they caught the *bluddy* murderer.

Behind him, he heard Showy say to them derisively, 'Are you thinkin' that feller'll walk in here any minute just to face you? Get yourselves across there to his house in that Godless place and show him he can't get away with it.'

Richie slipped out unobtrusively then raced to the stable, saddled up

Boru the Second and set off at a fast pace on the road to Shotwell. Catching up with Tommo and Pat a mile out of New Morven, he manoeuvred the horse alongside them.

'Leave it alone, Tommo,' he begged. 'They're up in arms in Showy's. There's plenty of them goin' across to get him. They don't need you.'

Tommo reached up and, not without a struggle, heaved Richie to the ground, lifted himself heavily into the saddle and set off, only turning round to say: 'Then don't I need to get there before them? Because he's mine!'

Richie and Pat watched him vanish in the lane, Richie confused by his own restraint. He could have whistled and made Boru turn round, but he didn't.

He pulled at Pat's arm and set off running, calling behind him, 'Pat, they were blackin' up in there, banging iron and talking of marchin' on the house. Sure there'll be murder done. Get hold of Biddy's friend, that Father O'Reilly. He might stop it. I'll get straight to Garth End. Our Biddy and Shona's there as well as those two little'ns. They'll be scared out o' their wits.'

'And Thoria,' said Pat with feeling.

'Ye've a soft spot for that one?' said Richie, breathless with running.

'So I have,' gasped Pat. 'But I'm not certain if it's the girl or her pies. Sure when I dream of her, aren't the pies always there too?'

'Right, Pat! For her and her pies, you'd better run. Run for her bluddy life!'

Tad Pinkney stood uneasily at his smoking hearth watching the heavy figure of his wife, her head obscured by her draped apron, rocking backwards and forwards on her chair. His three sons were jammed side by side on the rough settle, averting their gaze from the shrouded figure of their battered sister lying on the bed.

The tension was relieved by a rattle on the door which burst open to reveal Tad's closest workmate, a roofer named John Fell, whose face was blacker than usual, smeared with earth.

'There's a clamour,' he said. 'Folks from New Morven where another woman was did for, and us. We're gonna get that reprobate on two counts.'

Tad breathed out. His sons stood up. Here was something to do. Here was *the thing* to do.

John Fell handed Tad a sack which he put on his head, taking his knife to make holes to see through. Then Fell gave him the bleached skull of a large ram which he fixed to his head by means of cord brought under his chin then back up through the curling horns.

'Now!' he roared, his voice muffled by the sack.

Half a mile out of Shotwell, Tommo came on Stuart, now familiar as the man with the untidy fair hair and green jacket, the man whom Pat had called a prowler. He was picking his way over the scrubby half-moor past the last cottage in the wandering lane that was still Shotwell; crouching hatless on a rough brown cob, vanishing along a track that led to the high fell.

With delicate care, Tommo removed the gun from the sack and laid it across the saddle in front of him. He pressed his knees into Boru the Second and urged him forward off the road and on up the hill. By the time he had gone half a mile he was in a position to turn the horse and watch Stuart McNaughton coming towards him.

He cocked the gun and raised it.

Looking along the barrel and seeing the hunched figure of Stuart in the semi-darkness, his mind flashed to an image of the soldier alongside Lord Marsteen who had lifted his gun in just such a way before he had shot Tommo's brother Gerard, injuring him so badly that he had lain for two days before dying.

In another flash Tommo saw himself lying half-dead in Manchester, Matthew Granter leaning over him and old Septimus peering on with anxious concern.

He dropped the barrel slightly and shouted: 'Stop there, ye *bluddy* murderer!'

Stuart pulled up and peered towards him. 'What is it? I . . .'

'Ye killed Maudie Martin. Just stand still there and die, will yer?'

'That girl? That one? Why, she was only . . .' Stuart peered closer. 'Put the gun down, sir, please.' His voice took on the whining, wheedling sound so familiar to his mother. 'The girl . . . I didn't mean to do it. Some of the girls, you pay them and they . . .'

Stuart flinched as Tommo dipped into the sack, brought out Maudie's painted box and the twisted, shrivelled belt and threw them on the ground in front of his horse.

'Pick them up.'

Stuart scrambled down and picked up the box. 'Yes, this was hers. That money was wages of sin, d'you see?' He looked anxiously at

370

Tommo. 'It couldn't have been hers, the money, don't you see that?'

'And the other?'

Stuart picked up the twisted belt and drew it close to his face in the fading light, to see the blackened buckle end.

He looked hopefully towards Tommo. 'This could belong to anyone.'

He brought up the gun to set his sights down the barrel once more.

Stuart ran towards him. 'Don't shoot that thing, I beg you! Don't . . . shoot.'

Tommo pulled the trigger and the shot rang out harmlessly over the head of Stuart's horse. Stuart screamed and the horse reared and bolted across the heath, leaving him crouched in the heather.

Tommo put his foot down and booted Stuart's shoulder so that he fell to the ground on top of the belt and the box. Stuart lay there looking up at him, eyes glassy with a combination of relief and fear.

'I wouldn't even set Pat Daley's ferret at yer, Stuart McNaughton. Ye're worse than a stoat, lower than a worm.' Tommo smiled. 'Sure ye'd better keep runnin', though. The constables and half of New Morven is after ye already. An' that's just the start.'

Keeping his eye on Tommo, Stuart backed up carefully, step by step, until he bumped into a low stubby tree, then turned and ran for his life.

Tommo retrieved the belt and bag and placed them carefully in his sack with the gun. Then, as he turned Boru, he caught a glimpse of the hut with the stone tiles.

He went inside. The soot and sticks of the fire he had built for himself and Maudie were now scattered all over the floor. He closed his eyes and could see her there again, bright and teasing and fully alive as she had been that day. Try as he would, he could not picture her now as he had last seen her, bruised and battered and covered with a fine shawl.

He turned the horse's head again towards Shotwell. Becky . . . He would see her and tell her all the good things about her mother.

After Stuart had left, Thoria had drawn all the curtains tight at Garth End. The children were put to bed and the rest of them gathered in the parlour.

Douglas had just returned from Priorton where he had listened to Terry Kennedy's story of the robbery, from his own mouth. At a request from Biddy, so firm it could have been deemed an instruction,

371

Douglas had told the constable about the box and the belt, now in the possession of Tommo Farrell.

Now Douglas sat staring into the flickering depths of the fire. Margaret sat at the piano, turning the pages of her music and occasionally picking out a new tune. Thoria and Biddy sat opposite each other on hard chairs, winding wool. Shona and Greg sat side by side on the couch, not touching but each highly aware of the physical presence of the other: each wondering, even in the middle of catastrophe, when they could be alone together.

Shona was showing Greg the small pottery figure of the girl with black hair, sent to her by Mary Challoner on the day she died. And the fish-fossil which Shona herself had found among the stone and coal that same day, and given to Richie.

'One way or another these two have been scratching away together ever since, in bags and pockets. In Stables Street. In Manchester. In the attic here . . .'

There was a knock on the back door and Greg jumped up to answer, coming back with a dishevelled Richie in tow. He had fragments of bracken sticking to his breeches above bright leather boots flecked with mud.

'Shona!' He grabbed her arm. 'There's fellers from New Morven coming here to get Stuart McNaughton. To this house! They've blackened their faces and are picking up bleazers and pans and making a hell of a racket. An' here in Shotwell I can hear the same hum . . . Listen!'

Margaret stopped playing the piano. Biddy and Thoria stopped their winding.

They allowed themselves to hear it now, the noise: a menacing rattle backed by a cacophony of voices.

Shona stood up. 'Turn the lamps down, Greg.'

He did so and she opened the curtains wide. They all got to their feet and moved to the window. The clamour outside quietened.

A huge crowd of people stood in a semi-circle before the house. The intervening fence had been trampled to the earth. Flickering torches, clasped in hands or held high on sticks, found reflection in gleaming eyes made whiter by blackened faces. In the dark it was impossible to tell man from woman, boy from girl. At the centre was a small figure with a blackened face who looked vaguely familiar. Beside him was a great rearing figure with horns holding a heavy stick high in the air. He brought it down again on the ground and the clashing of iron started up again, the roar of voices blended to a threatening babble made up entirely of the word: 'Murder!'

'There, I told you, Biddy. The devil!' Margaret started to shudder.

'Daddy?' A tearful Lauretta stood in the doorway, hand in hand with Becky.

Margaret and Shona moved simultaneously to lift the children into their arms.

'We've got to face them this time, Ma. That's no devil. You've got to see it,' said Greg urgently.

Shona turned to her. 'Let's show them, Mrs McNaughton. Let's show them they can't frighten us. Stuart isn't here. There's nothing for them here.'

'Stuart, poor Stuart!'

'He isn't here! We need to show them.'

Clasping Becky tighter, she turned for the door, Greg close on her heels. Douglas came to one side of Margaret and Biddy to the other.

In a minute they were standing before the house in their own protective semi-circle, Shona and Margaret holding the children in the centre; Biddy close beside them with Thoria hanging on her arm; Greg, Douglas and Richie shoulder to shoulder behind them.

The devil figure raised its stick and the clashing of iron stopped though the murderous hum ran on.

Shona stepped forward and, taking a deep breath, raised her voice above the noise in the way she had learned from Marianne Villeneuve in Forster's Hall. 'This is no way to treat people. There's no one here for you. No murderer. He's long gone. Didn't he creep out ages ago?'

The humming faltered.

'The police know about the murder, and sure they'll get that man. That's the way, the proper way. Frightening a family out of its wits is not proper. It's the way of cowards; it's the way of savages.'

Greg pushed forward, took Lauretta from his mother and Becky from Shona and stood beside her, holding the two children high in his arms. 'I tell you,' he bawled, 'these children deserve new ways. The mother of each is dead. One through unnatural violence akin to the thing you've set out to do tonight. Another through the evil of the man you seek. These children are the future. They are both my . . . our . . . children now. Would you threaten them?'

The air stayed quiet, still heavy with threat.

Then there was a disturbance in the crowd as Tommo Farrell pushed his way through to the front. He laid his sack on the ground, then took his knife and slashed the cord holding the ram's horns to Tad Pinkney's head. Then he took Becky from Greg and stood by his shoulder.

'This is a family,' he shouted. 'No one hurts it. Anyone who tries gets it from me.'

From the edge of the crowd on one side came Father O'Reilly, followed by Pat Daley.

The priest looked very slowly round the people, searching each face before him. 'Go back to your homes now and leave this family in peace.' His voice was gentle, singing through the quiet.

Young Jamie MacQuistain came forward from the other side. 'There's been trouble here for all kinds of reasons today, I know it,' he shouted. 'About the women so savagely done to death, and working a week with no wages. I tell you, I'm just ahead of the Priorton police who are out in force. They have one of the thieves in their cells and they're on the track of the murderer. Neither man is here, so why are you?'

Tad raised his hand and removed the ram's horns and the sacking mask. He stood holding them a moment before he dashed them to the ground and stalked off. Then one by one the others clashed iron objects to the ground, extinguished their torches and crept away into the night.

Afterwards there were hundreds of pans and kettles, fireblazers and pokers, lying in almost orderly rows on the ground.

Then Margaret pushed her way past Greg and walked determinedly towards Father O'Reilly, her hand held out. 'Thank you, Mr . . . Reverend. Thank you for that. It was no devil, was it?'

He shook her hand warmly. 'If it was, Mrs McNaughton, it has departed forever from this house, you can be sure of that. A thing can't be entirely of the devil that brings our two peoples together, even as a consequence of such a perverse errand.'

She went to Jamie MacQuistain 'Thank you, Jamie. Your father . . .'

'He would have done the same, believe me.'

Finally she went to Shona and hugged her closely. 'And thank you, my dear brave girl.'

'Sure it was nothing, Mrs McNaughton. Nothing at all. Just a few lads on the rampage.' She smiled at Greg over his mother's head. 'Now can we all get inside before those children start sneezing and coughing? We've a family to take care of.'

Epilogue

Shona waited until she was clear of Shotwell to pull a leg up and over so that she was astride Boru the Second and could ride more comfortably. Under her fashionably wide skirts she was wearing the trousers from one of the suits Marianne had had made for her to serve and sing in.

She chirrupped at Boru, flicked him with her spurs and he started to canter.

The week since she and Greg and Tommo had faced down the iron band had been full of events.

Stuart McNaughton's horse had returned to the livery of its own accord. Stuart's body had been found in one of the brackish pools at Old Morven, less than a hundred yards from the pithead where Shona had worked alongside Mary Challoner.

Blundering in the dark, avoiding the searching police and the stragglers from the marauding iron band, he had wandered on to the blackened pit area, a much worked site with three disused shafts. These shafts had, through time, filled with water: water so dead that no plants would grow there, no fish swim.

Dogs, among them Tad Pinkney's old faithful, had finally led the searchers to the shaft called Old Leaky. The coal company provided a portable pump and they found Stuart's body fourteen feet down on a ledge, covered by black slime.

Shona and Greg had been there when they pulled his bloated remains out. She'd looked up past the crowd to the pit wheel which still spun over the place where she had once worked. She knew that it, like Ireland, was in the past: just as Stuart with all his badness and his sadness was in the past.

The funeral had been quickly and quietly disposed of on Thursday, with everyone there and only Margaret, with Douglas and Biddy on either side of her, crying copiously.

To her annoyance Shona had barely seen Greg all week. He spent Friday on some errand in Priorton and they had only managed to see each other briefly after supper. The idle life at Garth End did not suit her and she took it out on Greg.

'I haven't seen you all week,' she whispered at him on the staircase.

'I've been around all the time.' He grinned. 'You must be blind.'

'No.' She went bright red. 'I mean properly. To talk to, I mean. I want to find some work, I'm used to working. I've earned my own money since I was a pit-girl and don't intend stopping now.'

'You want to go back down the pit? Or on the stage at the Variety Hall at Priorton?' His tone was neutral.

She scowled at him. 'Neither of those. But something.'

He laughed. 'I know what you need! You need an outing. I've to go up to check Killock Castle. We could go there tomorrow. And we'll talk about it there, away from all this lot.'

She had sighed then, and nodded. 'Yes. Sure I thought that was a lovely place. Will we set out early?'

'No, not together. You go there for noon. I've business at Priorton. I'll meet you there.'

It was just on twelve when she tied Boru beside Juvenal, at the old tumbled gates of the castle wall, and walked up the great pathway. There was something strange about the building. The wooden shutters and curtains were pulled back and even at midday, light seemed to glow from every window.

The front door was open. She could smell woodsmoke. A great fire crackled in the fireplace. The drapes were off the furniture, revealing the dusty shapes of chair and tables.

'Greg?' she called. Her voice echoed through the hall and up the great stairs. She called at the top of her voice from room to room. There were fires in every room: some smoking, some burning bright. She mounted the stairs and tried the bedrooms. Each had its own glowing fire. She came to the small back bedroom last.

Here again a great fire was blazing. Greg was sitting on the bed, legs dangling, smiling broadly.

She flew at him, battering his chest. 'What's this game you're playing, wretch? Hide and Seek?'

He held her close. Then they kissed and rolled on to the bed.

376

After some confusion in disposing of layers of clothing, they made love slowly with well remembered expertise.

Afterwards they sat on separate chairs by the fire, just looking at each other in delight.

Then Greg slapped his forehead. 'Oh, I forgot!'

'What is it?' Alarm threaded its way into her lazy contentment.

He came across and knelt before her. 'There are two things,' he said. 'First, will you marry me as soon as it's possible?'

She ruffled his hair. 'No, of course not,' she said in a friendly enough fashion. She was only half joking. She loved being with him but was serious about finding work. Only if she did, could she be happily married to Greg McNaughton of Garth End Cottage. There was still thinking to do. 'What's the second thing?' she demanded.

He reached into an inner pocket. 'And here is the second thing.'

It was a heavy parchment envelope. She pushed him away slightly so that she could open and read it.

It bore an address in New York and was short:

Dear Miss Shona Farrells,

You will have had the news by now and this is to say it is serious and true. I knew when I first met you that our souls marched along. So the gift is to seal that perpetual journey. I know you have the wisdom to use it well and the humour not to take it too seriously. With the gift comes the freedom to make your own choices, good and bad.

Yours sincerely,

Benjamin Shakespeare.

'Gift?' she said, frowning at Greg.

He stood up and opened his arms wide, spinning round on his heels. 'This!'

'This bed?' she said stupidly.

'This castle. These lands. These pits. These villages. Is this work enough for you?'

She stood up. 'What? The man must be mad!'

'He's Russian and a great gambler. Full of grand gestures. But apart from that he's as sound as a gold sovereign. It's all yours by deed of gift. In the first place he sent papers to Moxham which were a will, leaving it to you. Then on its heels came more papers, making a deed of gift. Moxham says they're sound. Shakespeare's doing well in America now and will settle there. He wants all this off his hands.'

She remembered what a deed of gift was, and Marianne's words about independence. 'Why me? I still can't understand it.'

'Perhaps he fell in love with you like I did, the second he saw you. Perhaps, like he says there, he feels your soul's in tune with his. In his letter to Moxham he says Killock came to him by pure luck and it would perhaps be lucky for him to pass it on in that way.'

Now she believed him. She stood up and went to the tall narrow window, peering out at the spread of green with its punctuation of villages and pit heads.

'It's mine? There's work enough out there.'

'Yes.' He smiled and shook his head from side to side. 'It's yours. And the work that goes with it. I had a letter from him too, telling me to marry you, not to let you slip. He also said you were the independent type and would always be so.'

She turned round and leaned her back against the window with its wide views of her own land. She took a deep breath and smiled up at him. 'Didn't he say as well I was to make my own choices, good or bad? So, Mr McNaughton, good or bad, that means I can choose you and be glad of it.'